Leigh Hunt

The Foster-Brother

A Tale of the War of Chiozza

Leigh Hunt

The Foster-Brother
A Tale of the War of Chiozza

ISBN/EAN: 9783337074869

Printed in Europe, USA, Canada, Australia, Japan

Cover: Foto ©Andreas Hilbeck / pixelio.de

More available books at **www.hansebooks.com**

No. 66.

LIBRARY OF SELECT NOVELS.

THE

FOSTER-BROTHER.

A Tale of

THE WAR OF CHIOZZA.

EDITED BY

LEIGH HUNT.

NEW YORK:
HARPER & BROTHERS, PUBLISHERS,
FRANKLIN SQUARE.
1864.

Price Forty Cents.

HARPER'S PICTORIAL HISTORY
OF
THE GREAT REBELLION
IN
THE UNITED STATES.

PUBLISHING IN NUMBERS.—THE FIFTH & SIXTH NOW READY.

Price Twenty-five Cents Each.

The work will be issued in Numbers, as rapidly as is consistent with thorough and careful preparation. The Publishers hope to be able to issue two Numbers each month.

Each Number will contain 24 pages, of the size of *Harper's Weekly*, profusely illustrated, and printed in the best manner, from large and legible type.

The price of each Number, containing matter equivalent to an ordinary volume, will be Twenty-five Cents.

Four Numbers (Nos. I., II., III., and IV.) will be sent by mail, *post-paid*, upon the receipt of One Dollar.

Booksellers, News Dealers, and Canvassing Agents will be supplied on the most liberal terms.

Notices of the Press.

This is one of the great enterprises of the day. The value of the work becomes more apparent as the numbers advance. The historical matter is really valuable; the sketches of individuals and incidents are admirably drawn, not only by the pen of the historian, but by the pencil of the artist; and both combined will make, when bound, one of the marked histories of this war, if not the great history of the war. There are official documents on every page, at the bottom, which add much to the value of the work. It will be found on the centre tables of thousands of our countrymen.—*Boston Post.*

A careful, comprehensive, minute, and graphic record of the origin and progress of the war; and in the size and beauty of its pages and paper, in the profuseness, costliness, elegance, and completeness of its illustrations, far exceeding any other history yet attempted.—*N. Y. Observer.*

This long-expected serial has made its appearance, and no one will regret having waited for it, for it bears unmistakable evidence of having been prepared with great care. We congratulate the publishers upon their eminently successful commencement of so important a work.—*N. Y. Commercial Advertiser.*

It is edited by an accomplished scholar, a gentleman who occupies a good position for the collection of material, and one who wields a vigorous pen. He writes with strength and great spirit. It promises to be a very valuable as well as a very interesting book—one to which the eye of the child will turn for the illustrations of scenes with the names of which his young eyes have become easily familiar; and the eye of the older reader will be attracted by the careful, studious, and conscientious manner in which the editor prepares his historical matter.—*N. Y. Journal of Commerce.*

We speak confidently in praise of the manner in which the work is brought out. * * This narrative, embellished by the picturesque illustrations, affords an interesting commentary on the war, and will be of priceless value for preservation.—*Boston Advertiser.*

In entrusting the composition of this work to an experienced and intelligent scholar, whose labors both as a critic in the higher walks of literature and art and a journalist have given no small weight of authority to the productions of his pen, the publishers have adopted the wisest course to secure its accuracy, artistic construction, and popular success.

The writer judiciously combines the spirit of philosophical reflection with a vivid and picturesque delineation of

facts. His style is at once lively and polished, and every page gives evidence of careful study and preparation. As a specimen of his skill in character-drawing, we extract the aptly colored portrait of Jefferson Davis. * * *N. Y. Tribune.*

The work will always be valuable for the original documents embraced within it, and attractive for its illustrations.—*Brooklyn Eagle.*

The enterprise of the Messrs. Harper will certainly prosper. Their *Pictorial History*, simply written and profusely illustrated, will, we judge, be eagerly sought for by the Northern people.—*Albion.*

A careful, comprehensive, graphic, and minute record of the origin and progress of the war, and in the profuseness, costliness, elegance, and completeness of its illustrations, far exceeding any other history yet attempted.—*Christian Times.*

We have read the two numbers of this important work with great pleasure. They present the most intelligible, graphic, and impartial account of the events they detail, which we have yet read, and we have read a great deal. The documentary parts are thrown into notes. The illustrations are many, and very good. To the accuracy of a number of the likenesses we can testify, as we have seen the men.—*The Lutheran.*

Hurrah for the Harpers! They have started another splendid publication for the people, and such a one as is needed—a large, handsomely printed and beautifully illustrated serial, which, for the amount of matter given, and the style in which it is issued, and the quality of paper on which it is printed, is most surprisingly cheap—twenty-five cents a number. The serial will be one that will be popular with the whole public. The portraits in the first numbers are portraits, as those who ever saw the originals will recognise, and not caricatures, as is often the case in cheap illustrated works.—*Boston Commercial Bulletin.*

Profusely and graphically illustrated. It is altogether the most popular thing of the kind that is now before the public. The facilities of the publishers for carrying forward such an enterprise are unbounded.—*Philadelphia Christian Chronicle.*

Executed in the highest style. No expense, it is evident, has been spared to make the work attractive and instructive. It furnishes the best history of the times that we have seen.—*Pittsburg Christian Advocate.*

☞ Any Number of the above Work sent by Mail (any distance in the United States under 1500 miles), on receipt of Twenty-five Cents.

THE

FOSTER-BROTHER.

A Tale

OF

THE WAR OF CHIOZZA.

EDITED BY

LEIGH HUNT.

NEW YORK:

HARPER & BROTHERS, PUBLISHERS,

329 & 331 PEARL STREET,

FRANKLIN SQUARE.

1871.

This novel being the production of a writer whose name has hitherto scarcely transpired, the publisher is of opinion, that an introduction of it to the public by one who has been longer before them, may serve to procure it the speedier attention.

Thinking what I do of its merits, and the writer being one of my sons, the reader will conceive how willingly I have fallen in with a suggestion having such an object; though at the same time I must own that I felt myself to be in a delicate position, with regard both to the needlessness of my good word in the long run, and the suspicions to which fatherly commendations are liable. In reflecting, however, that my introduction is of necessity addressed chiefly to critical readers, I concluded that they would give me their best construction. Assuredly the new writer neither expected any such recommendation, nor intended, in the first instance, to have his name disclosed. He is not, indeed, a new writer at all, except as far as regards this class of composition, and the involuntary appearance of the name. He has written anonymously for several years, with the approbation of the best judges in the metropolis; and (to make use, in all modesty, of a saying of Johnson's respecting Goldsmith) has no more necessity, with those that know him, of coming to me for help, in any one respect, than he has to be "fed with a spoon." Still he does not hold himself superior to the pleasure or the advantage of having his father's good opinion.

I confess I think so well of the "Foster Brother," that I do not hesitate to mention a circumstance which might otherwise have told against it; at least with such as are accustomed to confound rapidity of execution with badness of it; and this is, that it was composed at hasty, though earnest intervals, during a pressure of work already too much for the writer's health, and only carried to that extreme from a sense of duty.

I am much mistaken, if the habit of a principle of this kind will not be recognized by the reader as originating some of the best things in the book; which, to sum up my general idea of them (for I am sensible that it does not become me to enter much into particulars) appears to me to consist of the heartiest male characters, such as Zeno, Luigi Il Grasso, and the Englishman; of the highly graphic nature of the descriptions, whether of scenes or persons, executed with all the breadth as well as minuteness of a painter, and above all, of the development of the graver elements of the passion of love, truly so called; that is to say, love founded on real or supposed goodness in the object, felt in proportion to the existence of the like worthiness in the person loving, and superior to all the chances, whether conventional or otherwise, of being confounded with what it is not.

I cannot conceive anything finer or more complete in this way, than the characters of Arduino's daughter and Morosini's son, of the younger Carrara, and the noble peasant girl Rosa Bardossi, my (I beg leave to say) favorite. All the scenes in which the affections of these individuals are concerned, I hold to be masterpieces; and no less such, of another kind, is the conveyance of the Venetian ship to the Greek island, by the undaunted Englishman.

The lesser "Queen of the Sea," and the imaginative, and therefore comparatively fluctuating nature of Italian courage, are there made to give way, though in the handsomest and most honorable manner, to that inflexible Saxon perseverance, the very pastimes of which, to this day, are partaken by a young English queen, in the excursions which she makes out to sea, at the head of her mariners.

I hold also that nothing can be truer to nature, or better executed, than the closing selfishness of Morosini's career, his sacrifice of his daughter's happiness, and the unexpected catastrophe it brings on our disgusted countryman. Truthfulness, indeed, and passion, appear to me to characterize the whole work.

To prove, however, to the reader (till he looks into the work for himself) that it is no mere fatherly partiality which makes me thus speak of it, I shall add, that the antique coloring occasionally given to its phraseology seems too little of a piece with the rest of it; that the introduction in English words, of Italian idioms, however confined to colloquial occasions, and true to the fact in one respect, defeats its own purpose in another, being not the simple presentation of one language, but the confusion of two; and that I would rather have had less of the history and politics of Venice, and more of its private life. But the author tells me, that should his first novel be indulgently received, he hopes to follow it with another, entirely of a domestic nature, and upon English life.

Pleased to have had this opportunity of introducing to the reader, in THORNTON HUNT, another of that family-name who has the welfare of his species at heart, and trusting at all events that no defect in the manner of the introduction will be allowed to operate to its disadvantage, I have the honor to be the public's old and faithful servant,

LEIGH HUNT.

Kensington, July 24.

THE FOSTER BROTHER.

CHAPTER I.

The sea breeze blew chill into the wide, dark hall of the palace Alberti, one of the oldest in Venice. Two torches, whose weary holders shifted them from hand to hand, threw a heavy glare on the walls in one corner, but left the rest of the hall in gloom scarcely broken. The glow fell full on the faces of the two men, whose big beards and swarthy skin belied their trim vests and well-fitting hose, and bespoke them rather soldiers of some roving band than the lackeys their dress betokened. Behind them stood a row of other men of a similar stamp, mingled with boatmen, who also looked as if they would have been freer in the loose vest of their craft, with arms and legs bare to the elbows and the knees, than in the liveries they now wore. A little removed from the light of the torches, and nearer to the door in the centre of the hall, opposite to the one that opened upon the canal before the house, sauntered three more servants, of less equivocal exterior. Their tongues were still, which alone would have told that they awaited some doubtful adventure—some fees to be won or lost. A hoarse murmur mingled with the glow of the torches : the stifled gossip and jesting of the careless band in the corner. Suddenly it ceased, and the sound of many feet was heard on the other side of the great doors: they were flung open, and a blaze of light poured forth, blinding the lackeys as they fell into a posture of vigilant and resigned attendance, and starting the pillars and copings of the hall into vivid relief. After a few men and boys, bearing flambeaux and candles, came a party of gentlemen, in easy, laughing chat, but keeping somewhat on either side, as who should make clear the way for their betters. Vests of silk or velvet, flaming with gold and budding with slashes, to show the white or gay lining underneath; hose, of colors chosen at the fancy of the wearer, and fitting the leg from the hip to the shoe, or eased in the upper part with looser trunks; small caps, of various makes and colors, with or without a falling fold or hood, and jewels in the fastenings of the dresses, shone all rich and glowing under the strong light. Then came some three or four more gentlemen, whereof one or two wore the red berret and robe of the senate. Behind them walked a man whose aspect, though little to be admired, at once arrested attention. He was of unusual height; his face was pale, solemn, and austere; his aquiline features, sharp and peaked, were wrinkled with an expression of peevish pride; his eyes, of a full gray, were glassy and unmeaning, the red lids giving them a look of weakness; yet the short black eyelashes imparted something like a noble fierceness to his fixed gaze forward. His small head was covered by the red cap of the senator, not unlike the lid of a flat, round box, with a fold of velvet hanging rather behind and on one side; beneath it scarcely showed the grizzled hair retreating from the forehead, cut close, to conceal its ragged scantiness, and for the same reason his thin, straggling beard was clipped as close as might be. His uplifted face drew out to its full length a slender, sinewy neck, which tapered from shoulders so broad and lean, that profane gibers compared him to a cross dressed in the old clothes of a gentleman. And in truth, his red cloak, grown brown with age and careless wear, black vest, and shirt scarce shown, looked as though they had learned to cling to his form from long use. Beneath his vest's skirt strode two legs, whose length seemed to enfeeble them, and his gray hose flowed in slender wrinkles to flat, spreading feet, that clapped on the ground as he walked. Yet was there vigor and muscle in that tall frame, doubly strengthened by pride, which scorned the earth he trod; a pride which the most illustrious Marco Morosini drew through a long line of noble and ducal ancestors from the origin of Venice.

By his side, and rather in front of him, walked a man not less remarkable; a being built on the same plan, but with all the details filled out differently. The high head of Alessandro Padovano was thickly clothed in black wiry hair, shorn like his lord's: his capacious forehead stood abroad, and frowned defiance at the whole world. His manly features mocked with a strange resemblance the other's sharp face; his dark gray eyes glowed with lawless fires under a stern cold stare; his solid beard cut short displayed a neck like a doric column; and his herculean trunk rested on hips so compact, and limbs of such gigantic proportions, that it was marvellous to see how active lightness combined with ponderous strength. As he stalked stride for stride with his double, he looked like a walking portrait of what the other ought to have been. The Morosini called Alessandro his foster brother, but all Venice called him a brother of another sort; saying that Marco's sickly mother was neglected even in the honeymoon, for the lusty peasant girl of the main land who suckled Marco with his half brother; and nature herself stamped the scandal with truth.

The party were crossing the hall when one of the lackeys in waiting, stepped forward, cap in hand, and bowing humbly to arrest the steps of the gentlemen in advance, passed them to Morosini; who stopped, and gazed on him.

"May it please your lordship," said the man,

"the boats are at the other side, through the calle, out at this door, if you will deign to go that way."

"How now!" exclaimed one of the other gentlemen, stepping back, (it was Alberti himself,) "why should these noble gentlemen walk down a dark and narrow by-lane, when their boats may come in front here!"

"May it please your excellency," answered the man with prostrate humility, "there is a boatman fallen into the canal—they seek his body, and would have none pass for a while."

"Eh! let the boats be brought. I will not have my house—"

"Noble sir," said Alessandro gravely, "my good lord would mourn most of all grieve if his progress did even the smallest hurt to the people of his Venice, and especially if it prevented the recovery of one single Venetian." He looked at Morosini, who replied by turning to Alberti, and saying, "my noble friend, we will walk by the calle."

The party now turned to a side door in the hall, which led into the narrow lane. The torch bearers were outside; the boatmen disappeared down the dark calle; the guests took leave of their hosts, and were soon walking along the lane in a lengthened file, Morosini and his brother bringing up the rear. As the slight lessening of the darkness and freshening of the breeze showed that they approached the canal at the opposite end, the pavement became very rugged and uneven. "Mind, sirs," said the spokesman lackey, "they have been repairing the path, and you will fall: stay, I will hold the light to the ground." The guests stepped cautiously on, each allowing his companion to get well in advance, that he might pick his way the better. The heavy sounds of feet as they jumped one by one into the boats, began to be heard, and "good night, Morosini," "good night, Tiepolo," "good night, Arduini," and other farewells flew from mouth to mouth. Morosini still stalked on in silence, allowing his people to guide him to his gondola without any vulgar vigilance. The subservient lackey almost burned his robe with the torch in endeavoring to illuminate each particular stone for the noble footstep; when suddenly they were in utter darkness. A stumble had driven the torch into the very earth. The small party remaining on shore halted. "How now, Nadale!—idiot!—dolt!" cried a loud voice, as another servant drove away his blundering fellow: "will my lord let me guide him—will my lord take his servant's hand!" The voice was a stranger's; but sooth to say, Morosini felt cold, and was anxious to be home; his brother made no demur; and so he took the hand which touched his in the dark. He was led down the steps into the boat, and then a large cloak was flung over his head, and fell around him in tangled, and still entangling folds. His hand went to his sword hilt, and there it was pinioned; his voice called aloud, but the sound was driven down his throat with a large mouthful of the cloak that served for a gag. One short struggle, and he relinquished the undignified and bootless contest, and lay motionless. The boat had already pushed off, and on it went—on and on, with a steady measured pull of the oars, as if the boatmen had a long task before them. Morosini's

twisted sword arm was very uncomfortable, and the cloak in his mouth was a very oppressive supper. He tried to mend his posture, when a voice said lowly at his ear, "if you stir not, I will uncover your face and loosen your limbs." He nodded—the cool night breeze visited his stifled nostrils, and the stars shone overhead. The round opening in the folds of the cloak just admitted a circle of the heavens, and the view of the living shadow of a man's face, big-capped, big-nosed, big-bearded, and stedfast as a picture. For some half hour Morosini debated with himself whether or not he should try to tamper with that imperturbable shadow; but the appearance of settled plan made him believe it hopeless; while he indistinctly felt that he was surrounded by others ready to gag and bind him again. So he gazed on the few stars within his scope, until the fixing of his eyes, and the fanning of the breeze, pressed down his eyelids with irresistible, leaden sleep.

He was awakened by being lifted from the boat; too heavy with sleep to think of resistance, even if his numbed limbs had permitted it; and he was borne by the steady tramp of many feet into a building, of which he could see too little to know its character; but he guessed it, from its massy and solid structure, to be of a military kind. Entering by a small door, he was borne along a dark passage, and up some steps, into a chamber; where they laid him on a bed. He preserved a sullen silence, while the bearded soldiers, by whom he now saw himself surrounded, unfolded his cloak, and left his cramped limbs at liberty. The senator had made up his mind to await the event, whatever it might be, rather than commit himself to any undignified position, by taking an active, and perhaps defeated, part. The men retired from the room. A long time he lay, half thinking half dozing, when he was startled by a soft voice close to his ear: a young girl was offering him food and wine, which she had noiselessly placed on a table near the bed; and without waiting for a reply, she withdrew as unexpectedly as she appeared. Morosini was now effectually roused: the warm air of the chamber had restored life to his limbs; his fasting voyage had made him hungry; and slowly rising, after due deliberation, and a more careful examination of the tempting viands,—the smoking dish of meat, disguised in all the mystery of the cooking art, the fair bread, luscious fruit, conserves, and sparkling wine, displayed in choicest silver and Venetian glass—he fell to. Appetite allayed, a glance round his prison amused him in the intervals of feeding. It was a small room, such as might be found in the turret of a fortress, somewhat crowded with handsome furniture, and too much filled up with hangings for the summer season. The small window looked on the sea, beach and a bare waste of water. To his suspicious eye every needless curtain seemed to conceal a door. The meal was soon over; the gazing on the walls and moveless furniture became a tedious pastime, and he rose to make a closer scrutiny. On the other side of his bed he discovered an open door. He passed through it; and found himself in another small chamber, bare of furniture, with another door, also open. Resigning himself to the decrees of fate, he walked on ; and seeing a narrow flight of steps, he ascended ; though not unconscious that an enemy at the top of the steep stairs would be resistless. None appeared ; but as he slowly passed up, he heard a murmur as of one reading aloud. A narrow door at the top of the steps, brought him into a small chamber, like those below, somewhat scantily furnished. Opposite to the door by which he entered, was a large picture of the Annunciation. Sitting near the small window, at a table on which were books and writing materials, was a man, whose large brown gown and corded waist, betokened a Franciscan friar. As Morosini entered, he left off reading, and regarded the intruder with an air of surprise ; and assuming a manner betwixt indignation and benign humility, he said, " How long, sir—for I presume I address the master of this my prison—am I to remain a prisoner, guessing only at the unrighteous cause of my restraint ?"

For an instant Morosini knew not how to reply ; but presently he answered, " In me, good father, you behold a prisoner no less than yourself ; now thinking worse of my kidnappers, since their hands violate the sanctity of holy persons. But perhaps you know who is our detainer ?"

" I crave your pardon, my son, for condemning where I should have pitied. No, I do not know, though I guess who is the bold man that can bend crowned heads and holy hands to his ambition."

A light broke on Morosini. His sallow face paled, and his brow contracted as he exclaimed, " You mean Francesco da Carrara ?"

" The same. Thou and I are under his eagle grasp ; I, with small hope, for who will miss the poor friar from the crowd ? But what must be the audacity of that man that can thus seize one of the lords of Venice ; for I cannot mistake your tongue and mien."

Morosini bowed. " Giovanni da Carrara could tell you from his prison how his nephew respects either piety or loyalty. But possibly he may repent this blow at Venice. You said you guessed his motives : might a fellow prisoner, not unused to secresy of councils, share your confidence ?"

" Is it possible, my son, that report has not told you of the immediate purpose of Carrara ?"

" I know, of course, that he harbors anger against Venice ; I know that for some paltry customs' duties which he would levy, and not pay. But I must not teach you how ill I can keep counsel. We suspect an enemy in Carrara ; though I did not know that he had gone so far as actual conspiracy."

" My son, you are right to maintain that discreet reserve which is the ornament of the Venetian senator. You cannot yet know that in the poor friar Marco, whose humble obscurity might have saved him in this hard imprisonment, you have a faithful friend to all that is true and great—you might at times injure yourself, injure Venice, by careless confidence. I can injure nothing, but this worthless body, by telling all I know. But the story must not keep you standing ;" and rising, he placed one of the tall straight-backed wooden chairs for the senator ; who disposed himself to hear the friar's disclosures.

The tale, often interrupted to explain this or that point, may be told in fewer words than its narrator chose to use. The friar professed not to know the precise reasons of Carrara's enmity to Venice ; but he had entered into a league with other potentates, also unknown to the friar, to depose the present rulers from their power, on the ground that their personal rancor against him had made them sacrifice the true interests of their city. He did not even desire to *conquer* Venice—far otherwise, but to convert her into an ally as friendly as he deserved to have ; raising among her own patricians other rulers. " To that end," pursued the friar, " Andrea Contarini is to be removed, and, if I understand rightly, the new doge is to be Marco Morosini ; whom I dare say you know well."

Morosini started.

" It was for refusing to be a tool to this scheme—for I would not stain my sacred calling with intrigues of worldly policy and guile—that drew upon me, as I suspect, the wrath of Carrara. Some of his people let me understand that I was to be a messenger to this Morosini ; but, I say, I refused. Carrara swore indeed that I should ; but I declared that I would rather rot in a dungeon. You see I keep my word ; and I laugh at the tyrant's threat that I shall be his messenger in spite of my teeth."

" Wonderful !" exclaimed Morosini. " But tell me, why did Carrara dare to suppose that Morosini would accept the dogate from his hands ?"

" Nay, I know not. They say that Morosini has the fault of all noble blood—that he is ambitious ; and perhaps Carrara thought, that to rule the queen of the sea, given into his hands in all her unstained power, might be no unwelcome task. It was, he said, really placing himself and all his potent allies at the personal command of Morosini. Who can tell ? Possibly it would even not be difficult to make the dogate a more permanent office—hereditary."

Morosini listened in a transport of tantalized doubt. He knew Carrara, and knew that he was capable both of the intrigue and of following it up with deeds. The dream of his disappointed life seemed realized. The almost royal seat, once occupied by his ancestors, seemed wrongfully withheld from him. Who among the nobles of Venice loved their country with a more devoted patriotism ? whose love was informed by greater wisdom than his own ? in sooth Morosini knew not. But to league with the branded enemy of Venice ! He turned habitually aside to take counsel of his double, the foster brother : his judgment was left unwontedly to himself. He folded his arms, he rose from his seat, and forgetting the holy friar, he traversed the narrow room with long quickly turning steps.

CHAPTER II.

In the little room adjoining that in which were Morosini and the friar, furnished much in the same way, also sat two persons. One was a man of some forty or fifty years of age, or he might be younger, but marked by the traces of an ambition so active, so vast in its grasp, and involved in such complicated intrigues, that the handsome face, which seemed naturally fitter to beam with wit and good-fellowship, was lined with care, and clouded with a severity almost fierce. The compact massy head was thickly clothed in black hair, that hung in careless locks waving almost to a curl, but slightly retreating from the bold jutting brow. Thick, but pencilled eyebrows edged a brow that hung over black eyes so deep that none could fathom them, yet piercing and vigilant. The straightish nose was just so much curved as to give a sharper boldness. The clear brown cheeks glowed with a fiery blood, that showed itself rather in fits than in girlish roses. The face looked the fuller for that it was close shaven; displaying a mouth of sweetness too strongly traced in its waving lines to be obliterated by the compression of lip which seemed almost habitual. A manly neck descended bare into a coat of mail which covered an ample chest. The stout rounded arms, issuing from the shoulder pieces, were cased in mail; beneath which a thick acketon, descending somewhat lower than common, covered a pair of brawny legs. The cavalier had thrown his gauntlets on the table; on which was firmly pressed one moveless clenched fist, while the other sculptured hand was firmly spread upon the dark skirt that covered his thigh. He sat like one in the possession of command. The expression of his face was austere watchfulness; but an observer might have traced in it, as he sat motionless as a portrait, cunning, high intellect, dauntless audacity, yet gayety, and even kindness. On the other side of the table, in a somewhat similar attitude, was the stalwart Alessandro Padovano. The position chosen by the two was singular: they sat before a little door, which stood open, but was blocked on the other side by some dark substance, and at that was their gaze directed. It was the back of the picture in the friar's room. Francesco da Carrara sat, with one of his willing instruments by his side, to listen, while another played his game upon the baited senator of Venice.

When Morosini, without replying to the friar's searching hints, rose and paced the room, Carrara glanced at the foster brother's face.— It changed not: he still doubted in which direction his brother would take the field. The silence was broked only by the agitated stamp of Morosini's stride. It ceased—

"No!" exclaimed he, "my commands must come from Venice herself, and in her own voice! Venice may spurn my highest services, but Morosini courts the indignity. Tell Carrara that he has the body, but the soul of the Venetian is still on the council seat in Venice; the humblest there, but still above his reach.— Let him kill me; freed, I denounce him." And he strode towards the door by which he entered.

"Stay, Messer Morosini," said the friar. "I have spoken on the faith of your unstained honor. My life is in your hands; you will not betray it."

"It is well. You are safe. I shall watch the traitor; but hold my peace for the sake of his prisoner." He departed.

Half mortified, the foster brother turned his flushed and frowning face to Carrara.

"Your brother," said the Lord of Padua, with a sneer, "is too honest."

"Had I but been there——"

"You would have been betrayed to the honest senator one of my strongholds in Venice,—yourself. No, Alessandro, it is a chance lost, but not more. Your brother may go back; it was worth trying, and no harm is done, for you will keep him quiet."

The picture was drawn aside, and the friar entered the room.

"Well done, cavallaccio," said Carrara. "Is the hall prepared for our next task?"

"At my lord's service," said the friar with a smile.

"To it then."

CHAPTER III.

Carrara and his two companions descended to a hall, not of great size, and totally bare of furniture; except that a table was put by in a corner and a few chairs were placed by the single window, which looked upon the sea-side. Carrara surveyed the room like one who saw that his directions had been fulfilled; then, signing to the friar to close the door, he took Alessandro's hand, and passed across to the window. He opened a narrow door, concealed by some wood-work at the side, and disclosed a small recess, made in the thickness of the wall. "Stow yourself here, Signor Alessandro; your whisper may serve me at a pinch. But reserve it for that; and whatever you hear, be it battle and death, do not show yourself." He closed the door upon the imperturbable Alessandro. "Now, Marco, place this great chair nearer to the window—more on this side—turn its back more to the light." He sat in it, and leaned back. "Let us hear your whisper, Alessandro."

"Is this too loud?"

"Did you hear it, Marco?"

"I heard nothing, my lord."

Carrara's face lighted up with satisfaction. "The contrivance has a worthy first trial. Bring to us these most excellent lords."

The friar left the room; and for a few minutes Carrara paced it with measured steps. The door was opened by Marco, who made way for four gentlemen; members of the senate, who had been kidnapped at the same time that Morosini was carried off—the fiery Jacopo Malipiero, seized in his own bed, by his own servants, servants of his no more; the grave majestic Soranzo, the lusty jovial Navagero, and the earnest Steno. Carrara halted in his walk, and drawing himself up proudly, bowed to the illustrious prisoners. They returned his salute with various courtesy; except Malipiero, who pointing his finger at the full extent of his long arm reprovingly at Carrara, exclaimed with a burst of rage, "For what, audacious man, are we brought here? by what right? by what—"

Slightly smiling, Carrara motioned to the chairs ranged near the window, opposite to his own: "Be seated, noble sirs. I will not long detain you; and will explain to Messer Mal-

piero why I have ventured, partly for his own
sake, to bring him here without permission first
craved."

The stormy flush on Malipiero's passion-worn
face slightly subsided, as he seated himself with
his companions. Carrara took his station in
the great chair, and throwing himself easily
back in it, signed to Marco to leave the room.

"First, I owe it to Messer Malipiero to explain how you came here. You will learn presently how needful it was that there should be
this conference; and you need not be told that
it was hardly safe for me to be seen in Venice
—Venice whom I would so serve, but who
wrongs me with suspicion, and oppresses me
with injury: to have invited you would have
been to court refusal, or to have placed you
yourselves under suspicion of favoring this poor
traitor Carrara. I saved us both that refusal,
you that suspicion. Sirs, I need not recount the
wrongs that Venice has done me; not I believe, of malice in the illustrious Council, but in
mistake that I was her enemy. When, in 1373,
the fortune of war went against me—or rather
against the Vaivode of Transylvania, who then
commanded the forces of the King of Hungary,
my very good ally, you compelled me to an
humbling truce—you compelled me to have the
bounds of my state defined by your own officers
—to pay an enormous fine—the poor Lord of
Padua to pay to wealthy Venice two hundred
and fifty thousand ducats: and you took from me
at the very time the means of paying—you forced
me to give up the tax at the gates of Padua—
snatched from my state the salt pools of Curano
—and made me take salt from your own Chiozza." A whisper reached Carrara's ear. He
added—"You, Soranzo, proposed that condition
in the senate."

The four senators started, and looked at each
other.

"Yes, think not that you can speak in the
senate, and I not hear you."

"The Lord of Padua knows," said Soranzo,
"what I have said, and that it was the interests
of Venice alone that I consulted. I am ready
to answer for having devoted to Venice all that
I have and am."

"I know—I know; Messer Soranzo is among
the most patriotic and respected of her senators. But worse, far worse than that paltry
tampering with the means of my poor state—by
great and wealthy Venice—you made me send
my noble boy to crave pardon, on his bended
knees, of the doge, in the Place of St. Mark;
and you forced me—me, suddenly deprived of
aid, by the mistaken discretion of the vaivode,
because he had lost a few prisoners, to be afterwards ransomed from your dungeons—you
forced me, forgetting all chivalry—but what
chivalry ever ruled the inexorable senate !—you
forced me to the bitter shame of razing all my
forts—built again, thank heaven! as this that
you are in. You Malipiero, dictated that base
and cowardly condition."

"I did," cried Malipiero, his eyes gleaming
under scowling brows, and his frame trembling
with rage, "I did and I am here to answer it."
He rose violently from his chair—"but why do
we talk of these old matters? You have us
here Carrara, unarmed; for you dared not leave
us our swords; do your worst. I did raze your

forts, and I will raze this, which audaciously
you have rebuilt."

"Malipiero," cried Carrara, starting himself
in his chair, "as you razed my forts so shall
your salt-selling town of Chiozza"—there was a
slight tap in the wall behind; the whispered
"have a care" had not reached him. He cooled
at once. "I did not bring you here, noble sirs,
to quarrel, nor as an enemy; nor do I call to
mind my wrongs to raise your anger. You
thought to save Venice; be it so—'tis past.
But this, I say, that you have not forgotten
your enmity to a crushed foe: you—all of you,
still nourish hatred to me in Venice; even now,
when the power of Genoa is turned against you.
I would have prevented it; I would have been
your ally, as our neighborhood made most proper, but you have spurned me. Be it so. But I
tell you farther, that I am not less powerful than
I was when Hungary aided me—I am more so;
yea, even the lowly Lord of Padua has for his
allies—(a whisper reached his ear)—Enough! I
will recover that station from which Venice
struck me down. This, then, is what I have to
say to you: Genoa, seeking her own ends, in-
creases my strength by weakening Venice—I
will permit it; but Venice shall not be lost:
when the hour arrives, I will succor Venice, and
stay the march of her destruction. Till then, I
will chastise."

Malipiero felt for his absent sword: he rose,
and paced the room.

Not noticing him, Carrara proceeded. "Be
assured that Venice is in my power, and that I
shall use my power; but mercifully. Now for
yourselves. You, my lords, of all the senate,
most hate me: others would exalt Venice;
you hate my person."

"Not so," said Steno; "we, like others,
think of Venice alone; and this I can declare,
that if Carrara chose to join the alliance of the
republic, none would be more welcome, and
no greater friend would he have than the
Steno."

"It is too late. No; things must go forward. But, Messer Steno, I know your words:
you yourself said, but last month, that 'If I
were seized, quiet as I seem, the enemies of
Venice would be paralyzed—lacking their genius.'"

Steno and his companions again stared in
amaze.

"It seems," said Navagero, "that some of
us are traitors: it must be Malipiero, by his
anxious look."

"Messer Steno," retorted his outraged friend,
"is this a foolish jesting, or is this some mad
dream, that I am here between friend and foe
alike ribald and base!"

"Nay, peace, peace!" said Soranzo.

Carrara continued — "Your words have
reached me, and to them I look. But I must
cut short that influence. Gentlemen, in brief,
I have two paths to offer you: think gravely of
it; remember who is before you, and what he
dares: one path is back to Venice, the other to
your graves."

Malipiero started forward: he would have
seized Carrara, in the desperate determination
to make the plotter himself a hostage in his
throttling grasp; but his companions held
back.

B

"Think not that you can serve yourselves by touching me. I might be mastered by four cavaliers of your prowess, but my defeat would be the signal for a hundred swords to pierce you. Let us be calm, sirs; the conditions are not hard. I ask you not to be my allies; you may, and will, perhaps, meet me in the field; but this you will swear—not yourselves to propose or support anything in the senate which aims at my hurt. You will swear this in good faith; and to-morrow you will be serving your country with your counsel. Let us say no more now. We have all been irritated, and I crave your pardon for my own hasty speech. You will be led back, noble sirs, to your apartment; and I hope it is as little incommodious as my humble means can make it. If the servants have neglected their duty, tell me, that my hospitality, and the deference which I owe to your station, and to your patience under this force which I am obliged to put upon you, may not be shamed."

Malipiero, who had assumed a sullen silence, made no sign. Soranzo replied for all—"Your servants, sir, are diligent and courteous. But we claim our freedom. Rather than be traitors to our country, we would for ever remain in your lowest dungeons."

"That," said Carrara hastily, "was not one of the conditions. I do not use to keep caged nobles."

"Indeed!" cried Malipiero fiercely; "will your uncle say as much, Carrara?"

Carrara, keeping his stedfast and unmoved look on Ardiano added, "we will talk no more. The conditions—the sole conditions are known to you: ponder them. We will talk again in the evening, and at night you can be borne back to Venice.—Ho there!"

Marco entered.

"Holy father, convey these gentlemen to their apartment, and see that they be served with the best. Let me beseech you, sirs, say nothing more till we meet again."

The senators returned his bow, and retired. Carrara bolted the door behind them and released Alessandro.

"Now," said the cavalier, "your foster brother must be fed, and let him be made sleepy; you understand. When these men have yielded, he can be taken back to Venice. It would be scarcely safe till then. Arrived, you will see him first."

"He will first seek me, and I shall teach him how tense it will be to hold his peace. You know that Morosini sits in the senate, but that I give counsel there and direct the vote."

"Chief of my Venetian corps, praise not yourself to me. I know my men when I choose them. And now, when your brother is served, let me see if I have a wine sparkling enough to make that sombre face laugh: it would be Carrara's greatest victory."

CHAPTER IV.

As they left the room, they met a man who was about to enter. Carrara, who walked first, hastily whispered—"not now, sir, not now;" and the other abruptly retired. The foster brother had seen him; but he feigned not to have seen anything. The man slunk into the room which they had left. He was a person of more than middle age; so dressed, that it would have been difficult to tell whether he was a gentleman or a servant; for his brown vest and dark silk hose, and blue cloak faded to a sombre gray, might have belonged to one of good degree; yet they were so worn and tumbled, that a servant would scarcely have deigned to exchange his livery for them. His limbs were meagre but sinewy, and his once handsome face was weather-beaten and care worn, and disfigured by a flighty expression, which harmonized with his restless manner. Presently Carrara returned, alone.

"It was unlucky, Jacopo, that you showed yourself. An Arduino should not be seen in these walls, or people might think that we were plotting against Venice."

Jacopo Arduino smiled in careless assent, as if he thought it absurd, that his movements could be of importance.

"To be serious," added Carrara, "we need, Messer Jacopo, to be careful in this matter. The gold is ready for you, and you will convey it to my excellent friend, Carlo Zeno. You need not tell him how I thank him, for Zeno knows it well; and never would my retribution visit Venice, if only for his sake. You may tell him that. And now, Messer Jacopo, let me thank you for your singular good will and trouble in serving me in this matter."

Jacopo eagerly interrupted—"Nay, nay, speak not of that: I am but too glad to serve so excellent a gentleman as yourself; for I never believed what they say of you in Venice—never. Moreover, I can never enough serve my kind friend, Messer Zeno. I am fallen in estate, Carrara; but to serve my friends is still some companionship with them, for which I am grateful." And Jacopo looked sad, almost dignified, as he spoke.

Carrara felt an unusual embarrassment, as he said, "Messer Jacopo, forgive me if I say, that you must not incur this trouble to lose by it too. You have spent money in this my service; let me repay it to you." He proffered a purse of gold.

"No, no," cried Jacopo, his face flushing, and his eyes filling with tears—"no gold!"

"You will not scorn Carrara's just payment to you, Jacopo."

"Nay, nay, I am not proud, Carrara; but if I take your gold, Carrara, I lose all I have earned —it is no more friend for friend."

"You are foolish. Take the gold—what is gold—could you pay Zeno in gold—can I pay you, do you think—or do you think that I think so!—Never, man! Besides, you need it for those at home, and I only make the excuse of your kind service to me, to send this gift to them. Take it as a gift if you will."

"As a gift," said Jacopo; and he took the gold.

Carrara added, "You shall sup with me to-night; and we will talk of Zeno, and our youthful days, Jacopo. Till then I must leave you. But keep to your room, my friend; for there are those in the place who must not see you."

CHAPTER V

AFTER the repast provided for him by the hospitality of Carrara, Morosini found himself awaking once more in a boat; and as he rose from the cushions in which he lay, he perceived that he was in a common fishing-boat, with an awning spread over him. The sun was bright. Seeing him wake, the steersman addressed him respectfully, and told him that he had been lifted while he slept from another boat of which the crew said that he was fatigued with travelling, and that he desired to go from Padua to Venice as privately as he might. According to his wont, when his foster brother was not by to prompt him in a difficulty, he said as little as possible, and sunk once more into a doze, until the steersman again asked him, whether he would not prefer entering the town in a city gondola? He assented; one was hailed; and in a few minutes he entered his own palace.

He passed at once to the principal saloon, from which the sounds of music swelled as the door was opened by the servant that had it in charge. Seated on a chair was a young lady, with a sheet of music in her hand, his daughter, but how unlike her surviving parent. She could scarcely be accounted tall, although a graceful length of limb made her look so. The light slimness of the girl was swelling into ripe womanhood; and the glow of her clear brown skin was such as in after days inspired her countryman the prince of colorists; shaming with its brilliancy the opaque whiteness of fairer skins. The jet black hair, which waved in clustering ringlets from her brow, the brightness of her eyes, the roses of her cheeks and lips, the joyous smile that disclosed living ivory, the dazzling transparency of her neck and bosom, which the dead white of the linen that enshrined it, and the deep green of the velvet bodice that embraced her fruitlike form, would have composed a picture too brilliant, had not a melting tenderness softened the lash-shaded eyes, and played on the curling lips. That dulcet mouth seemed made for the music that swelled the liquid-moving throat. If her unlikeness to her parent surprised, how much more wondrous was the likeness to him in the noble youth that sat beside her, so like and so unlike —a picture of evil painted in goodness. Scarcely of such lengthened proportions, his tall figure combined that ponderous strength with that compact lightness, which is the consummation of manly grace. A wreath of crisp curls adorned his commanding brow; the slightly outward-curved line of his nose gave to it a character of decision and courage; in his cheeks the fullness of youth had begun to give place to the sterner mould of manhood; a thick close beard on the upper lip and chin, had just assumed a more vigorous growth than the down that edged his cheeks; a neck like a stag's for graceful length and swelling strength, was rooted in shoulders, to depict which, Michael Angelo and Raphael must have borrowed from each other potency and grace. He grasped in his left hand the finger board of a lute, from which his right hand wrung music so full and loud, that his sister's voice was provoked to an emulous rivalry, and the harmony filled all the lofty room, curling about its florid cornices, and eddying in its

vaulted roof; while Sebastian gazed at the upturned face beside him, exulting with all a brother's love, in the might of song so sweet from lips so gentle. As Morosini entered, the spell was broken; the sounds ceased, and the brother and sister rose to greet their father— Sebastian with cheerful respect, Angiolina with a love that overflowed from her abundant heart, creating in its fullness the deserts of its own object.

A close observer of all the decorums of life, and especially those which are considered incumbent on the statesman, it was with something akin to pride that Morosini laid himself open to the imputation of a vice, which, he said, was common in the greatest statesmen; and widowhood had left him without scruples in respect to appearances, if unbending in the gayeties of celibacy. His absences were too frequent to cause surprise to his children. Sebastian guessed but avoided, knowing the cause; Angiolina implicitly believed that they were necessary for affairs of state. They formed for Alessandro a great convenience, first because they occasioned useful intervals of freedom; next because he was able to impute to them any absence of which he did not wish to seem to know the real reason; and chiefly because they furnished material for a very subtle flattery; callous himself, he was able to keep up a show of great austerity of life; which gave him opportunity to reprove "Marco," as on such occasions alone he thought it polite to call him, for his "libertine courses," whereat Morosini not only conceived an exalted respect for his brother's continence, but also was convinced of the bold frankness of the man, who made him believe himself superior in a hundred other really important matters; and even in that particular left a loophole, to imagine that his lordly relative erred from patrician habits of indulgence, and a happier turn for pleasing the fair. It was, therefore, the salt of life for Morosini to resign himself to the brief castigation of a frown and a solemn reproof, never made tedious. Of his daughter's innocent ignorance he quite approved; and that feeling made him reward her with some endeavor to display paternal tenderness, as he pressed her hastily to his bosom, and kissed her brow with mechanical emphasis. Sebastian's suspicions were matter of course, and of indifference; and the bow of the son was duly sanctioned by an approving bend of the head. Having thus performed his paternal devoirs, Morosini looking round the room, and saw the object of his search, sitting in a corner, poring over a large volume of classic lore; for Alessandro had from the first perceived the advantage which learning would prove to his tainted escutcheon; and he had so well profited by his labors, that he had enjoyed in the frequent sight of Venice the converse of Petrarch himself. Morosini laid his hand on his foster brother's shoulder, and he, closing his book, rose at the bidding of his lord's countenance, and accompanied him to an inner room; leaving the brother and sister to resume their music—Angiolina with a sigh, Sebastian with a sense of relief—until summoned to the morning meal.

Hastily and angrily Morosini recounted his adventure; but so confusedly that the Paduan could scarcely have understood him, but that he knew it all before—a frequent case with Morosini's disclosures to him. He had no difficulty in persuading the senator that it would most comport with his dignity, be safer to prevent suspicion, and be most politic for watching the future course of events, to conceal the whole; and he was considering how he could arrest the tiresome overflow of the noble's indignation, when they were interrupted by a servant, who told Morosini that a woman wished to speak with him.

"Again, Marco?" said the foster brother, in a low voice, with a frown.

"Nay," replied Morosini, with a latent smile, "I know not who it is. Did her send her message by you, Pippo."

"I told her so, my lord, but she will not be answered."

"You had better see her yourself, and not make confidants of babbling lackeys," whispered Alessandro, as he left the room.

Presently a woman was ushered in. Her tall figure showed, through the thick gray cloak and veil that enveloped her, a firm and dignified carriage; her face was so covered as to be scarcely visible. By her side walked a stripling of some sixteen years in height, but his boyish face might have seen but twelve or fourteen springs; his fair locks, carefully combed, were surmounted by an old velvet cap; his body was clothed in a faded gray vest of some indifferent stuff, and dingy dark hose covered his legs; but no meanness of dress could disguise the pleasing form of an active and well-grown boy; while the healthy glow of his handsome face, and the upright step, as he led the woman by the hand, his left resting on the short poignard that hung by his side, bespoke an honest and courageous heart. He stopped inside the door, as the woman advanced to Morosini. The senator gazed on her in calm attention.

"My lord," said a low, firm voice, issuing from the veil, "I am a messenger from a mother's bed of sickness. I come from the wife of Jacopo Arduino."

Morosini's brow contracted, as he asked, "Why does the wife of Jacopo Arduino send to me?"

"Because she is in trouble—reduced to the lowest misery, and believed that the Morosini would not desire the blood of his friend Orso Arduino to perish."

"How is this? what has happened? and tell me, girl, why is the wife of Jacopo obliged to beg charity? The man has been indiscreet—so reckless as to lose his station, and with it the countenance of his family; his very marriage with a common woman would have done as much. But he has means, he has at least hands, and why does he leave his family to beg? where is he?"

"My father has been unfortunate, but when my mother accepted his love she had health and strength to aid, rather than encumber him. You know that the plague struck her down, and that she never recovered that dreadful stroke."

"Why should I know? Where is your father?"

"We know not; but we are sure that he is absent for our good, or that some accident keeps him. We have not seen him for ten days,

and my suit to your lordship now is, that you would vouchsafe your powerful aid to have him sought, and spare to us, in our need, a morsel of your wealth, to be paid after our father's return."

"Girl, I have no wealth. My wealth belongs to Venice, and cannot be lavished to patch up the battered fortunes of shameless spendthrifts. You say you want, but that boy shows no signs of famine."

"He is the youngest, and we strive to keep him from feeling misery as long as we can. Oh! how hard you are. I would not supplicate, but that my wretched mother sinks with fear and weakness, and I dare not return as I came."

In the earnestness of her appeal, the woman allowed her veil to unclose, and display a face sufficiently attractive to please the critical Morosini. His tone changed.

"There is, indeed," said he, "one way in which your mother might be served. But then, fair one," he added with a forced smile, "services should be mutual. Can that sweet face repay kindness with kindness?"

The girl drew herself up, and fixing on his face one steadfast look, she said, "I fear we cannot understand each other. I take my leave of your lordship."

"Nay, hurry not away;" and he would have taken her hand.

"Ranieri!" she cried, quickly, but not loud. The boy was at her side in an instant.

"I shall give to my mother your lordship's answer—that is, the answer to her message."

She bowed and left the room; Morosini half wondering why he let her go so easily.

CHAPTER VI.

THE day proved hot and oppressive, and Sebastian, in aimless idleness, loitered from the Place of St. Mark, late after his evening lounge, into some of the smaller and deserted streets that branched off from it. His attention was arrested near the end of a dark calle, by a peculiar sound of struggling mixed with a woman's voice in earnest entreaty, and now and then, a sharp sound like a suppressed scream. It was like some one in terror yet afraid to call for assistance. He moved towards the spot, directed rather by the noise than by the moonlight which was now becoming more and more obscured by drifting clouds. In the deep gloom, he saw a man, with a woman struggling in his arms as if for life; while he embraced her with an occasional murmur of cajolery and a sneering chuckle. "Leave her, ribald!" cried Sebastian as he stepped briskly forward. The man desisted, and stopped for an instant, as if prepared to contest the matter; but as Sebastian came nearer, he turned quickly away, and with rapid strides disappeared in the dark lane. Sebastian would have followed; but he saw the woman stagger, and had he not caught her in his arms she would have fallen. Her weight told him that she had fainted; and in spite of his good nature, he began to reflect with some embarrassment at the awkwardness of his position, with a lifeless woman in his arms, not knowing whither to bear her. The moon again came forth, shining full upon his unconscious burden; and in spite of his perplexity he could not help scanning her somewhat closely, as her head lay upon his shoulder. She was worthy of his critical regard. The thick and somewhat coarse veil which had covered the upper part of her figure, had been torn off in the struggle, and hung loose around her. As she leaned against him, the folds of a sober dress of common stuff did not conceal the grace of a tall and commanding figure. Her face was cast in the finest mould: somewhat too thin for beauty, suffering of mind or body seemed to have slightly disturbed the regularity of its outline; but even the helpless prostration of the swoon did not mar the sweet dignity of womanhood; and the fairness of her complexion, the soft fair hair that waved in loosened tresses from her temples, and the extreme pallor, which showed yet more for the silver moonlight, imparted an air of delicacy and gentleness that made Sebastian hold her more tenderly and reverently in his arms. A sigh like departing sleep stirred her severed lips, then a low uneasy murmur; and a pair of soft blue eyes, in half awakened sense, met Sebastian's gaze. A sudden terror overspread her face; she strove to rise from his arms with scarcely articulate exclamations. "Fear nothing, dear lady," he said, in a low earnest voice, "you are safe, and there is none here to offend you with a thought of harm." She seemed to know by the voice that she was no longer in that audacious, cruel embrace; and terror no more giving renewed strength, again she sank exhausted. Sebastian felt no impatience now, as he held his arms unmoved, lest her rest should be disturbed. Another sigh and she rose slowly from his embrace; and putting her hand, bewildered, to her brow, she tottered forward. Sebastian again passed his arm round her, but so gently and respectfully, that she could not fear. "Suffer me," he said, "to support you; you cannot yet stand. Tell me where I can place you in safety." "Where, ah! where!" she cried; and clasping her hands together, she turned her eyes to heaven, and exclaimed, "Oh! can suffering goodness find no peace on earth! but must its servants be the sport of pitiless crime!" A burst of tears relieved her. Sebastian stood beside her in respectful silence. Presently she turned to him, and said, "I do not know how to thank you, sir, for this protection, or I would thank you with my soul." She was about to leave him, when he begged her not to reject his support and guard until she was in safety. For an instant she bent upon him a fixed and searching look, her unmoved eyes reading his countenance like a book. How much did that regard tell, of wrong known, of firm self-reliance, of practised judgment! No unworthy fear made Sebastian shun her regard: but, as he leaned forward, he turned his face up to hers, as one who would have his credentials read through every line. Unconscious of her stern scrutiny, her eyes dropped gently, and her countenance resumed its softer expression, as she placed her hand in his, and suffered him to lead her the way she turned her steps. "We have not far to go," she said; and then she suddenly added, "Tell me, in my terror did I scream!"

"Scarcely to be heard."

"I hope not; for it might have carried my terror to the bed of one who is sick and feeble."

She stopped at the door of a house that opened into the lane.

"Are you in safety now!" asked Sebastian.

"If any where," she answered sadly: then more cheerfully she added, "Yes, no danger could follow me here. Farewell, sir; never will your goodness be forgotten."

Sebastian relinquished her hand without the pressure that he was wont to bestow unreproved, on that of high-born damsels; and he bowed lowly as the girl entered the house. One grave kind look greeted him as she closed the door after her, and he heard it bolted. A few minutes he remained looking on the door; scarcely thinking, but in the mood of a man to whom an event has happened that he is hopeless of unriddling, and so contemplates without thought. The dark outlines of the house, which was quite unknown to him, and was of rather an humble kind than otherwise, had grown in those moments familiar objects. Not a sound was heard, save the ripple of the water and a distant hum of men. He walked slowly away.

CHAPTER VII.

As he proceeded, the hum which he had heard grew louder, and gradually he could distinguish shouts and angry cries. He quickened his pace; something was evidently the matter in the city. Entering the square of St. Mark, and going on to the piazzetta, he found the whole place in a tumult; and near the water side, from the midst of the dark mass of a quickly shifting crowd, he saw the glare of torches which were dashed to and fro. He hurried to the spot. As he drew near, a horrid spectacle reared itself from the moving mass. An old woman, more crooked than years ever bent the frame, her eyes staring rigid and glassy amid their wrinkles, her nose and chin forced apart by a ghastly grin of agony and terror, her stony cheeks and white hair dabbled in blood, was lifted above the heads of the crowd, and as she fell back again one smote her with a torch. With a cry of horror Sebastian rushed forward, and forced his way through the dense and heedless multitude. When he had done so, a new sight appeared. The old woman lay, half crouched up and resting on her hands, upon the ground, and over her stood a young cavalier, with his sword drawn, and both hands extended to keep back the enraged crowd. The person that thus braved them, seemed scarcely fitted to cope with such a foe. He was barely of middle height, and his light frame, fair complexion, short light brown ringlets, delicate features, and close, silken beard, gave an appearance of extreme youth. But a second glance detected in the full chest, the manly breadth of shoulder, the well knit joints and muscular limbs, and, above all, in the stern glow of a deep hazel eye, the vigor and courageous heart that made him front his unnumbered foes with an air of peremptory command, which held them back far more than the sword he grasped. "The Englishman! It is the Englishman!" shouted a thousand voices; "he is a traitor!

he is one of the gang! It is Carrara's ruffian." Sebastian recognized in the dauntless youth his friend, Edward the Englishman—in his protégée, an old crone known only by her nickname of La Gobba, so called from her humped back; the keeper of a low wine-shop, which was the resort of the bullies and all the refuse of Venice. In an instant he was by the side of his friend; and Messer Alberti, Messer da Riva, and one or two more, soon formed a little band that daunted the rabble rout by their high station. A rough fisherman tried cunningly to draw the old woman into the crowd behind Edward; who, not wishing, both for prudence and mercy, to shed blood, pushed him back with his open hand. The man drew a knife, but a blow from Sebastian's sword laid him beside the chattering crone at Edward's feet. The crowd made a rush; but one in front of them spread his arms and cried, "Stay, stay; 'tis young Morosini: let us tell them; let us speak."

"Stand back, men," shouted Edward, in their own dialect: "do you not know friends from enemies!"

"Yes, yes; it is the Englishman!"　"Hear Messer Odoardo!"　"Give us up La Gobba!" "There's treachery among the nobles!"　"Hear them!"　"Tell them!" Such were the discordant cries that beat the air about Edward's ears, as he still stood unmoved over the miserable wretch and the bleeding fisherman. There was a pause.

"Viva Vinegia!" shouted Edward.

"Viva Vinegia! Viva Odoardo!" echoed the mob. Another pause.

"Venetians, have I not served our city!" "Yes, yes!"　"Fought with you!"　"Yes, yes!"　"Shall I not do so again—against Carrara, if he appear against us!"　"Yes, yes!" "Let us then serve Venice faithfully; let us make her laws obeyed. If you know me to be traitor, you have me here, kill me now"—"Viva Odoardo!"—"But do not disgrace yourselves by warring on old women—worrying this miserable creature as dogs would a cat." He suddenly lowered his voice: "You, Zanni, tell me, what has this unfortunate done, that you were murdering her!"

"Carrara!" "the wells! the wells!" shouted the rabble.

"Let Zanni speak."

"Zanni speak! tell, tell!" was the shout.

Zanni, the man whose effort to stay the mob in their last rush had been observed by Edward, now shifted for an instant on his feet, half abashed at being the spokesman for injured Venice; and then, with a much subdued manner, he said, "By your favor, sirs, Signor Carrara has sent people here to poison our wells, and we found that La Gobba is hostess to the conspirators."

The nobles looked at each other aghast. Edward stooped down and asked the shaking hag if that was true. She stared at him with idiot terror, speechless.

"She confessed it," said Zanni. "Yes, yes, she confessed," echoed a thousand tongues: the storm was rising again.

"Stay, my friends," cried Edward; "if we have traitors among us, we must have the law; the Ten must deal with this." At that dread name, those immediately around him

were hushed. "Go," added he, "go, with a guard; let us not suffer her to escape in the disturbance." His humane artifice succeeded; and when the officers of the watch, who, in virtue of their office had been out of the way, now approached, Edward and his friends had no difficulty in consigning the trembling and guilt-confessing dotard to their charge. With a shout for Edward, and many another for Venice, the multitude dispersed, bearing away their torches, and leaving the place of St. Mark once more to the quiet moonlight.

———◆———

CHAPTER VIII.

NEXT morning all Venice rang with the detected conspiracy. Having discovered the plot before the wells were poisoned, everybody was convinced that there was poison in the water; and for the first few hours of intense suspicion, wine and fruit were at a premium. Morosini, after a consultation with the foster brother, went to the senate, to await the disclosures anticipated from the examination of La Gobba before the Council of Ten. With Angiolina and her brother there was no music, but she made him recount all that had happened; listening with breathless attention, and drawing closer and closer to the youth, as he told of the terror of the wretch, the fury of the mob, the bold humanity of the Englishman, and his own share in the scene. He was too modest and sincere to think of disclaiming his own merit, or to think of it all; but he revelled in the pleasure of seeing his admiring description of Edward's bearing reflected in the earnest emotion of his young sister's face. They were still thus engaged, when a servant hastily ushered in the hero himself. Angiolina rose from her brother's arms, blushing rosy red, conscious that at the moment the visitor occupied all her thoughts and feelings. Edward hesitated to approach, fancying that he had inopportunely intruded; but Angiolina advanced to him, and putting both her trembling hands in his, cried, "O Messer Odoardo, Sebastian has just been telling all your story, and—" she stopped, scarce knowing what she was going to add. Edward, struck with delight at so unexpected a reward from the lovely for his service to the hideous, respectfully put to his lips one of the gentle hands he held, saying, "Dear lady, my countrymen—indeed, no true men can forget, when any woman is in peril, those more lovely ones who are away." For an instant Angiolina suffered him to hold her hands: his set compliment recalled her to herself; yet there was in his manner a something more than mere courtesy. She was struck with one of those fits o undefined doubt and disappointment, which sometimes dull impulsive natures; too vague, however, to be known even to herself; and withdrawing her hands, she put her arm in her brother's, as he stepped forward to greet his friend.

"I am come," said Edward, "to summon you away: we must not delay."

"I am ready," answered Sebastian; "but we are fasting still; will you eat!"

"Nay, so am not I. But I must be cruel

enough to carry you away without food ; for our business needs despatch."

"You are sudden ; but I am with you ;" and taking leave of Angiolina, the two friends departed.

"In the boat Sebastian sought an explanation of the other's sudden and anxious manner. "And now that the brawl is over, dear Edward," said he, " I cannot believe this fierce rumor. Carrara never could have harbored such devilish intent. He has friends as well as foes in Venice—Zeno, for instance, whom he and all men love. Besides, is he not at peace with Venice ?"

Edward looked stern and grave, and did not answer ; but drawing from his pocket a paper, he said, " Hear what is written to me ;" and translating as he went, he read from English this letter.

" My very dear and esteemed friend, Master Edward of Ellyndenne, I have things to say to you that concern ourselves, and our friends in Venice. Signor John Fernandez, who is known to you as a very excellent soldier, and the captain of a goodly troop, as men go, hath been engaged for service near Venice, as he telleth me ; but not, as I suspect, for Venice. He told me, that I might have the like service, at very good reward. I told him I liked not such service as he thought of ; and he reddened, but did not deny it. This I said, meaning Carrara ; and that is what I say now, that Carrara is gathering troops. If Venice should want my poor services, I shall hold myself ready to your summons : if not, I will not fight against any whose bread I have eaten ; nor would, I think, many of my men. Tell this to whom you think proper ; and my service to Master Zeno ; and the same to you.

"From your friend,
"WILLIAM COOKE."

Sebastian was silenced. "To whom," he asked, " have you shown this letter ?"

"To none as yet but you ; to-day I show it to none ; but should Zeno not return from Tenedos to-morrow, I shall make it known to Messer Alberti, my countryman, as he calls himself. But dear Sebastian, you are desirous to take part in serving your country ; and if your father yet deems you too young to do so," added Edward, playfully, " your friend does not : you shall take me to whom you think best ; to Messer Alberti, if you will."

Sebastian's eyes glistened : the ambition which he inherited from his father, but in a more generous kind, was about to be gratified. Pressing Edward's hand with a tight grasp, he answered, " I would carry it, not to Alberti, but to the doge himself ; for none is so fit to know it as Andrea Contarini."

Edward agreed. In a few minutes his gondola landed them at the place of St. Mark, and presently they were in the hall of the ducal palace. Of the attendants waiting about, Sebastian desired one to bring them to the doge. The man replied that the doge was just then on the point of going to the council. But Edward interposed, saying that they must see him before he went to the council ; and the servant, hesitating a moment, retired. He soon returned, and ushered them into a small chamber, where they found themselves in the presence of the doge.

Andrea Contarini was seated in a tall straight-backed chair, both hands resting on the arms, in the attitude of a man who is waiting, conscious that his time is short. The weight of seventy years had not bent his back, nor shrunk the noble proportions of his form, clothed in a dark velvet vest ; and the cares of state, forced upon him as the dogate had been, if they had doubly blanched his hair, had not tarnished the benignity which illuminated his countenance A noble brow, and an air of manly energy and determination explained the reason why the republic had compelled him to be its chief in troublous times. The ducal cap lay on the table beside him, ready to be donned ; the red robe was in the hands of an attendant. As the young men entered, he exclaimed, "Ah ! Ser Inglese, is it you ?" Then ordering his servants to wait without, he added, " Be brief, my friend ; for I must be gone." Edward looked at his companion, who told, in a few words, the purport of Cooke's letter. Edward added, that Cooke might be fully relied on, as the doge knew, and that he must have very strong grounds for his statements, as he used not to speak lightly. Contarini looked grave, and paused : then he said, " This is the worst news we have had yet. We may want the services of your countryman, Ser Odoardo."

" So, my lord, I judged ; and therefore I have already written to Cooke, to say that I know he may hold himself engaged. The letter has not been sent, as I did not mean it ; but I thought it might be less harmful if my letter were intercepted, than one from a Venetian."

" You were discreet : you should know"—he stopped and glanced at Sebastian.

" My friend is young," said Edward, in answer to the look ; " but he has judgment beyond his years ; and if I may be trusted he may ; for indeed we are as one."

" You should know," proceeded the doge, " that this miserable old woman, who owes you so much gratitude, Messer Odoardo, has made confessions : her brutal son, one Nadale, was one of the malefactors who were, as it is said, to have poisoned our wells, and hopes of purchasing his life made her confess. He too had confessed before ; being a spy upon all—even upon his dotard mother. She admits that the crime found its executors at her house, and that Carrara inspired it ; but he has, she says, higher tools. She accuses some of the highest men in Venice, hitherto deemed Carrara's greatest enemies. Torture, sirs, and fear will force lies out of the mouth as well as truth ; and I cannot yet believe those noble gentlemen traitors on the word of this wretched hag. But there is something bad in Venice, something that threatens our lives even in our homes. Your news, Messer Odoardo, completes the circle of our dangers : Genoa is again in arms against us."

" Genoa again !" exclaimed the youths.

" Aye, Genoa ; and for a brave reason." The old man continued, with a twinkle of humor in his eye : " when they were crowning King Pietro of Cyprus at Famagosta, as Bishop of Jerusalem, our two ambassadors quarrelled for precedence. The Genoese, losing the coveted post on the king's right hand, fell to flinging bread at our officer ; the Venetians retorted by flinging some of the Genoese out of the window : and Genoa takes her revenge on our republic, unless she will humbly crave pardon for being insulted by the noble bread thrower. Venice," he added more gravely, "can meet them ; but her enemies are many."

"And so," said Sebastian, "are her servants."

"Good ; here is proof of it," said Contarini, laying his hand on a letter, "this tells us of service done by the best of her servants."

"Carlo Zeno !" said Edward.

"The same. In all parts of the world he writes his name in high deeds. He has seated Calojohannes of Greece on the throne from which his rebel son Andronicus had driven him ; Tenedos given to Venice is the token of the emperor's gratitude, knowing that Zeno prized no payment so well as that made to his country ; and on his way home he has stopped to drive out the Genoese. But we want him here. Young men," proceeded the veteran, "let that great man's life, let his fame, and the love of Venice, teach you how to live. Messer Odoardo will one day return to his own country, but not without our affection, nor I hope without marks of our gratitude ; but you, Sebastian, will grow up in these councils : be another Zeno, if you can."

"I cannot have a better master in that precept than Odoardo," replied Sebastian warmly, "for I believe that no man is prouder of being the chosen friend of Zeno."

"I know it. But I must not dally with you gallants while our grave senators await me. Say nothing of this matter to others, but you, Odoardo, send your letter, and speak as confidently as you please ; our good friend Cooke shall not lose ; and you or Sebastian shall advise me of his coming. Adieu."

The young men saluted the venerable prince, leaving the room as his attendants entered, and helped him hastily to assume his robe of state.

CHAPTER IX.

As the day darkened, Sebastian could not abstain from visiting the spot where he had met with the adventure of the night before. Some time he loitered about near the dismal looking house ; but all was dark and silent. The dull stone walls and dingy door gave no sign that they enclosed so fair and noble a creature as the lady whom he had rescued—for such he called her in his thoughts, despite her coarse gown and homely veil. It was as still next night ; only that some two or three men who stood round the door skulked away at his approach. His disappointment served to pique his perseverance, and he watched many evenings. At length, one night, the door opened, and from it appeared the form that he had so long looked for. All that had happened since the door had closed upon that same figure seemed like a dream. The woman fastened up the house carefully, and wrapping her veil round her, walked towards the spot where he

stood, with a firm and measured step, as if she braved a danger which she feared. When she drew near she caught sight of his tall figure, and stopped, in evident dread. He approached, saying, "I fear, lady, that I have done a wrong which I would be the last to do, and given you some alarm." Recognizing his voice, she again walked on, replying, "I ought not to be alarmed at that voice ; but weakness is fearful." There was something in her manner that fascinated Sebastian into forgetfulness of all but the stranger before him : a favorite with women, he never felt so diffident ; not inexperienced in gallantries, he never thought of the singular inconsistency of the woman's lowly garb with her speech and bearing ; he thought not of seeing her thus walking in the street, and alone ! He forgot his own habits, the customs and suspicions of society, the woman's strangeness—everything but that he was talking to one of the better part of the human race. Involuntarily dropping the tone of compliment, he said, in a low and earnest voice, "Would I were allowed to be your guard. I have kept watch here each night since I first saw you in your danger ; will you not let me attend you ?"

She stopped, and looked in his face. "No, it may not be. It should be right that your goodness should not be repulsed, but it is not right."

"Nay, the very thing that makes your danger is a shield for you—it is dark, and your attendant will be unknown."

The girl answered slowly, as if half thinking —"I am used to be unprotected ; I scarcely fear ; and in the worst danger I ever had, God sent succor. It is not I that need to dread being seen, whoever is my companion ; but no," she added, more decidedly, "you must not do this. You have served me ; and I never shall forget it ; but you must not bring reproach upon me."

"Reproach ! Oh, how little could I do so ? But you said just now that you feared not to be seen."

"You mistake me : no reproaches such as you think can touch me : I am beneath them—and above them." With a painful revulsion at these equivocal words, Sebastian's feelings were thrown back upon the world, as he looked at the unknown being before him. She proceeded, in the same low voice, as if it borrowed music from her heart itself, "there is none to reproach me, but me." Sebastian's breast was relieved of the uneasy doubt that cramped it with cold, though he was not much enlightened ; but still he listened. "Besides," she continued with a smile, which he heard in her accents rather than saw in the dim light, "I can give you plain reasons why you could not go with me now."

"Why !"

"I am going on a very humble errand—to fetch home some bread."

"And why cannot I wait upon you, and carry your food too ?"

"No, no ; you forget who you are."

"Do you know me, then ?"

"Only that you are of noble station, and that only by your manner. I shall meet no new harm. I do but what I do daily, though not always so late." And she moved forward

"Since you forbid me to follow you," said the youth, "I must obey. But you cannot forbid my watching you at a distance; and I am a better watchman for that I have studied the art lately." She walked on, silent. Sebastian exclaimed, "One word. I have not displeased you!" She turned her face to him—it was melancholy almost to grief; in a tone scarcely audible, she answered with the one word, "No." Sebastian fell back, and allowed her to pass on alone.

He just kept her in sight as she traversed a few streets, on foot; she entered a baker's shop, and returned. He stood aside in another street while she went by, and watched her to her own door again.

Attending to the public business of the day, in which Edward procured him a share, by throwing his influence and information into his stock, the young noble watched each night at the door of the house. He was more fortunate than he had at first been, for the journey for bread happened to occur at night more frequently than he had hoped. Gradually the girl seemed to grow more accustomed to the meeting; and even tacitly to acknowledge a kind of pleasure at his protection. Gradually, too, the mere passing word grew into a conversation, which extended part way to the now familiar baker's shop, and back again. His unknown friend did not take the youth into her confidence; but he gathered from things she let fall, that she was without male protectors, and that only one other woman lived with her; and that they were in great poverty. At the thought, the gold in his own purse seemed to burn against his bosom; he thought, not enviously, yet painfully, of the dainties which were his dear sister's daily food; yet he dared not even think of offering help. He kept a guard on every word he uttered, fearful of being exiled from a presence now becoming dear to him. Yet surely never was wooing stranger than his! The subject of their short conversations were few; and the colloquy usually consisted of such remarks as he found best calculated to draw from the veiled form beside him snatches of a simple wisdom which she seemed to have extracted from the very poverty that cramps and benumbs so many minds and hearts.

For some nights this lesson was denied to him; his friend came not. At length, the bread journey again occurred at night, and Sebastian saw the girl to her own door. Instead of entering, as usual, she stopped, and, after a pause, said, "I must now say farewell. This is the last time that I shall go out at night."

Sebastian felt a blow that a few weeks before would have been a marvel to himself. Turning as pale as death, he exclaimed, "The last time!"

"The last," she said; "it must be so." She took his hand—the first time that he had held it since *the* night—and her voice slightly trembled.

"The last! Why! why, the last time! May I know that! Have I done aught to offend you!"

"No, indeed. I have been only too little displeased. But do not punish me for not letting it be the last time, without bidding you farewell."

C

"You could not have been so cruel!" Sebastian, bolder than he had ever felt, firmly held the hand which had been placed in his, and with fervid entreaty persuaded her to tell him why it was to be the last time. Lastly, she told him, after he had seen her safe at home, he had hurried away to confer with Edward on some of the arrangements of the period; and on the night when he had last seen her, she had been obliged to go out again and again she met the ruffian from whom he rescued her. This time he offered no violence; but she had much difficulty in escaping from the outrage of his importunity.

Sebastian's cheeks burned as he listened. "What a recreant was I to leave you, and not to watch later! But why keep within, when you know that I am here to protect you!"

"No, my friend; you rescued me once, but I will not make dangers for you to meet."

Partly by gentle threats, however, that he should still watch on, though hopeless of seeing her, Sebastian wrung from his companion a promise that her determination should not be finally put in force that night. He left her, full of thought; for the process which any spectator could have discovered to him from the first, was now revealed to himself, and he knew that he loved, without knowing whom! Love at first sight he had laughed at, yet he was almost its victim. Love of a total stranger would have been equally ridiculous; yet, he asked himself, do not I, who have so often been that lovely, ingenuous face, and heard that truthful voice, know more of the being than of many whose names I know and have known for years. The answer of his heart was quite satisfactory.

The bread journeys at night, however, were stopped for ever.

CHAPTER X.

WHEN Sebastian approached the house next night, he was surprised to see the door open. So unusual a circumstance filled him with an undefined alarm. He drew nigh, and fancied that he heard the sound of men's voices. He entered, and found himself in as desolate a hall as he had ever seen. The sound of voices led him up stairs; but he went cautiously, and with a feeling of hesitation, like one who feared that he was trespassing. The noise grew louder as he advanced; it was a rude gabble; he was certain that there were enemies in the house—possibly the one whom he had repulsed, and he hastened forward. He passed an ante-chamber and two rooms bare of all furniture whatsoever, as though it were a deserted house. The next room had in it a table, a few chairs, and some few articles of domestic use. But he noted nothing, for in the next were the voices, loud and brutal. He stopped at the door, seeing that it was a bedroom. Not far from him, with their backs to him, were four men. One, the loudest of all, seemed a serving man; the others were an officer of the governor and soldiers of the police. Beyond them, near the opposite corner of the room, was a bed, bare of all furniture, and covered with the commonest clothing. In it was a woman of middle age, whom he knew at once to be the mother of the girl in whose fate he had grown so strangely interested. Her grayish brown hair had strayed from the white kerchief that bound it together; her hollow eyes glowed through the weight of sickness with a death-like hue; her nostrils and lips quivered with feverish emotion; and as she leant on one hand and stretched forth the other to forbid approach, the sleeve of her bed gown fell back and disclosed the ravages of disease in shrinking her once fine form. Beside her stood the one Sebastian now knew so well: the girl supported her mother in her arms, and looked towards the men as if expecting that the voice of suffering would cast a spell upon their ruffian rudeness.

"It is not our affair," said the officer; "Jacopo Arduino is in the house, and if we would not lose our own heads we must have the traitor."

"Jacopo Arduino," cried the sick woman, in a hollow voice, "is no traitor—unfortunate, miserable he has been, but you are traitors that call him so. There are none here but those you see; begone; let death and misery protect us—begone! I see," she cried more vehemently, "I see that you come here to torture me for the crime of my youth; you are sent here—I see it—I see it—to taunt me with the wrong I did to Jacopo when we were young, and to make me know all the bitterness the peasant girl brought to his proscribed house. Go, go; it is enough."

"Mother!" said the girl soothingly. The woman looked up in her face; and as the daughter bent down to reassure and control her, the two looked like a protecting angel and a penitent.

"Well, sirs," said the serving man, "if you are to be scared from your duty by a whining woman, you may chance to be the worse for it. I dare say the gentleman, like a worthy husband, is in his good dame's bed there, before our very eyes."

"Aye, Nadale," replied the officer, "truly there are not many other hiding places in this barren house. We will search it." He made a step forward.

The sick woman clasped her hands, and looked at the men in delirious terror. Her daughter quickly but gently put her back upon the cushions from which she had raised herself, and also making one step forward, so as to shield her parent, drew from her bosom a knife, such as the men had oftener seen in the hands of their fellows than in a girl's hold. Placing her left foot forward, she threw her armed right hand back, and firmly fixed her eye upon the group, ready to strike the first that advanced.

They paused. "Oh, oh!" cried the serving man, "the girl is a fighter. Bravo, let us try her mettle, masters." Again the officer was about to move, when a voice behind him called, "Hold, ribalds! what make you here?" They turned round, and beheld Sebastian. Submitting less to the stern voice and powerful form of the young man, than to his gallant dress and air of command, the man of law explained that they were in search of one Jacopo

Arduino, whom the man with them knew to be in the house; but his wife and daughter audaciously denied it. Sebastian looked to their guide, and in him he recognized, with small pleasure, a man whom he had used to regard as a kind of servant to the foster brother, though he had no recognized place in his father's household. A suspicion flashed across his mind that the ravisher whom he had encountered was no other than the cold Alessandro. He was about angrily to drive the men from the room, but the young statesman's deference for the law of the republic, and perhaps some desire to get rid of the men as quickly as possible, checked him. "You have found no one in the house!" he asked.

The men shrugged their shoulders. "This good man, sir," said the officer, "says that perhaps in that bed—"

"That bed is sacred, ruffian, even from your suspicions. Begone!"

Seeing that farther altercation was useless, if not dangerous, the bold assertors of the law retreated.

Sebastian looked towards the bed. Bianca Arduino had perceived the protection which came to her sick couch as from heaven, and she sank, half swooning, half slumbering into a state of placid unconsciousness. Teresa knelt by the bed, and bent over her mother in alarm. Sebastian too drew softly near, and gazed upon that care-worn face. After some moments, he whispered, "She sleeps." Teresa started round at his voice and looked in his face—"A second time!" she cried, as she snatched his hand, and pressing on it one passionate kiss, she leant her brow upon it in an uncontrolled burst of tears. For a few moments Sebastian permitted his hand to receive that unwonted and too delicious homage; then gently clasping one of those which held it, he raised his charge from the ground, and, for the second time, folding his arm around her, sought to soothe her with assurances of safety for herself and that dearer one whose case he now knew. Teresa buried her face in both her hands, and listened in silence. She trembled violently. "You are ill," cried Sebastian, "do, dearest lady, stay this passion of terror. Think that you have now a guard that never will leave you, except in safety." "Still she spoke not. He tried to take her hand from her face; but she yielded not. He used a slight force, and then she suffered him to take away her hand; but turned her head aside. "Unfortunate that I am," he cried, "whenever I seek most to serve you, my foolish heart makes me offend." Putting her hand again to her eyes, Teresa pressed her brow, and by a strong effort recalled her strength. "You could never now offend," she said slowly, and deliberately, "though you trampled on me. You have saved me twice, and twice again, in that dear mother; would that in doing so you could have saved something that would repay you." She disengaged herself from his arm, and turning her pale face full on his, she continued: "You now know that you have served the daughter of a gentleman, so unfortunate and so poor, that men dare not call him traitor —a race so wretched, that their very indigence stamps reproach upon them, and makes her

vice to them a disgrace. It is, too, the last
misery of poverty that it cannot be grateful;
having nought left but itself, it cannot even
give itself away, for it is a cursed gift. You
served me once, and I could think of no return,
but to leave you: you serve me again, and
still I have nothing but that—you must come
no more."

"Dear lady," cried Sebastian, with something more of obstinacy than he had yet ventured upon, "you have now a protector, one
too to protect your mother; and never again
shall you lose it. No, I can ask your own
heart, if I should leave you thus pale and trembling, or if I should not shield that poor sufferer's bed." With earnest persuasion, urged in
words so little akin to gallantry that they
might have been addressed from one sister to
another, Sebastian obtained permission to stop
for a time.

His foot touched against the knife which
Teresa had let fall in bending over her mother.
He stooped and picked it up; and for a moment
he looked upon it, thinking on the fears that
could have placed it in the hand that had held
it. Teresa seemed to divine his thoughts, and
she told him to put it aside. "You could not
have used it!" he said. "Oh, I could, I
could!" she cried; "you do not know what
the poor and helpless endure. How could
you? You do not do the wrongs they suffer,
for you are not base and tyrannous: you do
not suffer, for you are strong and powerful; you
do not see these things; and the poor have not
always such as you near them. That is a cruel
friend that one can always have. But put it
away—I cannot take it from your hand—I can
never touch it again."

"You should not need it again. I was to
blame in that I left you so unprotected." He
put the knife upon a table by him. "This hand
was not made to hold such things," respectfully kissing it.

"That hand," she answered, "must perforce
do things it was not made for; and its first
duty is to keep vileness and danger from this
house." She pointed to her mother's bed.

Bianca stirred, and he retreated to the next
chamber; where, after he had been down
stairs to fasten the house door, he was soon
joined by Teresa. Her mother, she told him,
slept more tranquilly than she had long done.

He led the exhausted girl to a chair, and
taking one beside her, he had that night a
longer conversation than any that the bread
journeys had afforded. Though she still ab-
stained from telling him all the secrets of their
poverty, he gathered from the snatches of her
explanations that her father, Jacopo Arduino,
was a decayed merchant, which indeed he knew
before; that since his misfortunes a wandering
disposition had seized him, his object being to
fall upon some enterprise to benefit his family,
and his occupation to serve every body but his
family; that in despair at her mother's increasing malady, her brave young brother,
Ranieri, had set out in search of his father,
whom they secretly suspected to be at Padua;
and that in the mean time a foul charge had
been brought against him by some humpbacked
woman, of being employed by Carrara to poison the wells of Venice! Sebastian listened

in mingled delight and agony. That the creature before him could be allied with treason
was impossible—her face was truth itself. He
was little inclined to believe ill of Jacopo,
whose name he had heard with praise in the
revered mouth of Carlo Zeno; yet his unconsciously acknowledged presence in Padua, the
undeniable existence of the conspiracy, Jacopo's vagabond habits and desperate fortunes,
crowded upon Sebastian's mind. Did he think
of abandoning the ill-fated daughter of the supposed traitor? He thought nothing of the kind
—he scarcely thought at all, except of her immediate safety, and of the strange progress he
had made in her confidence; so that midnight
found him still talking with her in the humble
room. Truly he had earned her confidence,
by the fraternal discretion of his bearing; and
when it is remembered he had not long reached manhood, the discretion of his behavior
will be admitted as more remarkable than the
indiscretion. At length Teresa declared it
impossible that the house could again be disturbed, and begged him to return to his home.
With a sigh he rose, and after many cautions
to her to admit none but those whose voice she
knew—should she know his? he asked—could
he doubt it? he kissed her hand, and took his
leave. But he went no farther than the street.
All night the house was still and safe. When
it was broad day-light, Sebastian repaired to
Edward's lodging, wishing to be first seen
where he was safe from inquiries.

From that time Sebastian did not wait outside the house. Bianca had no recollection of
his appearance, scarcely of the scene at all;
and Teresa hesitated to agitate her by introducing to her Sebastian. There was another
reason that deterred her: Sebastian had never
told her his name, and without positively in-
tending it, she was not reluctant to defer the
introduction of her anonymous protector. The
trouble to which she had been exposed had
taught her self-reliance; and perhaps it was
too great confidence in that which made her
admit the visits of her new friend. Destitute
of all that is usually taken to constitute comfort, she had in some sort resigned herself to
the course of events; reconciling herself to the
solace of passing good; confident that when it
did pass, and the evil followed, she could bear
it, as she had so well learned to do. It was
the course of the profligate's philosophy; but
none was more opposite to the profligate than
Teresa, whose self-denial eked out the slender
means of her family. She thought that she saw
Sebastian's character open before her, as a
book: he hoped that it was so; and in fact it
was. She received him as he deserved to be
received; content to see him no more when
the tide of time should have borne him to a
distance. Of that Sebastian took no thought:
she did.

CHAPTER XI.

WITHIN the hour, the account of Sebastian's
rescue of the women reached the foster-brother.
The cunning bully Nadale told the story, not
without an effort to raise his master's choler
against the untoward arrogance of the young

man, but Alessandro listened as if all went as he had ordered it. Nor was he altogether displeased. The tale finished, he dismissed his retainer, and patiently waited until the senator should next seek him. Accordingly, it was not long before Morosini roused him from the reading of the Latin manuscript which he held in his hand. He turned his head, and quietly listened to what his lord had to say.

"Alessandro," said Morosini, "I fear me that there is something astir which we know not. It was told us in the senate, to-day, that the ports of the Lagune are to be defended. Do they look for the Genoese so suddenly?"

No look of surprise escaped the stern countenance of the foster brother. He replied, as often was his wont, by passing beyond the question to another. "And you, Morosini, have charge of the defences?"

"They are not yet settled."

"Who spake of it?"

"Piero Mocenigo, and the doge after him."

"Then it will be done. You will have charge of it?"

"I know not: they seemed to look to Pietro Romano."

"Nay, he is of the doge's council, and none of the signory can be spared from Venice. Of all the statesmen of Venice,—those, I mean, of trust and power,—Marco Morosini alone is unemployed in preparing for her defence; and not to give him this service, were to humble him in the very eyes of Venice. You claimed it?"

"Indeed I did not. I had not spoken of it yet to you, and it did not strike me, as now it does. I was to blame."

"True. But it can be done to-morrow. Morosini, I have something of more importance to treat of. You know, Marco, that on one only thing do I hold you foolish, even to your own disgrace."

"I know," replied Morosini, with the ease of a man confessing to a sin of which he feels no shame; or rather with the satisfaction of one, who, in suffering the penance for an acknowledged fault, earns a title to a thousand other virtues.

"I fear me that in this,—would it were in all things—but in this I fear me your son is but too like you."

"Sebastian," said the senator, philosophically, "is like others of his years; but I have noted in him no excess of indulgence. Alessandro, on these matters you are too austere. You seek, friend, in this austerity to exalt yourself above some stain, which men have said is in your blood, though I believe it not; but Sebastian needs no such rigid care: he knows that things are forgiven to his blood, which are denied to the baser; and who shall tell him it is not so?

"At least, then, if he must inherit the vice in his race, to which the Holy Virgin be thanked—am too humble to pretend—at least let him not, in his vile passions, oppose himself treasonably to the decrees of the state. And at least," continued the foster brother, with a show of increasing warmth—"at least let him not cross his father in these pursuits of shame. If you, Marco, will not be an example to teach the boy, let him not come where you are an example to him of folly and wickedness."

"What mean you!"

"I mean that, if you must have the laughter of a proclaimed traitor for your vile plaything, Sebastian must not be the bully of that shameless wench, to defend her from the consequences of her father's crime."

Morosini turned pale and red by turns; but he still awaited further answer.

"You have told me yourself, that the Ten have detected the one that disgraces the name of Arduino, in league with the traitor Carrara, or I should not have understood what has happened; the officers of justice were seeking Jacopo in his house; when Sebastian entered and drove them out—entered as if it were his accustomed home—into Bianca's very bed-chamber! Think you it is Bianca that your son visits! Now do you understand me?"

Morosini's glassy eyes glowed with rage, and his scattered beard bristled from his face, as he clenched his lips and teeth. He was about hastily to leave the room.

Alessandro called him back. "Stay, do not betray yourself, Marco, to the boy."

"Nay, the boy crossed me there once already. I thought he knew not; I could not hold him to be so audacious—I thought it but a chance; but this is past endurance."

"Stay, stay: Venice claims your first thoughts. About this matter, Morosini, of the defences—you must possess the management, by teaching the senate how to do the thing."

Morosini listened. His rage subsided, while Alessandro described to him a method of closing the ports with piles and chains; cautioning him to begin at the port of Lido and the openings to the north of it; as a stranger might naturally seize those first. The senator was diligent in his lessons.

"And Sebastian!" he asked, as the foster brother finished.

"We will watch him. Meanwhile, you can employ him at the sea-shore."

CHAPTER XII.

Sebastian seldom sought the company of his father, and for two days after the conversation between Morosini and the foster brother, he saw him not at all. On the third morning, his father suddenly entered the saloon where he sat with his sister, and desired him to attend upon him. Sebastian obeyed in silent surprise. With the foster brother, they entered a gondola, but at the place of St. Mark they passed into a galley, which rowed swiftly away. Uneasy thoughts beset him as they left behind them Venice and its palaces, and stretched forth in the channel of St. Mark. At Lido they landed, and here for the first time he learned that he was a prisoner in the service of his father, who was charged with superintending the construction of the defences. They took up their lodging in a small house on the shore, which had already been begun. The evening wore away, and it was past midnight, before

Sebastian was released to resign himself to bed, —sleepless, but not because the bed was hard as beseemed a camp. The unprotected Teresa haunted him all night; and the thought more than once crossed him, of escaping in the dark, and returning before dawn. But the fear of attracting notice to his frequent retreat, deterred him. He rose betimes, impatient of his bed; and leaving his father still asleep, sallied forth to busy his thoughts about the works; which proceeded night and day. As he approached the water-side, he saw through the mist, which drifted in from the sea, Alessandro already at his post, as Morosini's messenger; and with him was a man much shorter than the tall Paduan, though still no dwarf in height; and what he wanted in height he had in girth, for his belt would have taken in two or three of his stalwart companion. A close cap was on his head; and his gray hair and beard, thickly curling, were cut close to his full and ruddy cheeks. A large brown cloak, drawn tightly round, made him look, as he slowly carried himself along, like an animated bale of goods.

"Holy Virgin!" he exclaimed, with a loud voice, and all his jocund face beaming with delight, while he flung his arms and ample cloak apart, "is there not our dear Sebastian, leaving all the plung fair of Venice, to brave winds and waves among sailors and workmen! Embrace me, boy; by Bacchus, it turns business to a holiday to have our dear Sebastian with us."

Sebastian embraced his uncle Luigi—surnamed Il Grasso, from his fatness,—with more than usual warmth; so did it gladden him to see one loving friend in what already seemed his long exile.

"Here is this learned man, boy," cried the noble, with such a voice as if he would make all Venice hear him, "would persuade me that we must stay at this port till we have finished it; but let Alessandro, our brother, read his books, and leave galleys to them that have studied galleys: we will begin all at once; for see you not, young man, that a galley can enter at Malamocco for all our chains here at Lido! But I cannot convince this reverend gentleman of the same. I have ordered men to follow me, Messer Sebastian. Dost not see the thing so!"

"In truth, uncle mine, if Messer Alessandro can teach us more than we dream of, you can teach the sailor's arts to any man in Venice."

"We talk not, Messer Sebastiano," said Alessandro, "of galleys, for who could teach our most excellent lord, Messer Luigi!"

"True, sir, true. Sebastian hath taught us wisdom; but says Messer Alessandro, Sebastian, that your father is bent upon stopping here: believe it not, man; Marco is our leader, sirs; is he not a senator, one of the most excellent fathers, in truth? Let us go in and break our fast; we will break our fast, and then our father shall go with us, my son, to look after these our other ports. But stay—ho there!" he cried, as he ran back, with an agility rendered marvellous by his bulk, and shouted to a party of workmen a quarter of a mile off, "bestir, boys, bestir—or when I am back—" he shook his fist at them with a broad grin. Obeying the signal, the men answered with a shout of laughing obedience, and at once moved more quickly, in earnest that they would fulfil his wish.

"Now, my friends, for a little bread,—Messer Alessandro,—and a little wine, Sebastian, and then to the south."

Marco received his brother Luigi with dignified displeasure. He suspected that he was sent after him by the senate to be his lieutenant and master; a suspicion not far from truth. The foster brother, however, gave no sign of displeasure; but seemed suddenly to have adopted Luigi's view, so far as proceeding with the works at the next port; strenuously, however, resisting further progress to the south.

"We will do so, Messer Alessandro," said Luigi; "we will leave Malamocco to-day; and we can begin all along in a month, say."

Alessandro was silent; so was his lord and foster brother; and the breakfast suffered little, except from the repeated assaults of the fat noble, who stuck his knife into the loaf as often and as deeply as if it were an enemy. Before it was finished, Alessandro disappeared.

Soon after he had gone, Luigi exclaimed, "now, sirs, that our good scholar has gone, let us to our trade. I go to the port of Malamocco —you will go with me!"

Sebastian looked at his father; but he made no reply. Alessandro did not re-appear; and while the boat was prepared, Marco Morosini gave no sign of his intention. The fat man made no stay in his proceedings. The boat was announced to be ready; Luigi entered it with a look at his brother; and Marco silently followed. Their voyage would have been cheerless but for the constant talk of Luigi, which not even the continued fog could choke. At length the air began slowly to grow clearer, as they approached the strait which separates the island of Malamocco from that of Pelestrina. They landed on the southern end of Malamocco. It was in silent solitude. "These caitiffs," cried Luigi, "have not yet come, lazy dogs!"

"Who are they?" asked his brother.

"The cunning workmen, Marco mine, whom I had ordered here. We shall wait for them, for we must not leave this till the first pile is in the ground. Luckily the fog is blowing off."

They paced the ground for some time; Luigi pointing out the way in which he, with Morosini's assent, would dispose the barrier. The assent was neither given nor withheld; but for that Il Grasso seemed to care little. At length Morosini's long strides grew slower with weariness, and he sat down upon a stone. The other two continued their walk, gradually stretching more seawards. Suddenly Luigi stopped, and pointed with his finger,—"See there!" Sebastian looked, but saw nothing. Luigi kept his arm stretched out; his jovial countenance was grave even to fierceness; his eye gleamed under his drawn down brow, as though he would pierce the fog by an effort of the will. Sebastian looked again, and saw some dark body moving towards the lagoons. Luigi seized his arm, and drew him behind a slight projection of the ground; still watching in breathless silence. The slow and measured sound of oars came muffled through the fog, which now floated by in quickly waning thickness. "I knew not," said Sebastian, "that any of our galleys were near." The vessel steadily pursued her way. After a long pause, Luigi replied, "It is none of ours. See, Sebastian!" A break in the fog showed a column of smoke rising in thicker clouds from the opposite shore. "Look, look again!" Another dark body emerged from the seaward fog, with the click of oars, and followed its consort into the laguna. A third—a fourth! they counted six.

"Quick, boy, quick!" cried Luigi, "take my boat back to Venice, and tell them that we have seen six Genoese galleys in the waters of Venice, and that there are traitors there. We are bare indeed: but let them send what force they may, I will stay here; my men will be with me presently. Haste."

Sebastian flew to the boat, without a thought of aught else; and in two minutes the men were straining forward on their oars, as the bark cleft the roaring water at its bow.

On their way he gave the alarm to a boat which they met passing towards Lido, and issued order for other boats to be sent to Il Grasso. As they neared Venice he grew more circumspect; but he took from a boat which they encountered, fresh rowers. The sun was already in its downward course ere he landed at St. Mark's: in two minutes he was in the presence of the doge, and Contarini had heard his startling tale. Next minute the great bell of St. Mark's campanile was tolling; the people poured into the square, and already shouts of "the Genoese! the Genoese!" rang through the city. While the doge repaired to the senate, Sebastian flew at his bidding to the arsenal—roused the astonished workmen from their labor, toiling with his own hand; and with a quickness passing belief, he made them prepare two of the readiest galleys for service. In one of them he returned to the great square, where already he found her crew under their appointed leader, Alberti, eager to depart. He went to wait outside the senate chamber. Edward was there—ever among the first when Venice was in need. Presently the venerable prince came forth; and with a manly cheerfulness waved his hand to the shout that greeted his appearance. His stride was firm and youthful, as he walked to the water's edge, where stood the two galleys ready manned, the rowers at their posts—bowmen crowding the deck between and the forecastle. "Messer Alberti!" he cried; Alberti was pointed out to him in one of the galleys, waving his cap. "Messer Inglese?" Edward stepped forward with a glowing face, but a brow grave and firm. Contarini pointed to the second galley: "Venice owes your patience the occasion of winning new laurels." Sebastian drew near his friend; but the doge beckoned to him. "Young man," he said, laying his hand on Sebastian's shoulder, "we may need you here. You have done your share of service. Often have our galleys come to this familiar place, but never I think so quickly at a summons as to-day. Stay now for me. Tell me, as to the second part of your message—that there are traitors in Venice; what ground had Luigi Morosini for that suspicion?" "None, Monsignore, that I know, but that strange smoke. Yet we have heard be-

fore things which make even matters so light as smoke wear a look of foul suspicion." "True; but you know no more? Good. Attend me here, or at the palace gate, until I send a message."

Before the Doge had retired, the three galleys were out of sight; and not long after, two more, for which he had given order, followed. Sebastian loitered about, answering, with what discretion he thought fit, the thousand questions that beset him on all sides. Messengers passed to and fro; the nobles, first in numerous parties, then by single stragglers, hastened to the Ducal palace. Both the senate and the Doge's council were sitting; and orders were sent out from time to time, to put the city in a complete state of defence. The sun began to sink: Sebastian felt the weariness and chill that follow on violent exertion; but no message came from the doge. At length a new shout was heard at the water-side; there was a bustle in the crowd; some one had arrived from the sea-shore! Mounting on a step, Sebastian could see a knot of men approaching the palace through the crowd; the multitude opening a ready way for them. He descended, to meet them and learn their tidings. The last rank of the crowd opened; and pale with vexation and anxiety, his dress disordered and damp with the spray, his father stepped from among the crowd, and passed hastily into the senate. As he went by, he looked round, and seeing Sebastian, a scowl of hate and rage came over his face. The senate had already broken up, ere Sebastian received a summons to the doge's presence, in his private apartment.

He was led to the same chamber which he had entered with Edward, to disclose the less formidable danger of the conspiracy of la Gobba. Carrara's dark intent had been frustrated; his miserable tool was supposed to be passing her waning days in the Piombi, the prisons under the leads of the palace, terrible from their intolerable heat; one of the bravos, whose life had been spared, was in the more shocking Pozzi, the wet well like dungeons under the palace. So suffered the enemies of Venice: would not this greater danger pass away! Such were the thoughts that crossed Sebastian's mind, as he followed the attendant up a private staircase, and along the corridor, into the little chamber. Contarini was reclining on a couch, wearied though not conquered by the anxieties and fatigues of the day; as his cheerful smile betokened when Sebastian entered. "Be welcome," he said, "worthy servant of Venice. Sit, Sebastian mine. Well, boy, your father told you, I should believe, what happened after you came away with such good speed."

"No, my lord; he told me nothing; but passed straight into the senate."

"He is a discreet father! but he hath a discreet son. Know then, that you counted but six of the seventeen galleys that passed into the waters of Venice! Ay, Sebastian, the city is threatened by a fleet of the Genoese. But we are ready for them, praised be St. Mark. We tell not this thing in Venice, lest it needlessly affright the people; but your zeal deserves a full knowledge, and will profit by it.

Now, my son, have you aught else to tell me?"

"Nothing, my lord."

"Then, Sebastian, you shall go rest you, and so must I: for age does for me what toil does for you, and my old eyelids sink in the watch that Venice has forced upon them. But others watch for us. Be here betimes in the morning; and now, good night."

Sebastian took the doge's proffered hand, and was about to salute it, when he stopped, and hesitating, said, "If I were not reproached with folly and presumption, I would tell you, excellent prince, a thought that crossed me as I stood waiting in the court of the palace."

"Tell it me, my son: you have no presumption in you; and I dare say, no folly, where the ladies are not. Say on."

"Thinking of this danger that besets us, and looking at the nobles, as they passed in to the senate and to the council, I could not but remember one away whom most we want; seeing none that could fill his place."

"Carlo Zeno!"

"Carlo Zeno. And the more, seeing that the Ten have adjudged that Vittor Pisani should lie in prison, because the weather lost him some ships in Pola, after he would have left it, if he might."

"Hush; we must not say these things, Sebastian, even though we are young. Holy Mary! my son, would you win for yourself the honor of a dwelling above." And he pointed upwards with his finger, towards the leads of his palace. "But I am no spy. Young man, you have made me remember something that haunted my thought, yet so dimly, that it could take no shape: Zeno it is whom we want."

"Why, then, should we not have him?"

"Nay, he is at Tenedos."

"But can we not fetch him? Give me a galley—or rather give it to Odoardo, and let me go with him."

"The Genoese would intercept you."

"Not the Englishman, for he is a more cunning mariner than any they have, and almost than any in Venice. Vittor Pisani said that he would yield to none but Zeno in the art, and he did not know that Odoardo need yield to himself."

"We will think of it. But now, Sebastian, hie to bed, and bring to Venice a readier man in the morning than you can be to-night."

The youth took his leave, and wound his way by the private entrance to the court, and thence into the still crowded square; but in the darkness he passed unknown.

CHAPTER XIII.

RELEASED for a time from all care of Venice and her fortunes, but one thought took possession of his mind—Teresa, unprotected, unseen for a whole night—for two days and a night! His weariness was gone; and if his cheek was paler, an unseen smile played around his mouth, as the distance between them grew less. Once more the old house-door sounded to the well-known knock of his knuckles. It opened with a string from above, and he entered. In his haste, he forgot to close it, but hurried forward in the dark. As he mounted the stone stairs, a strange sound struck on his ear behind: he listened. All was still. "Who is there?" he asked. No answer. Then he remembered the open door, and laughed at himself for his foolish fear at the sound of footsteps in the street. Nevertheless he turned back, for all his impatience, recrossed the hall, and carefully closed the door. That done, he repaid himself for the delay, by running more quickly up the stairs, and across the empty rooms, which poor Bianca's narrowed fortunes had left desert. A dim light shone as he entered, and he saw Teresa standing with one hand on the door of the bedroom, as if alarmed at his delay, and awaiting the issue. At the sight of him her alarm fled, and she moved towards him. Suddenly she stopped, and clasped her hands; and her face became rigid with terror, as she strained her eyes in the direction from which he came. He made a quicker step to soothe her fears; when, yet more terror-stricken, she pointed at the door by which he had entered. He turned, and as he turned, he saw in the darkness of the room he had just left a figure moving: Sebastian's sword glistened in his hand; he remembered the sound on the staircase, and the officers of justice whom he had driven from the house. A tall form emerged from the obscurity into the dim light of the room, and came steadily forward, with an air of such right and authority, that Sebastian hesitated.

"Who is this?" he asked, turning to Teresa, but still keeping before her.

"O heavens!" she cried, "it is he—he from whom you saved me!"

A torrent of fire rushed through Sebastian's veins as again he turned and raised his sword against the intruder; who now stood full in the light of the solitary lamp, also with his sword drawn.

It was his father!

Ten years had fallen on his father's head since he had seen him—discomfort, neglect, disappointed lust, and rage, had withered his brow; his hair straggled wildly over his forehead; his glazed eyes were scared and bloodshot; his ashy cheeks were furrowed with grim wrinkles; his dilated nostrils trembled; and as he spoke, his voice was hollow, hoarse, and broken.

"Out of my way, idiot," he cried; "hypocrite, out of my sight, and mock no more; playing the cavalier, and fighting with thy father for a girl in the streets."

Sebastian stood unmoved. "Approach not, sir; for I do forget that I have a father, and see none but the oppressor before me."

"Oh ho! this, then, is what the child has learned from my coy mistress! Begone, fool! or I must teach you what a sword is, that you handle it so boldly." He raised the hilt of his weapon, and pointed it at Sebastian's breast. For an instant they stood eyeing each other. A world of thoughts—or rather feelings too vague for thought, dashed across Sebastian's brain; but most he thought that he would rather his poor sister should hear that her father had killed him, than that he himself had desecrated their love with a parricide blow He flung his sword far away; but still stood firm and moveless before Teresa. Morosini slightly drew his hand back. Teresa rushed in front of her protector, and threw her arms round him; offering herself as a shield against the father's sword. Sebastian made an effort to unclasp her arms, and push her from him; but she clung with all her soul; and looking round, she gazed upon the bad man. The youth folded his arms as tightly round her. For a brief space Morosini's eyes glanced fiercely on each of the marble faces before him: he could not endure that statue look—his eyelids dropped; his arm fell; then his eyes again flashing, he said, in a choking whisper—"Evil-begotten child, I have then detected you in these your shameless haunts! Stay; be they your home; you have none other. No, I renounce you; accursed be the day I first saw you. I say to you, Sebastian, enter not my house again—you have no father." And thus in the act of paternal malediction, fixing a calmer regard on the son, he recovered more of his accustomed dignity: and strode out of the room.

Sebastian looked down upon the suffering creature in his arms. She did not relax her grasp; but pressing him yet more tightly to her breast, she buried her face in his bosom. Oppressed with grief, and still more with pity for his companion, he remained silent for a time. At length the stillness alarmed him. The sweet girdle still tightened round him told him that she had not swooned; yet there was the stillness and silence of death. He whispered in her ear—"Teresa—dearest, we are alone. Fear no more; there is none with you but Sebastian." Without moving from her posture, she slightly shook her head. A little moan escaped her; her brow pressed closer to his bosom; again she moaned, and uttering inarticulate words, that seemed to cleave to her palate, she writhed in his arms. "Teresa, dear Teresa! you terrify me. Let me see your face, sweet. Teresa, I cannot see you so, sweet; you are ill; let me see your face." She suffered him to unclasp her arms, and place her in a chair. In gentlest accents he repeated assurances that her terrible persecutor was gone. She leaned her elbow upon the arm of the chair, and, resting her head in her hand, seemed to strive to collect her memory. Her hand hung more gently by her side. Sebastian took it, and softly kissed it. She drew it from him. A pang shot to his heart: "You do not," he said, "hate me for—what you now know."

"Hate you!" she answered, in a whisper; "Oh no, it is not that that I cannot bear. No," she continued, uncovering her face, and turning her now tearful eyes full on his; "it is that the curse on my house should fall where it does, on others; it is that I should first learn your name, Sebastian Morosini, when it is too late to prevent the ills which I have brought upon you. Misery is like a crime, that taints all who touch it. You have touched one that has the plague, a stranger; and I, too, I have let you do it."

"No stranger, dear Teresa; call you strangers those who have seen and known together what we have known? Do you forget what you have taught me, that it is not the fame and

pomp of a thing that make it dear to us, but the good which is in it."

"No, I do not forget; but you needed not to learn the lesson."

"Indeed I did, for your sake; and more for my own. Think you that life to me, before it, was what I live for now!" There was a pause. He broke it by saying—"Teresa, you have not told me, as you did in your mother's chamber that night before, to leave you for ever."

"It is too late."

"It is too late. Just now, when I stood with your arms round me, I felt that I could not unclasp them, and when I in turn took you in my arms to brave that sword together, I thought that you would not bid me leave you afterwards."

She suffered her head to fall on his shoulder. Presently, raising it, she said, "Sebastian, in a rough life I have learned a strength on which I have relied too much. You suffer for it. I thought I could have seen you, and let these days pass, yet again to be alone with my poor mother and Ranieri, should he ever return; but fate would not have it so. And you, dear Sebastian, who might have laid your heart in some noble shrine, have given it in charge—to whom, but a beggar! I know you will forgive me now; but will you always? Will you not some day spurn me, and say I loved myself too much and you too little, when you loved most."

"Forgive you, Teresa!"

"If you do retract—if you do desire revenge, do but tell me so; and my death will avenge you."

Sebastian clasped her in his arms, and the first kiss upon her trembling lips sealed the betrothal.

A sound from the bedchamber roused them from their dream. Teresa would have flown to her mother; but Sebastian telling her that he should go down the stairs and fasten the door of the house, she would not suffer him to go without her; not, she said to protect him, but to protect her own thoughts. They went hand in hand. All was quiet, and the door was made fast for the night. Teresa entered her mother's room.

Bianca was sitting up in bed. "Teresa," she said, "what is amiss! I called, but you, who always hear me, heard not. You are agitated, my daughter! What has happened!"

"Nothing is the matter, mother. Could I smile as I now do, if there were!"

"And yet your eyes are red with weeping, child. What is it!—your father is returned!"

"Would he were, for your sake, mamma mia. It is not that—it is nothing." But the girl could not, even for the invalid's sake, master herself; and bursting into tears, she cried, "O mother, take me in your arms;" and into those dear arms she fell. It was but for a moment: ashamed of thus breaking the quiet of the sick couch, she withdrew herself from her mother's caresses; and answering her adjurations, to tell all, by saying that presently she would, she returned to the saloon.

"Sebastian," she said, taking his hand, "I have come to crave a strange boon: it is to take me, or to renounce me, once for all." Sebastian would have folded her in his arms, but she drew back. "Hear me. With what right I know not, nor with what wisdom, I have suffered you to link your fate with my fortunes, bad as they have been, except—except in many things. Now dear Sebastian, if your courage fails, if the danger, the reproach which I see for you, affrights you, say it. Think not that I shall reprove you. I will still love you for what has been, for things done cannot die , and I can bear the loss of a happiness I almost dread ; but I dare not disclose it to one who must know all, afterwards to strike down her hopes !"

Sebastian was silent. Teresa looked upon his face with that fixed regard which he had encountered twice before, as though she could see through his eyes.

"You do not answer me."

"Do you need an answer !"

"For this I do."

"Then, Teresa, I am yours for ever. If ever I forsake you, mine will be the punishment. To lose you would be despair ; but to lose even the love for you, and the knowledge of all that makes life itself what it is, were madness— were to renounce heaven for hell itself. You know what I mean, and what is my gage to you."

"I do indeed. Then bear with me while I leave you for a little while. I shall return, to summon you where I may see two of my best friends joined ; and some day, Sebastian, I will tell you why they have been my two best friends."

He kissed her hand, and she left him alone. In quiet delight he listened to the murmur of their voices, as Teresa told her wondering mother their story ; suppressing however the most alarming passages, in pity to the invalid. That done, she called him to the bedside, and making them both kneel before her, Bianca joined their hands and blessed them ; bidding Sebastian be as like his own mother in heart as he was in face, for then she could without remorse bequeath to him her child. They then left her to repose.

It was broad daylight before the two had exchanged the thousand explanations to which the events of one day and night had given rise, and then Sebastian took leave ; promising to keep a watch upon the house.

———————

CHAPTER XIV.

ıт was not without anxious thoughts of those he left behind, that Sebastian repaired to the private apartment of the doge, not sorry to avoid the possible encounter with his father in the public part of the building. As he entered an ante-room the venerable Andrea Contarini came forth on his way to the senate, as upright and as fresh in face as though years and trouble sat not on his brow. With a smile of approval on his faithful attendant, noting within himself his haggard looks, which he attributed to weariness, the doge desired a servant to take him to a chamber to await a summons.

Contarini entered the vast saloon devoted to the sitting of the grand council, where the senate now assembled. It was not then quite finish-

ed ; the space between the windows that looked upon the piazza was as yet unadorned by the painted record of his own exploits, and the inscription that afterwards stood there—"Me nulla tenebæ ætas, quum Januenses profligaverim ;" but Tintoretto's picture of the heavens and the blessed already glowed above the throne that the doge ascended ; and the walls and ceiling were rich with gold and colors. On the benches which stretched from either side of the throne were seated a crowd of senators, in various garbs, as habitual splendor or plainness anxiety, fatigue, or eagerness animated the nobles ; the senatorial robes were in many cases forgotten ; and the assembly would almost have seemed a council of war, but that the solemn bearing of its chief, the presence of the grand chancellor, distinguished by his red stockings, and of the procurators of St. Mark, restored its august and deliberative character. Other senators continued to enter as the doge took his seat, and there was a buzz of voices, as many, seated in little knots, or speaking as they passed, repeated the latest tidings of the last night. One alone sat silent and abstracted— Marco Morosini—who had taken his place at the extreme end of one of the benches ; with his arms folded, his body stiffly drawn to its utmost height, his shoulders leaning against the back of the seat, he kept his eyes fixed high up on the opposite wall. His hair was grayer, his wrinkles harsher, and his skin sallower ; but a purple flush seem to spread from his blood-shot eyes a little way upon his cheek ; and the tight embrace of his own arms, with fists clenched under them, showed the conflict of passions which was raging within that moveless form. At every lull in the murmur of converse, or sometimes rising above it, was heard the echoing murmur of the increasing multitude without, in the piazza ; and the frequent shuffle of feet in the adjoining halls, which sounded loud and sharp as the doors occasionally were swung open by an entering senator, indicated the bustle of messages, orders, and preparations among the subordinate officers of the state and the retainers of the nobles.

All sound was hushed in the Council Chamber as the doge rose. In brief and plain language he described all that had been done over night to despatch forces for the repulse of the invaders, and to put the city in a thorough state of defence. "But, most noble senators," he said, "though Venice can always defend Venice from this sudden assault, more is needed to defeat her enemies. This attack is but the first blow : you are already possessed of the reasons which make me fear that our arch enemy is raising a league against us, of which the Genoese are a part. Already have we offers of service. Milan will lend us her strength ; our faithful friend William Cooke, hearing of our danger, is already marching to our aid, and shall we repulse him !"

The murmured "No" rose to a shout, so many were the answers.

"Others may be summoned. But in this service of uncertainty, where the first need is quickness of action guided by wisdom and discretion, the thing we want is a head for this our gathering strength Of sage and valiant leaders we have abundance—I speak now to many ; but the difficulty is the choice. While I am in Venice, with the help of this grave senate and of my most excellent councillors, I doubt not we can devise plans fitting and just for all occasions ; but there needs some trusty person to direct on the scene of battle. In this great peril it would ill become us to betray Venice by too much despising our foes ; they are many and powerful ; and therefore it behoves us to choose for our leader—"

"I claim the service," cried Morosini, with a sudden start from his seat that turned every face upon him ; some indignant at his interrupting the doge, others wondering at the man's heat, and many more curious to hear him. The doge remained standing. Loud calls reminded Morosini of his discourtesy ; and he sat down. But Contarini, saying that all such zeal for Venice should have a voice, took his seat, and Morosini rose again. " I claim the service. Forgive me, illustrious prince, and most excellent senators, if I somewhat too suddenly press to the service of your republic ; but I owe to Venice and to myself that you should not forget, while you remember your need, the servants that you have. How can I say to you, most excellent fathers," continued the senator, his voice growing steadier as he spoke, and as the exercise of his high office warmed and soothed his heart with its accustomed pride, " how can I say to you, that for this service Marco Morosini is the fittest ; since I know too well how great it is, and how unworthy and lowly am I ! Most excellent fathers, there is none in Venice that thinks more meanly of Marco Morosini than himself. Yet his name hath some weight with you. Was the name of Morosini not heard when the great Arrigo Dandolo took Constantinople for young Alexis from his uncle ? and was not Tomaso Morosini elected patriarch of that imperial city ? Was it not Ruggiero Morosini who ravaged Pera many years after ? and though Messer Carlo Zeno was our leader, did not this feeble arm drive before it the Hungarian hordes whom Carrara used in the last war ? But I speak unworthily of the house when I tell of these few acts. Nevertheless, most excellent fathers, remember that to have a good name is not to be despised ; and that to preserve the dignity and glory of our state they must be called upon to whom that dignity and glory in part belong ; for glory is the monument and shrine of deeds valorously done, which you can with no wealth purchase ; but men of high birth and rare virtue are penetrated with its power, so that, without guerdon and without watch upon their acts, they will spare neither fatigue nor danger. For the which thing it behoves you to ask the greater account of the gage which you have in the name of him you choose. Say whether Marco Morosini has not ever stood with mind intent and ready, and vigilant to watch whatever should befall Venice ? Say whether I have ever been backward in your counsels—whether my counsel has been valueless ? The last—the last given was by you taken—to defend the ports of our waters ; given in time, but taken too late ; for had it been taken when given, the port of Brondolo would have been closed against those very ships that now violate the lagoons of the republic. Yet tell me, when has Marco Morosini been repaid, by having the command of plans which himself has suggested ?" He sat down.

The doge rose again, and said, "Most excellent senators, it is in such zeal as this that Venice finds her strength and safety. But I can believe that none present will not feel equal ardor, though with less eloquence to make it appear to us than Messer Morosini ; and now in time of trouble like this, it behoves us, who hold the fate of Venice in our hand, though it pleaseth God to keep us dark and unknowing whether we judge wisely for that fate until the event—it behoves us, I say to you, to take those acts of God that have been shown, to see whose valor and skill he hath already favored, so that we may the better judge for the future ; and therefore, believing many, and Messer Morosini among them, equal to this service, still let us take those whom we know to be equal to it. Let me have your advice, noble senators, and say whom you judge fittest. If it be Messer Morosini, let me have your will to say so to him."

Morosini again started from his seat, but he resumed it as many others got up. Several called out that Marco Morosini should have the command ; others named Malipiero ; others Saracino Dandolo. A voice behind the crowd of senators, many of whom were standing, called out " Vittor Pisani." " Hush, hush !" cried a host. The doge held up his hand, and in the silence said, gravely and sadly, " Vittor Pisani is a prisoner by the decree of the Ten, having commanded when the ships were lost at Pola." There was a pause. The doge, still standing, continued. " There is one, who, were he present, would at once be named by all. He is abroad, fighting in the service of Venice ; he has won for her the alliance of the Greek Emperor, newly reinstated on his throne ; he has gained for her her newest possession, the island of Tenedos, where he waits to strengthen her power ; but do we not rather need him here ? Is not Venice herself more precious to us than Tenedos ?" Loud cries of assent answered these questions.

" But," cried Morosini, angrily starting up, " the Zeno is not here—why discard those whom we have, for those whom we have not ! Why are our senators silent ! Many who are wont to aid us with their counsel, now unclose not their lips. Here is Navagero, who will let Venice be lost without a word." Navagero flushed a crimson red. " Here is Malipiero."

In an instant Malipiero was on his feet. Navagero and Steno, who sat near him, as men cling together that have a common burden on their minds, dragged him down.

" What says, Malipiero," continued Morosini, " whose tongue of fire has so often urged the valor of our senators beyond the discretion of cooler hearts ?"

Malipiero would not be held down. Hastily whispering to his companions, " Fear me not, fear not !" he turned to Morosini. His eyes flamed, and his lips quivered, as for an instant he gazed on the man who pressed unconsciously on his wound, which he dared not avow ; then looking towards the doge, he said, " Let Venice put a sword into this hand, and see then whether I have forgotten how to use it for her." A murmur of applause soothed his hurt spirit as he sank back on his seat, amid the whispered reassurances and cautions of his less eager companions.

Seizing the short pause, Lionardo Morosini rose among the collected senators; a man not unlike his cousin Marco, but of stouter proportions, with a cloud of black hair over his brows, from which he looked forth with a serpent's eyes. He urged the claim of his relative; and in a distant part of the hall arose successively Marino Barbarigo and Pietro di Bernardo, with the same purpose; Marco expected not their support. His cousin and he were old enemies; and the other two were partizans of Lionardo. But the ambitious senator sat in moody majesty, while his claims were advocated by strangers.

Again the doge motioned for silence, and continued, as though he had from the first meant but one speech which had been broken by the interruptions. "Though we have not Messer Carlo Zeno here, noble senators, he might be with us speedily: you have but to send for him." The senate murmured concurrence. "And in choosing our messenger, let us have one whom Venice can spare, yet trust."

"Venice," cried Morosino, once more interrupting the prince, but with forced calmness. "can, it seems, spare one of her citizens: if Zeno is always to command, and Morosini never, let him fetch this second doge!"

"Venice," replied Contarini, speaking through the sounds of rising displeasure in the assembly, "can better spare those who are not in her councils. Already has a messenger been suggested to me, whom Venice has trusted."

"And who, sir, is this other, for whom is despised"—an angry burst of voices silenced the intemperate senator.

"The message of the senate could not be more safely trusted than to the Englishman, Messer Odoardo. Messer Odoardo has the confidence of Zeno; he has learned from him the mariner's art; and one discreeter, bolder, or more eager and rapid in his duty we could not have."

Paler with rage, Morosini exclaimed, "The illustrious prince says that he was advised to name this messenger; was it in his council, that the advice was given? Or if the signory does not send this advice to the senate, are there other councils in Venice, at which the doge sits unknown to the senate, that advise placing her in the hands of strangers? It is said, indeed, that there are traitors among us—here in this hall: are they near the throne?"

A shout of fierce displeasure drowned the voice of the senator; Malipiero and Pietro di Bernardo drew their swords: some rushed towards Morosini, and others called for the officers to seize him.

The uplifted arm of Contarini again allayed the tumult. "Senators," he cried, "we will pardon to Messer Morosini the folly of his too great eagerness. The advice he scorns came almost from himself. It came, artlessly and in honesty of heart, from one who, like himself, burns to serve the republic; from one to whom the republic already owes high services, and of whom a father may be proud—from his own son Sebastiano Morosini.

Morosini, who had glared upon the doge while he spake, started like one stung at the sound of the name. He shook his fist high in air, and his shirt of mail jangled beneath the robes upon his swelling chest, as he cried with frantic voice—"There are traitors then, not here alone—in the house of Morosini." Placing his strained hands convulsively to his side, he stared wildly around for an instant at the hundreds of faces, that watched him in speechless amaze, and stalked from the hall.

Before the senate had recovered from their amaze, a loud shouting without announced that something had happened: it was repeated again and again, and the swelling noise showed that more people were running into the piazza. Some senators went out, and presently returned, announcing the arrival of the Englishman, with tidings from Brandolo, of the retreat of the Genoese. The whole bearing of the assembly changed; the scene just past was forgotten; faces were jocund on all sides; and it was decided by acclamation that the Englishman should be admitted.

He entered with the quick step and fixed look of a man who has hurried forward with his utmost speed, eager for the goal. Courteously saluting the senate, he awaited the bidding of the doge; by whose permission he told his tale. The galleys found Luigi Morosini watching the Genoese from a distance; the number of the enemy's ships that had entered the lagoons was in all seventeen, and he was too discreet a soldier to risk his men in a bootless contest. The arrival of the two galleys enabled him to do no more; and he could only console himself with the determination of resisting to the last any attempt to approach Venice. The Genoese landed a party at the eastern suburb of Chiozza, and repulsing the scanty garrison who were led out against them by Pietro Emo, the Podestà, they succeeded in setting fire to some houses; and re-embarking, the whole set sail for sea through the port of Chiozza. While Luigi Morosini remained to watch the approaches of Venice, he sent back Edward in a ganzaruolo, or lighter bark, with the good tidings. Having finished, the Englishman was desired to retire, and the senate remained in calmer deliberation to devise further measures.

It was not very long after, that the departure of the senators, first by ones and twos, and then in numerous knots, told that the sitting had closed. Presently an attendant came to summon Edward to the private apartment of the doge. He found the prince in converse with Sebastian, and their discourse was of him. The doge told him, that the senate had determined, under certain contingencies, to send for Carlo Zeno, and that he was to be the messenger; the question being who should go with him, as a kind of Provveditore. In the meantime, thirteen other galleys were to be prepared with all possible speed, and placed for the present under command of Taddeo Justiniani. The friends were then released from their attendance on the doge; who gave Sebastian a parting injunction to hold himself in readiness at the first call.

CHAPTER XV.

During the long time that he was detained in the doge's apartment, Sebastian had been torn by anxiety and impatience in thinking of those whom he had left undefended. This encounter with his father threw an unpleasant light on the previous encounter with Alessandro's servant; and while he was confined, and even his father detained in the senate, he felt that their most dangerous enemy was at large. He had however full time to ponder the means of providing some protection. The first thought was to engage in his own service one of his father's attendants, who was especially attached to himself; but that was at once rejected. His next was to admit his friend Edward to his counsels; and, though many times relinquished in the shame of exposing his father, and still more in some fear lest his love for Teresa, or her's for him, should suffer the misconstruction which seemed so unavoidable, that thought he fulfilled. Therefore, when they arrived at Edward's lodging, with some difficulty Sebastian disclosed to his friend the whole history of those events which had so unexpectedly crowded upon each other. As he spoke, he felt more than ever how hard it was to tell a stranger Teresa's bearing in the matter, and to describe that force of truth which he saw in all she said and looked. When he had done, Edward held his peace, with his eyes cast down; and it was with a beating heart that his young companion watched his face. Edward knew at once what must be Sebastian's trouble; and he saw how readily suspicions would arise to his mind which had no ground in truth, and how the mere hint of them would hurt his friend. Discarding them therefore, he thought only how he could serve him as he wished. Presently laying his hand on his shoulder, he said, "Sebastian, you should sooner have told me of this, for some of the ill might have been prevented, had we taken counsel together. But now, the first thing is to set a guard on the helpless ladies." He called an attendant, and desired him to bring to them the English soldier who had just come. He turned to Sebastian, and continued: "This man is a messenger to me from William Cooke, who is already on his march to our aid, and has sent him forward to announce his approach. The man is an honest and faithful fellow, with much courage, little Italian, and little care what becomes of him, so that he be fed."

The door opened, and the soldier entered. His bare head was round and small; and the once yellow hair, shorn close, seemed bleached by the heat of the alien clime. A patch of skin so fair that it looked like a white light, showed where his steel cap had sheltered it from the sun; but below, the hue was burned to an Italian tint, which contrasted strangely with the sandy eyebrows and bushy beard. On his upper lip the hair was close, short, tender, and silky, as it often is in very fair men; but round his cheeks and chin was a bush so thick and full, that his broad nose and mouth, thick firm cheeks, and sullen eye, made him seem like a bull looking through a bunch of hay. The mail which covered his ample chest swelled it to a giant's breadth; and his shoulders, spreading abroad in emulation, gave to his brawny hips, clothed though they were in the rusty red vest of coarse cloth, and to the massive mahogany legs that showed beneath, and stood in loose leather boots, an air of lightness marvellous for their size and strength. The weight above seemed almost necessary to stay the activity below. Answering Edward's beck, he came near, and after a hasty salute stifled by mingled bashfulness and a careless indifference, he stood with one broad hand on his hip, and the other hanging in moveless weight by his side. Sebastian surveyed him curiously, and thought that he would alone be almost enough to guard a castle; but he mistrusted the dull look of the man's face. He was reassured, when, at the first word from Edward, a smile beamed over his face and lighted up his wrinkling cheeks, like a burst of sunshine from a thunder-cloud.

"Well, Master John," said Edward, "is service as gay as ever! Dost look for sport in thy new sojourn!"

John Turnbull, as he claimed to be called—John of Maidstone, as his comrades called the sturdy man of Kent—or John Maid, for shortness and fun—grinned a yes, which said more than words.

"Wilt do me a service, John!"

"Aye, Master Edward. I should like to see the service I would not do to thee, by leave of our captain."

"Nay, I will promise thee the captain's leave and a good guerdon to boot, and easy service too, John. Didst ever take care of ladies!"

John grinned again; but what his grin meant he did not expound.

"This man," said Edward, turning to Sebastian, and speaking again in Italian, "will do better for your purpose, than some more cunning knaves that you might meet in Venice. He will guard the house like a dog; and yet, for all his rough bluntness, he is no fool."

"Can Cooke spare such a man?"

"Indeed, he is worth any five men in his band; but he must stay here till Cooke arrives, and we have not fighting to do yet. Possibly before we need him, Jacopo himself may return."

John Turnbull was sent to find the loosest clothes among those of Edward's servants, that his dress might attract the less notice: and then, a very brief lesson from his countryman sufficed to explain that he was to follow Sebastian, and to keep guard where he should be posted daily, until relieved by Sebastian. John bluntly signified his assent, and did not even look a wish to know more than was told him.

Sebastian led him forth; and for the nonce he stationed him to watch the house of Jacopo Arduino from the street; making him understand, in the English which he had learned from Edward, that if he saw others enter the house, he should enter too; and act as he found them enemies or friends.

Another duty then lay on Sebastian's heart, and as he walked through the least frequented streets to enter his father's house for the last time, by a side door, many were the bitter thoughts of his dear Angiolina that crowded on his mind. He almost reproached himself that aught should have happened to drive him from the charge which he felt to have been bequeathed to him by her mother; and he approached the palace, more and more lost in the bewildered doubt, whether he should disclose all to her or not—leave her to be possessed perhaps against him, or make her at once know the vice of her father. He entered the house undecided; his thoughts for the time diverted by the desire to escape seeing his father. He met none but a few servants passing through the halls on their accustomed duties; and luckily he found his sister alone, in a chamber more especially consecrated to her use.

In the three days that had passed since he had seen her, what events had happened! He had endured the most violent fatigue: two sleepless nights, one most wearisome, the other hurried along by the strongest passions; he had become a renounced son; he was affianced to a bride whose safety, and even life, he felt to be in jeopardy; he had come to bid farewell to the sister with whom he had grown up from the cradle. Angiolina looked round. His face was as altered as if years had gone by since their last hasty separation; and his haggard and troubled look, as he hurried forward to embrace her, struck her with affright. She had however heard of his exertions, and there was a feeling of pride as well as pity when she folded him in her arms, and exclaimed, "Dear Sebastian, how weary you are! But now you shall repose awhile; rest on this couch, and we will talk when you have slept away this paleness and that little frown." Sebastian pressed her to him in silence; and kissing her cheek, suffered her to lead him to the couch. But instead of reclining he took her hand, and made her sit by him. His solemn look alarmed her anew, and she thought of some unknown danger. "What ails you, brother mine? have not the Genoese yet left us."

"The Genoese, Angiolina," he replied, putting on a less troubled air, "need give you no more fear—there is indeed no fear of any kind. But, sister mine, my time is short; yet while I see you look so glad and kind, I hardly dare begin to tell you what takes me from you again."

"Sebastian, something has happened to you!" she cried, looking anxiously in his face. "What is it? tell me, my brother; for whatever ill befalls you, falls also on your sister."

With many efforts to break the shock, and many words of reassurance and consolation, Sebastian told her so much of the story as concerned himself; but he dared not scare the fond face that looked at him through its tears with the knowledge of their father's wrong. Besides, in that father's care he must leave her; and it was on every account safer that she should know nothing more. He told her, indeed, that his father had discovered him, and renounced him; and when he came to that, and added, that he must now leave her, never perhaps to return to the same roof, the agitated girl flung herself into his arms, and nestling close to his bosom, vowed that he never should leave her. What should she do without him! What friend had she in the world! Sebastian could not answer; but endeavored to pacify her with hopes, that the trouble would pass by, and the day would come which should reunite them.

A deep voice spoke his name close to them;

and looking round, Sebastian saw the foster brother at his side.

"Messer Sebastiano, I have a message from your father, which I believe I may tell you here?"

Sebastian listened in silence.

"The Morosini has commanded me to say to you, that grave as your fault has been—he said so, though he did not vouchsafe to tell me what it was—the son of his house must not want the means of keeping up his proper estate, and therefore you will have set apart for your separate use and maintenance one-third of all the money which our lord reserves, in these times of doubt and trouble, from the service of Venice."

Sebastian paused for a moment. And then, while Angiolina looked up in wonder and dismay, at his bitterness and audacity, he replied, "Messer Alessandro, tell Messer Morosini that when he suffers me to live in his house, I do not refuse the gifts of a father; but he has made me a stranger, and a Morosini accepts no alms."

Alessandro was not surprised; first, because he knew more of Sebastian's provocation than he pretended, to either son or father; next, because he knew the fire and courage of the young man's nature, though it had hitherto had no scope for display. Alessandro admired him with all the warmth of a congenial temperament in so far as an indomitable audacity was common to both; and he would have strived to use the growing senator for his own ends, but that Sebastian's nature was of a kind which made it incompatible with the use of Morosini himself—already in the senate, and a reader if less powerful tool. Thus it often is with men of more talent than instinctive feeling: had the ambitious bastard determined to make a tool of his nephew, probably it would have been his policy to be partly as virtuous as he seemed, if only to support the scrutiny of his ally; but Marco Morosini he despised so much, that his mind felt alone in his company, and he scrupled not to unbare it of its dress before him, knowing that the eye upon it was as unknowing as that of some household brute. Virtuous or vicious according to his means, the selfish profligate dullard whom he had chosen for a tool made him more infamous; and he almost disliked Sebastian for reminding him of what he had abandoned. It was when—even while rising against him as an enemy—Sebastian exhibited that boldness of purpose, that energy, and that keenness of intelligence which he himself still possessed, and which seemed still to link him with the noble nature of his kinsman in blood, that he felt towards him something almost like affection. That feeling as well as an astuter wish to retain some show of alliance with the departing son, made him now offer to be a mediator. "Sebastian," he said, "I know not at what thing your father is angered; perhaps it is some fault of youth; perhaps some rigor of his age, or some mistake of his parental care; a little submission might soften him; and you need not humble your high spirit before him, but suffer me to put some such words into your mouth, in the answer you give me—without making me more a party to your secrets than you may pleased."

Angiolina eagerly seconded the foster brother's counsel; entreating her brother to remain or to return to his home. Sebastian looked at his sister, at first, doubting, but then resolved. He turned to Alessandro, and looked up in his face. Alessandro answered him gaze for gaze: he was sincere, in part at least, and knowing that for once he could meet his kinsman's eye, he seized the opportunity. Still Sebastian was not unmindful of his meeting Alessandro's servant in Bianca's bed-chamber; and though he read no confession of it in the foster brother's face, he could not relinquish his suspicions for a look. He said, "If Messer Morosini has not told you the quarrel there is between us, none other can. But I have no other answer. I shall not many minutes trouble him with my presence here."

"He heard from the servants that you were come; but he said nothing to hasten your departure. I shall convey your message, wishing it were less difficult to deliver." So saying, Alessandro left the room.

Angiolina urged her brother to recall him; and asked eagerly, whither he would go to take up his abode? Whither, he asked in reply, but to their excellent uncle Luigi; who had himself already been driven by Marco's overbearing behaviour to the other palace of their family, where Michele their cousin dwelled. "Then, dear Sebastian, I shall at least know that you are in good keeping, and may see you at times; but how shall I pass the days which do not begin with seeing you? how sleep after the days in which I see you not!" It was long before Sebastian could break away from his sister and leave her to her bitter solitude; while he for the last time crossed the halls of his fathers and suffered the great door of the palace to be closed against him—now welcome in every house but that.

CHAPTER XVI.

DAYS passed by, and Edward received not the final command to set out on his voyage. The Councils of Venice seemed paralyzed. The general terror died away with the removal of its immediate cause; but yet the aspect of affairs daily grew worse. No efforts of the signory could check appalling rumors of the preparations of the Genoese immediately without their waters. Istria was invaded by the enemy, and Rovigno and other towns recorded, by their surrender, the disgrace of Venice. The Genoese were reported to have some fifty galleys in the gulf of which the emperor had named Venice the queen. One day's degradation was more than rumor. A ship belonging to Aluise dalle Fornasi, laden with cotton, approached the port of Malamocco from Syria; and a crowd of people, swelled by those engaged in completing the works of the barrier and fortification, and others who had come to the shore to see their progress, stood to witness the entry of one among the many ships that used to bring riches to the city, now, in times of war and trouble, a rare sight. But the ship was not alone; behind it were three others: they were Genoese war-galleys. The bold and

fiery Aluise stood to see his ship chased. Two galleys that had been so hastily prepared were now all but unmanned, and were at a distant part of the lagune. Shouts arose to summon them; men ran hither and thither with loud cries; everybody urged others to do something, as if helplessness were a mere weakness of his own. Amid the noise and tumult the vessels neared the shore. Those in the cotton-ship were evidently on the alert: it suddenly turned, and awaited the approach of its pursuers;— Giacomo Vendramini was preparing to fight. A loud shout arose on the shore, but the wind beat it back, and in the crush against the first of the Genoese galleys Vendramini and his men heard it not. The watery joust was not in favor of the Venetian; the beak of his galley missed his foeman, while the Genoese came against his side with such force that the timbers crackled and started, and in an instant a stream of fighting men ran along the flat though narrow bridge of the beak. Six of them fell dead as they leaped on to the deck, but some behind succeeded in engaging the foremost of the Venetians hand to hand; a little space was made behind the boarders—more rushed in; and though one fell now and then under the shower of arrows which swept the prow of the galley, the number of the Genoese on board soon equalled that of the Venetians. Vendramini burned to signalize his young prowess, no less than to save the treasure of his friend and patron Aluise; and the Genoese felt all the force of his desires. But suddenly a shout arose behind him—the second galley had approached unobserved on his other bulwark, and already were a crowd of fresh swordsmen making havoc in his rear. Inch by inch he fought, as he was driven to the stern: some of his men were urged into the water by the press which he in front could not resist; until sinking with a mortal wound, he could no more head the resisters, and the crew yielded. A short time sufficed to carry their treasure, the profits of their voyage, into the Genoese galleys, with part of their cargo: a smoke rising from the hold spoke the fate to which the rest was doomed, as the Genoese, with shouts of scorn and triumph rowed off from the burning ship. With desperate energy the disabled crew manned a few of their oars and pulled for the land. Black smoke and lurid flames rose from the wreck, as the bleeding mariners bore their dead captain on shore among the angered and shame stricken multitude who had witnessed the fight in helpless impatience. Many and deep were the murmurs heard, that Vittor Pisani was in prison, because he had been conquered by the weather, while the citizens were left to be conquered by the more terrible Genoese. The report, that Pietro Doria had dragged in the water at his galley's stern, the flag of St. Mark, taken from Pisani, less shamed them than that rout before their eyes.

The event gave an impulse to the activity of the signory, and with great exertions fifteen galleys were prepared. But only six could be manned: for many of their seamen were away with Carlo Zeno; many were discontented at the imprisonment of their favorite leader; and for the six that they did man, the officers of the republic had to hunt out and force the reluctant r.arincrs. Thus however were the violated waters of Venice placed under some guard, and Taddeo Justiniani was enabled to protect at least the city itself from immediate assault.—Again the excitement somewhat died away; yet Venice was full of malcontents; and rumors grew rifer of traitors, even in the senate, though none could find them out. Marco Morosini appeared singular only in the incontinent utterance of his love for his country, not in feeling it. The works to fortify the approaches to the city were increased and hastened. The port of Venice was closed with a bastion of wood, and three large vessels were stationed across it, 'bound together by strong chains, and filled with armed men, with bowmen, and with the rude artillery now first used by the Venetians. The like fortifications were completed at the Fort of Malamocco: and a fortified ditch and palisade were hastily constructed on the Lido. Troops now began to answer the summons of the senate, and were encamped on the long islands that inclosed the lagoons, and placed under the command of Jacomo de Cavalli, a Veronese. Thus the signory provided for the present safety of the city; but why, asked the people, was Vittor Pisani still in prison, and why was Carlo Zeno unsummoned?

Such was the question that haunted Sebastian as he repaired one evening to the house of Jacopo Arduino. It was one that disturbed his present happiness; for in other things he was comparatively at ease. His uncle, Luigi il Grasso, had ever been to him more like a father than his own parent, except that the good man had no jot of sternness, called paternal, in his nature. He almost rejoiced at the youth's quarrel with his father, although he forced himself to deplore it on principle; but he loved to cherish his adopted son. And he unreservedly delighted in the chance which, as he said, had given him the child in the world that he would soonest have chosen, without the trouble of a wife. Sebastian had always loved his uncle for his overflowing kindness; he had now fathomed that kindness; and he found it inexhaustible and enduring. He almost blamed himself for keeping any secret from him, but he feared to trust the history of Teresa to the outspeaking bachelor, lest all Venice should know it.—He had therefore some trouble to escape his uncle, and when he did, he not seldom noticed a humorous wrinkling of the fat cavalier's eyes, which he would have chased away with the grave truth if he had dared. Occupying the congenial post of Provveditore over de' Cavalli, his father now gave him little uneasiness, and in the cares of state, the senator seemed to have forgotten his amour: or at least to have sternly withdrawn from an enterprise promising so much disagreeable embarrassment. Teresa herself had become, as one woman does at sometime in each man's life, the sunlight of his existence. To him however the change was really like a second birth. Growing up from childhood with his sister, he had viewed her eager affection less critically: it was only what he was taught by his religion to expect. His early remembrance of his mother painted blood relationship in the same colors. His father's rigor was a mischance to be borne, not deplored; but Morosini's angry nature had caused so much dissension with his friends, that his children were almost alone, except on state and ceremonial occasions; and the youth's free and engaging demeanor had procured him entrance to many gay saloons,—aye, even to some more secret retreats, where bright eyes and rosy lips were neither coy nor repelling. Home then had been to him the abode of tranquil happiness, disturbed but not destroyed by paternal rigor; society had been a region of thoughtless pleasure, thinking not of its own vanity and decay. The first sight of Teresa's face, as she leaned fainting on his shoulder, read him a new lesson of life: it told him that happiness, such as he and his sister had known, might be invaded by crime and misery, and yet survive in the noble heart; that pleasure, as he had known it, was mortal in itself, and destructive to more than its enjoyers: and that there were some things in existence yet unknown to him, and not then to be interpreted. For a time Teresa was a riddle that he scarcely dared to solve. What she was, her way of life, he almost dreaded to know; and then again, he scorned himself for the dread before it had gone. He found her accept his kindness with a simple willingness that in any other woman would have made him bold; yet he was held back by a calm firmness, a knowledge as well of what ought not to be, as of what ought to be, which surprised and alarmed him, yet still reassured him. Helped by the events already narrated, he surprised the girl out of her history; and then he rather felt than knew that Teresa's knowledge was the birth of adversity, exalted by full faith in the goodness of God, and of God's last work, human nature. The natural reflection of the intelligent but untaught peasant girl whom Jacopo Arduino had united to his troubles and disappointments, and the affection of the children who grew up and answered to that steadfast love which the vacillating and ruined gentleman could not appreciate, had taught Bianca a primitive philosophy which made her reject much that passes for truth in the world, and cling only to those elements of goodness that man has in himself, naked as he comes into the world: in all else Bianca had been disappointed. Her native wisdom, and such learning as Teresa could gather in her father's passing time of prosperity, and from the lips of the man himself, less unaccomplished than unstable, fructified in the daughter, who in turn strengthened the faith of the mother, and found new strength herself in teaching all she could to her brother Ranieri, too young to have reaped any profit from their father's better days. This was Bianca's great stay in the weakness of her malady. It supported Teresa under assaults to which her unprotected condition exposed her; and of which Sebastian had rescued her from the worst. To her Sebastian came in the time of her greatest danger: misfortunes had taught her a decision approaching to a fatalism in judging of character: she thought she read his nature in his ingenuous face, his earnest words, and his understanding of her faith: she accepted the risk, put trust in him, and all bar to their mutual intelligence disappeared. From the time that she had accepted him as her affianced, she received him as one of her own little circle in the great crowd of the strange world, and had no more reserves of her heart. A new region was disclosed to Sebastian, who entered it in a reverent spirit. Her whole soul was opened to him; from her he learned to love humanity, of which she seemed the purest type; and the tenderness of love was exalted by becoming the exponent of sympathies which had their birth not less in a grateful intelligence, than in the affection of fast and tried friends. Sebastian knew what existence was, and he was not remiss in attending his new school.

CHAPTER XVII.

It was dark one night when Sebastian issued from the house. He heard footsteps behind him as he walked towards the ducal palace, but they seemed only those of a passenger, who like himself preferred walking to interrupting his thoughts by taking to a gondola. As he approached the square, the steps behind him hastened, and involuntarily he looked round. Alessandro's tall and ample form met his eye. The foster brother drew nigh, and said in a tone of mortified kindness, "Messer Sebastian would not vouchsafe to answer my salute as he left the house."

For an instant Sebastian felt vexed, and almost alarmed. But dismissing the fear which surprised him, he answered, "I knew you not —indeed I saw you not, Messer Alessandro, or I should not so far have forgot myself. You can give me tidings of those most dear to me: how fares my sister?"

"Your sister is well, though not so gay as when her brother was by her side; and your father," added the foster brother, affecting to understand the question as meant for both, "is also well. State cares keep him from smaller ones, which should fret him not. Sebastian," continued he, assuming a graver manner, "I would that you were not apart from your house —from your father, who best can bring you to your right station in Venice—from your sister, who grieves in your absence."

"I would so too; but you know, Messer Alessandro, that I did not depart of my own accord."

"I know, I know. These things have passed, Sebastian, and it is not well that you should live in exile from the house of your fathers. If you would suffer me,—if you would allow my humble aid to be given, it should not be so."

"Nay, sir, it has been, and it is. I told you before, that I could not disclose to you the reasons—but if you knew them, you would know also that it lay not with me."

"It might be, Sebastian, with you and me. Could I have grounds for it, my counsel might prevail, as you know. Though absent from your family—or rather from your palace—you have lived at peace—there has been no farther trouble to you where you most would feel it?"

Sebastian was silent. He neither cared to tell anything by answering to these hints, nor to check anything that the other might have to tell.

Alessandro proceeded: "There are things, Sebastian, which men do that they ought not, yet we must give them license, except it be

that indulgence is against their own determined judgment; and then we can use them against themselves. I speak to you openly, for I know you to be ingenuous and of good faith. Then, I say, that though you are young, though you feel the spur of passion, yet are you in some matters less vehement than your father; therefore should you somewhat pardon in him what you would not in me—nor in yourself. Yet must we not talk to him of pardon, or his hasty nature would take offence. But, truly because I do not often cross your father in matters of which I have little experience, for my station is less suited to gayety and ease than if I could boast the noble name of a Morosini,—for that very reason have I more influence; and could I back it with reasons to him, I might so move him to your desire, that the path of father and son should not unseemly justle each other."

Sebastian still was silent.

"I should grieve," continued Alessandro, "if your pride or my unworthiness debarred from you the service that you most would desire; and you know what it is when I say that. Sebastian, I fear my uncouth and too grave dispositions have not gained for me what I have so often hoped for—your good will."

"Nay, Messer Alessandro, you never gave me cause to withhold it; but—" Sebastian hesitated: the foster brother indeed had not his good will; he believed him sycophant and traitor; yet was there little more than bare suspicion. He might wrong the man; and right or wrong, he had nothing to tell for his dislike.

Alessandro accepted the unsaid disclaimer. "We shall know each other better. I do not mistake what you most would wish?"

"Not if I understand, where your words are so dark."

"I feared to offend you by speaking too suddenly. To be frank, then, you would have no bar to your passion—you believe that you have the worst in your father; but, if I boast not in saying so, I could remove it. I could remove it, having reasons."

Sebastian still hesitated. He liked not even to be served by one whom he so suspected; both for mistrust of treachery, and for shame that he should hate, where he would take a debt of gratitude which he scarce could pay. He had turned back with the foster brother to avoid meeting any friend in the piazza; and they walked for a while in silence; Alessandro at times stopping, looking at the stars that peeped through the slowly moving clouds, and carrying himself like one that was in no haste for an answer. Sebastian suddenly stopped, and said, "You speak of reasons, Messer Alessandro: if I could serve you, it might be less difficult for you to serve me."

"You are even prouder than your father, Sebastian! There might be reasons, and I need not tell you that there are reasons, which weigh much with your father. Sebastian, I must, chiefly for his safety, hold you pledged to secrecy in what I say."

"If the secret be one that a Venetian may know, say on."

"Nay, a Venetian knows it—your father. But the secrecy must be without condition."

"I will be secret. I will be secret in all that you tell me—in all as it is told me by you; but

I will not pledge myself to secrecy in all that I may know hereafter, even though it should touch what you disclose."

"Enough: I trust to your good honor. You know that Venice is menaced by a mighty league against her; and that her most powerful foe—the foe most powerful against her, whose power is on the sea, threatens this very city with destruction."

"Genoa."

"The same. You know moreover, that Genoa is the hand that strikes the blow, but that it is not the head that moves the will."

"Carrara is the most dangerous of our enemies."

"These are no secrets. True, Carrara is the most dangerous of our enemies, and the most wicked; but he is not the most obstinate. There is even some manner of justice in his anger; for has not Venice humbled his proud spirit past bearing? And were we right, could we trample him in the dust, and look for his blessing upon our work? He hates Venice because Venice is terrible to him. But, I know this man, Sebastian, and I can say to you that he is a vain proud man; haughty under oppression, elated with little courtesy to him. Without stooping to him, but rather casting to him some favor as from on high to one below, Venice could make him her slave; and so could make all this danger that threatens her, wanting its head and spirit, disperse. All these great works that we build up, all these armies that we collect, all this vast cost which wastes our substance, might be spared by one word to this man, who is our enemy perforce, and who might be our slave."

Sebastian listened in silence. He cast a glance on Alessandro's face, the sounds of his powerful but subdued voice still vibrating in the air about his ears: the foster brother was erect, with his face bent to the young man; a little lamp cast on it from the shrine of the Virgin a glooming light, and its expression did not wrong that holy gleam. It was austere, but earnest: Sebastian doubted whether any guile lurked there.

Alessandro continued: "Now, it happens that, though Venice might well pardon the offender, those who rule in Venice cannot do so; for they it is that oppressed him, and to do otherwise now were like a confession of wrong. Venice and her rulers are not one: Venice will survive the men that govern her; the men themselves might survive their counsels. Other rulers might chase away all this peril to our beloved city, without dishonor to the Queen of the Adriatic."

"I doubt, Messer Alessandro, whither you would go, or whether I ought to listen farther. This, methinks, draws near to something too dark—too intricate for my judgment. At my age men act; at yours they take counsel and direct action. Therefore should you rather say these things to my father than to me."

"They have been said to your father."

Sebastian started.

"And farther, you have heard too much not to hear more. Sebastian, the highest post in Venice has been offered to your father."

Sebastian was alarmed—" And he refused it?"

"He refused it. It was offered to him wrongfully, and he nobly refused it. Yet are there those in Venice, neither few nor powerless, who would rather that he should have it. Were it bestowed upon him by Venice, there could to her be no wrong done; the safety to her you know. Now for the bearing which this has upon your fortunes. Were Marco Morosini Doge of Venice, he must of necessity put a curb upon those passions which disfigure even the senator; for the doge lives in the world's regard, and Marco Morosini would never consent to mock the fate of Pietro Candiano, who perished in revolt, because his lawless love had wronged a woman of Venice. Contrary wise, if he knew you to be engaged in the state as befits the dignity of your birth—if he knew you useful to me—to me as his lieutenant, or rather as his humble servant, seeking no rank nor fame, but only his welfare—there would be nothing that he would refuse to my counsel on your behalf. Sebastian, you see that I put all trust in you; that I trust my own safety—which indeed I regard not—but that also of your father, in your keeping. Traitors ever gladly suspect and charge treason against those who, hiding from treason, are fain to put on a disguise; and were what I have said to you known by others, that life might be forfeit which gave you yours. Of all the youth of Venice, Sebastian,—and I say it almost with a father's pride—you are the one most sure to reach fame and high station. Your choice of a path is before you: you might help me most signally to shake off this weight of trouble on Venice, if you will not hastily spurn my proffered friendship; and, doing so, you might most safely and suddenly pass to the end of all your desires. I have said all, until you bid me to say more."

A long silence followed, broken by Sebastian, who said:—"Well Messer Alessandro, I have heard, and I will be secret. If I were to answer you now, I should say what would little satisfy you, but I will stay till the morning. I say again, that at my years it is rather for men to act, directed by those whom they find to guide them. But I will think of it; so now, good night."

"You answer as I hoped. Farewell. Consult your own heart and honor, and I fear not. Heaven bless you, my son." Alessandro abruptly walked on to St. Mark's place; and Sebastian saw him making his way straight across it into the gloom, with the measured speed of a man confident in his purpose. Going a few steps towards the square, Sebastian stopped. Relieved of the foster brother's imposing presence, he now thought only of his words rather than his own answer; the rumors against Alessandro rose fresh in his mind; he was shocked though he almost knew it before, to find how great was the sway which the Paduan exercised over his father. He was alarmed for two reasons: though his father repulsed him so far from his side that he thought not of interposing, he liked not to see him thus bound to a suspected traitor. Alessandro's plea for Carrara; his knowledge of a treasonable offer made to Marco Morosini—his sudden disappearance at Lido—filled Sebastian with suspicions to which he could not give shape. On the other hand, the

E

foster brother's knowledge of the father's lawless passions—his playing with them—the presence of his retainer in Bianca's chamber, suggested worse suspicions. Yet, again, there was a show of reason in what the man said. Sebastian was perplexed. The bond of secrecy prevented his asking counsel of Edward. By a little prevarication he persuaded himself that it had one exception; and after some hours' pacing up and down in the dark streets, he retraced his steps, to advise on this mystery of state which touched him so nearly, with the young and artless girl who had become part of his being.

He knocked at the door of the house, and a gruff voice within asked, "Who goes there!" "'Tis I," said Sebastian softly, "your friend, Master Turnbull." The Englishman cautiously opened the door, offering his broad chest as a stop gap. Seeing Sebastian, by a little light which he held in his hand, he drew back, saying, with a broad grin, "You begin to come oftener, Master Sebastian; I think you had need to set a porter at this door, to save more tender feet than this"—and he gave a little stamp on the ground which might have crushed a man to death. Sebastian smiled: "Good Master Turnbull, I fear you are like to die here rather of weariness for want of company, than of trouble in opening the door." "True, master, true. But I fear me they have gone to bed above—though I ought not to—" "Never mind, good Turnbull, if they are a-bed I will go out again quietly, and you shall open the door again by daylight. But let us see." And he passed up stairs.

Bianca had long retired to rest; and Ranieri's tired limbs were gaining strength in sleep: Teresa was reading one of some few books that Sebastian had lent to her, partly for love of all knowledge, partly because he had lent it to her, and because she liked to render herself more worthy of the love which she had created. She turned to him as he entered, in some dismay at his return, with a grave and thoughtful face. He told her all that the foster brother had said, all that he suspected him to mean, and his belief that the man had the power to bend his father's will to sanction their union. Teresa remained calm, though her color changed often as she gazed on her companion's face.

"Tell me," said he, "for I am bewildered between wishes and mistrusts—suspicions and doubts, whether those suspicions are just—tell me what I should do."

"Why do you, who are practised in the world and in its intrigues, and so well practised that you have avoided them, come to me for counsel, who know nothing of such matters? You are fitter to teach me than I to teach you."

"Because, Teresa, in learning the world's ways, we also unlearn the instinctive habit of looking at men's acts in their simple truth, so that our taste, more practised, is less discriminating, especially when we desire to escape from a maze of cross reasoning by some clue of natural sense and goodness; and I seek it where I have ever found it. You are the wisest of us all, because you have preserved to yourself the faith in which you were born. Why do you look into me so! you did it when I first saw you, just as you do now."

"I looked into you then, I suppose, that I might know what you were; and I look now, I believe, because I love to see you as you are. Nay, if you blush, I shall think that we have unseemly changed places, and that you are the maiden."

Sebastian kissed the hand he held. "But you do not answer me."

"If this man is what you suspect, there is no safety in him. Listen to him no more; or listen to him only, if he consent that your compact shall be made aloud in the market-place: for be sure, if you venture with him into the secret abodes of his own dark mind, he will ensnare you there."

"It was my thought, and therefore I scarcely for a moment hoped for what he seemed to promise."

"Dear Sebastian, such a man as he cannot give anything half so precious as you can take for yourself. Be it that we were married in all your father's state, and lived ever after in a region of fraud and treachery. Would that he union! Would it not rather be separation—estrangement of our trust in each other! Can we, by letting this Alessandro come between us, draw our love closer than it is! Listen to him no more."

"I can listen, dearest, only to one voice. But if we may not be united as he would help us, the greater the reason why you should give me the best of rights to protect you always, to be your guard night and day, though I cannot bring you the wealth and splendor of my forefathers."

To this plea, however, Teresa would not listen. She would not suffer him in so much haste to forego the condition to which he was born; nor would she, while her father was wandering in exile, set his parental authority at nought. She had never, she said, been so well protected—never so happy as now; but her father must share her happiness. Sebastian was unconvinced: but the kiss which Teresa suffered him to take from her trembling lips—and which those trembling lips returned—was so sweet, that he forgot the hard future.

Teresa's cheek still lay on his shoulder, when the loud sound of a bell startled them. It was the bell of St. Mark's: some new danger threatened Venice. Listening with knitted brow, Sebastian rose from his seat. Teresa clasped his hand—"What is it!" she asked.

"I know not; but there must be some heavy danger, that the bell should sound at this hour. Dearest, it cannot threaten you, or the place would not be so quiet: it is some news from the shore. But I must be at my post—I must leave you, when most I would stay."

"And when most I would have you stay: it is worse when the danger which you go to meet does not threaten me." Her brow again sunk upon his shoulder, and spell-bound him to the spot. But the toll of the bell went on with its loud summons. He obeyed it; and tore himself from the agitated girl.

A heavy presentiment made him give Turnbull a purse of money to supply his wants till he should return; with a new admonition not to leave his post, though Venice should be besieged.

"Fear nothing, Master Sebastian," said the soldier, "Master Cooke loves Venice, and no a girl in Christendom could draw him from the fight : now I have learned to love the face we know so well, that Venice might go to the winds before a hair on that blessed head should be hurt."

"Master Cooke is right, friend ; but you are more right. And so good night."

CHAPTER XVIII.

As he issued from the door, the loud clangor of the bell swelled to a roar ; and he could already hear a growing bustle in the city. He hastened towards St. Mark's. As he entered the place, Alessandro stood before him.

"Well, Messer Sebastian, day begins again betimes, and you have had a short night for your resolve."

"Short, yet long enough."

"It is made, then—you consent ?"

"No, Messer Alessandro. I have come back to the place whence I started, and say again, that my youth is best for action under those whom I find as the guides set over me ; and least of all now can I stop to parley while that bell is calling all Venetians to do."

Alessandro's face assumed that absolute nullity of expression, a mask-like passionless regard, with which he had taught himself to conceal all surprise and anger. It gave for an instant to his stern features, strongly marked with the thick black hair that adorned his brow and face, even a more inhuman aspect than rage itself.

"'Tis well. You have your choice, Sebastian. I grieve that you will not make your happiness and safety part of my plans ; but you will not suffer it. Still, though you will spurn me, I will serve you all I can ; but I fear new dangers where you most would fear them."

Sebastian's footsteps were again arrested—"What mean you !"

"Nay, I know not. Your father has a headstrong will, and is difficult to thwart."

"You mean something ! What does my father threaten now !"

"Nothing, I say. I speak in doubt only of the future."

Sebastian could not stir. In Alessandro's calm profession of fear he read the threat that lurked in it : he remembered the ill-defended state in which Teresa remained. A world of thoughts crowded to his brain ; whereof the most distinct was, that longer uncertainty was intolerable, and that Teresa must surely be his on the morrow.

Alessandro partly guessed his thought ; but partly mistook it for yielding. "You do well to ponder, before it is too late. A few steps more, and you might have entered on the path that you could not recall. Think you that naught unworthy is required of you. Rather is everything honorable offered — power, fame, love."

Sebastian still hesitated. He had become almost used to the swinging roar of the bell ; and he fell into a sort of waking dream, in which the bell, the foster brother's voice, and the shouts of the people sounded like remote and alien noises. For an instant the dreadful tolling

ceased, to ease the ringer's arms, and he awoke. He started forward, saying—"At least I cannot stay, till I know what that bell means."

"Nay, then I can tell you, without going farther."

"What !"

"It means that the Genoese hold Chiozza."

Sebastian rushed on, and entered the palace

CHAPTER XIX.

When Sebastian left the foster brother so suddenly, Alessandro remained for a while as if amazed and angry ; then shaking off the weakness, he turned and walked away at a quick pace. For some time he pressed on, like a man bent on reaching the goal ; passing over many bridges, and threading the narrowest calli that he could choose. He did not stop till he reached a house in an obscure part of the city, by Canareggio, in the midst of others occupied by fishers, and such poor persons. He knocked at the door. It was speedily opened by a woman bearing a light in her hand. When she saw her visiter she gave a scarcely perceptible start, but at once opened the door wider, and let him enter. He did so, and passed through the first kind of little hall into a room beyond, as if he were familiar with the path. The woman having closed the door, the foster brother turned and embraced her somewhat hastily, and then proceeded to lay aside his cap and cloak. That done he again eyed his hostess. She was a young woman, but tall and large, of proportions like his own, such as furnished models for the art then rising in Italy. Her brow was fine and compact ; her cheeks nobly rounded ; and through the dark brown of her skin the blood glowed in its ruddy course ; her features were regular, but boldly rounded, and her large black eyes were so shaded by long lashes, and so finely bordered by the even arch of the eyebrows, that their intentness was solemn rather than stern ; her throat rose like a column from her well curved shoulders and ample bosom, the luxuriant form of which was veiled, but not hidden, by the coarse dress she wore ; nor did it hide the turn of the limbs, whose just proportion gave a look of smallness and delicacy to hands and feet, with which Ceres might have grasped her dragons' reins, or pressed her yielding axle-tree. She suffered Alessandro's salute in silence ; watched his movements with an expression betwixt curiosity and indifference, and returned his more leisurely gaze with a fixed look of tranquility, which seemed more habitual than constrained.

Alessandro was the first to speak—"You give me a silent welcome, Rosa."

"I had a warmer one ready for you, Alessandro ; but it died months ago for want of use."

"As beautiful as ever, and as cruel ! But you know that it is not discreet to reproach a lagging lover, for love is the only passion that cannot be spurred."

"I do not reprove you. The loss is more yours than mine."

Alessandro smiled. "If you boast, I shall think you proud ; and if proud, you may be flattered into kindness."

"You do not understand me, or you would not think me boastful, when I say that he who leaves love of his own free will, loses more than he who has it taken from him."

"My books do not teach me that he who throws away a thing loses more than he who cannot help his loss."

"And you have no wisdom but what you find in your books !!"

"But who talked of leaving love ?"

"I *talked* of it; you have *done* it."

"Why, am I not here, the same as ever ?"

"Yes, you are the same as ever, perhaps ; but love has starved while you are away, and I am altered."

"Rosa mine," said the foster brother, laying aside his bantering air, and speaking with his customary stern precision, "you talk folly. I have been away solely because the whole fortunes of Venice have weighed on my shoulders ; I come, even now, because I need your help—and partly, perhaps, silly girl, because I was only too willing to come." He was about to take her hand, but she drew back a step.

"Alessandro, I looked for you again. I knew—I have seen it well enough, that even your cold heart must have its fits of love, and I knew that you had already chosen her who in all Padua, and Venice too, best pleased your nice taste. Therefore I expected you. But two wills go to all bargains. Ours has hitherto been a cheat ; for I gave love, you gave—your own pleasure. I expected you : you have left me leisure to think of all that I could do ; and I was ready for you long ago. From this time I will love just as well as you—no more ; and you shall do my pleasure before I do yours."

Alessandro paused. His passion rose at being crossed ; and starting from his seat, he cried, "Fool—fool—beware !"

Her color changed not, as she answered :—"Do not threaten. You could not so soon subdue these limbs, if they were once unwilling, but what I could proclaim you before I died. But I am the fool to threaten. I say again, that while you have staid away, I have taken thought, and what I have resolved, I do. I shall force you to nothing ; but I will not be forced neither."

"What mean you ?"

"That I will be your wife."

"And do you not call this folly ! My wife ! would you be content to be nothing but a wife ? Why, Rosina, I love you—aye, doubt as you will—I love you. I have told you that a wife may have to serve my turn in other things. Let my plans answer, and perhaps I must wed to crown them : but Rosina shall always be my love, and at her feet shall I lay my triumphs."

"You are choice in compliments, Alessandro."

"Do not be the fool you are not, Rosa. Because habit makes me speak after a fashion, do not believe, as common women do, that I do not feel it too, even as well as those who have not the art of saying what they feel."

"It is difficult to divide men's thoughts from their speech ; and there are some kinds of learning that one moment's sorrow can unlearn "

"This is idle. Do not be mocked, Rosina. If I were a noble, I would at once give all to purchase you."

"I believe that."

"But I must first be noble. You are silent—you do not deny that. Let us not waste sweet moments in quarrel." He approached to caress her, but she calmly put him back with her hand.

"I have said what I have resolved, Alessandro ; I am your wife, or not your wife. You said you wanted my help—what is it !"

Sooth to say, the foster brother was rather relieved by the question ; for although his love, as he pleased to call it, was not all affected, and the sight of Rosa had revived recollections which tickled his fancy, he was just then bent on other enterprise, and her coldness cut short his road to the end he hoped to gain by flattery. Bidding her sit down, therefore, and listen patiently, he recounted to her what he knew of Teresa's history, Morosini's pursuit of her, and Sebastian's love. "Now," he continued, "you know well that much that I do is done through this brother of mine—that losing him, I lose half my power in Venice. He is as much my servant as I would have him. But in this Sebastian I have a more powerful man to encounter. I could almost doubt whether the same blood runs in Marco and myself, but that in Sebastian I see my own strength. I have tried in every way—I told you how, when he parted from his father—to bend him to me ; but he escapes me. I tried him through his love, but the fool does not see his own danger. There is one way left, before I try to crush him ; I would rather win him—and that, Rosa, may tell you how little cold I am—I would rather win him ; and there is one way left—to win the girl. You see that !"

"Aye."

"But how ! I dare hardly go near her ; for I suspect that already she thinks of me as if I favored that aged libertine Marco, and I swear that I have hardly done so. How then to approach her? This is where I want your help, Rosa."

"Do you believe that she has power over your nephew ?"

"He would abandon everything for her—rank, power, glory—all."

"But how has she such power, if she loves not him !"

"Why she does love him—madly. When Nadale was in their house to seize Jacopo, she looked when he came in as if her good angel had returned."

"And you would have me spoil this love !"

"Folly, girl ! can they not love because I am fortunate ? Love can have its hour and the state by turns."

"What should I do then !"

"Go to this Teresa, tell her that a danger threatens her Sebastian ; that unmeasured power is within his reach ; that they may wed tomorrow, and almost reign in Venice. Will you not do this for me !"

Rosa looked angrily at her companion—almost with hate. He did not seem to notice the look, but continued to await her answer. After a long pause, she said—" I will go "

Disregarding the praise which burst with unwonted warmth from Alessandro's lips, the girl rose from her seat, and bringing forth some bread and fruit and wine, she laid it on the table for her companion's supper, as if she were performing a familiar task. When it was ready, he began to eat. Rosa did not join him, but sat apart, taking up some work which his coming had interrupted. She was making a large net. Alessandro was a temperate man, and but a little of his frugal meal sufficed to appease his hunger. He watched Rosa at her work. Suddenly his face changed, but he spoke calmly as he said—"It is just as it was wont to be, Rosa, except in one thing—do not you eat?"

"I have eaten," she answered, as she continued her work.

Presently he said, "That is rough work for fair hands. Do you often do such work, Rosa?"

"Every day, till this be done."

"Have you turned fisher?" There was no answer; and Alessandro hesitated before he added, "That is a thing that must be used by stouter hands than yours, Rosa; I fear that I am the less welcome since you have begun to make fisher's nets." Her silence seemed to anger him, and he said more fiercely, "It is not that I have been absent in great enterprises, that has changed you, Rosa, but that you wish me absent always, for some other's sake."

Rosa lifted her head, and turned upon him a look of unspeakable scorn.

Alessandro was half ashamed. "I did but jest," he said; "I know you, Rosa, too well to be jealous of any fisherman in the lagoon But tell me, girl, for whom is it that you work?"

"For Pierotto. He is an old man that serves me much; would I could reward him better."

"You shall; surely you have not wanted gold, Rosa! I have sent it you as I was wont."

"I have not wanted gold, Alessandro."

"But you have not had enough. You shall have more.—You know that you shall have as much as you desire."

"I desire no more than I have."

Alessandro seemed daunted by her short answers; and for some time he said nothing. The darkness of the night grew less thick, and he started to go. He gave Rosa renewed instructions for her mission to Teresa, urging her to dwell on the happiness which the couple might at once reach, if Sebastian would join with those who offered him their alliance. He would have embraced her, but she gave him her hand to kiss. Smiling at her humor, he yielded, and presently she closed the door on his departing form.

CHAPTER XX.

FROM the time of the attack on Aluise dalle Fornasi's vessel, Doria had been collecting a strong fleet at Zara, numbering some fifty fighting-ships, and hundreds of lighter craft, with victual and troops. With this force he anchored off Chiozza, on the 6th of August, 1378; at the same time that Carrara descended the Fiume Vecchio with a hundred ganzaruole and a large land force. Their approach was known in Venice; but Pietro Emo was well fortified in the town; and it was thought safer to intercept all alarming rumors. Chiozza, like the younger city, on which it is dependent, was

built on little islets, and partly on piles, within the entrance to the lagoon between the island of Brondolo and the littorale of Pelestrina. A long embankment, severed by a drawbridge, connected it with the island; on which Doria landed his forces, in three divisions, under Gerardo da Manteloro. Their numbers, descried from the walls of Chiozza, created little alarm, for the walls were strong. Therefore the army which Venice already had assembled on the island of Malamocco was undisturbed; except that Marco Morosini insisted upon relinquishing his command, and sharing the perils which thickened round Chiozza. Emo was cautious, and did not venture far from the town; wishing to render Doria's harmless possession of Brondolo uneasy by keeping up a point of attack from the town. Gerardo seemed scarcely to perceive his aim, and as the weather-beaten veteran advanced nearer and nearer, until at length, with hardly any resistance, he seized the entrance to the bridge from Brondolo, he prided himself upon his victory, instead of fearing the danger in which the Venetian desired to trap him. A day he was suffered to remain in quiet possession. In the meantime, Doria advanced ten large galleys to the side nearer to Venice, whence he opened upon the town a fire from the arblasts and the rude artillery then newly invented. The people began to murmur, and to say that the three thousand and odd fighting-men in the place had better be sent to their homes for safety, since they were afraid to face the enemy.

So stood matters, when, on the night of August the 13th, or rather, early on the morning of the following day, a party of men were assembled in the house of the podestà. The room in which they were seated was larger than many even in Venice itself; but its furniture was rough and simple, as befitted a hall open to men engaged in the toil of daily combat, and too careless of comfort to disarm or seek the couches of the more splendid saloons in the ancient palace. The grave and hardy podestà was seated in a chair at the head of a table, but turned aside to give more ease to his crossed legs. His basinet and steel gloves lay beside him; the rest of his body being cased in mail, over which was a jupon of silk, reaching to the hips, and richly worked with gold. On it were blazoned his arms—barred in six pieces, of argent and gules. On the table were the remains of a hasty meal, at which some dozen persons had been seated. A few still remained at the board. Nicoletto Contarini and Giovanni Mocenigo had withdrawn, and sat on chairs near Emo, dressed in the long black vests which they had not exchanged for actual war: their office being to watch the warriors in the execution of their duty. Baldo Galluzzi, the captain of the forces, still sat at the table, his wine-cup by his side, and his bronzed face glowing with ruddy health and the exhilaration of his favorite pastime—the deadly dance of war. Three others stood apart. The tall figure of Marco Morosini, clothed in black armor of the plainest kind, leaned against the side of a window, open to the blackness of a dark and gusty night. His arms were of the oldest kind in use: his basinet had no visor, the mail reached even to the steel gloves, no plate showing on his arm; his surcoat was long, blazoned with the ancient arms of his family—argent, a bend azure—unadorned with the cross that some of his kindred assumed when Fornasa Morosini wedded with the king of Hungary: for Marco deemed that all augmentation of the arms of his house was an abasement, as confessing that the race was less noble, if it could be made more so by mixture with others. He bore the listless look of a man who is waiting for something which will happen too soon to leave him leisure for thought, though he had nothing to do meanwhile. Malipiero bent his fiery visage to the ground, hugging with folded arms the thought that in the approaching fight he could make amends with his sword for fierce counsels withheld from Venice by his oft-repented submission to the bargain with Francesco Carrara for his life. Watching both was Lionardo Morosini; his face turned away, but his piercing eyes often glancing under his clustering black hair at his unconscious cousin, and marking the excited face of Malipiero. He, too, like most in the room, was in arms.

"This wind," said Galluzzi, subduing his potent voice almost to the low tone in which their consultation had been held, "will serve our turn; for it will keep Doria busy while we deal with his friends ashore."

"Aye," said Emo; "and the dark too. Will Messer Nicolò, think you, have his men ready in time?"

"Doubt it not. If you hear no bustle, it is because Nicolò is just the silent man we need."

Nicolò da Gallicano entered as he spoke, and addressing both the captain and the podestà, announced that all was prepared.

Emo desired him to summon the prisoner whom Messer Lionardo Morosini had taken two days before. Lionardo remained behind until all the rest had gathered near the podestà's chair. The man was brought in. He was a bold and sturdy fellow, with a bluff, soldierly bearing, as though the rough life of the camp had broken through the cunning that peered from his eyes; he would have been the secretest of inquisitors, but, being a soldier, he had grown frank and careless. The man's mail was dented and broken, and his dark gray vest was soiled like that of one who had not been nice in his sleeping places on the bare earth. He was unbound, and had no look of a prisoner, except that a guard brought him to the door, and that he was weaponless.

"Well, my friend," said the podestà to the man, "the cavalier that spared your life yesterday is willing to take service by way of ransom, and you say that you can lead us to your captain's sleeping-tent?"

"He is no captain of mine: I am not a Genoese, though I am a Genoese soldier."

"So much the less care need you have in giving him up to us. Can you do it?"

"If you can take him," answered the prisoner, bluntly, "you may, and I will show you where. But I cannot give him to you, who have him not."

"But," said Galluzzi, turning to the podestà, "what security have we that this man is honest?"

"Nay," said Emo, in a lower voice, "we know him not to be honest, but a kind of traitor. Let us not, however, disclose our counsels before our prisoner. Messer Lionardo said, and he said it truly, that we have the gage of the man's own life or this much of honesty, that while we hold him by the throat he will not brave death by angering us."

"I agree," cried Marco Morosini, harshly, "with Messer Galluzzi: let us rather attack the whole of them, than waste our time in a doubtful chase. Were it Doria himself, indeed, it would be different; but who is Gerardo da Manteloro, that we should hunt for him?"

The prisoner started at the sound of Morosini's voice, and looked at him uneasily. The senator also looked hard at him, and the man's eyes turned aside, while his color fled. There was a pause; and the man's harder breathing was visible in his heaving chest. By a strong effort he was calm again. "I will not believe," continued Morosini, "that the man is honest."

"I thought from his look just now," said Mocenigo, in a whisper, "that you knew him."

"I, Messer Mocenigo! they say that there are traitors in Venice; but I do not make friends among her enemies."

"Nay, nay, Messer Morosini," said Emo, still in a soft voice, "it also seemed so to me; at least I thought the man looked as if he knew you."

"The cavalier," said the prisoner, who overheard them, "struck me just before the other threw me down: this cut,"—pointing to a gap in the mail on his shoulder, "was made by that sword"—and here he pointed to the one on which Morosini rested.

"I had forgotten it; but now I think I do mind me of something that I should know in that face."

The prisoner smiled, and added, "I rather should remember best."

"We waste time," said Galluzzi. "If my lord the podestà and the provveditori approve of this adventure, there is nought to do but to obey; and I shall not strike a whit the softer, because I like not the plan."

"We know it, Messer Galluzzi. Let it be so. Honest man, keep near to me; and when I call upon you, lead us on the way, without a word. Silence, for your own life."

He called; several attendants entered the hall; and with their help Emo and his friends laced on their helmets. Following the guidance of the governor, they passed out into the street, and thence to the gate that opened on the bridge. As they neared it, an occasional clash of iron, and that half heard breathing which tells the presence of men, made them know that the large body of soldiers under the command of Nicolò di Bernardo were posted there; but the silence and the darkness, for not a light was allowed, might have left less practised ears to fancy that there was solitude. Arriving within the archway of the gate, Nicolò was sent to the top of the gateway to see that all was clear without. He descended, and a whisper satisfied every doubt. With as much care, however, as if the enemy lay with his ear to the door, a little postern was unbolted, and Emo stepped forth with the Genoese. Gal luzzi, the two Morosini, and Malipiero followed him ; and advancing a few paces on the bridge, they turned round. With great care and silence an officer stepped forth, and then the men, one by one, in small parties, each headed by an officer, until a hundred stood upon the bridge in a compact band across it. With some anxiety, Emo bent his ear over the bridge ; for a boat might have crept near in the darkness, and might escape to give the alarm. No sound reached him between the beat and roar of the wind, save the beating of the waters as they were dashed by the wind through the bridge. The body of soldiers advanced ; and that guard placed in front, the gates behind them were opened as cautiously as the postern had been ; and while the first band moved on steadily, four other bands, each of equal number, followed at short intervals. Their pace now became more rapid, but still it was steady and noiseless—the feet of the men being bound in tow or whatever else they could procure to deaden the sound. After a longer interval, another division passed along the bridge. The dawn had already begun ; and the leaders could see the tents at the other end of the bridge ; when the dark figure of a man who was walking to and fro at the end, suddenly stopped in the midst. A loud voice cried, "Who goes there?" There was no answer, as Emo pressed forward, those behind imitating his movements. The sentinel paused for an instant ; then stooping down more distinctly to catch the outline of the moving mass of heads, he raised a trumpet to his mouth and sent forth a blast so sudden, loud, and clear, that it seemed to cleave the night ; for just at that instant the clouds burst asunder. Before the note had died away, it waked a hundred echoes ; and while the trumpets still blew on, there was a stir, a clashing of arms, a shouting, growing and mixing in a wild uproar. Ere it had well risen to its height, Emo and his band were on the drowsy guard, and few escaped to answer for their fault. The sleepers beyond, startled from their beds, hastily snatched up what arms they might, and blindly fought without aim or care, or ran to the rear to arm them better. "Now," cried Emo, to the Genoese soldier who stood by him, "now for your captain's tent." The man stepping briskly forward, took the lead, keeping rather to the left ; and Emo followed him at a running pace, with the other nobles and the first hundred men. Their guide, seeming to avoid the places where there was the greatest sign of bustle, led them past two buildings of which the Genoese had possession, to the outskirts of the little encampment, and then seemed about to strike into the country, when Emo stopped him.

"You told us, fellow, that you would show us Messer Gerardo's tent ; but whither do you lead us now?"

"To his tent, my lord : it lies just beyond here ; in another camp not a mile on."

"How is this? we meant the captain of this force that lies here at the bridge."

The man looked confused for an instant, and was about to speak, when Morosini exclaimed, "There is treachery here ! let us go no farther or our return will be cut off."

"It is true," said Emo, "seize the fellow."

"My lord," said the man, sullenly, "I am your prisoner already. If you will not permit me to do your wish, why call me traitor?"

"There is none here to oppose us," continued Morosini ; "yet the Genoese are not wont to be so heedless !"

The prisoner looked about him, as if seeking help.

"Seize him," said Emo, turning to the men behind ; "he is going to escape."

As he spoke, Lionardo Morosini rushed forward from among the soldiers, and was the first to grasp the man's arm. As he did so, he whispered fiercely, "Fool ! run, run for your life !" A short struggle released the prisoner from his hold—and he started off like a deer. But his hesitation was fatal to him. Two of the men had got the start of him, and one tripped him up. He rose with the dogged look of a desperate man ; and yielding to his fate, he advanced resignedly towards the drawn swords of the cavaliers.

"Bring him hither," cried Emo ; "we must force his treachery from him. Prick him with your swords."

"The villain," cried Lionardo Morosini, in a loud and angry voice, "owes a debt to me, who have spared his life. Was it for this, rascal, that I delayed your death?" And he stepped towards the prisoner, who regarded him with astonishment.

"Nay," exclaimed the man, "if it be so, I will confess all."

"It is too late." And Lionardo raised his sword.

"Hold ! hold !" cried Emo and others, "he will tell us the plot."

The prisoner drew back, and called out, "Stay, Messer Lionardo. What ! will you murder me ! Stop him, for the blessed Mary's sake, my lords—let me tell." Before he could be prevented, Lionardo, saying in a low tone, "Your blood be upon your head !" plunged his sword into the man's throat above the gorget of his mail. He fell choking and sobbing with the blood that poured into his throat ; and stretching out his hands wildly, to catch some hold as he felt himself drifting away from life, he tried to call for help. He ceased, and the blood flowing for a few moments in a silent flood, stopped as it froze in death. Marco Morosini who bent over him with others, knew the features as they sunk to moveless repose, and he exclaimed, "Ha ! I know the traitor !— it is the monk ! he is a spy !" The cavaliers looked at him with surprise. "You knew him, then?" said Emo. "I knew him for a traitor : no more. But it is no time to tarry now. Lionardo's haste has left us to learn for ourselves why we were brought hither."

At that hint, the party redoubled their speed back towards the bridge. On their way, Emo whispered to Galluzzi—"Let some of your trustiest men watch Messer Lionardo. We must take him back again to Chiozza, and doubtless he will tell us how this strange soldier knew his name, and why he stopped the man's tale."

As he spoke, they approached two houses which they had before noted as being so still. They had barely reached them, when Marco Morosini, pointing to a wall that stretched a little way from one, made a sign for the band to stop. They saw above the wall the point of a lance. It stirred. It was hastily lowered. Galluzzi, putting his finger to his lip, waved his sword in the direction of the lance, and rushed round the corner followed hard by his companions. The ambush stationed for their surprise, was in turn surprised; and a sharp short struggle, hand to hand, ended in the flight of the Genoese towards the bridge. Not far; for as the Venetians opened the view of the bridge itself, they found a more numerous body stationed to receive them; while the uproar and dust of battle marked the line of the bridge for a long distance from the island.

"Now, sirs," cried Emo, grasping his sword more tightly, "is the struggle for our lives and for Chiozza. Viva San Marco!" "Viva San Marco!" shouted the little band behind him; and in a minute their swords were crossed with the Genoese. Their compactness and the fury of their assault carried them into the midst of the press, like a spear head into solid flesh. Now Galluzzi showed that power which had placed him at the head of the army in Chiozza: his gay and thoughtless face had grown stern and heavy with the weight of purpose. Putting himself in front, his ponderous form bore down all before him; and his big arm hacked and hewed down the steel-clad men, like a woodman clearing away the saplings and underwood that stop his way to some tall trees on which his real force is to be spent. Inspired by a holy phrenzy in his love for Venice, Morosini fought with reckless valor; and Emo with the single purpose of making good his path to the bridge. The men pressed forward; the Genoese before them yielded inch by inch, when their young captain, Andrea Fazio fell cleft to the chest by Galluzzi's sword, their power was unloosened, and the Venetians fell upon the backs of their fellows who were driving the close mass of Venetians towards Chiozza. The shouting behind told Gerardo da Manteloro of his new assault; and leaving the van, he struggled to return through the packed ranks of his own men. He met Morosini, driving in the Genoese to their own destruction, and trampling on the bodies of two of the many already sunk down upon the bridge. With mad fury, Morosini struck at the Genoese chief, his blow falling full upon Gerardo's sword, which shivered into pieces. The stalwart Genoese rushed within Morosini's long reach, and grasping him with both hands by the waist, lifted him from the ground, and turned to push him over the rail into the water. Morosini fell with the small of his back on the ridge; but seizing in his hand the vizor of Gerardo's bascinet, he dragged back his head, so that he lost his power. While they struggled, friends came to the rescue of each. Emo grasped Morosini's left hand, and pulled him from the water; while a Genoese strove to tear Morosini's right hand from Gerardo's head. The press around them became hotter; Venetians and Genoese still seeking to prevent each other from slaying the entangled warriors. At length the two once more stood face to face upon the ground, still grasped in each other's arms, their teeth clenched, their breasts heaving with exhausted breath. As the Venetians

on the one side slowly gave way towards Chiozza, and on the other pressed forward in the same direction, the knot of combatants round the two was carried on and on, until they felt the looser wood of the draw-bridge beneath their feet.

Suddenly a smoke arose from the very ground and a glow of heat. A hundred voices shouted, "the bridge is on fire," and so it was. While the battle waged hottest, and men forgot all but the foe before them, Giovanni Saluzzo had brought a small boat under the bridge, and with a torch had set fire to the woodwork near the water, meaning to cut off the retreat of the Venetians. He did better than he meant. The two wrestlers, turning their astonished eyes to the smoke, released each other. The Venetians led by Galluzzi, taking advantage of the surprise, gathered up their strength like fresh men, and striking right and left, soon ran in among their friends. Those, alarmed by the smoking, and taking the speed of the new comers for flight, also began to fly, calling "fire! fire!" The alarm spread. At that moment a cavalier on horseback cantered on to the bridge, followed by a force of untired men. His head was unarmed, and covered only with a small cap; his face was gay, as he pointed onward with his sword. It was Carrara. "Forward Messer Gerardo!" he cried, "In—in to Chiozza, while the way is open!" Gerardo needed no second word. Recovering from his surprise, he too shouted. "Viva San Giorgio! —Chiozza for San Giorgio!" The Venetians were followed close by the running Genoese; and they so crowded up their own gates, that they could not be closed. Emo turned to make a stand—twenty hands seized him in every part, for he was among Genoese alone; and so he was carried to the rear. Venetians, mixed with their foes, ran along the street; and the few that kept round Galluzzi, on reaching the piazza, found themselves surrounded by Genoese and Carrara's men, who poured into the town like locusts. Resolving to die hard, Galluzzi stood at the head of his men; but no one molested them; all moving past, taking stations here and there, until he stood amid a wall of soldiers. It opened, and Carrara rode in. Courteously saluting the Venetian, he cried, "Messer Galluzzi, you may if it please you, kill some more Genoese in selling your own life; but you cannot save Chiozza, which is ours already." And he pointed to the flags which waved on every tower and many a house top. "Let us not have savage war for the sake of blood, after victory is won by no fault of yours; for you have conquered to day in valor—we in numbers."

"Noble sir," answered Galluzzi, "you say true. But we are now free, and mean to be so while we live."

"Good! be so then; for we will not spend our men's lives in taking some hundred others, when we have won a whole town. You may depart."

"And may I seek my wounded friends? I fear me that Ser Pietro Emo is among the wounded or slain, and that the Morosini have fallen somewhere."

"The podestà is our prisoner and guest; and so is Messer Lionardo Morosini; I hope that

Messer Marco still lives : I shall thank you to aid in searching him."

Galluzzi stepped forward and held forth his sword, saying, " It shall be given to one only." Carrara took it, and instantly returned it : " Keep your sword, sir," said he, " we have plenty of our own ; and when you again use one, you will strike less cruelly with that which you take from my hands." Turning to some of his followers, he added,—" Conduct these men to the shore ; and guard Messer Galluzzi, while he seeks his friends."

He was obeyed ; and Galluzzi retraced his steps towards the gate. As he drew nearer to it, he saw the man he sought, slowly rising from the ground, amongst heaps of bodies, which lay with their faces from the gate, having been struck down in flight : Morosini's own face was towards it, and he was still with the wounds from which he had fainted.

" Ah, Messer Morosini," cried Galluzzi, " I grieve to see you so. Help me to raise him, some of you."

" Is the town still ours, Galluzzi !" asked the wounded man.

" Alas, no : it is held by the Carrara."

" Carrara ! I had rather it had been Doria ; and rather have died than hear either. But how comes it then, that you are here and at liberty !"

" It is the generous courtesy of Carrara ; who leaves me free, and the small troop that stood firm with me, to leave the town, and to bear you with us."

" Under no pledge to remain disarmed prisoners in Venice, to be laughed at by our fellow citizens ?"

" Under no pledge at all," said Galluzzi, smiling at the helpless man's nice valor. " Let us bear you to the boats."

" Morosini hesitated ; but growing still paler, his faintness made him fall back in the arms of his friend ; and they carried him tenderly to the shore.

CHAPTER XXI.

Late next day, the hall in which we found Emo and his companions, was occupied by a very different group. At the table, moved to one end of the hall, were seated the two leaders of the armies, Doria and Carrara ; and as they conversed in a low tone, their officers and a host of cavaliers who stood around, mostly armed, except their heads and hands, confined their voices to a whisper ; which ceased when Doria cried, " Bring in the Venetian Ambassador."

Pietro Justiniani, the procuratore, was ushered in, accompanied by Nicolò Morosini his brother procuratore, Nicolò di Bernardo, and some score of attendants led among them seven Genoese gentlemen, prisoners, who with a few others had been carried off by the Venetians before they were driven back on the bridge. Justiniani, a grave and dignified man, seemed to steady his troubled eye with an effort. Approaching the table, as his companions stopped behind, the two leaders courteously returned his salute.

F

" My lords," he began, " I come the bearer of a message from Venice, who neither denies the wound which yesterday inflicted on her, nor forgets that she has still strength to resist a foe ; there it is thought that her valiant conquerors in that one battle may rather forego their full desires, to obtain some part at once, and without farther battle, than desire still to waste their blood in our waters. The more especially is it thought so, in that Venice and Genoa are sisters of one race, one country, and one faith ! blessed be the virgin ! and there is in this wide world room not only for both, but battles to be fought in which they may share with a common interest."

" Say on, Sir Ambassador," said Carrara ; " we listen."

" Know then," said the procuratore, " that the signory are willing in this hour of difficulty to offer what Venice never yet offered. They believe, noble prince and most excellent lord, that the victory which you have had must content you, no less Christian, than noble and valiant, and that you are willing to use it with moderation befitting your high fame. In peace leagued with Venice, Carrara and Genoa would each double their power, and while the most excellent prince would strengthen himself on this our fair land of Italy, and be independent of aid from distant and strange regions, the ships of Genoa and Venice might help each other in the conquest of new lands, for their trade and glory ; so that a league of such might, of such magnificence, should never yet have been since the tramontane hordes ravaged the whole land, and drove into the lagoon of Venice those fugitives who have raised it into its present estate and dignity. No, Messer Carrara, if you used Genoa and Venice, not to waste their strength on each other, but to aid you in loving fellowship, the honourable ambition which has made you in your single person equal to the most powerful princes, more powerful this day than the great republic—would I reach to things more worthy of it than the destruction of one ally by another ; that other perchance getting its death wound in the struggle. See what trust the signory puts in your noble honor, Messer Francesco ; you are the only sovereign present — the signory is not here—the doge of Genoa is not here ; but only Messer Doria and I, servants of the two republics ; to you, therefore, Venice submits her desires, consulting as you please with the great commander that sits with you. My lord, here is the bond of Venice, for you to subscribe."

Justiniani drew a roll of parchment from his bosom ; and stepping up to the table, he unfolded it, and laid it before Carrara. The Lord of Padua started, and his deep eye gleamed with triumph. The parchment was blank.

The procuratore continued. " One word more. In token that Venice desires no ungenerous bargain, but only her freedom and your friendship, she sends you by me the highest present that she could devise—seven illustrious gentlemen of Genoa, whose valor led them too far into our ranks, and betrayed them into honorable bondage." And he pointed to the prisoners, as he drew back a few steps, and awaited a reply.

The two chiefs conferred together. Carrara

seeming earnestly to press upon the Genoese something to which he listened coldly, and with dislike ; until gradually Doria became the earnest speaker, and the Paduan sunk back in his chair, like a man who unwillingly abandoned his wish. Justiniani watched the converse, thinking to himself how the fate of Venice hung upon their words. Losing his caution, in his heat, the Genoese leader cried, " No; let us hold what we have firmly, and we may step on to take all." Then rising hastily from his seat, and speaking rapidly and loudly, he said to Justiniani, " By the faith of God, Signori Veneziani, never shall you have peace from the Lord of Padua, nor from our commonwealth, until we have put a rein upon the unbridled horses of your St. Mark. When we have broken them in, we will be at peace. That is our will. These my brothers and countrymen, whom you have brought with you, I do not want them : carry them back ; for in a few days I will come and take them and the others out of prison."

Justiniani started, with an angry gesture ; but keeping down his passion, he turned to Carrara : "Is that, Lord of Padua, your answer to Venice ? You, I think, would counsel otherwise."

"Sir Ambassador, I have none other to give than my good friend hath already told you."

"Then, my lords, this is all that I have to say more ; make your best speed to Venice, if you would break the prison of your friends ; for you may find it too well guarded—or," he added, in a lower tone, " you may find it no longer a prison of the living, but a tomb."

" Be it so," cried Doria, " I speak as I would speak were I myself in the prison ; but this I answer, that if we find it a tomb we will light such a pyre above them and offer such a sacrifice, that it shall be more glorious to lie buried there than in the greatest monument."

Justiniani eyed the threatener for an instant, then, recollecting his quality of ambassador, he saluted the chiefs, and retired with his train.

CHAPTER XXII.

The night had passed, and the sun was high, when Sebastian landed in the place of St. Mark, from one of the eight galleys left in the arsenal by Justiniani, which his exertions had helped to put in complete readiness. A band of rowers was drawn up at the water-side, and some bowmen ; but as his eye glanced at their scanty numbers, and at the galleys behind him, he blamed the carelessness which had brought so few together. Edward met him, and exclaimed, " You have come too soon : the Venetians have lost their spirit, and I will not go out against the Genoese." He spoke aloud ; and one of the men, with an angry flush, cried out, " You do us wrong, Messer Odoardo ; Venetians have not lost their spirit ; but if they serve well, they are paid with prison !"

" I spoke not of you, friend, but of those who have not come as you have."

" Nay, I do not know but those who have staid away are wiser."

Sebastian looked from one to another with surprise, then saying that they must not hear such things, he walked towards the palace with Edward. " What does this mean ?" he asked.

" Some say," answered the Englishman, " that it is treachery, that it is the treachery which lurks in the city, and threatens it in every corner ; but I believe that these men have a grievance, that the senate has not pleased them in some way. But see, here comes Marin Barbarigo to take the command of the galleys. Let us watch."

Barbarigo came from the palace, surrounded by a party of nobles who were to take command in the galleys, with which he was to reinforce Tadeo Justiniani. Little knew the senate what leader they were sending. At the head of the steps Barbarigo stopped, and looking surprised at the almost empty galleys, he drew back and said to one near him, " Let the men enter first." His messenger walked towards the assembled mariners, and pointed to the galleys. The men were motionless. He drew nearer, and said to those in front, " Bestir ye, friends, Ser Marino waits ; you ought to have been at your posts already !" They moved not. After a moment's dead silence, while Barbarigo and his companions looked on in angry amaze, the men shouted with the burst of one deafening voice—" Vittor Pisani."

" How ! What is this ?" exclaimed Barbarigo, as with angry face he went up to them. His projected expedition was threatened with failure. " Know you not," he cried, " that the senate has ordered us to join the Justiniani without delay ?"

Another pause—" Vittor Pisani, Vittor Pisani !" shouted the men.

" Messer Vittor Pisani is unable to lead you : the senate has commanded me to guide you to Justiniani."

" Aye," cried Zanni, whom we saw active in the riot of la Gobba,—" Aye, to Justiniani, who let in the Genoese."

" So, there is rebellion, is there ! Here, some of you," said Barbarigo, turning to his own attendants, " seize this fellow."

Men started forward, to defend their spokesman, but Zanni put them back. " Yes, seize me ! I shall do as well for a prison as Pisani ; and more of us will go if you like—all. What good will that serve ?"

With instinctive discretion, Barbarigo's attendants stopped halfway, and looked for farther orders. He himself was silent, his eye fixed stedfastly at the men, gaining time for his own thoughts. The shout of the mariners had drawn to them all the stragglers in the square, who pushed forward from behind to see what was the matter, while many ran back again to tell their fellows. The outburst of feeling had not been unexpected ; and as Barbarigo glanced over the heads of the crowd, he saw the unceasing motion of heads behind, as fresh crowds poured in to join and abet the mariners, while there was a perpetual clash and jarring of voices, as men called to each other with that fierce hilarity that animates a multitude when there is something amiss, and the basest order feel themselves of political importance with the highest.

Barbarigo made another appeal. " Is this

your will, Venetians, that the Genoese should sail up to the very Rialto, undefied! Have you so little courage left—so little love for your city—so little for yourselves, for your wives, your lovers, and your children! Shame, shame! Let us begone, and show the Genoese how Venetians defend their city." A pause. "You are silent: is that your only answer!"

"Vittor Pisani," was the stunning answer of voices such as grew strong in battling with the winds; and the shout was repeated in a hundred echoes; until the windows of the senate shook, while the place resounded with "Vittor Pisani;" more and more crowds running into the open space, and catching up the cry; so that it spread like fire about the city. Barbarigo turned back to his companions, and the two friends at the same moment joined the group. Edward advised them to send for the doge. Barbarigo hesitated; but Sebastian at once hastened to the palace. The men stood still, in dogged calmness, watching the effect of their rebellion.

Before many minutes had elapsed, Sebastian returned, and said a few words to Barbarigo; who, speaking to the men, desired them to follow him to the palace, and they entered the court; which filled till more could not come in. As they marched, the red robe of the doge caught their eye, issuing forth on the giant's stair; and they respectfully stopped, leaving an open space between their front rank and the stair on which stood the prince.

Raising his open hand, in token that he addressed them all generally, he said in a loud voice,—"They tell me, my friends, that you stay when you are asked to go forth against the enemies of our city. I cannot believe that Venetians are chilled by fear, or that they have forgotten their love for the Queen of the Sea. Tell me what it is you want."

The shout arose again—"Vittor Pisani."

"Vittor Pisani is not our commander, but Messer Tadeo Justiniani. Is he not brave and generous! Some of you have served under him, and can tell. I can see one,—there—Beppo da Murano; because I remember that Messer Justiniani told me how Beppo had torn him from the grasp of two soldiers at Pola."

"Yes," cried Beppo; "and Justiniani gave me this knife for it; and I have not sold it yet, nor ever shall." And his rough hand held up a jewel-hilted dagger.

"Will not Tadeo Justiniani serve you for a leader! Has he not, with so small a fleet, kept back the Genoese who might else have taken Venice itself; and shall we shamefully hold back when we ought to bear him succour!"

The men were silent.

"Answer me!"

Zanni stepped forward, and with rude reverence, said—"It is not, monsignore, that we dislike Justiniani; but Venice cannot be fortunate while her best leader is away, and the other best leader is punished with prison for the fault of the tempest. There are few of us here; and we came out because you and the senate ought to be told what it is that makes so many more hide themselves like cowards, as one noble said to-day,—which they are not. Let it be said that Messer Vittor Pisani is to lead us, and you will see ten willing men in place of every one of these."

"And I can tell you," said Beppo, pushing forward, "that I have persuaded some eight or nine here from Murano, because I have yet to earn this pretty knife that Justiniani gave me of his bounty; but they told me there, that the town should be emptied into the galleys, if Pisani were to lead them."

"My friends," said Contarini, "I would do your will before it was uttered, if I were able, but the Ten—"

"Tell the Ten—tell the senate," cried several of the mariners; and they turned round to those behind, calling "Messer lo Doge will tell the senate to give us Vittor Pisani!" "Vittor Pisani, Vittor Pisani," answered the multitude.

The aged prince gazed at the animated scene before him for an instant, and then turning back, he retreated to the palace. The band of mariners kept together; while the multitude fell into little knots about the court and the square outside; children running about between and playing at shouting for the favorite leader; while a few nobles walked the space before the stair and loitered at the entrance above.

"They will give them what they want, if they are wise," said Edward to his friend, "if they thwart this law of the people, they will make Venice destroy itself."

"And all might have been otherwise, if Carlo Zeno had been here: yet you are kept back, who were to have fetched him! There is not a man in Venice that would have refused to follow him."

"True. I have suspicions. Nothing that the senate does, seems done in time, and when it is first talked of. They do say much about treachery in Venice,—"

"And not too much; it meets one, even in one's own home."

"Sebastian! your father—"

"No, no, Edward; my father is too proud a man ever to be a traitor. I have said too much. I am so used to speak to you as myself, that I forgot others will not think of us as one. Forget what I have said."

"Forget I cannot. I understand you, and what you say can scarcely increase my own suspicions. I will be silent, but be you guarded. It is the worst mischief of treachery, that even those who are not traitors, yet live familiar with it, are after accounted criminal when it is discovered. Sebastian, I have fought in many fields,—at home, the debasement of many of my race you know—even so long after the Norman seized the crown of England, has made us objects of injury and suspicions: I have, like my father, lived much abroad to escape indignity. In Italy I have been among those who have crossed their treasons more often than their swords. But never—not once, did I ever listen to a traitor; never did I promise to keep secret aught that it was not honest to know. What has become of it! I might have filled my chest with wealth, and perhaps, have been found a bloody corpse in the Arno or these lagoons; or I might have been a hunted alien, driven from every house. But I can say, that no man is safer than I am to be where he lists: and that be it in Venice, in Florence, or in Milan, or in Westminster, people suffer me to pass unsuspected. I am older than you, and bred perhaps among those whose suffering made them covet the solace which the poorest may have in an honest life, which state and intrigues somewhat mar; and I do believe that an unsuspected honor is the greatest power that a man can have, even among traitors."

"I do believe you. I see it in you,—I see it in Zeno; and I feel it"—Sebastian stopped and blushed a little. Edward smiled and said, "Where all lovers feel it. But," he added gravely, "that is an idle jest, which every man can say to others, and be offended if they say it to himself. You are right, Sebastian, and I offered violence to my own wisdom when I jested because you gave it its best sense."

"Nay, I was not offended."

"I know you were not; and that it was that reminded me how like an idle gossip I was, and how different were you. But see, here comes the doge again."

Contarini again came forth, and raising his voice, cried, "Venetians, the senate desires to pleasure you in these times of our common trouble; Messer Vittor Pisani will lead you. He is free."

Long and loud was the shout that burst upwards; a solid mass of sound, in which the words that made it—"Viva Pisani, Viva Contarini," could scarcely be heard. As the doge again retired within the palace, a rush was made to it, and habitual respect for the abode of power could scarcely restrain the people from forcing their way up the great stairs. The loud buzz of voices was hushed. A man appeared on the stairs alone. A square built man, in clothes of soberest hue, carelessly put on. He wore a grave and thoughtful countenance, like one who could bear all things with equal mind—triumph to the full as well as defeat. He came slowly and steadily down the stairs, but at the first glimpse of him, the shouting renewed: it glanced hither and thither in the multitude, as those at a distance in the piazza knew what it was those in front saw: others filled up the intervals, until at last the whole city seemed shouting in chorus, "Vittor Pisani."

Pisani stopped before he descended the last few steps, and stretching forward his hand, with the broad palm towards the people, he hushed the storm of welcome. As it died away towards the skirts of the multitude, his well-known ample voice came forth—"Venetians, you have mistaken: the only cry for Venetians is—'Viva San Marco!'"

"Viva San Marco!" answered the exulting people; as Pisani's friends, high and low, hastened towards him, struggled for his hand, and pressed forward for a word or look in salutation. "I see," he said, smiling, "that I am still a prisoner; though I would never be free of such bondage. Will you take me to my home, sirs, that I may prepare me for my enterprise?"

Those about him formed themselves into a kind of guard; the whole people joined in procession, some one, as they did so, striking up a hymn familiar to the waters of Venice, and the people changed their shouts for the sacred song. Thus was Vittor Pisani escorted to his house at San Fantino.

CHAPTER XXIII.

As Sebastian and his friend were about to follow in Pisani's train, one plucked him by the sleeve. He looked back, and knew an attendant of the doge, a grave and aged man, who had served Contarini nearly all his life, and now served him not as prince but master. He gave Sebastian a letter, saying that the doge wished him to man one of the galleys ?? the instant, to bear that letter to Justiniani, and to wait with the commander until Pisani should arrive, and the doge would then give farther orders. Turning to the Englishman the messenger desired him also to be ready to set out that night on the voyage he knew of; and then the man left them.

Sebastian turned pale. "Little did I think," he said, "that I should dislike any service that Contarini would appoint; but it is so sudden."

"Nor should you this," said his friend, "sudden as it is. The same fate that has prepared for you this sudden absence, and which has prepared for you the reasons why you dread it, will also prepare for you a return."

"True enough," said Sebastian, as they walked to the water's edge; "yet I would have foregone a little glory for one hour's delay. Edward, you have still a little time and you must be my messenger." And he begged his friend to see Teresa, and explain his sudden departure; and to give Turnbull a new charge to be stedfast to his post. His sister also was to be told the reason of his sudden absence. They found a galley ready manned by the now willing sailors, eager to bear to the outer shore the tidings of Pisani's release; and in a few minutes Edward was watching the vessel as it glided swiftly away.

He turned to obey his friend's first injunction, and in a short time he knocked at the door of Jacopo Arduino's house. The door was cautiously opened, and the massive form of Turnbull blocked up the opening. "Ah, Master Edward," he cried, "is it you! Truly, it is a comfort to see an English face again."

"Well, let me enter, good Turnbull, and you shall see my face more at ease."

"Nay, nay, Master Edward, I have no order for that. I am put here to keep folk out, not to let them in."

"Good; but you are not ordered to keep me out?"

"All, Master Edward, all; and there was no account taken of you: they said not, keep out all save Master Edward."

"Nay, good Turnbull, you know me, and you know that Signor Sebastian would not shut me out. Why I brought you to him; and you know me I hope for an honest gentleman."

"Aye, and I will make it good against all that gainsay it; but so you know me for an honest man, Master Edward, and true to my word; and I have said that none shall come in."

Although vexed at his awkward plight, Edward could not forbear laughing at the untimely fidelity of the guard. Presently he bethought to ask the soldier whether he would take the orders of the lady Teresa? The man consented, and shut the door for a time. It was then opened, and the smiling Turnbull admitted his countryman, closed the door, and ushered him to the room where Teresa usually sat.

She rose as he entered, and advanced to meet him. Though he had put more faith in Sebastian's account of her than he would in any other lover's description of his mistress, he was little prepared for what he saw. Since Sebastian first met her, the diminished pressure of poverty and anxiety had shown itself in her form: her face was not so thin ; her color not so pale but a delicate tint signified the place where the rose of her cheek would bloom in a more propitious season. The almost despondency, which pained while it melted Sebastian's heart, had given way to a more contented calm. But departing grief had left all the dignity and self-possession which surprised Edward in one so humble and so little proud, until he knew how her nature had trained itself. As one of a disinherited nation, he cared little for the dignities which were lost to so many of his race, and to the highborn dames of Venice was wont to show no more courtesy than became a man to all women ; but as Teresa advanced towards him, in all the unconscious dignity of vanquished trouble, he felt a respect which had never before possessed him, and bowing low, he kissed the hand she held out to him with more reverence than a courtier some great prince's. "Dear lady," he said, "I fear that I am an unwelcome visitor, where another was expected ; but the seeing you seems to give life and presence to all that I have heard and known for some time ; and where you had one, you now have two faithful servants."

Teresa held for an instant the hand that had taken hers, and pressing it gently, she answered, "Never could you be unwelcome, Messer Odoardo. Rather say, that to see you where another was expected is some solace. But Sebastian !—these strange noises in the city have alarmed me !"

"There is nought to fear ; only that Sebastian is hastily sent to a distance,—so hastily that he could not even stay to tell of his departure, and take his leave. I believe he would not have heeded a little more danger to himself, if it had kept him in Venice."

"In Venice ! has he then left the city !" cried Teresa, as she hurriedly returned to her chair, not daring to trust her trembling limbs.

"He has gone to the seashore ; but only as a messenger. Though he knows nothing certainly, he hopes that he may soon return."

"The Genoese !—"

"The Genoese have taken Chiozza, and Sebastian is sent to Messer Taddeo Justiniani to announce the coming of a larger force under Vittor Pisani."

Teresa covered her face with her hands. It was her first separation since she had loved ; the first time that one she loved so well had left her to seek danger at the sword's point. She had foreseen the time ; she had thought herself prepared for it. She had even once prepared herself to dismiss Sebastian, and to be again in the world with no stronger protection than her own firm mind. But since that time she had tasted the luxury of a tranquil reliance on more powerful defence. Resting on Sebastian's manly bosom, she had somewhat forgotten the uses of solitary fortitude.

The blow was worse than she had feared ; but covering her eyes—looking steadfastly for an instant on the blank which his chaste endearments now made more desolate—by a strong effort she suppressed the chill shivering that unbound her limbs ; when she uncovered her face, its old paleness had settled there: but her eyes were dried ; and if her brows were slightly contracted in an upward frown, her lips were firm. "These griefs, Messer Odoardo," she said, "are the price we have to pay for happiness. We should think them too great, but that with happiness we buy two other things—memory and hope."

"Excellent lady ! Sebastian told me true—" Edward stopped.

"Sebastian loves you too well, Messer Odoardo, not to make you believe that all about him borrow from his own goodness. He has made me know you as more to him than a brother, and that is why I speak thus freely to you. Tell me, what is his danger, and when he may return !"

"Would I could. He has gone, as I said, a messenger from the doge to Taddeo Justiniani, to await with him for farther orders from the prince. Should the doge think fit, he may remain with Pisani."

"Until !—"

"Until any time—to the end of the war. But that is not likely. As he went, he desired me to give new charge to your guard below, and to tell you why he came not."

"It is like him. He thinks of others, who think too much of themselves. Do you stay in Venice ?"

"Alas ! no ; or Sebastian would less have cared for it. I am bound on another errand, still more distant."

"And you too ! Yet how little should I repine, who have those watching for me while braving such trouble and danger."

"Sweet lady, fear not that Sebastian will forget what he leaves in Venice ; and although he may not leave his post, he will more than you yourself care for your safety."

"I know it—I know it ; and let him not hear that I am troubled at his absence."

Edward promised her, and took his leave, with fresh assurances that Sebastian would return without long delay. Nor did he forget his charge to Turnbull, whom he found very well disposed to so easy a garrison.

CHAPTER XXIV.

Edward had scarcely departed, when another knock summoned Turnbull to the door. He opened, and before him stood a tall woman, closely veiled. She at once stepped forward to enter, pushing back the hand which he opposed to her. Had it been a score of men, they would have found some difficulty in forcing an entrance ; but Turnbull could not put forth his strength against a woman ; and, in sooth, he encountered a more vigorous push than he expected. Having made good her entrance, the woman motioned him to shut the door, and desired him to guide her to the lady. With many signs and a few unintelligible words, the soldier tried to make her understand that she could not be admitted; but she would not depart. At length the veiled visiter made signs that he should crave audience for her, and again he repaired to Teresa. He returned, and carefully fastening the door, he beckoned the woman to follow him to his mistress.

Teresa surveyed the unknown form before her with curiosity, not unmixed with something like fear: nor when the man had retired, and the veil was slowly unfolded, did she know the beautiful but severe and mournful face of Rosa. In turn, the stranger regarded her like one who is comparing a picture with its description, and seeing that all is true. As she looked, Rosa seemed to take heart; and breaking silence, she said, "Pardon me, if in my eagerness to speak with you I have shown so little courtesy. When you have heard me you will forgive."

"I do not know that I have anything to forgive; I must rather ask pardon of you, for that my defenceless state makes me slow to admit any to this poor house."

"I am rude at answering, as such kind words should be answered, and must rather show you that I would serve you, than strive with you in compliments. Do you know Alessandro—Alessandro Padovano, he is called?"

Teresa started, and turned pale. "You mean the foster brother of Messer Marco Morosini?"

"The same. He it was that sent me here. But fear nothing. I came because he sent me. I will tell you what he told me to tell you; but I will tell you something more. Promise me only that what I say shall be secret to us two." Teresa hesitated. Her companion added, "It concerns the safety of more than yourself—why should I not say it—it touches Messer Sebastian most nearly." Still seeing Teresa hesitate, though her color changed, Rosa said—"Well, I do not deserve that you should make bargains with me: I will tell you all that you should know, and you shall be secret in mercy."

"You are too good for me," answered Teresa; "I cannot, though I would, promise to be secret before I know what must be concealed; but rather, though you speak of names most dear to me, let it be unsaid than danger befall you."

"The worst has befallen me. Be patient, then, and listen to me." And Rosa repeated Alessandro's discourse faithfully, dwelling upon the happiness which the other might enjoy united to Sebastian, a great and powerful man in Venice, with all the high influences now arrayed against his native city bent to his service. "Think," she said, "how you now see your lover seldom—in secret—in danger; how the word of others may part you, as it has done, for ever; how, when you do see him, though your heart melts until you are blinded with love, you dare not give it way, lest he who adores should scorn, and love itself turn from its excess to its own undoing and shame. And think how, if it were as I say, you would have power to claim him in the face of Venice; how none should part you; how your arms being honored by clasping him, there should be no bounds to check your passion. There are

times, fair lady, when women can command men, if those minutes are but seized. Say that it shall be—tell him that it shall be so, and your happiness awaits but your own consent."

Teresa listened with her face looking down; and when silence awaited her answer, she turned her eyes on Rosa, saying, "I scarce can tell what power I may offend: I should grieve to displease one who pleads so well, but you have shown me yet nothing that I can do?"

"Yet, do you not desire the union I spake of?"

"Why do you ask?"

"Lady, suspect me not. Why do I ask?—aye, indeed, you could not know that. But you cannot fear one who is poor and friendless."

"Madonna," answered Teresa, "I do not well know in what fashion to speak to you; from your bearing, I should believe you a friend; from your face, I could swear that you mean me no wrong—nothing false; but you are a messenger from one whom I have learned to believe neither true nor my friend."

Rosa took her hand, and kissed it. "I will not task you farther," she said. "If there is risk to run, let it be to me and those who deserve it. But tell me first—and I swear to you that I mean you nought but humble service—tell me, to content my mind—do you not love, that you refuse the union with Messer Sebastian?"

"I do not refuse it, but only the way to it. I do love."

"Tell me, farther, does Sebastian love no less?"

"I believe so."

"And he too refused." said Rosa, musing. "Strange, that love should be so true, and yet so willing to be denied."

"Is it strange, that love should be true, and yet refuse to join with secrecy and falsehood? for if love be joined to falsehood, it soon ceases to be true."

"And thus it dies, poisoning itself with what it takes to be food." There was a pause, and Rosa seemed lost in thought; while Teresa regarded with sadness the sorrow in her face. Suddenly recollecting herself, she spoke in a firmer voice, "I have given you Alessandro's message, and now let me speak for myself—obey it not. Alessandro would sacrifice everything, all that is great and true in the world, to his schemes. He it was that told me—me!—to describe to you the happiness of successful love. I consented, but I did not promise to tell you no more. See then—but have you patience to hear a long story?"

"I will hear anything that you wish to tell."

"See then if I have not cause to bid you beware of him. Alessandro, as you know, comes from Padua, and so do I. His mother gave suck to Messer Marco Morosini, while Alessandro was still a babe. The old Morosini was wont often to visit the mother, even when he was aged, and Messer Marco came very often. When Alessandro grew of a fit stature, and he was early a tall and strong man, Messer Marco begged of his father that his foster brother might be his servant. The two went to the wars together, and all that Alessandro could do he so contrived that it should add to the fame of his young master. It is said that he delighted to be mistaken for Marco; and though Marco is brave, Alessandro was ever more powerful; so that many an achievement done by the servant was told of the master. Marco was proud, Alessandro taught him how to be discreet. In time, the servant grew to be the master, and Messer Marco would not even suffer him to be called a servant; so that when they returned to Venice after long sojourn in other lands, the contadina's son was called Messer Alessandro da Padova, and men treated him like a gentleman, even if they did not believe him to be such. He also studied, so that he is very learned, almost as learned, people say, as Messer Petrarca. He used to come to see his mother often. My father's vineyard was next to his mother's. Her husband had died years before, but she kept the vineyard, and my father managed it for her, with his own; and I have heard him say that she paid him well. I can remember Alessandro when I was quite a child, but he says that he cannot remember me—not before one day. Santa Maria! how I was terrified that day! Afterwards, I thought it was the first day of happiness, the first day of life! yet now it terrifies me again, for I begin to think that I do not understand what has happened since, and the end is dark to me. I was cutting the leaves of a vine, to let the sun get at the grapes, and Alessandro was passing by, from where he had been lying in the shade, to the house. He stopped to look at my work—I was just then growing to be a woman. When he spoke to me, I left off working. Did you ever see Alessandro?"

"I am not sure; I believe I have."

"It is not very many years ago; but he was then still a young man, and still looked young; now he is harsher and severer; you could now scarcely believe that he could speak so softly and kindly as he did then. I was then very young, and only a simple child. I do not know how it was, but while we were talking he drew me towards him and kissed me. I had been kissed before, in sport, and thought no shame of it; but at that kiss my heart seemed stifled. I turned from him in fright, and ran away. But I did not tell any one. I always worked at cutting leaves from the grapes while there were any to be cut, and Alessandro used to watch me at my work. My father—he died; and another man came to work for Alessandro's mother. But she said that she would not leave me alone, and she took me to live with her. When I asked her why she was so good to me, she laughed. I believed that it was Alessandro's kindness, and I loved him all the more; so that when he reproached me for not loving him, it made me very sad—and I never thwarted him more. I loved him with all my heart, and I thought that he loved so too. I asked him one day why he did not wed me, as others did their lovers! He said that he had not the power, and that I should know why when I was older. But he persuaded me to come to Venice, for he could not leave it so often. Not long after, his mother died; and he said that she had some little property belonging to my father, and that suffices me to live now; though I think Alessandro does not stop to count my property when he has money to give me; for he was ever generous in such matters. After I had been in Venice a long time, I asked him

again why he did not marry me. Can you guess why!"

Teresa did guess; but she answered not.

"It was—that he might wed another. Some one powerful and rich. Not that he had yet forgotten to love. It was gradual. While I lived only in him, he forgot me. He was silent, thinking of greatness, and of wars, and of sacrificing love. He staid away, and left me to think. I remembered, that while I had loved, that is, all the while, I forget everything but Alessandro; he forgot nothing of his own pleasures—everything else. I cannot tell you how it was or what agonies it cost me, but I seemed to learn to understand him. I thought that ours had been love. I doubt it now—his—and—O God!—I even doubt my own." Rosa covered her face with her hands, and bowed down, swaying to and fro, as if in an agony of pain. Teresa took her head with her hands, and laying it on her own shoulder, passed her arm round her companion. After a few moments, she recovered. "I thought that I had learned to know him. He came again—he came again but last night; it was to send me hither! I had seen his own love fade and turn to something monstrous—he now talked of your love as a jest, a trifle in his way, and he sent me to destroy it! I came not for that. I came to see if all, like him, would destroy themselves for power—or if there were love and truth abiding in the world."

"And why did you not look into your own heart to know it, poor girl!"

"I did—I did; but it was only one; and oh! if I were mistaken. But I know it now; and though I am more certain that I am wretched. I am not so wretched as I was; and I am stronger to endure. But, dear lady, I have now told all; had I mistrusted you I might have done my bidding more artfully. I am at your mercy."

"Fear not—but you have not told me your name."

"Rosa Bardossi."

"Fear not, Rosa; no harm shall reach you through me."

"Nor Alessandro?"

"Nor Alessandro. But do you return within his power?"

"I must obey my fate."

"And do you not fear him? What will you say of your enterprise!"

"Nothing; I shall be silent."

"But you will anger him. Is he not violent?"

"I do not fear him. He has already done worse than kill me. And besides," she added, with a bitter smile, "he is not yet so wicked."

"And what, Rosa, have I to fear from him?"

"I know not. I think, nothing as yet; but I will know, and you shall hear if any danger threaten. You will let me see you again?"

"And, tell me again, what can I do for you, that come so far to serve me?"

"Nothing either—unless—it will not offend you? I feel to love you so that I cannot tell—it will you, dear lady, let me kiss that kind mouth?"

Teresa took her in her arms, and kissed her many times. The first tears for a long time bedewed Rosa's eyes as she drew herself away, and folding her veil around her, she left Teresa alone.

CHAPTER XXV.

It was night before Edward set out on his second mission. He delayed, partly because he did not wish to be observed entering the palace of Morosini in the absence of his friend, partly from some dislike to his errand. While yet he was a child, the young Saxon had been the playmate of a fair girl; who, Norman herself, was destined for a Norman lord; and when her father, noting the growing earnestness of Edward's looks, had caused him to be shut out from the accustomed sport, and when he saw that the proud little beauty smiled joyously as she passed him in the distance, easily waiving his service, he conceived a new hatred to the land where his race was humbled. He had not yet loved; but the cutting blow prevented his ever loving after; and though he had found beauty complying, he had never wooed it to relinquish wealth and high estate for his sake. When he first knew Sebastian's sister, he forgot his armor of pride; and he remembered it too late. Yet he refused to yield to the feeling that had stolen upon him. Not that he believed Angiolina cruel, or unfavorable to his suit, had he made it; but he judged that it should not be made. Of her father's enmity even already he was sure; because he was poor, because he was the friend of Zeno, whom Marco Morosini deemed a sort of rival; and most of all, because he was not of Morosini's own train. Like her brother, Angiolina, frank, unsuspecting, and eager-hearted, had shown the Englishman that she was not indifferent to him; but he had seen her gentle, and what was more, her spontaneous submission to her father; he dared not woo to disobedience, nor one so delicately nurtured to a rougher and more uncertain life; and he would not woo to be again the sport of a filial obedience which his lowly station could not distinguish from pride. Angiolina had learned to like the Englishman in her brother's description, and that bearing which gave testimony to the description; while she wondered, and almost grieved, at that strange constraint which she thought belonging to the coldness of his northern country. Had she been older, she might clearly have seen that he did not hate her, nor have attributed his distant bearing to humble timidity, which she pitied and tried to reassure; her kindness wondrously making it only worse. Now, Edward had never yet seen her in grief; he had not seen her since Sebastian left his father's house; and he had, in a manner, to play the part of that brother. Conscious of his own conflicting thoughts, he fancied that he should be suspected. As he drew near to the house, however, he had cast aside all these doubts, and had well-nigh persuaded himself that they were all of them no more than sickly fancies; that the lady was as heedless of him as the little Norman that haunted him like something of a first love; and that the servants would let him pass like any other messenger from their young master—beloved by them all. Strange to say, he not only found the door of the palace open, but the hall seemed deserted. He walked straight to the saloon in which he had usually found Sebastian and his sister. Though dark, its utter stillness told him that no breathing thing was there. At the top of the palace, on a terrace, was a little space filled with plants, and called a garden. Little was it frequented; for few entered Marco's solitary palace, except on state days. Thither Edward repaired, going more softly as he approached the door; for he heard voices. As he went on, however, he heard footsteps also behind him in the ante-room that led to the terrace; and not wishing to be seen, he stepped into the garden. The most had been made of the little space, and it was filled with a few tall thick shrubs, that hid the talkers from his sight; while he also concealed himself from the person that came behind. He had scarcely done so, ere he was vexed; for if he were discovered, some color would be given to the suspicions that he feared; whereas he needed not to hide at all. The person that came behind him partly closed the door, as if he had come on purpose to do so; for the footsteps retreated again. The voices that had ceased with the sound, again went on. One was Angiolina's, the other a man's. Moving cautiously, so as to see them through the shrubs, Edward observed the lady sitting on a seat that usually stood there. By her side, with one arm resting on a tall flower-pot which was raised on a stand, was a young man. He was dressed in the tight vest and nether garments of the time; a tightly buttoned sleeve issuing out of the looser sleeve that hung from the elbow. The cloak which he had worn was thrown across one end of the seat. As he leaned carelessly against the flower-pot, his head supported by the fingers of his bent hand, the other hand resting on his hip, and one leg easily thrown across that which sustained his weight, there was an air of agile strength and grace of the most pleasing kind; and yet withal a dash of hardihood and recklessness little to be looked for in a lady's suitor. His voice it was that first struck Edward's ear.

"I had thought that they were coming to drive me hence! so Angiolina—I cannot help calling you Angiolina, as if you were not cruel."

"I am not cruel," answered the girl, with a sweetness and kindness that never before displeased the hidden listener. "Call me always Angiolina."

"I do intend to. I used to call you so when we played together at Messer Zeno's house. You have chid me often; and especially when I kissed you; but never for that; and I do not think you have yet grown so cruel."

Edward listened for the answer, but there was none. That Angiolina had a lover he had never heard a hint, and to find one so familiar almost passed the belief of his senses.

The youth continued. "It all comes back to me again. We are strange creatures, Angiolina! I have been away from Venice. I have passed long dreary months beyond her waters. I have been in camps and halls, fighting and revelling; I have left off thinking of you, rather than think of you and not see you; I have been as heedless and sportive as any; but now, when I come back to this quiet—hark! you can hear the water ripple, it is so still—and I can hear you sigh, carina—when I come back here, all that time seems like a dream in sleep, or rather death, for there was nothing living in it. When that is gone, and one thinks of it, it revives no more—there is nothing that remains of it; but when this short hour is gone—though I have been so still that my arm is numbed with not moving it,"—and he did move it, and sat on the long seat, half beside, half opposite his companion, "and though I have scarcely heard the sound of your voice, yet will this hour remain to me a living thing through life. It will be the light from home to the traveller that has set out on the long winter's journey, and looks at what he has left. And you have sent me that journey, Angiolina!"

"Francesco!"

"Aye, and you pity me! But that only makes it worse. I do not know but what it were better to lie down here, and move no more. Or bury myself here under your orange tree. I could do it in a night; and so be food to the fruit, and creep to your lips that way."

Angiolina had hidden her face with her hand. Francesco took the other; and Edward saw that she did not withdraw it. Suffocated, he wished now to leave the place, but he scarcely dared move, lest the noise should disclose him; and he was still uncertain whether his retreat was free. His rival went on.

"How is it, Angiolina dear, that you are so merciful while you are so cruel!"

"How can I resist when you talk so sadly."

"But how can you be so cruel too!"

"I am not cruel."

"You do not love me, Angiolina."

Edward's life seemed to hang on the answer.

"I do."

"Then why deny me! I do not boast myself to be all that you should have; but if you love me, what can be said more! Your father will not refuse you a throne, poor as it may be."

"A throne!" thought Edward.

"Nay!" said Angiolina, "I love you not for thrones, Francesco; and I want none of them. It is cruel of you to say that I do not love you, and to speak as if I desired your life to be unhappy. But—but—it is useless to say more. You know my father never would let me wed an enemy of Venice."

"I am not so sure of that, if the enemy of Venice could become its friend; make all other enemies its friends; and give him a sovereign for a son-in-law; or at least a sovereign's heir. I fear not the father: what would the daughter say, if the father consented!" No answer. "Would the daughter too consent!" Angiolina shook her head. Dropping her hand, the youth rose from his seat, walked a few paces, and resumed his station by the flower pot. "And yet you say you love me, Angiolina, as well as when we used to meet—as well as in that long sojourn with Madonna Zeno!"

"As well, Francesco."

"As well—and no better!"

"Why should I love you better!"

"Are we not older! Do not I love you better! I once thought indeed that you did—when I performed that hateful office, and knelt for my father before the doge (Edward now knew that it was the son of Carrara who spoke,) and when I looked around, I saw triumph on all faces—on all but one; and there a sad and pitying mirror of the shame I felt—my mortal suffering mirrored in an angel's pity That deceived me, Angiolina, and I thought you loved me."

"And so I did, and so I do. It is because I love you, Francesco, that I tremble for your being here, while all Venice cries out against your house."

"Aye, with horrible stories of its crimes—as if Carrara could hire men to poison the wells of which Zeno drinks; as if I would suffer him to poison your fountains, Angiolina! There are traitors that borrow my father's name, whenever they are plotting: and I wish I could unstrip them. You love me! but when we say love, you talk of one thing, I another. What hard fate is it that makes me love and not be loved!"

"Perhaps it is Heaven, that will not let me love an enemy of Venice."

Francesco smiled. "Are you too, so bitter! But is there no other reason, Angiolina! You do not answer: I suppose your silence means yes. Could I guess the reason! Should I have been more lucky had I been born a Venetian! Ah, I see! I tis a Venetian then." The girl again shook her head. "So, then, I have discovered your secret, Angiolina. Nay, hang not your head. I do not know why—it is strange, but I feel less angered to think that I am not scorned merely for your coldness, or for fear of your father. And what great lord offers you a higher fortune than poor Francesco!"

"None, Francesco."

"None! what, is it then some wretch as mean as I am! But I will not torment you. See, I am not so cruel as you are. But why not tell me sooner!"

"Because I had nothing to tell."

"Nothing! you are a riddle, Angiolina, which I cannot read. But I must be gone on the winter journey I spake of; and with the light shut against me too. Would I had said farewell long ago, and carried away a longer deceit. I seized a few more moments, and they bear this fruit! Well, Angiolina, I was to choose one of two lives—should I learn to live of you, or of my father! You have left me but one choice, and when you hear of Francesco Carrara busy in the world, among wars and profitless plots, say to yourself—I made him so; and blame me not." He put his cloak round him; and putting his arms through the short sleeves in its sides, took both her hands as she rose from her seat. "Farewell, dearest!"

"Farewell, Francesco,—Oh! if you did but know"—she leaned her head upon his shoulder. Francesco pressed her to his bosom; and turning her face round with gentle violence kissed her on the mouth. Then carefully placing her on the garden seat, he hastily entered the house.

During the scene that he had witnessed, Edward had been swayed by a storm of passions, that seemed to assail him from all sides; a dangerous despair was followed by a still more dangerous hope; and when he was alone with Angiolina, the memory of what he had heard, seemed to render her sacred against his approach. But night darkened, and the wind began to rise; reminding him of his enterprise, and of the duty to Sebastian which he must first perform. He stepped round from behind the shrubs, and stood before Angiolina.

G

She started. "Back again! Oh, do not so tempt danger."

"It is I," said Edward; "your servant Odoardo, with a message, Lady Angiolina, from your brother."

"Ah heavens!" she cried, as she rose from her seat, "what strange night is this! Tell me, how did you come?"

"Through yon door."

"And did you meet any one!"

"None."

"None! and yet you came but now! Did you not say that you came but now?" Edward was silent. "You do not answer me!"

"I would not answer you, lest I should offend."

"Offend, Messer Odoardo! but say, did you enter this moment!" .

"I did not: I have been here many moments; longer than I would, but that I was, as it were, a prisoner."

There was a pause, which Angiolina broke. "You heard then, sir, more than was meant for your ears; though I am assured that it will be safe with you." Edward bowed. "You said that you had a message from my brother!"

Edward delivered it; and with a little artifice, the girl did not hide her grief at her brother's hasty departure, because she had other feelings which she was glad to hide and make pass for that.

"And you, Messer Odoardo—do you follow my brother!"

"No, lady, I am bound on a more distant journey, and must say farewell for myself."

"More distant! Surely you do not leave Venice;" and Angiolina again sank upon her seat.

"Only to return."

"And for how long," asked Angiolina, in a faint voice, "shall you be absent!"

"Not for long; but sea voyages are uncertain. May I have your prayers for its shortness!"

Angiolina gave him her hand. "I seem to be losing all my friends at once," she said, and he could guess from her voice that she was trying to smile. Her hand trembled, and when she tried to withdraw it, and found that he still held it, she still left it in his; and it trembled more. She leaned her head upon her hand. Edward, carried away by what he had heard,—by the night—and the finding of himself thus alone with one who appeared to rebuke his pride with a generous tenderness,—could not speak, but stooping down, covered that trembling hand with kisses; then pressing it to his eyes, he held it so for some instants. A gentle voice whispered—"Messer Odoardo—Odoardo—leave me!"

"Leave you!" cried Edward, all his resolves vanished. "Yes, Angiolina, when I have told you all that this bosom has striven with; when I have made Sebastian's sister know how the love for her brother dares reach herself—dares to forget its own lowliness—even her fortunes which it mars by crossing—and to make the wretch it sways injure that which he loves, because he loves." And Edward told the trembling girl all that he had suffered from his own pride; his doubts of her favor; all that he had felt while hidden among the shrubs; his doubt

even—but by this time his arm was round her waist—of her own courage to brave the precarious fortunes of so powerless a lover. He was not repulsed. Though he could boast no childish plays together; though he—Angiolina felt it—was even less likely to obtain her father's favor, than the powerful enemy of Venice; she leaned her head on his shoulder, and talked of his love for her brother, and of her brother's love for him, as if to excuse her own. Long would Edward—how changed from what he was when he entered the palace,—have remained thus; but he did not forget his dangerous enterprise. Had young Francesco Carrara witnessed that farewell which happened so soon after his own, he would have been less patient than Edward had been; for the first kiss which he took on those ripe lips, gently but hastily yielded, was worth all that Francesco had ever had, and he would have given them all for it.

Re-entering the house, Edward proceeded slowly along the ante-room, towards the downward stairs. A lamp in one of the rooms, shed an uncertain light across the broad hall. Just as he entered it, the figure of a man appeared before him. By the size and gait he knew that it must be the foster brother. As he stopped, uncertain what to say, Alessandro whispered in a harsh quick voice. "Fool! fool! know me not. If the servants see you, I must seize you, Francesco. Pass on, buy, pass on. I thought you had gone long ago." Edward obeyed, for the moment rejoiced to be so mistaken; but as he again issued into the open air, he was ill pleased to find the house in charge of a traitor—a detected traitor to Venice, and a double traitor to Angiolina: both as a Venetian and as her foster uncle.

CHAPTER XXVI

Edward had tarried so long, that he half feared lest his absence should have been observed; and he was pleased when he reached the great square to find an attendant of the doge who had just been sent to seek him. He repaired to the prince's apartment, to which he was at once admitted. The newly released prisoner, Pisani, was taking leave and his last instructions. His captivity was still marked in the settled sternness, almost gloominess, of his face; and his plain and sober deportment did not cover the pride of injured desert. In addressing him the courteous Contarini seemed half-abashed, as though, but for his station, he would have humbled himself before the ill-used prisoner. But, a true Venetian, he would not, by doing penance for the republic, admit her to be wrong. Desiring Pisani to exert all his art and strength to confine the Genoese to the points already gained, and to make even their hold of Chiozza uneasy, he dismissed the commander; whose arrival among his men was announced by the shouting outside.

Contarini turned to the Englishman. "Well, Messer Odoardo, if your stout heart is still with us, Venice desires your services."

"They are her's, my lord."

"To-night!"

"This instant."

"It is well. The senate have long determined, as you know, to send for Messer Carlo Zeno, whose skill has often driven from Venice dangers almost as great. The task will be difficult, as the Genoese possess the sea; and therefore we must give it to some one who is as bold a man as can be, and withal discreet. Messer Odoardo, when our Sebastian advised me to send for Zeno, he advised also that you should be the messenger; the senate consented, and the signory thinks that the time has now come. We believe Messer Carlo to be at Tenedos, which he has acquired for Venice; and you will sail straight thither with all the speed you may; bringing back the Zeno in your own galley. That there may appear no putting away of Venetian authority, a noble gentleman will go with you—your friend Messer Luigi Morosini. The galley is ready, and Messer Luigi awaits you."

"I will depart at once, then. The night is dark, and the approach of Messer Pisani will draw the Genoese to Chiozza."

"Do so, take the fleetest galley in the arsenal, and what rowers or bowmen you will."

"There is a galley that belongs to Messer Pietro Caresino. It is not of the largest, but he had it made only to carry goods of price: it is two-masted, and there is none so fleet in the arsenal. He will give me that. And for men, we shall need more to row, than to fight."

"Do as you will."

"But before I go, my lord, let me crave to say to you one thing, and saying it to you, to be allowed to tell no more."

"I will buy what you have to tell—which is indeed your free gift—by promising not to put you to the torture, Odoardo, for more, before you go on your perilous service."

"Do you know the man they call Messer Alessandro da Padova? He is best known as the foster brother of Messer Marco Morosini."

"What of him? Yes, I know the man. I have heard of him often. They say, indeed, that he sits in the senate, when we poor fools fancy we see Messer Marco—that Morosini's body is only there, but Alessandro's spirit."

"Would Messer Morosini had a more honest spirit as indeed I believe he has, if he would only use his own mind instead of his foster brother's."

"No one speaks well of that man, Odoardo. But what were you to tell me?"

"This, my lord. I would not accuse the man to those who would harm him, because it is impossible that I could say how I know it, or in what it lies—but I *know* him to be a traitor. Let him be watched."

"Odoardo, he is watched. Everybody suspects him, everybody says that he is traitor; yet he is the most faithful of Venetians, for all that we know. Morosini, his servant, in the senate—there is no more ardent and faithful man for Venice. He it was that intreated to command the works at the ports."

"Aye, and Alessandro commanded in his name."

"True. Yet no treachery of the man is known."

"To me it is."

"And you cannot tell it? Is it impossible, Odoardo?"

"Impossible, my lord; I must die first."

"When youth talks of dying for a secret," said the venerable prince with a smile, "we always suspect some sweet secret in the case."

"There too, my lord, I must ask you to forbear. I do know Alessandro to be a traitor—a double traitor; and I would not leave Venice without telling you to let him be watched."

"It shall be done; and I ask no more. Farewell: be your return speedy."

Edward took his leave, and went forth into the place. The wide place was filled; many torches lighting up the night, and showing clear the lofty walls of the palaces and the bell-tower, which reared upward into the darkness above. Some of Pisani's galleys were still taking their departure, and exchanging loud farewells with those on shore; while the water driven by the wind and beaten by the oars, danced and foamed in a thousand shades of white froth, red torch-light, and black shadows. Here was a group of women, giving the last caresses to a couple of mariners, their grief blown away by the storm of bustle and hurry. Here was a young noble pointing his farewell with a jest, the more bravely to set off his chivalry. Here again a sturdy number carried on board the last store of arms. As he drew near the water's edge, the broad form and jovial face of Luigi il Grasso emerged into the light, with hands held out.

"Well, foreigner, here am I waiting like a dutiful commander to learn the pleasure of my lieutenant. We are as ready to see you as your mistress is, boy; and all right to go on board. I did not forget your dress of gala, lest you should need to go a courting where we shall be, you know; or we may pick up some syren—very fine women they say, and very seductive."

"We shall need little holiday clothes, my friend. But you are as careful of your friends as if you were the father of us all."

"And so I am, Sebastian—I mean Odoardo, default of a better. A father who has brave sons, but never a wife to prevent his sleeping, or eating in peace; and that is the reason that sleep and food do me so much good;" stroking himself complacently.

"Nay, I think it is charity that fattens you; and on your credit I shall ever say, that content and kindness are your only physic."

"Boy, boy! you never flatter the great and wise, so I know that you take me for a poor fool. But let us go aboard."

"We must seek our galley first;" and despatching Luigi to pick out a full number of the best rowers and bowmen in the city, he repaired to beg the fleet galley of Pietro Caresino. It was soon standing with its stern at the steps of St. Mark; and the men led by Il Grasso walked in. Edward surveyed the crowded vessel from the poop; and then sending all the rowers to the front, he made the bowmen stand before him.

"Who among you can work at the oar?" he asked aloud: "let such go to the left here, and the others stand on this side." Most stood still, either unable to do the work or scorning it; others, guessing that their commander had some secret motive, moved apart as he directed : about a score or more claimed to be rowers as well as bowmen. "Good!" he cried. "Every bowman that rows shall have a rower's pay, besides his own, four ducats a month besides his eight : those that cannot row, or like it not, may go on shore, for we have too little room for nice workers. To the shore." And as he pointed with his finger, the discarded bowmen walked through the covered poop, and regained the piazzetta. "Go you forward," said Edward, "and let me speak with the rowers." The sturdy mariners gathered behind the mast in front of the poop. Are there any among you that cannot fight, my friends? If so, let them go on shore; I say fight, and I mean fight well." None stirred. "Good. You rowers while you are out with me shall have bowmen's pay—eight ducats instead of four. Nay, shout not. Hush! we must learn to go as quietly as we may. To your places, and let us be off. Who is that—is that you, Zanni?" he asked, as he saw the man that helped him to appease the crowd, when he rescued La Gobba. "I am glad to see such as you on board. Keep your fellows from tumbling over each other in their hurry; for we must make good speed."

In short time all was disposed. The few bowmen leaned or reclined about the deck; the rowers stood to their posts on either side, lost in the gloom, and seeming but parts of the vessel. Edward fell back, leaving the command to Luigi; who, wrapping himself tightly in his cloak, to keep out the wind that raked the deck, issued in his loud bell-like voice the orders to man the oars. A few seconds more, and the galley shot from the quay, swiftly driven along the canal of St. Mark. They made directly for the port of Lido. A messenger had already been sent, and the watchword given; they stayed for some time while beams were raised and; clanking chains that barred the entrance to the lagoon were lowered. The night was so dark that they could barely see a single figure; except when, now and then, a solitary torch shed a passing glare upon some busy number. Two lights were placed upon the works, to show the passage, and the galley went forward; until at length it left the lights, and the snatches of voice which broke through the wind, and stretched into the outer darkness.

"This north wind," said Edward, "blows the favor of Heaven upon our enterprise. Its strength will beat off the Genoese, and carry us past them like a spirit."

"It blows lustily, in truth. If I had a choice, I should say that I should choose a trifle less, —just a breath less."

"Not a jot, not a jot. It is less dangerous than one Genoese; for though we might drive him down, we might lame ourselves in doing it. I would have up a sail, but the white might be seen."

"A sail! why that is tempting the devil—St. Mark help us!—to drag us down. However, boy, you are answerable for it all, and I will drown with you as cheerfully as any man. As for the seeing it, I think this darkness may console the only fear you seem to know."

"Aye, as yet, but look there." Edward pointed to the east, where already the gray dawn had encroached upon the upward sky.

"Well, but the Genoese are between us and the light. If they are abroad, we should have the dark longest."

"True. Forward there! up with the foresail."

There was a stir in the galley, as if the mariners gathered round the mast farthest from the speakers. But no sail was raised. Edward shouted again—" What stays you, boys! up with it." A crumpled dark mass danced up the mast, and gradually spreading abroad like a cloud opening itself, it bellied before the wind: the white canvass scarcely reflecting the scanty light. Motioning the steersman to put the galley a little more before the wind, to ease the leeward oars, Edward proceeded to the side of the vessel, to see the effects of the sail upon her speed; while the passive Luigi walked to the mainmast, and leaned against it to ease his legs, and catch a strip of shelter from the wind. He had not remained long, ere Edward called to him. He joined his friend, and following the direction of Edward's finger, he saw a heavy mass moving along the water, not far out of their track.

"It is a Genoese," he said, in an undertone.

"Zanni," cried Edward, to the man who was near him, "run foward, and tell them to keep the silence of death. Some Genoese are near us ; but we will fight nothing in this hour, save time and the weather."

The sturdy sailor obeyed; while the friends watched the moving mass. It went steadily on its way. "They do not see us," whispered Edward. "Whither can they have been!"

"On a fool's errand; perhaps, to Tre Porti, to see whether they could not enter there to take possession of the swamps within."

"Venice must thank St. Mark for this darkness, which shields her messenger. Stay, there is another : perhaps they take us for companions?"

"Hardly, on this course; unless they think that Messer Capitano is drunk."

"Not an impossible guess. I cannot see the first one now ; can you!"

"Scarcely the second. This Zephyr—"

"Boreas, you mean."

"Well, it is Boreas,—carries us along like a dry leaf down a forest path."

"That shall be in the sonnet you shall make, Luigi, when we get back. We are very like a dried leaf, and I will be your witness. There, the place of the second galley can only be guessed at now. They are well passed, and my heart beats no more."

"Your heart beat! Why I should have thought that it could beat at nothing if this storm could leave it still."

"Storm, Luigi! why you should know storms too well to call this one. But my heart must beat, when the safety of Venice depends upon a ray of dawn, a glance of a stupid sailor's eye, or a turn of the wind."

"You are more Venetian than the Venetians themselves, Messer Inglese! And see, the storm has punished you, for it has blown your cap away. Aye, it is gone, Edward : you are as bad as a Genoese at catching what was before the wind."

"I am of no country, Luigi ; but most a Venetian ; for in Venice—"

"Aye, in Venice!" chuckled Luigi as he returned to the mast.

For some time the galley pursued its way in silence. Near the bow of the vessel was gathered a knot of men, some few rowers whose turn had not come, and who spoke in hoarse whispers, partly because of the order for silence, partly because they were half ashamed of their discourse.

"You talk," cried one, "as if we had a good and true Venetian over us; but this gentleman, is a foreigner."

"Well," answered our friend Zanni, "has not Venice been well and faithfully served by foreigners; and does not Messer Odoardo do in all things like a Venetian."

"No; I say, no. No Venetian would have come out in such a night as this. He would have known too well."

"That is calling the Englishman a bolder man than the Venetians."

"Not at all—I say, he would have known better. But it is not the coming out that I complain of; it is the setting sails in such a wind."

"And do we not go the faster!"

"Aye—to the bottom," cried a third.

"And if it were to the bottom, Pippo, is not an Englishman as likely to love life as well as any one of us, and will not the Englishman go with us?"

"I do not think he can love life at all, by his deeds. I propose that we should say we will go back. I said so before, and I think you are mad if you do not say it too. You say it, Zanni; for you know him. You wish to see the Sandracca again, don't you, spouse; and the little ones—four or five, you cannot tell which this blessed night."

"That's true, Pippo. I should not mind going back; but I am ashamed to say that we are afraid; especially to yonder Englishman, for I do not think he understands what this is, to be afraid."

"Well, tell it then to Messer Luigi: he is kind, and no one need fear him."

"I shall say you send me."

"Aye, say we send you. We will go with you."

They walked to where Luigi stood; but there they remained silent, their spokesman lacking courage to speak out. Luigi saw that they had not approached him for nothing; and he partly guessed their errand. "Well, friends, how goes it with you?" he asked.

"Why, Messer Luigi," replied Zanni, "it has gone better in other times."

"How so, boys; do we not go on bravely?"

"Somewhat too bravely. These men want to go back. They do not like the wind, sir."

"And still less," cried Pippo, "this hoisting of sails to brave the punishment of our sins, and break our mast."

"Eh! eh!" cried Luigi, with a good-humoured affectation of contempt, "you are forgetting time, friends, and think yourselves still little frightened children."

"I told you so," exclaimed Zanni, turning to his companions.

"Aye," said Pippo, pressing forward; "but Messer Luigi does not see all the danger. If this wind were against us, you would then know how the waves would beat over the bow, and blind us with spray."

"Oh! but this is good! why, here is a fellow afraid of what is not! Why, man, the wind is not against us. If it were, indeed, I might say that you have reason. Besides, see, boys—suppose we go back to Venice: then the weather alters, as it always does alter; and then we set out again directly, but having to go all the way we have already come."

"Why, that is true," said Zanni.

"True! it is only sailor's wisdom. Let us wait here for good weather. And while we do wait in open sea, you know, my sons, we may as well be going on; for it is as safe ten leagues forward as it is here."

"That's true again."

"Yes," cried Pippo; "but we need not have a sail to bear us down."

"Oh! it is the sail, is it! what would you do with that!"

"Have it down, sir: see how it strains the mast. It is a mercy that it has not broken it already."

"But it has not broken it."

"That is true, Pippo."

"Well, I know it is. But there is no talking with Messer Luigi."

"Then," said Luigi, "go and tell Messer Inglese there, that you want the sail down." He pointed to Edward. Unconscious of the dispute, the Englishman stood fixed to the position in which Luigi had left him, before the poop. Regardless of the wind, or rather impatient of its entangling his cloak, he had thrown the cumbersome garment aside, and remained in his tight vest; of which the looser sleeves fluttered and beat as though the wind would blow them off. His head was still bare: the blast had swept his light hair all forward, and it streamed from his forehead like a flame of light blown from a torch. He stood firmly, resting more on one leg, and his hand on that hip; while the other hand, the fist clenched, was placed upon the bulwark as if in mastery of the fleet ship. His brow was fixed with the intentness of his regard, which looked out into the sea, forward upon the path they were pursuing; his face and body moveless. He seemed to hold the ship and to urge it onward in his grasp, as though he would thrust it into the distance with mere might and will. Luigi held his arm out, pointing with his finger to the steadfast commander while he scanned the faces of the men. He took them by surprise, when he proceeded with a severe voice that had seldom been heard from his genial lips—"Go, my sons, and tell that Englishman that you are Venetians, who are not used to sails, nor to high winds, and that you want him to pull down this one sail and take you home. Go, and say, even while the wind is now growing less, that still you are so afraid that you dare not go on. Go, and tell him, the Englishman, not to mistake you for Englishmen; and, in order that you may be less ashamed, I will allow you to say that I too am afraid, for I am only a Venetian, and that I too will take you home and be your captain back; because I do not think that the Englishman would be your captain back—I do not think he would go home because he was afraid of the sea. So that, perhaps, if you do not persuade him that I am willing to go back, he might resist, and you would have to try to kill him first! and I doubt whether you would not be afraid of that too. Go and tell him, my sons; and I will share your shame, rather than you should die of fear. Why do you not stir! You do not seem so eager to do it, now you may. I see it, I see it! you are ashamed to speak so ill of Venetians. Shall I go and say it for you! Shall I go and say, Messer Inglese, we have not Englishmen on board, but only Venetians; and they are all afraid!" He continued, in his usual good-humored tone—" Let me go and tell him, boys. I think he would laugh. I think he would not believe me. I think he would say, ' I have been out with Zeno in fiercer winds than these, with none but Venetians; and then the Venetians laughed and gloried in the wind that went their own way—the more the better. These men must be no Venetians.' Shall I go and play this jest, my sons!" He made a step, as if to go.

Zanni stopped him. "Stay; do not tell him anything. It was only a dream of Pippo here, who mopes because his girl cried till her tears took the starch out of his courage."

"You are the liar, Zanni," cried the abashed Pippo; "it was when one talked of your babies and your wife, that you said you should come and speak to Messer Luigi."

"You talked of my wife yoursen, Pippo, to make me come."

"Nay," interposed Il Grasso, "quarrel not among yourselves, because you had all taken a little of the girls' fears along with their last kisses, lads. You have grown men now. Go to your posts—stay, Messer Odoardo comes. Perhaps it is to take down the sail, without asking."

Edward had turned his head, looking towards the wind, which now blew in much less force. Starting from his place, he came forward, shouting—"More sail there—up with the mainsail."

The men stood still; Zanni looking half abashed—half amused; and Pippo, turning a doubtful half-angry glance at Luigi; who cried, " What do you stand for, boys! You have what you asked for. Run, run!"

"Up with it," shouted Edward.

The men started; renewed courage thrilled in their busy arms; and in a minute, pressed by another swelling sail, the galley cleft the roaring foam with added speed.

CHAPTER XXVII.

It was a cloudless morning, and the sun was yet low, as a party of Venetians assembled on the shore of Tenedos. The greater number were soldiers in arms; with here and there a follower of Zeno's forces, more mariners, and some few islanders whose eastern dresses varied the group. The road that swept near the sea was crowded with other groups, who seemed as if watching for the approach of something by the land. The attention of the first group, however, was directed so intently to the sea, that even the shouts which arose behind them, and the sound of trumpets that blew nearer and nearer, scarcely made them turn their heads. That which they saw was a vessel in the extreme distance, making for the island; its white sails glaring in the sun, and the water sparkling like jewels as it was thrown up by the oars. Meanwhile, a new spectacle appeared on the road behind—bands of soldiers came first, with all the marks of fierce battle upon them. These looked heated —those others were pale with blood lost—and others again were more hacked in their surcoats, their mail, and steel caps, than hurt in their flesh. It was Carlo Zeno and his little army returning from their last victory over Andronicus, who had attempted to revoke the gift of Calojohannes; but he found the Venetians more powerful than his imperial enemy. The Greeks had been utterly discomfited after two days' fighting, which had not left the Venetians altogether scathless. As the men marched by, their looks were turned to the sea, for they knew that the galley, which was now more distinctly seen, came from their own fair city. After them moved another band, bearing their wounded; the eyes of the sick men were turned to the open sea and solitary sail upon it. They passed on, obedient to discipline and fatigue; but on reaching the spot where the road ran near the water's edge, a number of cavaliers left the body of the army, and joined the group by the shore. A few were mounted, and one among them was greeted by the loudest shouts, so that you might know where he was by the sound of the voices. As he dismounted from his horse, his hands were seized by many of the Venetians, who for a moment forgot the sea; and many of the islanders came around to make their obeisance. He was of an aspect to command and to be loved; so manly and agreeable his countenance, so strong and graceful his frame. He was of moderate height, but his just proportions made him seem taller than he was. His shoulders were broad and square; his chest was large; his limbs were muscular and powerful, but the extreme compactness of his well-knit joints gave an appearance of singular lightness and activity to his figure. Albeit, suffering from a wound in his leg, while one hand was tied to his chest, that another wound across the back might the sooner heal, the lameness did not quite hide the dignity of his carriage. His face was somewhat large and broad; his forehead —for his head was covered only with a light cap—was compact and straight; his eyes were large, dark, and brilliant, their steady gaze taking now a look of sternness, now of benignity; the nose was neither straight nor aquiline, but something between the two; the thick black beard on his upper lip parted to either side as it flowed into the manly crop that clothed his chin, displaying a full and genial mouth, that seemed ever ready to smile. His cheeks, burned to the deepest brown by the sun, and slightly paled by the weakness and pain of his wounds, yet showed the quick glow of health. Having looked around him, and pleasantly answered the salutations that reached him from all sides, Carlo Zeno fixed his eyes upon the sea. The Venetian galley still drew nearer. Suddenly two other vessels appeared, coming along the shore. They were Greek galleys that had been left rather behind their fellows; and they steered so as to cross the course of the Venetian. Zeno was the first to see them, and bidding one near him to hasten to his own galleys at the port, and send two out to support their countryman, he watched with anxiety the motions of those upon the sea. The Venetian kept its course as though it had been drawn by rule, the wind favoring the skill of its mariners. It now became evident that the Greeks, one of which shot ahead of the other, meant to hazard a parting blow against their solitary foe, by way of scoff to their victors on shore. The Venetians still made on.

"Our countryman," cried Antonio Veniero, "is not easily daunted: his message would be more surely and safely delivered, if it avoided the Greeks."

"Be not so sure of it," answered the full, clear voice of Zeno. "He that begins a flight, may never say whither it shall go, where end, or how. And it is no countryman of ours except in love."

Veniero looked surprised. "Whom do you think it, then, Messer Zeno!"

"It is the Englishman."

"Why should it be no other! Surely our sailors are as skilled as any, and as bold."

"A Venetian would have done as you counselled, Veniero, and would have thought rather of state reasons than a short blow. None but the Englishman would have kept so straight a path to his purpose."

"Nay, I know one Venetian that would not have taken my counsel."

"Who is he!"

"Carlo Zeno; for he said so but now."

"You have trapped me there," said Zeno, laughing.

"And I know another, too: Vittor Pisani never takes any but the straightest road."

"True, but Venice can hardly spare Pisani just now to be sailing about in a single galley. No, it is the Englishman—but see!"

As he spoke, the foremost of the Greek galleys was about to close with its enemy, which had not turned a hair's breadth from the straight line to the port. Suddenly the Venetian stopped, the oars arresting it in the water; the Greek, taken by surprise, still floated swiftly along on the smooth water: the Venetian again shot forward; a few strokes sent it right on the galley as that crossed it—it touched it smartly in the stern, breaking a few oars as it passed over them, and making the stricken vessel lurch so that it well nigh filled with water; and then, floating clear, it resumed its rapid course towards the land, passing in front of the other galley, whose people had stopped in surprise. Before the Greeks had recovered from their dismay, the Venetian was far off; and as they turned to pursue, the two other galleys ordered out by Zeno began to move from the shore. So abandoning farther contest, the Greeks turned their prows, and put quickly out to sea after their comrades. A loud shout arose from the land.

Zeno and his party went leisurely along the shore, and came to the landing place as soon as the galley. Presently descended from it the two strangely-matched companions, il Grasso and his friend Edward. Having embraced them, Zeno conveyed them to the palace in which he lodged, eager to learn the tidings which they had for his private ear. As soon as they were alone, Edward told him all that had happened in Venice, and the desire which the doge and senate had for his return.

"But where," said Zeno, "is Vittor Pisani! Is he still in prison doing penance for the wind's fault!"

"No," answered Edward, "the people would not be of good heart without their leader — indeed they would not go forth."

"Good! the populace know too little to be led into mistakes by state reasoning."

"But the senate are not content without your counsel and aid, both in the chamber and in the field."

"And they shall have it, for we should all give it. Your mariners will be fatigued, and we will have a fresh set; but methought your galley came in at a flying pace."

"Why Edward," exclaimed il Grasso, "would drive a galley to the world's end faster than any other could come here. Storms hinder other men, him they serve."

"If we would conquer in this world, Messer Luigi," replied Zeno, "we must learn to turn our mishaps to good use, as well as our good luck, or we lose half our power: the invader drove our forefathers into the lagoon, where they have built our fair city and all its power."

"Well, Edward is good for using mishaps; in sooth, I think he prefers ill luck; just as your patriotism, Messer Zeno, grows all the more for being ill used."

"A country, Messer Luigi, cannot be said to ill-treat its children, for all that they enjoy beyond savages is the gift of the country; all that they can do, they owe to it; and all that they throw into the common treasury is repaid to them with interest. We must not gauge that free gift by our desires, and say that it falls short, when naked man, by himself, would be but a brute to whose life we should prefer death. All of wealth, and power, and fame that a Venetian has he owes to Venice."

"And Venice again to Venetians."

"The more reason why they should bestow on it all they can. But I will not contest with so skilled a casuist as Messer Luigi. Let us rather talk of our departure. Are you sick of the sea, my friends, and shall I leave you; or will you convey me back in that same fleet galley of yours!"

"But," said Edward, "you will not depart before your wounds are healed!"

"Why, they will heal best at sea. But in truth they are nought; and as neither of you are new to the sea, we will go forthwith. But first I must take order for the proper care of this our new possession. It is fortunate that we have chased away the Greeks before you came."

Causing food to be placed before his friends, he was closeted for a time with Antonio Veniero, whom he left governor of the island. Then making his servants carry a few clothes on board the galley, and pick out fresh mariners and rowers, he summoned his visitors; and in a little time the galley was again ploughing the waters.

"The wind is against us," said Zeno.

"The more praise to our rowers for sending us forward so fast, maugre the wind," said Edward: "if they are as willing and as tough as those that brought us out, we need think little about the weather."

"Ay, willing as they were," cried Luigi, "now you have parted with them, my friend, I may tell you that they were near rebelling, because you thought them too willing."

"How so?"

"Why, scarce had we issued from the lagoon ere some dozen of them would have forced you to return."

"But they did not," said Edward.

"No, they were ashamed, and I made them more so; and after they seemed as if you could scarcely go fast enough for them."

"It is ever so," said Zeno; "those men who have never made trial of their own mind, are ever bolder than they think themselves, and grateful to whomsoever will discover it for them. A leader is seldom abandoned by his men for being too bold; but often for not being bold enough. Those who are to follow must ever be sure that those who are to lead will keep in front, go those behind as fast as they may."

Edward started: "The wind has come round on our side," cried he, "a sail will help us now." And presently a fresh spur was given to the straining galley.

CHAPTER XXVIII.

Hard was the fate of Venice after Edward had left it in quest of Carlo Zeno. So environed was it by enemies, that provision could scarce be brought to it, and while the grain ran low in the stores, food carried in with peril and difficulty became costly. Though Pisani kept the Genoese employed, the citizens of the lagoon grew accustomed to hear that the foe had made slow advance: with bastion and manganel they encroached upon the littorale. As the days passed, many an eye was turned to the coast, in hopes of hearing that Zeno had come to breathe new life into the dispirited soldiers. While the great trembled for their wealth and high estate, the poor were scanted in their food. Men collected in the streets and in the great square, gloomy and angered; and women staid at home, to soothe hungry babes and weep away the day. Turnbull had been well provided by Sebastian, and he often jested to Teresa on the princely prices that he paid for his bread and wine. Little did he think that he alone in that house fed well. Jacopo's long absence had left Teresa's purse quite exhausted. The gold which Sebastian had forced upon her, to furnish better food for her sick mother, had been husbanded, until only a little remained, not for better food, but for as much as Bianca would eat, while Teresa sat with her almost fasting. Jacopo came not; there were no tidings of Ranieri; Sebastian, whom they had hoped to behold a few days after his departure, was not suffered to leave the front of the advancing foe. Bianca had again grown sick and weak, and kept mostly to her bed; and Teresa began to think of teaching herself to ask charity of their guard, for her mother's sake; when one day as she sat beside her sleeping mother, she heard footsteps in the next room; not the heavy tread of the English soldier, but lighter, and the steps of more than one. At first the blood rushed to her heart, as she thought that it was Sebastian; but the steps were not so marked and steady as his. There were voices. She rose to prevent her mother's being disturbed, and as she did so, the door of the chamber opened, and Ranieri entered, followed by her father! Starting at the unexpected sight, she rushed into his arms; but the next moment she motioned for him to be silent, lest her mother should be surprised. It was too late: Bianca was awake, and she had turned round. Nor was she surprised; for every day and every hour had she looked at the door, expecting to see the wanderer. She was not surprised that he came not, neither that he came. Jacopo approached, and taking his wife in his arms, he wept to see her weak condition. When Ranieri had embraced his sister and mother, Jacopo sat down by the bed; and the long separated husband and wife, father and daughter, looked upon each other.

"Bianca mine," said Jacopo quickly, but sadly, "disease has hastened the work of time with you, as travel has with me. You look as kind as ever, sposa mia, but your cheeks are pale, and your brow is wrinkled. And, though I have not been absent many months, you never saw these locks so gray before." And he stooped down as he shook them half playfully into his wife's face. She smiled; but no one told Jacopo how much he was altered. His face was pale and thin, and had the dry skin of a much older man. His gray eyes were lighter, more glassy, and more restless than ever. Yet there was still about his slender frame the air of activity and liveliness. His dress was much worn. The black was now, like his head, turned gray. He had no cloak: and one of his outer sleeves was torn off at the elbow, the other hung ragged and soiled; and the point of his sword peeped through a scabbard that had knocked against many a floor.—"And Teresa!" he continued: "she is altered. She, too, looks older; but she is too young yet, sposa mia, to be the worse for that. I do not think that she is taller, and yet she looks so. Per Dio e Bacco, I think that she is a more stately damsel than you were, Bianca, before you spoiled a princess of the vineyard by marrying an unlucky gentleman. Ranieri is more grown, and is more manly; and yet there is a change in Teresina that more surprises me."

The others, saying little, looked on while he talked, surveying their lost one. Without much bidding he told them all, enjoining secrecy, how he had a message of importance to carry from a great prince to Carlo Zeno; how he had taken ship and voyaged to Constantinople; how there he fought to restore the emperor, not being able to get a ship back; how, at length, the Zeno had found a ship in which he might return with an answer to the prince; how he did so; and at length he had met Ranieri, who was seeking him even in the lion's den—in Padua. "The boy got in and out with one of the country women going into the market, who passed him as her son; and he paid her in kisses, the wicked rogue." Ranieri had laughed when he told his father; but he did not mean to have it told to his sister. "The noble prince," said Jacopo, "gave me money for my wants. I thought to have brought the most of it back to you, Bianca; but in so long a time it is all gone; and he was so much in haste when I last saw him, that he did not think of it again. So I have returned, as I went—a beggar."

"You are returned, and that is all we want. Teresa, my child, give your father to eat."

Teresa moved a step as if to obey, stopped, and hesitated. She staggered. She was dizzy, and would have fallen, had not Ranieri caught her in his arms. He set her on the bed, and supported her head on his shoulder.

"She is faint, too, for want of food," cried Bianca. "She eats nothing. Daily she schools me to eat, and yet I cannot force her. Or is it," she added to Teresa, in a lower voice, passing her arm round the girl's waist, "that when your father returned, you thought that another——"

Teresa pressed her mother's hand, to make her silent.

"She lacks food," said Jacopo; "go you, Ranieri,—you know where it is kept,—and fetch her some."

Teresa held her brother. "There is none," she murmured.

"None! Go, then, my son, and buy some. Give him the money, Teresa."

"There is no money."

"No money! Alas! and have I left you thus helpless while I have been wandering on other's business! Fool that I am." And for the twentieth time in his life Jacopo was lost in anger at his own folly, in destroying those he most loved while he did the behest of strangers.

Her father's grief aroused Teresa, and she did her best to console him. Again she thought of craving help from Turnbull; but she could neither bear to let him see Sebastian's mistress in such need, lest Sebastian should dislike it, nor to take the bread of the simple soldier, uncertain whether she could restore it. She persuaded her father, that fortune would soon be better with them; and he was willingly consoled. When he was calmer, Bianca made their children retire, and her husband sit once more by her side, while she recounted what had befallen them in his absence. She told him how she had sent for him, because their daughter was not safe; relating her message to Marco Morosini craving aid; and Morosini's pursuit of Teresa. She told him nothing of Sebastian. Teresa did not wish to conceal aught from her father; but when she motioned her mother to be silent, she did it because she liked not to hear her tale told in her presence, and because, in sooth, she was not sorry to delay her father's knowing. Perhaps Bianca misunderstood Teresa's sign for one of secrecy, though Teresa was not wont to keep secrets from her father; perhaps the mother too had little wish to make a disclosure to Jacopo for which Sebastian had not yet signified his consent; perhaps she even shared Teresa's dislike to tell the strange story to the uncertain and hasty Jacopo. "But," she said, "we must leave Venice, my dear husband. This house, if sold, will give us money: it is our last, but it will carry us to a place of safety; and it is less hurt for your pride to sell the house of your fathers, than it was to marry a poor peasant girl, my Jacopo. We must not part again, for Teresa's sake; but you are not safe in Venice."

"How so!"

"I know not; but since Ranieri left us to seek you, you have been accused as a traitor to Venice." And she told him of the conspiracy of la Gobba, and the hunt for him in his own house; and of Sebastian's coming to their rescue.

"And who is this man that I see below!"

"It is a guard who was left with us by Messer Sebastiano Morosini."

"And could not this same Sebastian aid us? Why have you not asked him?"

"Nay, Jacopo, he is no longer in Venice, but is away to Chiozza, and we cannot seek him. Nor could he give us much aid; for his father is our enemy, and would prevent him. But we must leave Venice."

"But why, dear Bianca! Let me lie concealed here, and I can still protect you."

"No, no, Jacopo; you are not safe in Venice: they have offered a reward for you."

"A reward!"

"Yes."

"And for what!"

"I believe for joining in the conspiracy of which I told you. They say that you are a traitor in league with that worse than traitor, Carrara."

"That is a mistake; nor is Carrara traitor. But truly, something must be done, and that speedily. I will not leave you more; and we will eat or starve together, Bianca mia; or rather we will eat, for food you shall have before night, though the house go for it."

For some time Jacopo was lost in thought, his restless eye often wandering to Bianca's faded form. When Teresa returned, he again asked who was the strange man in the house. She looked to her mother, and was about to explain, but Bianca again told her husband as before, that Sebastian had left the man to guard them in his absence. Then Jacopo said there was no reason why he should remain longer, as he himself should not be absent any more. Teresa hesitated; but she left the chamber to obey. Making the most of her English, she told Turnbull that his protection was no longer wanted; and much thanking him, dismissed him, with the injunction to seek out Messer Sebastiano Morosini, and to tell him secretly, that the protector whose return she expected, had come. Turnbull left his quiet and easy duty with regret; and kissing her hand in more courtier-like tenderness than she could have expected, he departed. She too had her regret; for his presence was endeared to her by Sebastian's care, and moreover she had little confidence in her father's protection. Formerly, she had less fear of encountering the dangers of her defenceless state; but now she regarded herself as something which she held in charge for her future husband.

Having returned with Ranieri to her mother's room, the next hour passed drearily. Suddenly

Jacopo rose, and led his son into the hall, that they might confer alone. After a few hasty turns, Jacopo stopped, and exclaimed, "Your mother, Ranieri, is sorely borne down by sickness!"

"I fear so!" cried Ranieri, alarmed at the re-echo of his own dread.

"My son," began Jacopo, and paused, looking earnestly at the youth, who still waited for his father to proceed. "My son, could you make some great trial to save her!"

"Ah! If you could tell me how! I can devise nothing, though none were too great. If I could serve her by dying, I would. And Teresa—I marvel how she can bear herself up as she does. I have watched her, and she seems at times to be more afflicted even than the mother."

"You need not die, Ranieri; but I can show you how you can achieve something which shall bring home plenty of gold, so that your mother may live, and all of you have abundance."

"Tell it me, then, and it shall be done at once."

"Hear me. You should know that the Ten have declared me traitor, and have offered a reward to whomsoever shall bring me captive. I am not traitor, as I can one day show. It is not because I have served Carrara, as I have done, that I should be traitor to Venice. I will discharge myself of this reproach one day. But now it shall serve us, boy. I would have this reward for your mother's use."

"But how, father mine! Rather let it be had by no one."

"Nay, nay, Ranieri, Venice shall pay to your mother and sister, for having called me traitor; and that is the revenge that I will have of it."

"What is it you mean!"

"You shall have it, Ranieri!"

"How, my father!"

"You shall claim it—you shall give me up."

"Never."

"Ranieri mine, you said that you could do any service for your mother, yet you start back at the first you hear."

"It would not be serving her to betray my father and disgrace her son. No, my father; let us bear the misfortunes of our house; but I am sure that if crimes disgrace it, my mother would die."

"Ranieri, it must be done, and without hurt to your mother. Fear not for me: the worst for me would be a few days or a few months in prison; for as soon as I choose to speak, I can prove that I am no traitor, and shall be free. But I cannot bear this misfortune, of seeing your mother perishing for the want of that money of which my ill-fortunes, or my follies, have deprived her. If you have so much fortitude, I have not; and rather would I perish in a prison, and be happier so, than stay here to see her die in helplessness."

"No, father, never could I do it. I am certain that Teresa would cast me off if I did; and the bread thus bought would be poison to us all."

"But it should not be known, my son. You must do it, and you alone must know it. You shall say that I have gone again to the main land, and that I have sent the money which I have got for them."

"Never. I will not stay to hear you. I will tell Teresa, and ask her if I should do it." And he was about to walk away.

His father held him. "Stay, Ranieri; Teresa has not taught you to despise and disobey your father!"

The youth stopped. His sister had been careful in her lessons, to counteract what she silently felt to be the effect of her unstable father's conduct, and to teach her brother ever to respect him. Jacopo, therefore, was armed with the influence of Teresa in urging what the boy felt Teresa would have forbidden. He hoped that his sister would interrupt them; but, unconscious of her father's sudden project, she came not. Ranieri looked, now to this, now to that open door, and listened for his sister's firm and light footstep; but all he heard was the low murmur which the desert rooms echoed to his father's half-whispered persuasion. Wanting counsel, he stood still and silent, almost hoping that it was a bad dream; and slowly he yielded—the father had bent the boy to his will.

"And now, Ranieri," cried Jacopo, "dry your tears, and summon the courage your sister has taught you. It must be done at once."

"No, not to-day; I cannot have courage yet."

"Yes, at once; for your mother needs food each moment; and as time goes on, they may discover that I am innocent, and so the reward may be withdrawn. Let us come at once, while we are alone, and before those we would serve, have seen your pale face." Jacopo went on to instruct his son how to contrive his surrender.

Ranieri stared at his father, half stunned with fear and horror. He pressed his hand on his eyes; then, saying, "I am ready," he stood to follow. Jacopo moved towards the house door; but before he opened it, Ranieri stopped him by crying—"Father, embrace me." Jacopo took his son in his arms, and pressed him to his bosom, with a muttered blessing; but he did it hastily, eager to be gone; and they issued into the street.

CHAPTER XXIX.

YIELDING to the fate which over-mastered him, Ranieri now thought only of the task imposed upon him; and he made the best speed he could to the house of the governor of the city. He had entered the hall, and was looking about to see whom he might best address, when a serving man, dressed in half soldier fashion, as many then were in the city, came forward with a swaggering carriage, and cried, "Olà, youngster; what do you here! There are too many guards here for thieves, and Venice wants all the money that beggars crave. Run, run!"

"I wish," answered the youth, nothing scared by the big lackey, nor his big beard and big words,—"I wish to see my lord, the governor."

"You see my lord, in sooth! My lord is never at leisure to see idle boys Run, I tell you. Go to his office if you want him, at the palace, in the morning."

Nay, Messer Soldato, my affair is pressing, and I must not be refused. If you turn me back, it may be worse for you."

"What, do you threaten, puppet? then I must whip you." And he drew his sword to strike the intruder. Ranieri's face flushed ; he drew the small poniard that hung on his left side, and with flashing eye stood his ground. But another attendant interposed, and saying that even so young a boy might have real business for the governor, moderated his fellow's wrath. The big man sheathed his long sword, nothing loath to avoid cutting his fingers with Ranieri's sharply-drawn little weapon ; and he retreated with dignity, saying to his companion,—"Do as you will ; be the damage yours."

The other man went at Ranieri's bidding, to crave admission to the high functionary, and presently returned. The boy stopped, and asked the man his name. "Cecco," replied he. "Await my coming out, then, for I may need you ; and you shall not lose by being civil."

Ranieri found the governor in a large room, at a large table ; with some people sitting at it, and others walking about ; all the officers of Venice were engaged at that hard time. Some were busily talking ; others looked at him carelessly as he came in, but looked away directly. The man led him by the governor's chair. Messer Orso Quirino continued reading a paper that lay before him ; and then turned round suddenly, and said in the abrupt severe manner of one whose time is too scanty to be wasted,— "Now, boy, what is it?"

"My lord, I came to ask for aid in seizing a man who has been proclaimed a traitor.'

"Ha! who is he?"

"Jacopo Arduino."

The governor leaned towards a gentleman that sat near him, and said, "Has any Arduino been proclaimed traitor?"

"Yes," replied the person who was spoken to : "Jacopo Arduino. He is accused with others in the conspiracy of la Gobba. There is a reward offered for him."

The governor turned to Ranieri. "Is he in Venice?"

"Hard by, my lord : if I have aid now, I can bring him to you forthwith. Give me this man that is here, and another, and we could master him."

"Go with him, Cecco," said the governor, "and take another with you. Bring this boy and the other person into my private room."

Ranieri saluted the head of the police, who had already turned his back upon him, and left the saloon. As they went, he desired Cecco to take any one with him but the bully whom he had met in the hall ; for they might need one who could fight. Presently he was again in the streets, with two stout fighting men at his back. The encounter with his opponent had stirred his blood, and in checking his progress had spurred his intent ; so that in place of grieving, he now almost desired to accomplish his enterprise. He walked briskly along until he entered a small wine-shop, where he knew that he should meet his father. Jacopo was sitting on a low stool, with a flask near him ; the wine-seller, an old acquaintance, having forced a cheering draught on the unfortunate gentleman, whose kind and easy manner made him liked by all. At a table near were the master of the shop and another ; who, with arms folded on the table, were trying to draw from the talkative Arduino where he had been and all that he had encountered. As Ranieri entered, the wine-seller rose, and came towards him. Without heeding him, Ranieri turned to Cecco, and pointing to his father, said, "That is the man—seize him !" The governor's men advanced as they were bid. Jacopo drew back, as if he mistrusted them ; but Cecco, crying, "Now, master traitor, it were useless to try escape ; let us go quietly," took him by the arm.

"Stop, stop!" exclaimed the wine-dealer. "What is this? What rude fellows are ye, that think to brawl in my house. This is an honest gentleman, and my good friend, and he shall get no hurt here."

"Meddle in what concerns you, Signor Vinaio," said Cecco, carelessly ; "the less you call Messer traditore here your friend the better for you. I reckon you do not wish to take up your lodging with la Gobba under the Leads?"

"What ribaldry is this? Have we la Gobba here, rascal? Get out of my house, or I may chance to chase you."

"Now stand aside, honest man, and do not bring yourself into trouble. Well, if you resist—Stefano, come forward; here is a fool wants to keep company with our prisoner to the governor's custody, as proclaimed traitor by the Ten."

At the title, the wine-dealer let fall the hand which he had placed upon the knife in his belt, and looked at Jacopo ; who now, anxious to close the quarrel which might interfere with his project, came forward, and asked Cecco by what right he seized him. "By the governor's order, to seize you for a traitor," answered the man.

"Messer Jacopo is no traitor," cried the sturdy wine-dealer, whose terror of the Ten again died away at witnessing the injury to his unfortunate friend : "Who accuses him?"

"Oh, there are many that accuse him," replied Cecco ; "and one is this young gentleman."

"That !" cried the wine-dealer, his voice harsh with surprise and disgust. "Why that is his son?"

"May be so. Son or no son, he has done a service to Venice in giving up a traitor. Come, Messer Jacopo, if that is your name, you know you had better not resist."

"Well," said the wine-dealer, grinding his teeth, "if you will go, Messer Jacopo, you must ; but we will keep you, if it so please you. And at least we will keep this good son here ; a little washing in the lagoon may get out some of his starch virtue. So virtuous a boy, that he must think his own father a traitor, is too good to live. Help me to hold him, Nadale," he added, to the man who had sat with him.

Ranieri looked towards his father ; but Jacopo, uncertain what to do, turned away his head. Seeing the angry wine-dealer advance,

Ranieri, half sorrowing to be reproached by one that showed so staunch a friend, half fearing for himself, drew back, and put his hand to his poniard. The other man, who had hitherto remained silent, had before risen from his seat to look at the son that betrayed his father; and he now came behind the youth and suddenly seized him by the arms, which he drew tightly together, so that the elbows met. Ranieri struggled to free himself; but the hands were too tough for his more youthful limbs. He had almost felt inclined to declare his scheme a traitor, by disclosing his scheme; but now the cense of danger to himself was uppermost, and provoked him to resistance. His cheek glowed, and his eye gleamed steadily as the sturdy fellow grasped him roughly by the clothes at his breast; but just at that moment Ceceo again interfered; striking down the other's hand, and saying—"Nor that neither, galant' uomo. If we must take the traitor, we must also take the witness. Besides, this young man is our captain for the nonce, and we must not let him come to harm. Loose your hold, man, loose your hold, I say." The man laughed, seeming to be cowed by Ceceo's loud tone of authority, and Ranieri's arms were again free. He stopped for an instant, reluctantly yielding the desire to resent the violence; but more discreetly followed the men as they led his father from the house, returning with cool defiance the scowl of those he left behind.

"What a pity," cried the host, "that such a smart lad should be so base a son!" The silent man laughed again, and reseated himself to listen to his friend's copious commentary on Jacopo's adventures, and this last the most perilous of them.

By good fortune, Ranieri and his strange train encountered none of the few people whom he knew, before they were once more in the presence of the governor. Two other gentlemen sat by that high officer, and near him was a younger man writing. Messer Orso Quirino looked to Ranieri in the same impatient and peremptory manner; and the stillness of the room, the strangeness of his enterprise, again oppressed his heart with dismay. Ceceo placed Jacopo before the governor, who exclaimed, "Well, is this the prisoner?"

"Ay, my lord, this is the man."

"What is his name?"

"Why, Messer Jacopo; but more I know not. This young gentleman can tell you."

Quirino looked to Ranieri; but his tongue cleaved to his mouth. His father, who kept his eye averted from him, but guessed from his silence that he could not answer, said in a firm and cheerful voice, "My name is Jacopo Arduino Of what am I accused?"

The governor leaned over to the man who was writing, and after a brief whispering, said, "Jacopo Arduino, you are accused of treason to the state, being one of those who engaged in a conspiracy at the house of la Gobba to poison the waters of Venice."

"It is a false accusation," answered Jacopo.

"Will you prove it false."

"Not yet But time will help me to the witnesses I want."

"It has been proved that you were in conference with the principal enemy of Venice just before the conspiracy—with Messer Francesce Carrara of Padua; but enough—I fear the only doubt is whether this is the real traitor. How do you know, Ceceo, that this is Messer Jacopo Arduino?"

"Nay, my lord, I know not; but this young gentleman ought to know, for he is his son."

"His son!" cried Quirino; and he looked in astonishment at the two who sat by him. Then turning to Ranieri, he said, sternly—"Is this gentleman, your father, the person whom you accuse as the traitor Jacopo Arduino?"

Ranieri was silent. His knees shook, and again he thought that to confess the whole scheme would be the best. Now for the first time, his father looked at him gravely and steadily, and with a peculiar expression that made him understand that he was to persevere in his task. To gather courage, he thought of his mother and sister, and their need.

The voice of the governor again struck on his ear. "Answer, boy; is this the man you accuse as a traitor?"

Ranieri recovered his voice: "It is Jacopo Arduino."

"The reason," said Jacopo, "that Messer Orso Quirino does not remember the host that had the honor to entertain him soon after he was married is, not only that the entertainment was so humble, but that time and misfortune have altered this face so that even those of my own blood have forgotten it."

The governor looked at the prisoner with compassion; and in a milder voice he said, "Let him be removed. He shall be examined hereafter."

Jacopo turned once more to his son; he had not yet had the reward. Ranieri would not suffer his father to be sent to his prison without knowing that his purpose had been answered; and he said, hastily—"My lord, there was a reward promised when the prisoner should be secured."

The governor stared at the youth, and was about to speak; but checking himself, he turned to the secretary, and asked in a low voice what the reward was.

"A hundred ducats of gold for Jacopo Arduino, my lord."

"Let the boy be paid, then, for giving up his father as a traitor against the state. Let him be paid at once, that he may go."

The secretary went into another room; and presently he returned with a small bag, which he gave to Ceceo, and he gave it to Ranieri.

The governor cried to Ranieri—"Count the money, boy."

"My lord, I make no doubt that it is right."

"Count your wages, young man; see that you have your due."

Ranieri emptied the bag on the table. All kept deep silence as he counted the gold; and he so longed to hear some sound to break that odious quiet, that his thought wandered, and he could not count.

"Count it before him, Ceceo," said the magistrate.

Taking pleasure in the youth's shame and confusion, the serving man stepped to the table and did as he was bid, saying to Ranieri, in an undertone, as he swept the coin into the bag—"If giving up a father is worth a hundred ducats, doth not he that helps deserve interest?"

"Keep what you please," said Ranieri.

"What is it you say, Cecco?" asked the governor.

"Nothing, my lord," said the attendant, alarmed at the angry voice provoked by his idle joke.

"Nay, I almost heard. Take not one coin of his money—give it him all, and let none of it stay here, nor among my people. Now, remove the prisoner, and send away the informer."

One took charge of Jacopo, while Cecco led forth Ranieri. When they were in the hall, the youth again took some gold from his bag, and said, "You should not lose your fair fee: take this."

"No, messer spy, yours is forbidden money; our master wishes you to keep it to fatten yourself withal; so, a good appetite to you."

Ranieri returned the ducats into the bag; and with a flushed face and knitted brow, he took his way home.

CHAPTER XXX.

Rosa had just finished her net. A large part of it lay in a heap, while a portion was spread out upon the floor, and raised by two chairs, so as to show the girl the work of her hands. She had spread out all that she had done since Alessandro had visited her after his so long absence. For some hours she had worked hard, that she might complete her task before dark; and as the last gleam of daylight shone upon the fruit of her industry, her grave face was not devoid of satisfaction. The symmetry of the lines as they crossed in forming the meshes, the newness and stoutness of the cord, the pleasure that it would give to old Pierotto, the use that he would make of it, were thoughts that pleased her. How the green and blue waters would dance and play in and out of the supple trellis! How the silvery scales of the fish would glisten! Poor things! their captivity would be fatal; yet are there worse sorrows than fatal thraldom. This much work, she bethought her, had been done in her solitude: the time might have been worse employed. Even life that is not as we wish it, need not be fruitless of good; and if not fruitless of good, it is not without a happiness. Rosa was not learned in books. Alessandro had never thought of teaching her; and if he had, he would not; because not only he took a pride in possessing that which was the more valuable to himself, the fewer about him that shared it, but he took a delight in her ignorance,—he admired her unaltered nature, so strong a contrast to the vain knowledge which multiplied his desires faster than his powers. He would have kept her for ever a spot of wild luxuriant nature to retreat to; but the fool forgot that he could not weed his own speech, least guarded when with her, of the thoughts that he learned in books; and moreover he taught her grief. He showed her how to think; but as her thoughts were not tinged by worldly ambition, as they arose from nature, his from art, theirs was the more

vigorous growth. And Teresa had given a new turn to them—a new dominion of thought. Strange, that as she mused over her netting her feelings toward him had grown less tender, and at the same time less bitter. She felt less dependent on his love. She judged him. As she stood gazing on her work, her thought wandering from it to other things, a knock at the door startled her; it was Alessandro's. Unlike her poor neighbors, Rosa kept her door fastened. She opened it, and the foster brother entered. As before, he would have embraced her; but drawing back, she held out her hand to him. Without seeming to notice her humor, he obeyed, and kissed her hand with more than his wonted devotion. In truth, though she meant it not, her new distance gave to her a new interest in his eyes; and as she stood, drawn up to her full height, her chest expanded, her arm held out majestically, and a slight sternness mingling with the pensive sweetness of her face, he thought that in all Venice there was not, nor in all Italy, so noble a woman to look upon.

"Rosa mia," he said, "I have hastened here before some others my companions, to crave your pardon for a license which I have taken with what is yours."

"My pardon, Alessandro! Have I anything that is not rather yours than mine?"

"Yes, sweet; all is yours more than mine, if you will believe it, especially this house. But it will not lose you aught. This it is—I have occasion to meet some gentlemen, and one of them must not be seen to-night by any that know him in Venice; therefore have I appointed that we shall meet him in this remote part of the city."

"Here—in this house?"

"In this house. You are not offended, Rosa?"

"The house is yours, Alessandro; but it was not well done to bring any where I am, who am not yet——. Can you not meet in this part, yet in another house?"

"They will be here anon. Moreover my life is periled. But they know not of this house, and you shall not be seen, Rosa. Forgive me, and I will not offend again."

"You are too courteous. But, be it as you will."

"You are angered that I have not sooner again paid my homage to you; but I have been away, lady mine, and in the midst of war and turmoil; and that is another part of my errand to crave your forgiveness also——"

Another knock at the door was the welcome announcement that his friends had arrived. Rosa hesitated, and looked at her companion. He pointed for her to leave the room. She obeyed.

As he opened the door, four men passed into the room, wrapped in large cloaks, with their caps drawn much over their eyes, as though they felt the chill of evening. They had little chance of being known in that quarter by any who would question them: even the gondolier who had taken them up, after they had dismissed a boat of their own, neither knew them, nor cared to wonder what brought nobles so far among the poorer people, or else he settled it in his mind that some bright eyes and youthful charms, disguised in coarse attire, had attracted them. As they entered from the darkening night, into the still darker room, they looked around in vain to see who was there.

"You are dark here, Messer Alessandro," said the strong voice of Ser Luigi da Molino, the Avvogadore del Commune, a man large of body and limb, with an insolent and over bearing manner. "Darkness is convenient sometimes; but sometimes it is too convenient, in concealing more than one knows. I never talk in the dark, except in mine own house."

"You shall have a light, Messer Avvogadore, since you are afraid of the dark; but in truth, the night has come somewhat suddenly while I awaited you alone."

"Nay, Alessandro," cried Ser Pietro di Bernardo, whose bright gay eyes almost shone in the feeble shade of light from the windows,— "there are more who dislike dark than those who fear it. If now we had our fair friends here, it might be pleasant; but it will be dull work not to see Messer Luigi's portentous countenance while he is plotting away our republic——"

"Hush," interrupted Marino Barbarigo, a chief of the Forty; "did you learn that careless speech in the grand council, amico mio?"

"Why, the grand council has its varieties of eloquence, and mine is of the playful kind, you know, Barbarigo; as when I asked what the Ten had done with la Gobba, and recommended, for our credit, that you and Molino should be appointed to see her quartered. I thought it would shield you from suspicion of being a conspirator to poison the wells. You quite overreached me there; for I never heard of the plot till I saw that heroic Englishman, whom we all love so well, defending the lady like a true knight; only knights do not usually straddle over their ladies while they defend them. I suppose I was too heedless to be admitted to that project?"

"Silence, Messer Pietro," said Molino, angrily; "here are we in the dark, and know not who may hear you; yet you talk of these wickednesses and plots almost in a manner to plant horrible suspicions of the illustrious gentlemen with us in the breasts of any that may overhear your idle speech."

Pietro di Bernardo laughed aloud, and said, "Hasten, good Alessandro, for a light, or Messer Luigi will die with fear of eaves-droppers—or ghosts."

"You are too incautious, Messer Pietro," said Barbarigo. "Why can you not imitate the silence of your excellent brother here, Messer Niccolò! He has not spoken a word since we left my house. But I think I heard Messer Alessandro go for a light when the Avvogadore first spoke."

"Niccolò is silent," said the incorrigible Pietro, "because you know he is in love with your daughter; and as she is very imperious and very young, it is most difficult for him to contrive what to say that shall be magnificent enough to satisfy her, and yet that her years may understand. I can vouch for it that he studies night and day. I know he will be glad when his courtship comes to the fondling stage, because then there will not be so much fine speaking to do."

"Silence your idle tongue," muttered his brother, "or we will thrust you out."

"Aye, to alarm the neighborhood! But your fears may be calmed, Messer Avvogadore, for here comes Alessandro with the light. How it shows out his mighty countenance in the dark. One of us was born to hold Venice in his grasp; and if Messer Avvogadore drops it, in his fear of goblins, I say that yon Alessandro is the man. Does he not show the very model of a conspirator!"

"Cease your idle talk of conspiracies," said Molino, "or I will take my leave."

"Aye, cease," subjoined Barbarigo. "However," he added, turning to Molino, "all Pietro's indiscretions are committed very sagely in secret; for none is more discreet abroad."

"Thanks, good friend. My imprudence is not so dangerous as Messer Luigi's tremendous silence and suspicious frown. If there is a man in Venice that would be picked out by guess as a conspirator, it is Luigi da Molino."

"Cease this, Bernardo," cried Molino, feeling for his sword, "or I will silence you perforce."

"O Messer Alessandro, defend me!" exclaimed the threatened man; "here is Messer Luigi da Molino, Avvogadore del Commune, going to kill me outright for talking faster than he thinks suitable to this your hall, with one small lamp in it, and some doubt of listeners or devils in the corners!"

"Peace, my noble friends," said the foster brother, gravely; "there is none in this house to interrupt us, and as for danger, you may talk as you list; but our time is precious. Sit you here, Messer Barbarigo, president of this council for the welfare of our beloved Venice, your authority will moderate our gay friend."

"Aye will it. Now does that light disappoint me of one amusement that we might have had, to hear each other break his shins over the furniture in the dark. But let us leave play, now that our Master Alessandro bids." And the careless councillor took his seat at the table with the rest.

When they were seated, Barbarigo turned to Molino, and said, "You already know that we have met to receive some advice from our friend Messer Alessandro da Padova. The ambitious dotard who now unhappily rules in our councils, with a power never meant to be entrusted to the chief servant of the grand council, persists, in spite of the ruin that he has actually brought upon Venice, in waging a cruel and profitless war on its best ally, the Lord of Padua. But he and his faction will be defeated. Messer Alessandro has just returned from Chiozza——"

"From Chiozza!" exclaimed Pietro di Bernardo.

"From Malamocco," said Alessandro, "which is almost the same thing."

"True," continued Barbarigo, "from Malamocco; and he has learned how this unjust and injurious war may be ended." He turned to Alessandro, who took up the discourse.

"I need not say, that were Andrea Contarini defeated, it would be a triumph for Venice. The way now seems clear. In ten days from this time the allies of Carrara will make a combined attack on the port of Venice. When that is once in their possession, nothing can hinder their entrance into the city, to surrender its possession to those who will govern it for its own sake. There is but one difficulty in the way—the inner barricade. I know that the captain of one cocca is of our party; but the other is Galluzzi; to attempt his faith would be madness; and he will fight to the last. One of us must contrive to get some other man appointed, within the ten days. Has not Ser Pietro di Bernardo claim to it, if he choose to solicit so poor a post?"

"Surely," said Barbarigo.

"And all the more willing to have it," cried Pietro, "in that no fighting is likely. Messer Alessandro forgets the outer barricade at the entrance of the port."

"Alessandro seldom forgets," said the foster brother, with a grave smile; "and this council should know, that when Messer Marco Morosini was appointed to superintend the works, he was convinced that the best economy of his resources would be to make those posts which forbad assault by the least show of strength, in reality stronger than those which were made to look impregnable." A low laugh ran round the table; and the four nobles looked a demand for clearer explanation. "In fact, though timbers and chains were piled up most at the entrance of this port, every other barricade is stronger; because Messer Marco knew that the Genoese would believe it to be as strong as it looked. And so of course they did, until they learned otherwise. But that is not all. One part of the barricade is really strong: it is the three chains which fasten the outward beams to each side. That part is guarded carefully; but on the tenth day, the guard will——"

A low knock at the door interrupted him. He rose from his seat, and admitted a stout, square-built man, wrapped in a cloak. His heavy tread caused a slight jingle, which showed that he was clothed in mail; though the small steel cap on his head was disguised with a velvet hood. The door having been carefully closed, he approached the table.

"Lionardo Morosini!" exclaimed the four.

"The same, sirs," answered the man himself, as he disengaged himself from his cloak, and took a chair set for him by Alessandro. "Your poor servant, and none other; though he must not be seen in Venice till the morrow."

"But," said Pietro di Bernardo, "we thought that you were wounded and taken prisoner at Chiozza."

"Wounded, no; taken prisoner, yes; and a prisoner I have been ever since. At first I was in prison with the rest; but they put me into a separate cell; I suppose that it might be more severe," he added with a smile.

"Aye," said Pietro; "that was because you killed Carrara's man—Marco the Florentine: that was a great mistake."

"Hush: who says that I killed Marco? Had he not chanced to be mortally wounded by some one, indeed, he would have been brought back, and perhaps put to the question by Emo; and it was very fortunate for all of us that he died—for Carrara himself. But not a word did any one say to Carrara that I had killed him."

"Truly no," observed Alessandro; "the less said of such things the better. We are not judges, and all may make mistakes in the moment of difficulty."

"Messer Alessandro is ever the discreetest," said Pietro. "But how, Messer Lionardo, if you were kept so close, are you here?"

"Aye, close indeed; for I was not allowed to stir out of the lodging that was provided for me, lest I should be seen in the town. However, I thought it most advisable for me to escape; and so I just came away, travelling by land, lest I should be seen crossing the lagoon."

"Let us not," interposed Alessandro, "inquire how Messer Lionardo came, but only rejoice that he is here, and remember that none of us must have seen him in Venice till tomorrow morning."

"Good," cried Mulino, solemnly. "But of course Messer Lionardo Morosini came to tell us something."

"I came to tell you, with what speed I may, that Roberto da Recanati has arrived at Lido, having joined the Venetian forces."

"We knew as much before," answered Molino; "we in Venice hear things as soon as prisoners in Chiozza."

"Nay, Messer Avvogadore, you ever hear things at the properest time: you heard that the Recanati had arrived, and now you should hear how he arrived. He was engaged by the Lord of Padua, who offered him higher pay than the senate; but somehow he suddenly altered his mind. He has joined Venice, and I suppose will not lose by the bargain. But farther—some of his men are appointed to guard the outer barricades of the port of Venice on the tenth day from this, and for six days longer. Do you understand now—for I suppose that Messer Alessandro has explained to you the plan?"

"'Tis well," cried Barbarigo. "Truly are there but two Carraras—one now in Chiozza, and the other here at this table, our good Alessandro. All this then understood, nothing remains but to determine how our forces shall be disposed for the enterprise."

Into the details of their counsel it were needless to enter. The dawn disturbed them in their discourse, and they hastily dispersed, again carefully muffling themselves as they went forth in the still gloomy streets.

Left alone, Alessandro again sat down at the table, and leaning his head against his clenched hand, assumed the posture of one who busies himself with thinking of future action while he waits. He had not long remained so, ere he heard the cautious step of Rosa, who peeped into the room, and seeing him alone, entered. He did not stir till she spoke.

"I thought that you had gone with the others."

"No, Rosa, I am here still; but I will not trouble you long. Some few things, however, I had to say before I go; for when I leave this house I cannot tell when I may return, if ever." There was a pause. Had he looked, he would have seen that Rosa turned pale. He expected her to answer, but she remained silent. "Much is to be done in these few days, Rosa mia; a great turn in my fate, and yours, may be at hand; and you will forgive me if absent, when you think that dangers and troubles alone keep me so."

"Pardon is easy, Alessandro. I will promise it you beforehand."

"I am assured that you will," he answered with something of a sneer, "since you speak of my offence so calmly beforehand. Have you seen Teresa Arduino—the girl that has enamored Sebastian?"

"I have."

"Well! Did you explain to her how Sebastian might join our league to his own great glory and honor?"

"I did."

"And she—"

"What if she consented?"

"Consented! Rosa mia," cried Alessandro, starting from his seat, "say that she consented and ask me what you will—I can refuse nothing. Rosa," he continued, his eyes glistening under his tightly contracted brow, while his lips smiled with pleasure, "that boy could command all I want. He has powers such as few men have in Venice. He may command his father's high station; and in him I seem to see myself born to the honors of the blood that is called debased in me. Yes, let me possess Sebastian Morosini, and I can draw on Carrara with another ally—I can even, if it so please me, laugh heedless and independent of Carrara. Marco Morosini, from his own weakness, continually fails in mind; Sebastian were another kind of tool. Yet is he young, and this girl's manner has so subdued him, that her will is law to him. Of all that have ever served me, Rosa, you have done best."

"How will this so serve you, Alessandro? I am dull; tell me how."

"Why this way, sweetest. Sebastian is rising to be accounted one of the discreetest of the young nobles in Venice—far beyond his years. He enjoys the full confidence, already, of the doge; nay, his counsel has been echoed by the doge in the senate, and acted upon by the senate. He is above suspicion—his fame is made—his intellect masters those that encounter it—and this while yet he is young and passionate. Could I but have such an instrument to my will, bastard as I am, I should not need to be a servant to Carrara, but rather ally."

"But you would use this Sebastian in your enterprise with Carrara?"

"Surely, Rosa: you know, carina, that I conceal nought from you. You have my life in your hands; and if you will go now to the Palace at St. Mark's, and tell what you know, you can command my death ere that rising sun sinks in the sea."

"You are safe for me, Alessandro. But tell me—if Sebastian did your behests, he would use the good fame he hath, to do the very opposite of those deeds by which he earned it?"

"Truly; or rather not the opposite, for it would still be for the good of Venice; but in some sort it would be the opposite."

"And it is to force him into that, that you would use his love for Teresa Arduino?"

"It is so. What is in your head now, foolish girl? His love would not alter; his love would remain as it is, just the same—no less. You look as if you had more to tell. Did she say when or how she would signify her will to the gallant? What ails you, Rosa, that you keep dumb, and look so strange?"

"What if she did not consent?"

Alessandro, unused to alter in color, turned deadly pale. He looked at Rosa as if he understood her not. "Not consent! but wherefore ask 'What if she did not consent,' when you say she did?"

"I ask you, what if she did not consent? It is my humor to know."

"It is a foolish and a dangerous humor, Rosa. By so much as I rejoice to hear that she did consent, so much should I—I will not for your idle humor unveil anything so horrid as what I would do if she did not."

"You threaten yourself, Alessandro, with what I could do if I were to proclaim you, and I regard it not; you threaten me now, and I regard it as little. See here." She drew from her bosom a knife, which she unsheathed. "This I keep that no rival of Alessandro may be too bold; take it—we are alone, you can use it as you will."

He took it, his troubled eye darkening as he grasped it, his thumb firmly resting on the tip end of the handle. "Rosa, you are safe for me. I do not put my life in your hands to play at morra with you for death. We are away from the world—I a bastard, with no rights; you mine, body and heart; but not more mine than I am yours. When I say that I love you, I say what is; and let my great love suffice you, without wishing to have in me what I am not: I am of no worth to you as a wedded husband —I am no lord; all that we have must be in spite of the world. I do suspect that you have some scheme to tame me. Better kill me outright, than take to your arms a mere worthless lackey, without power or name. You are safe. But I say," he cried, with a louder voice, his pale cheek trembling with rage, "that if my will be thwarted, those who withstand it shall as little resist destruction as this wood can resist my arm." And as he spoke he raised his hand, dashing the knife into the table. It broke not nor bent against the massive and tough-grained slab; but such was the strength and just aim of the blow, that the blade passed clean through, the point showing on the other side, and the handle trembling as the echo of the crash vibrated in the roof.

Rosa's voice was calm and deep—"There are things which strength cannot destroy, Alessandro—Teresa did not consent."

"Let them perish then!"

"No, nor let them perish; rather will you perish. You have said, Alessandro mio, that we are away from the world; but it is not so. Would I could talk as you do, and I would show you how it is that you are a beggar to the world, while you might retire to another and a better with none to reign but you. You say you love me. I am baffled, Alessandro; for I believe you, and I do not. Yet if you love, why does that not suffice you? And why will you force love, that lives only on truth, serve to make traitors for your use? Alessandro, this Teresa is too strong for you."

"We shall see."

"Ay, we shall see. I know you may kill her, as easily as me. Do so, and I follow her."

"What folly is this, Rosa?"

"Stay, I have not told you all. I did help to strengthen her resolve."

"You? Fool, fool that I was, to send one love-sick girl to another, when I was thinking only of a country and its gain and loss."

"Therefore, revenge yourself on me. You it was that made me do it. You had taught me to doubt all—life, love, everything. You made me an instrument to undo love with falsehood. I made good what you would have destroyed; and in Teresa, in myself, truth lives on though you abandon it."

"Rosa, you have half-learned these things of me, and talk like one who has gone mad with the smell of fantastic books that you cannot read. Be content; you have done your worst to defeat me, and I shall suffer. Farewell."

"Nay, I am not content. I cannot say farewell when you depart with revenge upon your lips of my causing. Believe me, I speak truly when I say that my life shall hang on your revenge. By that faith will I cling."

"I spoke wildly. You know not how you have troubled me."

"Would it were not so, Alessandro. But in this I have more than common care, since it is I who have moved you. You must forbear your revenge, Alessandro, for my sake."

"Be it as you will, lady mine. You shall rue no revenge of your making. Will that content you? and what shall be my guerdon for casting my fortunes at your feet to trample on at your humor?"

Rosa gave him her hand to kiss; but ere he relinquished it, it returned his pressure. He looked at her for an instant as he held the open door in his hand. Never had her face seemed nobler; yet never had he so little understood it. He could see men's characters at a glance; yet the young peasant-girl whom he had shut out from the world, the creature of his will, was a riddle that he could not solve! Rosa closed the door upon the audacious man who had joined their fate before she knew him. She went to the table in which her knife was sticking, and grasped the hilt. Her powerful arm failed to stir it. She took a piece of wood that lay upon the hearth, and struck the knife a few blows on the back and front of the handle, so that the sharp steel, swaying backwards and forwards cut for itself a wider and looser opening in the wood, and then she drew it out easily. She looked at it: so true had been the blow, that the blade was as straight as ever. But the mark on the table was passed all mending. That which is firm, she thought, being wounded, can never close and be whole again. She sheathed the knife, and returned it to her bosom; and then she replaced the chairs as they had been before they were disturbed by the intruders of the night; again disposing the net so that her old friend might best see its make when he should pay her his early visit.

CHAPTER XXXI.

Teresa's fear that her unsteady father would not stay long to protect his family was realized when Ranieri returned alone, and, with troubled eye, avoided her questioning. The better to conceal the truth from her, he told her that her father had undertaken an enterprise which was secret, but would bring him profit; that he had already gained some money; and that Ranieri would know how to get more. And he gave her ten pieces of gold: concealing the rest on a broad cornice over the door in his own sleeping room. Teresa too well knew her father's wont, to be surprised either at the suddenness or secrecy of his new enterprise; and she would not make her brother disclose what their father had told him to keep secret. Though she mistrusted, therefore, she sought to know no more; and Bianca was now ever content to do as Teresa thought fit. Yet as time passed on, the anxious girl watched her brother's altered demeanor with uneasiness. Though their actual want was far less than it had been, his youthful gayety, which had never failed before, was quite gone. He would scarcely eat a mouthful of food, saying that in the dearth he wished to save all that he could for their mother; so that he began to waste away. And when she urged him to share their bread, he turned from it with such loathing, eating a morsel just to satisfy her, that she suspected verily that there was more in his dislike than mere love of saving it for his mother. So that ever and ever she was pressing him to say what it was that occasioned his trouble and dislike of the food.

One day when he had laid down, scarcely tasted, some wine that she had forced him to take, she said, "How is it, Ranieri, that you not only leave this food, but look at it with such hate! If it is not fit for you to take, neither can it be for me, if I knew the reason." And she fixed her eyes upon him.

He started up from his chair, crying, "Teresa, I can bear this no longer. You mistake—it is right for you to eat what I cannot. Now, listen to me, sister mine. I have never but once done what I knew you would dislike, and once more I must do so. Therefore, tell me now that you will pardon me that I may at least carry that with me."

"What mean you, Ranieri!" exclaimed his sister, astonished at his passionate answer.

"Never mind my meaning—say that you pardon me. Say it, Teresa, if you would have me less miserable."

"I do, Ranieri; but what strange intent possesses you?"

Ranieri embraced her; and then still holding her in his arms, he went on—"Now, hear what I say to you. The money which I told you I should fetch, I have already—all of it except two pieces, that I have taken. Your use will bless it. It is on the cornice over my door. It will last some time; and then I will be with you again. Farewell." And suddenly releasing her from his arms, he rushed from the room.

"Ranieri—Ranieri!" cried Teresa; but he was gone. She followed him to the ante-room, but he had already left it; and as she rushed to the stairs, she heard the door of the house close, and knew that he had quite departed. Her sense was bewildered with this new abandonment. As if fancying that it would tell her something, she repaired to his chamber to find the money She counted eighty-eight pieces; which, with the two that Ranieri had and the ten that he had given to her, made a hundred; A terrible suspicion cast a shadow on her soul! but she chased it away. Nothing but that gold remained for her mother's sustenance, and should she avow to herself before she knew it that the gold could not be used? Again, on the thought of her mother, she trembled at the fear lest she should not be able to conceal Ranieri's absence till his return, for which she still hoped. And now she blamed herself for having scared away their only guard.

Bianca's very helplessness made it easier for Teresa to turn aside her questions until night approached. But when it became dark, and the sick woman saw not her husband, she looked still closer in Teresa's face. She asked where he was? Teresa saw that she suspected, and told her that he had gone upon some secret enterprise, and that he had already sent them some money. Bianca sank back upon her pillow in silence. She thought no farther but that Jacopo had gone; and she asked no more. So passed that night; and next day when she saw not her son, she asked, "And has Ranieri gone too?" Teresa rejoiced that she had put no closer question, and answered "Yes." Bianca's face turned still paler, and she pressed Teresa's hand, as if to thank her for that she did not abandon her mother. Now that Teresa suspected the source from whence the money had come to them, she too loathed her food as Ranieri had done; but she took almost the greater pleasure in buying for her mother those dainties which would provoke her appetite and restore her strength. Bianca attributed the girl's melancholy to their forlorn condition, and did the best to console her with hopes of Sebastian's return. Alas, the bedridden woman scarcely knew the extremity of Venice, or how Sebastian was bound to his post. Teresa's worst fears, however, arose when she was obliged to leave her mother alone in the house, while she went to buy the necessary things. She dreaded to hire an attendant, lest the money should not last out their time of need; and because of her suspicions, not liking to spend it in anything but her mother's sustenance; besides that she mistrusted strangers. For these reasons she would delay to buy what they wanted till she last moment, and it so happened that on the third night after Ranieri had left them, her mother asked for bread when there was none, Bianca would not let it be fetched; but fearing that her hunger should come again in the night, after she was asleep, Teresa went forth. Not long after, Bianca awoke, and called her daughter. The house was still as death; and the sick woman waited, thinking that Teresa would return. At length there were sounds as of tumult in the streets; but still within the house all was silent. Bianca called again and again. Fearing some mischance, she rose up in the bed and at last put forth her trembling limbs, and went forth into the next room. A light was burning, and a book was open where Teresa had sat; but all was solitary and still. Bianca tottered over to the other door, and listened: nothing struck her ear but the increasing tumult without.

CHAPTER XXXII.

For some days before he did so, Ranieri had thought of escaping from his sister's questions.

He distrusted his own power to keep his secret, and he dreaded lest some suspicion of the truth should defeat the very purpose of his father's sacrifice. For that it was that he had taken the two ducats, which he kept to enable him to get away from Venice; for he thought that if he could reach the littorale, great part of his trouble would be over. He had heard of So bastian from his mother—too fond to deny him that secret; and him he would seek and serve. He repaired to Canaregio, near which lived a fisherman whom he had known, and whom he had accompanied in his boat, both for pleasure and for help. The man was away from home, his boat having been taken from him to use for carrying some provision, with others, to Lido; but his wife let Ranieri stay till he should return, thinking that some fault of the youth had sent him away from his family for a while. In their poor house Ranieri remained three days; and still the man did not return; and the youth did not like to take from the poor woman's scanty store. For the ways to the lagoon were so blocked up by Carrara's people, that there had been a long and grievous dearth in the place. The fisher's wife, whom even Ranieri remembered a girl, had suddenly looked older, from hunger and fear. He already began to feel the gnawing at his own young breast. As the third day closed in, he stole out, and wandered towards St. Mark's. Many of the streets through which he passed were more silent than even Venice should be, for they were quite deserted: and no gondolas were skimming the Canaregio. As he approached the square, there were more boats and people astir. Groups were collected in the streets, of grave and careworn men, from whose talk as he passed, he gathered that Pisani made no head against the Genoese; but that more danger pressed upon the city than it had yet known. As he drew near a group, one spoke sullenly and fiercely as if he scarcely cared how it should end, and almost hoped that the Genoese would soon triumph, so that the ways for food to enter the city might again be open. The other men seemed to agree. Ranieri listened, but he said nothing; and he longed to be at Lido, with Sebastian, fighting his first battles against the strong foe that had so struck his native city.

While he stood, one man touched him who had so spoken, and pointed to the youth, saying—"Take heed what thou sayest, Nadale: it is not always safe to tell one's judgment aloud. The Ten have ears to hear all that is said in that fashion. Who knows!"

The sullen fellow turned round on his heel, and stared at Ranieri as though he would learn by examining him what he was. Ranieri knew the man at once—he it was who had sat in the wine-shop when Jacopo was seized. The youth moved on.

"Aye!" cried Nadale, "thou sayest true: here is one of the self-same people thou spakest of. Olà, master spy! if you can sell your father, you are not to sell honest men, who speak wider than they mean, thinking no harm. Stop, I say."

Ranieri, instead of obeying, would have hastened his steps; but the man who had already followed him, seized him by the arm. The youth snatched himself from the grasp, and drawing his poinard, stood ready to defend himself. But the spirit of the chase had already animated the other men, and he was now surrounded too effectually to escape. "Stand back," he cried, "or I shall hurt some of you before you take me."

"Oh ho!" laughed Nadale; "this is a gentle spy, perhaps a noble gentleman that follows the craft for pleasure."

"What wouldst thou do with him, Nadale?"

"Do! why silence his vile tongue. It is a spy, friends; a fellow that will sell his father. I saw him with my own eyes, and I would have helped old Boccolone the wine man to pay him his wages; but some officers of the council were with him then. Where are they now, master spy?"

"How knowest thou that he is a spy? Who is he?" cried another.

"Who is he! why perhaps he might not have been so wicked, if he were not the son of a traitor."

"Thou liest, ribald!" cried Ranieri.

"Oh yes! I lie—of course. Yes, signori miei, I am a liar: you that know me know that. And this gentleman tells no lies! Oh no! he tells only truth, because he is paid for it by the Ten; blessed be they. This gentleman is very noble in blood—oh! very noble indeed. He is related to Messer Marco Morosini, as I believe; also to the noble and puissant Messer Lionardo Morosini; also to Messer Michele Morosini; also to Messer Georgio Arduino, that died at Candia; yet is his father traitor. His father is the excellent Messer Jacopo Arduino; once a most powerful merchant, now a prisoner of state for conspiring with the Gobba to poison the waters of this poor city. I believe," said Nadale to Ranieri, gravely doffing his hat with mock reverence, "I believe Messer Jacopo is not of the grand council! Perhaps he is. Pardon me if I did not mention it, but I believe the excellent gentleman is not in the grand council, but only in prison."

Stung by the fellow's insolence, Ranieri struck at him a straight, sharp blow. Nadale started back, and caught the blow on his arm; and when the knife returned, its blade was red and wet. The other men had instantly seized the youth, while his arm was still stretched forth, and in a second he was disarmed, and held fast in the grasp of four or five, his arms held out on either side; while his detainers looked at Nadale as if for orders what to do. Ranieri also looked at him. The man's face blackened with rage; his heavy features contracting in a scowl of hate, as he felt in his bosom for a dagger, which he slowly drew forth. As Ranieri stood in bondage, his breast was exposed to the blow which the ruffian meditated; but he shrunk not, nor did his eye quail. As Nadale stepped closer, his foot struck against the poniard which had been dashed from the youth's hand. He picked it up, and looked at it. He held it against his arm, where the blood had soaked through the sleeve. "Aye," he cried, "it is the same. Pity that gentle steel should be soiled with such vile stuff! Nor must one mix it." He wiped it carefully on the dry part of the sleeve, and then drew back his hand to strike.

"Hold!" cried one of Ranieri's detainers,

"What art doing! Do you want to get us all in prison!"

"No, no; when I have washed this same knife in the stripling's own rosy blood, we'll let him fall, by chance, into the canal."

"A fine scheme, truly! No, no, Nadale; no more blood: let us give him up to the Ten ourselves, and bring your blood against him."

"Give him to the Ten! Why, he is their own servant. Has he not heard what I said! Have I not seen him give his own father up! Aye! while they drive us to war with the Genoese, they worry us out in Venice itself with their spies. Tell that, signore mio, to the Ten, and give me up. Has he not the gold in his pocket that he sold his father for! Seek—see if he has not."

"Look you yourself," said one, "while we hold him."

Ranieri knew that resistance would be hopeless, and he chose rather to maintain a proud stillness. He therefore stirred not, while Nadale thrust a hand into the bosom of his vest, and soon found in his pocket the two pieces of gold. "What!" cried the ruffian, "only two! didst sell thy father for two ducats!"

"He has given the rest to his mistress," exclaimed another.

"Like enough; though gifts generally pass the other way with pretty boys like this. 'Twere a pity to have lost this gold though in the canal."

"Aye," said the man that had staid him when he was about to strike; and now that you have the gold, do not let us save him from drowning any longer. No blood; blood tells tales."

"Be it as you will. But how, think you, is he likely to fall in, so that none shall see!"

"We will give him a turn in my boat, and perchance he may slip over; and we may be so anxious to save him," added the man, laughing with his comrades, "that we may only hinder each other. Hark—what is that!"

It was the bell of St. Mark's.

Nadale answered—"It is the old bell that they ring almost every day now. Something has happened. Let us hasten, or they will prevent us. Where is thy boat!"

"Close at hand, bear him along."

Ranieri derived some comfort from finding that he had respite; and already he watched for a favorable moment to call out for aid. As they came to a bridge, a number of men who were hastening to the great square crossed their path. With a sudden effort, Ranieri shook off the grasp of the men, whose thumbs began to ache with holding his arms. He ran forward, crying, "Help, friends, help! Here are traitors that would slay me. For the blessed virgin help me." In an instant, however, the grasp was again on his arms, tighter than ever. The new comers stopped, and pressed forward; they were friends of his captors; who, pointing to the blood on Nadale's arm, loudly told Ranieri's crimes, and laughingly whispered the punishment that they meant for the spy. Again they led him forward, across the bridge, towards the place where lay the boat that was to be the instrument of execution. The youth's heart sank within him as he looked at the darkening night, and imperfectly saw the rough and unimpressible faces that surrounded him. Already he felt cut off from the world. But he strung his trembling limbs with all his fortitude, determined to give no triumph to his murderers in any show of weakness. He thought of the fallen fortunes of his house, of his mother's dying state, his father's imprisonment; and in bending to the common fate that crushed them despair steeled his heart against regret. Yet again he thought of his dear and loving sister, and a tearful passion seemed to swell up from his heart when he thought that he never, never more should see her. But she would be protected by Sebastian; and his loss would still leave happiness on earth for her. As he walked along, Nadale came close and whispered in his ear—"How sad, that Messer Sebastiano Morosini cannot protect the brother as he has the sister, so grateful for the care! Ha, ha, ha!"

Ranieri turned to the speaker in angry amazement; but he had moved farther off, and the youth could hardly discern the twinkle of his eye, as the man looked at him with brutal cunning.

They had not gone many yards, ere a woman, who was walking rapidly towards them, stepped aside to let the band pass. Ranieri started, and felt a moment's joy, as he knew his sister: he was about to call aloud; but he checked the sound, and turned away his face; rather suffering alone, than desiring to drag her into his cruel fate and rude persecution.

But it was too late. Teresa had drawn herself as close as possible to the wall so that they might not push against her, and she looked at them as they drew nigh; not timid, but watchful. Suddenly her eye glanced upon the prisoner. By his youthful tallness, by the slender grace of his form, and the firmness and spirit of his tread, she knew her generous brother. A low cry escaped as she rushed before the march of the rude mob; for such the crowd that had now gathered round Nadale's prisoner might be called. Throwing her arms round his neck, she asked why he was thus led along.

"Oh, ho! this must be his mistress," cried Nadale's friend, the gondolier: "this accounts for only finding two ducats."

More bewildered by the words, though she scarcely heeded them, Teresa turned to the speaker, and again asked why the youth was detained!

"Stand back, girl, stand back," cried Nadale, "we want not to harm you, but we may chance to do it if you stop our way."

"Trample me down, then," said Teresa as she drew herself up, still keeping her arms round her brother. "I will not stir till I know wherefore he is your prisoner."

"Is that all," said the ruffian, whose voice Teresa fancied to have heard before: "then see here why he is prisoner." He seized her hand roughly, and dabbled it on his soaked sleeve. "Dost feel that! It is wet; it is getting wetter and wetter. Bring that torch forward, now look at thy hand, girl; is it not red? Ay, 'tis an honest man's blood, thou need'st not loathe it so; 'tis mine. If thou must shudder, let it be at thy gallant's crime; ask him whose knife cracked my flask here!"

Teresa sickened as she looked on her hand, and saw that the warm moisture was red! She turned her eye to the wounded man. Heavens! it was the same who had intruded into her mother's chamber in search of her father, and whom Sebastian had chased away. She looked at Ranieri: his face was pale and stern, but her questioning eye read no confession of guilt. "There was," she cried "some cause for the blow. Tell me, Ranieri; for your enemies are silent."

"Teresa mine," replied the youth, "you have given to my danger its only bitterness in being here. This is but an idle brawl, and I being the weaker, cannot resist numbers. But it shall all end well. This is no place for you. Leave me and I will soon follow you home."

"Not so soon as you think, young sir," cried Nadale; "but he says well, my girl, in telling you to leave us. We will not harm him; no, truly we will do him no hurt; so go home, and wait for him." And the man laughed.

"He says well," added Ranieri. "This is no place for you, Teresa mine; and as for me, fear not; justice will be done to me, and that will leave me harmless."

"Think it not," answered Teresa, turning to Nadale; "I leave him not, until I see him in the care of the law, if he has offended against the state. Who is it that accuses him!" And leaving her brother, she drew back and spoke in a louder voice: "Who is his accuser! Did you all see it done, that you are here as enemies against him! Were you all present! What is that you would do with him! If he has done a wrong let him be carried before his judges. Is it in Venice that you will help one of your fellows to revenge on one so young! Is that your pride! Or do you forget that the Ten will allow no encroachment on their power, and that those who steal the justice which it is their right to bestow, must suffer for their daring!"

"She says true," cried several; and a man, who pushed his way through the crowd, came forward to represent the number that had newly joined the group round the disputants, strangers who had no interest on either side, and began to be entertained by the thickening plot. Nadale frowned with a darker scowl: hoping to remove the obstacle to his wishes by bearing it down, he went towards Teresa, and pushing her rudely, cried, "Stand back, girl, or you will be hurt; for we will trample you down."

"Stay, stay, good man," said the new comer stoutly. "Who are these that you handle so roughly!"

"Who are they! why here is a boy that has run his knife into a better man. Who is he! he is the son of a traitor—one Arduino who plotted at la Gobba's wine shop to poison our wells. He is a child you would cherish, friends, is he not!"

"But this girl!"

"The girl! cannot you guess. Ha, ha, ha, did you not see how she hugged him!"

"His sister, his sister!" cried Teresa. "Think you not that a sister can cling to a brother in the face of danger and death! Will you let this rude man use violence to a woman of Venice, because she claims justice for her brother!"

"No, no," cried her new friend, "have no fear, lady."

"Oh ho!" said Nadale, disappointment making more bitter his malignity, "his sister! Why then we have two traitor's children. What is this!" he cried, picking up something from the ground. It was a new loaf. "What is this! what was the traitor's daughter carrying under her veil!" He held it up. "Do you know what it is, men!"

"It is," said Teresa, firmly, "bread which she, who is no traitor's daughter, was carrying to her sick mother. Is that a crime Venetians!"

"No, no, no," shouted many voices.

Nadale cried out fiercely, "She is a traitor's daughter, ay, and a traitor's sister. It is bread, is it! They feed well then, these traitors! How many of you, honest men, have bread to throw about the streets at this time! The Genoese keep the bread from us true Venetians. Do you feel hungry, any of you! I do. We cannot get bread. But these traitors—these half Genoese—they have bread to throw about our streets! Have you gold! How many of you have gold! Has any single one of you one piece of gold in his pocket! One piece of silver! No, it has all gone to buy bread, long, long ago; and now there is neither money to buy bread, nor bread to be bought. But these traitors have bread: and they have gold too. See here." He held up the two pieces that he had taken from Ranieri. "Two of them. That lad is young, is he not, to have two good golden ducats, all solid and unclipped! But then he is a traitor, and they get gold, these traitors do. And how think you that he got it!"

A faint sickness came over Teresa as she glanced fearfully at the gold and heard Nadale's coarse brutal voice. In terror she listened for his next words.

"He is the son, remember, of the traitor that was paid to poison our wells: good, how should the youngster get some money for himself! How! Why, he sold his father to the Ten."

A shudder, sharp and convulsive, rushed through Teresa's frame, at hearing out spoken what she had already learned to thrust away from her thoughts.

"Is all this true, my girl!" asked her stranger friend.

Teresa sought an answer in her brother's face. He had remained motionless throughout the scene, mastering his rage, and watching for a moment when he could burst from the grasp of his detainers. But the hard fleshy fetters at his wrists and elbows relaxed not. He answered Teresa with a firm regard, which seemed to say, It is true and yet I am falsely accused. She knew it all. She turned to the questioner, answering—"It is more false than true. There is so much truth in it, that the devil may use to make us believe his falsehood. But, true or false, we ask no favor, but only justice. And while the bell tolls to the danger of Venice"—the ringing still sounded solemnly from the tower of St. Mark—"shall we tempt Heaven by injustice!"

"The girl says well," said the stranger: "let us bear them to the square, and deliver them up."

"Aye," said Nadale, furiously, "deliver them up to the Ten that pay them!"

"Hush! hush!" cried the whole crowd, struck with fear at his audacity.

"Besides," he added, "who will attend to do justice to a poor wounded silk-weaver like me, in this hour of alarm!"

"All," answered Teresa eagerly striving to improve the friendly disposition among the mob; "the more the danger the more need to be just before Heaven. Bear us to the square."

"Yes, yes," shouted the people; "delay here no longer. Bring them along."

Nadale yielded perforce; and the whole multitude moved forward. The cunning ruffian, however, did not so easily relinquish his prey. Teresa walked free; but she observed that as they crossed a bridge and passed along the narrow streets, Nadale and his friends contrived to draw close round her and her brother. They entered the square, where the thickening night was broken by many a torch flitting hither and thither. There was some commotion near the palace, and in the piazzetta; and numbers of the crowd that accompanied them hurried forward with the impulse of curiosity. She listened; but could not gather from the confused sounds which reached her what it was that threatened the city with new calamities.

They had now come in front of the palace; the greater part of their escort had gradually mingled with the throng that filled the place; when Nadale thinking that his time had come, whispered to his adherents; and, approaching Teresa, said in a low voice, "If you would be safe, now, go: I have no quarrel with you."

"I leave not my brother," answered Teresa, foreseeing the attempt that was about to be made; and she hastily moved back towards Ranieri.

Nadale seized her roughly. "Stay then, and your blood be upon your own head. Turn back, boys; they have forgotten us now."

"Friends," shrieked Teresa, "help! help! Ranieri, stir yourself; let them not bear us back."

Strong with new power at her call, Ranieri shook off the hold of the man that held him, and his sister was in his arms; while he struck madly right and left with his clenched hand.

"Fool!" cried Nadale, "cease this noise. You will not!" With his fist he struck the girl violently on the head, calling to his companions —"Seize the boy; lift him off his legs. That's it. Tear him off her. Fool! fool! And as the youth was dragged from her, Nadale struck her again and again, now on the face, now on the chest. Bravely she strove to ward off his blows and to follow her retreating brother; but her blanched lips quivered; the man's hard blows seemed to batter the breath out of her breast; her sight began to swim; and she staggered and reeled as the sobs of agony and despair burst from her compressed lips.

Suddenly there was a change in the tumult round her. The blows ceased; the voices grew louder, the strife fiercer; and as consciousness left her terrified soul, she was aware that she sank into the arms dearest and safest to her in the world. It was Sebastian.

He it was who had brought tidings how the

Genoese had burst through the barriers in the port of Venice; how nothing remained between the city and its foe but the loose and floating force of Pisani, driven back almost to the house walls; on his arrival with that terrible report was it that St. Mark's bell had tolled. He had just left the palace, and was piercing his way through the crowd, when Teresa's shriek struck close at hand on his astounded ear. In an instant he was by her side. Closely hemmed in, and engaged with one arm in clasping his dear love, he could not draw his sword; but the brutal Nadale scarcely profited by that. Before the ruffian was aware of his new foe, a terrible blow shattered his jaw as he looked round. Turning like a wild beast to attack his more than equal enemy, a second blow came like a rock thrown at his forehead, and sent him blind and stunned, at the feet of her whom he had so cruelly used. Sebastian called for aid: he was well known, and without asking what his quarrel was, many soon joined him, and drove Nadale's band away.

The multitude was still swaying to and fro around them, some stopping to gaze at the pair so strangely grouped, when Sebastian looked down on the burden in his arms. He was struck with horror at thinking of the cruelties from which he had just snatched a thing so precious. Teresa's veil had been thrown back: her hair floated in disorder on her shoulders, and where the gentle fair locks waved from the head, a few stains of blood still oozing forth showed where the coward's blow had struck, while her soft lips, slightly parted as she lay in her swoon, were fuller and redder with moist blood. In an agony of tender rage, Sebastian felt a hot gushing glow as though his heart's blood had forced itself to his eyes. As he looked, a hand was laid firmly on his shoulder, and a voice said, "Is this Sebastian Morosini?"

"The same;" and he looked round to see who thus addressed him.

It was a tall woman, whose face was concealed by a veil drawn closely around it. "It is well," she said, "or I should have asked your claim to hold what you have in your arms. But tarry not here. How shall we bear her home; for she must needs return with all speed?"

"We will convey her to the nearest boat."

"Have you any servants here?"

"None; and there are none at hand that I would trust."

"It is all the better. Tell these gazers not to follow us. Lift her gently."

Leaving Sebastian to bear the fainting woman's head, Rosa, for she it was, gathered Teresa's clothes carefully round her, and raised her legs. Sebastian whispered to one near him to prevent the others from following them; and his courteous speech at once made the stranger so trusty a servant, that in a few instants the two were threading the way through a part of the crowd who knew nothing of the disturbance; which had attracted the less notice, since all were intent on learning the cause of the ominous toll. Rosa led the way with a light but firm step, from the great square, and so to the water side, higher up the canal at a more private place than at the steps of the piazzetta: presently they were seated within the awning of one of the many boats which even in that troublous time plied in the watery streets of Venice. Rosa fastened back the curtain of the boat so as to admit the night breeze. She had laid Teresa on one of the seats: Sebastian still held her clasped in his arms, her head lying on his breast. The repose of the boat and the fresh air on the water seemed to revive her.

"Speak to her," said Rosa; "it will rouse her; and she should not reach home thus."

Sebastian whispered Teresa's name, and pressed her gently in his arms. Her eyes opened for an instant; and then closed again; but she knew him, for she nestled her bruised head closer to him, as an infant presses against its mother to be reassured of safety. Presently she opened her eyes again, and putting her hand to her brow, seemed to collect her memory. Suddenly snatching Sebastian's hand, she pressed it to her lips: "The third time saved!" she whispered. Then looking round she saw in the faint light that some one was near them. "Ranieri!" she cried.

"It is not Ranieri," said the other drawing nearer to her, "but Rosa."

Teresa stretched out her hand to take Rosa's, but suddenly starting, she exclaimed, "And Ranieri—is he not here! It is so dark, I cannot see him."

"Ranieri, dearest," answered Sebastian, "is not with you; but you are safe."

"Alas, alas! Sebastian, let us go back. That was what I staid for, but that I was so weak. Alas! they were bearing him I think to death. Let us go back; it may not yet be too late."

Sebastian would have obeyed her; but Rosa prevented him. "Ranieri is not here," she said, "but you must go homeward, dear lady."

"Nay, nay, not without my brother."

"Indeed you must," said Rosa, pressing her arm as if to make her yield—"your mother—"

"My mother! what of her! Oh! it is so dark, Rosa, that I cannot see your face to tell what you mean."

"Your mother is safe, but, sweet lady, in sore fear at your absence. You must go back." Rosa's voice was low and forced, as if she tried to seem calmer than she felt.

"Rosa, your voice is altered," cried Teresa; "tell me what it is."

"Why, no more than I have told you. I went to your house, hearing that something was amiss, and as I came to the door I found your mother—"

"My mother! in the street!"

"Aye, with some women round her, half terrified at her, and—the fools!—half taking pleasure to tell her what they had heard—"

"And that was!"

"Of Ranieri, whom they knew."

"My poor mother! but you left her not in the streets of Venice, Rosa mine."

"Indeed I did not. I led her in, and to soothe her, set out to find you; for you it was she asked for when they told her of Ranieri. But stop the boat, Messer Sebastian; for it were better to land here. Can you go with his support alone, lady mine?"

Sebastian paid the men; and they were soon on shore. It was dark, but a slight glimmer of moonlight showed the path. Teresa suffered Sebastian to pass his arm round her to support her, but she stepped hastily forward; and a few silent minutes brought them to the door of her house. It was unclosed; but all was silent without. Teresa entered. Sebastian followed her close; and while they passed on, Rosa staid to fasten the door. On the stair, Teresa stopped and listened. She hurried forward. At the top of the stair she listened again. A light in the distant room gleamed faintly through the open doors; but all was still as death. Teresa turned to Sebastian, and took his hand; she shook so, that he could hear the quaking of her limbs.

"Sebastian — Sebastian!" she cried, in a choked whisper; "this silence! I shall go mad with terror."

"Dearest love, your mother is worn out and sleeps. Stay you here and let me go forward."

"No, no; I am stronger now that I have heard your voice." And she went on, but more cautiously, until they reached the saloon now so familiar to Sebastian. Never had sight made Sebastian's stout heart quail like that which then met their eyes.

At the opposite door stood Bianca, in her white night-dress, holding in her hand above her head the only lamp that lighted the place: her attitude was fixed as stone; her face was more pale than marble, and strained forward as her glassy eyes pierced the gloom beyond, her thin hair gray, before its time, hanging in lank locks on either side; and she held her left hand up with the finger extended, as though she had bid her breath be more silent, that she might listen for her children. So she had stood, listening to the distant tumult, ever since Rosa had left her, vainly hoping that she would remain in her bed. As Teresa entered, Bianca's eyes glared for a moment with a wilder stare; for she doubted her disordered senses, and thought that she saw in her daughter's pale and terrified face and dishevelled hair a vision wretched as herself; but when she saw that it was really Teresa, her rigid form relaxed; she essayed to step forward. She tottered; the lamp fell from her hand, leaving them in darkness; and after the clang of the falling brass a heavier and deader sound told them that Bianca herself had fallen. Teresa had already come so close that she could take her mother in her arms. She called to her; but there was no answer. Sebastian had found them, and helped to support the lifeless form. There was a pause; in the darkness and the silence, Sebastian almost fancied that he was alone, dreaming of what he knew was doing near him.

"I will fetch a light," said Teresa. Her voice was so hoarse, that at first Sebastian knew it not. He heard her go, and Bianca remained alone in his arms. Presently Teresa returned with another lamp. She bent over her mother, and looked earnestly in her face; starting back with a shudder, she placed the lamp upon the floor near her, and taking her mother's hand, prostrated herself before her on the ground, and placed that hand on her own head, as though she would make it bless her. Sebastian looked round upon Bianca's face, as the head leaned back in his arm: he closed the upturned eyes. A hand pressed on his shoulder again made him look round. Rosa pointed to Teresa, as she herself kneeled down to take Bianca's body from his support. He lifted Teresa from the ground. She tried almost roughly to tear away his grasp; but at the sound of his voice she suffered him to place her on a chair; while Rosa, tenderly raising the body in her powerful arms, bore it from the room to the bed where its life had withered away so long

---

CHAPTER XXXIII.

After the first stun of her grief had passed, Teresa again bethought her of her brother, and would once more have set out in quest of him; but Sebastian appeased her, with a promise to search for him; and leaving the sufferer in Rosa's charge, he went to the scene of conflict. Nadale was still lying there: some one had dragged the wounded wretch to the side, among the stones set for building in the yet unfinished part of the piazza; but no one had fetched him away. Sebastian called a man to him, and gave him a piece of gold to strive to restore his fallen foe to consciousness and bear him home; promising him another reward on tidings of the man's recovery, and on learning his name. But Ranieri could nowhere be found. Sebastian returned to Teresa, to console her as he best could, with hopes of Ranieri's safety, since the neglect of Nadale showed him how completely their enemies had been routed.

That night, while Rosa remained with Teresa, he watched in one of the lower rooms of the house. Early in the morning he renewed the search for Ranieri, but still without success. Providing himself with money which his good uncle had left at his disposal, he returned to the house of mourning. Rosa admitted him, and stopped him, as he would have passed on with a courteous salutation. "This," she said, "is no place for Madonna Teresa." It was the very feeling in his mind; but he had not yet bethought him of any safe retreat for her. Rosa continued—"She must be removed with all speed."

"Have you then a place where she can be safe?"

"Alas! no, I have not—not in my house—anywhere but there. Still I can find such a place."

"And how—forgive me, dear damsel—how shall I be assured of her safety?"

Rosa looked at him proudly, but not angrily. "You do well not to trust one so precious to strange hands. Ask Teresa who I am; she will tell you—all; and then trust me, and I will bless you for it. I know not how it is, Messer Sebastian, but on the success of your love, or rather of Teresa's, rests my hope that happiness in the world is possible; not mine own, perhaps, but some happiness. But I speak without your understanding. Let Teresa tell you, and then trust her to me; for in all that I can serve her, henceforth she is my mistress.

It is the blessed power of the good, that even when unfortunate themselves, they can give happiness and consolation to others."

She left him, and he repaired to Teresa. He found her more composed, and for the first time he heard the story of what had happened, so far as she knew it, to make the danger from which he had rescued her. "I once told you, Sebastian," she said, "to abandon a fate so doomed as that of my house; little did I think then that yet worse mischance and degradation would visit it; and yet, though I have stronger reason, I cannot now bid you abandon me: why did I not use the power while I had it! But I have it no longer."

"I will not, sweet life," answered Sebastian, "scold you for such disloyalty as to wish you had done what would have destroyed me though it had not killed me; but rather let it be the stronger reason why you should suffer me to take you to myself in the face of the world, so that your fate may be made more fortunate by being made mine, and mine more blessed by being made yours."

"Not so. I will not rob Venice in the day of danger of the best among its servants—I am not so craven as even to desire your safety at such a price. I will not risk the trouble to you which so strange a marriage might bring upon you, from the displeasure of your father or of the grand council. No, Sebastian, before I consent that you wed the daughter of a traitor, and the sister of a traitor, let us try to discover proof of the innocence I believe. Besides, I dare not, yet trembling with the sight we saw last night, and while my unhappy mother still lingers on the earth that was so cruelly matched with her angel nature—I dare not take to myself so much happiness, lest it drive away the sorrow that I ought yet to suffer as a sacrifice to that sainted spirit."

"Be it as you will," said Sebastian; and he told her of what Rosa had said. Teresa in turn told him Rosa's history; saying that in her own life she had run worse risks than she feared from trusting Rosa. Sebastian perforce consented.

That night the body of Bianca was silently interred; none but a few holy men, and three mourners, a man and two women, witnessing the dismal ceremony. Teresa returned not home, but guarded by her two friends, she was placed with all possible privacy in the house of Pierotto, Rosa's ancient friend and neighbor. Before he again suddenly took leave of her next day, Sebastian, summoned to the sea-coast, felt more certain of her safety than he had yet done.

CHAPTER XXXIV.

WHEN Nadale was so suddenly attacked, his friends, remembering his audacious words, to which they almost as audaciously had listened, and fearing that the officers of the Ten were upon them, made such good use of their heels, that in few minutes no two were in sight of each other. Those who had held Ranieri, hastily let him fall. Although slightly stunned by striking against the tiles, with which Venice was then paved, and somewhat bruised by the feet of those hurrying to and fro in the dark, he soon recovered. He had heard from the attack, and the manner of his captors' flight, that there had been a rescue, and he hoped for Teresa's safety. Drawing to the side of the square, he sat down with his back against the wall, to rest from the pain he suffered, and to think what he should next do. He more than ever feared to go home, lest the guilt that he could not disavow should be visited on his mother and sister; and he was more still bent on striving to reach Sebastian, at the sea-coast. But his money was gone. As he sat, he saw a gentleman stumble, and presently stoop down, and drag something towards the place where Ranieri sat; he saw that it was the body of a man, and he guessed that the other had stumbled over it, and now dragged it out of the way for the sake of pity. As the youth sat, he was in the dark, to which his eyes, better accustomed, could see without being seen; so that the gentleman dragged the body close to him, and left it there without speaking. Ranieri bent towards it. It was Nadale; and by the warmth and hard breathing, the youth knew that he still lived. As he looked, he remembered that the ruffian had robbed him of the two ducats which he had taken, and he bethought him that he might recover them. So opening the man's bosom, he felt for them; and he found them in a pocket; and also in the man's girdle was Ranieri's poniard, which he took back again. He left the man's vest open, so that he might be the more likely to revive from the air; for he did not wish to have blood upon his head. Then leaving the square, he returned to Canareggio and the house which he had left that evening. At first the woman refused to let him enter; for she had heard of his misadventure, and she feared to bring trouble upon herself if he were found in the house; but he besought her so earnestly not to leave him to perish, and promised her so sanctily that he would pay her with kisses, if she would not tell her husband, that the good woman, who perhaps liked his gay spirit and young beauty better than it would have pleased her to tell her husband, though she thought that there was no real harm with such a child, opened her door, and let the wanderer in. Be sure he did not forget the promised guerdon; for the fisherman was not yet returned. For two days the tender-hearted woman concealed him; and so well did he tell his tale, and so skilfully put the offer of his two golden ducats, that on the third day the man consented to convey him to Lido.

They waited till the night was far advanced, and then the fisher set out with a helpmate and Ranieri, as if for his daily toil. They cleared the city without hindrance from the guards, who recognized the man's voice; and using their best speed, though they made a wide bend to avoid the Genoese, they arrived at Lido at early noon, and the boatman offered some fish to the soldiers that gathered round his boat. "Nay, we want to buy no fish," cried one; "the republic pays for us." "But it is fine and fresh; no republic can have fish so fine and fresh as that; for it must get bad and stinking before it can possibly pass through the offices." "He says true," said another; "but I care not for fish. Come, you must not stay here. And what are you landing for, youngster!" he said to Ranieri. "Oh!" answered the fisher, "he is going to his master. You do not think that young gallant is a fisherman, do you!" His master! And who is your master, Senor Ragazzetto!" "Messer Sebastiano Morosini." "Nonsense, what can he want of boy lackeys like you! Push off again, I tell you; get into the boat, or I'll throw you in." "Stay;" said Ranieri, subduing his anger, and passively resisting the rough soldier—"See, there is one who knows me—that English soldier there, with the red sleeves under his mail. Olà, Turnbull!" Most fortunately, Ranieri's sturdy friend was loitering by; and after one look of astonishment, with more ready wit than his broad face gave him credit for, he suddenly understood Ranieri to be a page to Sebastian, and stoutly vouched for the fact; moreover, seizing the youth in his arm, and interposing the weight of his massy form between his friend and the guard. By this time the boat was far on its way back to Venice, and the Venetian soldiers suffered their English comrade to bear off his prize. "And now, Messer Arduino, that I have helped you ashore, what am I to do with you?" "Lead me to Sebastian!"

As they passed along, Ranieri's inexperienced eyes were astonished at the change which had been made on the island. Besides the fort which guarded the entrance, now beyond his view, the whole place was fortified. Vines and fruits were all gone. Palisades, and walls, and ditches were seen on every side; and here and there rose towers, strangers to his sight, some of wood, others of solid stone. They seemed to be within a very extensive palisade which stretched far beyond his power to distinguish it; and all around were the tents of the soldiers collected by the republic. "There," cried Turnbull, pointing, and patching up his broken Italian as best he could with scraps of English, muttered to himself—"as far as you can see to the left, those are the men of Robert Recanati; he came ten days ago. New tents he wants, I think, for I never saw such a ragged fair. Yonder are our tents. Some have got brown enough, but they are all sound. And I will tell you, signor, if ever you are a captain, give your men sound tents and sound food, and teach them your sword exercise, and never mind these new artillery things: let your men sleep well, feed well, and fight well, and you will win the battle, though you may make less noise. These tents before us are yours. Not all your men, but only some put here, I think, to be guards over the foreign soldiers. There are not many, you see, for Signor Cook's men will do as well; but I guess those Recanati want a good guard, for you will not see a stranger set of brigands—that is, to the look. They fight well enough sometimes, they say. Now, here is Messer Sebastian's lodging. I will wait to see you again before you go." "You will see me again, and often; for I hope I shall not go."

The tent was empty, and the youth wasted some time alone. At length a cavalier entered He was tall, and stout-limbed, and clothed

K

in armor richly dight with gold. No visor was on his bascinet, which showed a face somewhat flushed with the heat of his arms. On the front of his jupon was blazoned the blue bend dexter on a white field, of the Morosini: and Ranieri knew that it was Sebastian who gazed in surprise upon the unknown tenant of his lodging.

"Messer Sebastiano," said the youth, who would not mar his enterprise at the last for want of bold speaking—"here is one who would thrust himself upon you for a servant, if you will have him—who is ready to serve and die for you. I am Ranieri Arduino."

"Ranieri! Your sister!"

"She is safe," answered Ranieri, "and hath wherewithal to live. I have come to you, Sebastian, only for my own sake. Sebastian, Teresa gave you her faith: Teresa herself has reared me: I have come to ask for your faith. I have come to you because I dare not live in Venice. I must be secret—so secret that I must not even tell you what you will hear told of me. Yet I ask you for a while to believe me innocent in spite of all, and to let me stay in your service. I swear to you that I shall bring no disgrace upon you, and that Teresa shall one day thank you. Do you believe me?"

Sebastian surveyed the boy. Although his fair face was naturally ruddier than his sister's, and now of a manly brown: although his aquiline nose, dark brown eyes, and rich curling hair gave a more commanding beauty to his aspect, the lover saw something of the same earnest simplicity that had mastered him in Teresa; and with a firm and kind voice he answered, "I will."

Ranieri hastily recounted much of what had befallen him, already known in part to Sebastian; and so far its truth confirmed the belief of the boy's honesty. He finished by saying, "And will you take me to be your servant?"

"For my brother, Ranieri. Say no more; I know more than you think is known, and will await the rest."

"No, Sebastian; not yet for your brother. When I can make it known that I am undisgraced, even in seeming, you shall call me so; till then, if I am your meanest servant, I have more than my right, and more than I myself can thank you for."

Just so Teresa had spoken. Sebastian answered, "Be it as you will: you shall be to me my brother; to others my page: and right fortunate am I to gain so trusty a friend."

CHAPTER XXXV.

GREAT was the consternation of the Venetians at the defenceless state of their city. Many charged the advance of the Genoese on the ill-used Pisani, and blamed the indulgence of the senate which had released an unsuccessful commander from the punishment of his fault to resume the lead. Others hinted, cautiously and stealthily, at treachery; fearing that the very people they spoke to might themselves be the traitors, and revenge the suspicion in some dreadful way. More thought they read in the reverses of their arms the displea sure of heaven, and the doom of a sinful people. It was with the gloomiest countenances that the senators assembled in their spacious council-chamber, to deliberate on the next step to be taken. Not a few had come from Pisani's fleet, or from the scene of war on the sea-shore; and under their robes might be heard the clank of arms, covered, as in the last meeting that we recorded, by the senatorial robes, but not laid aside. Among these was Marco Morosini. Erect he walked, and seldom was his mien so cheerful. The large scar on his forehead, still redder than the skin around it, was an honorable ensign of the obstinacy with which he had resisted the foe at Chiozza. His cheeks were slightly tinged with a ruddy flush, so well had the sea air and camp life suited his health. The robe he wore hung open, and displayed the mail on his breast, which was cut and bent in every part, but only mended where most he needed it. His gray eyes flashed with more than common fire, so that to look upon him raised the courage of the timid.

When a goodly number had assembled, Andrea Contarini entered the hall, and walked to his throne. He also was upright, and his swelling chest seemed thrust out to stem the tide of trouble. His face was grave, but calm and steadfast, as that of one who knew the full danger, but feared not to meet all. The gray hair, that showed the whiter for the red cap which covered it, was thinner; but the snowy beard was thick and deftly trimmed; age could bleach its color, but could not in the smallest trifle chill the life and energy of the veteran. He seated himself on the throne, and for a few moments surveyed the assembly, while the last stragglers were coming in; then rising and speaking in a loud, firm voice, he said, "Most excellent fathers, few words will tell you the purpose of our meeting. The time has come for Venice to achieve her greatest glory, for now is her danger greater than ever it was. Our foe is in the lagoons; our advanced posts have been passed; our means are well nigh run out; and nothing remains to Venice, but the Venetians; nothing but the strength and wisdom of her sons. It is your part to say how that strength and wisdom shall be used, for all must be used, or all beside be lost. You know that the barrier at the port of Venice has been forced. How, we know not; but this we know, that at that post there were men more zealous, more faithful than almost any in our whole city. It was the fortune of war."

"Your pardon, excellent prince," cried Molino, rising with a flushed and angry countenance, his heavy loud voice ringing in the vaulted roof; "your pardon, if I say to you we must not be so easily content to lay the fault to the fortune of war. No, others must answer it to Venice. We must not—it is no time for us to dally with compliments, and parade our affection and respect, while Venice is threatened with destruction. Be it cowardice, be it ill-fortune, he that fails in her defence merits no pardon. He is not fit to be a citizen of Venice; but he that has been Venetian can be nothing else in this world. It were his best fate to die. Yes, I say it, though my friend should be the victim. There is one yet who must answer to Venice—there he sits: I accuse him to you, most excellent fathers. Let him defend himself if he can. I accuse him, my friend, Pietro di Bernardo, of treachery to Venice, for that he was too weak in her defence."

A murmur arose as the Avogadore took his seat. The doge had remained standing; but he also sat when Pietro di Bernardo stood up. The gay Pietro looked sad and downcast, and he leaned for support on the back of the bench behind him. "I do confess it," he said, "and crave nothing but that the pleasure of the state may be done on this worthless frame. It is true that numbers, who had escaped our guards at the outward barrier, poured upon us suddenly in the darkening day; it is true, that we fought until the chains themselves gave way, until our own dead lay heavy on many who had fallen and could not rise, and our own arms were faint with the loss of the blood that bathed the waters as they flowed in upon us; but had more valiant men possessed the post that we, in the pride and ardor of love for Venice, had thrust ourselves upon, they might perchance better have resisted; or if the unstable chains had defeated even them, they might somewhat more have thinned the number of the invaders. Let us, as we could not serve Venice with our arms, serve her in being examples of punishment." Ser Pietro covered his face with his hands.

The doge lifted up his finger, and stilled the murmur. "Messer Pietro di Bernardo's grief," he said, "is but the testimony to the zeal and devotion with which he resisted the dangers that close on Venice. But it is not our part to help ill fate in destroying the number of our faithful citizens. Rather let us devise the means of escaping—or rather of thrusting back this danger upon itself. We must throw the whole strength and wealth of Venice into the struggle; for better were it to spend all that she is worth—to spend Venice herself—than to let her fall a prize to the Genoese."

He was silent, and there was a pause, when Malipiero rose and with a pale face and quivering lips, cried—"Long enough have we suffered this oppression; too long have we looked to councils, and to generals, and to common stratagems of war, which settle nothing. Let us finish this. Let a sword be put into the hand of every Venetian, and let us rush upon our enemy. If man for man be killed, enough Venetians will remain to people these lagoons, and to make the city more terrible than ever."

This battle cry took the grave senate by surprise, and great numbers rose, shouting aloud. Contarini again raised his hand, the tumult was hushed. As the senators again sat down, Barbarigo remained standing. "I rejoice, most illustrious prince and most excellent fathers," he said, in a calm and pleasant voice, "at this outburst, so unused in our grave halls. I accept it as proof that the love of Venice and the courage of her sons are strong as ever. But it is not for us here in this senate to forget that we are something more than soldiers. It is not for us to scoff at the manifest displeasure of Heaven—for what but such high displeasure could thus have made the Venetians weak before the Genoese; what could have disarmed our noble and most brave defender, Ser Pietro di Bernardo ; what could have prevented even the powerful Messer Vittor Pisani from conquering with his accustomed skill the mariner's old enemies—the winds and waves ! What else has removed from us—we thought it mischance, but what else than the terrible wrath of God—St. Mark and the Holy Virgin intercede for us !—what else could have removed from us at such a time, our chief reliance—Messer Carlo Zeno ! Heaven has taken from us the means of victory. We have sent for our great captain ; but does not destruction march upon the city, even before he can possibly arrive, though the Englishman should have outstripped the winds ? Nay, do we know that our galley is still above the waters ? Did it not leave us in time of storm ! They do say too that there is treachery amongst us—the Englishman is a stranger—Nay, nay, excellent fathers, think not that I accuse that most noble stranger ; rather let me say that such accusal is base and not to believed except on proof. But shall we risk the fate of all our doomed race in defying Heaven ! Is Venice all that we possess ; or are these small islands in which we are now cooped up really Venice ! We are Venice ; and Venice is where we abide. We have fairer lands even than this. Candia is ours. A new empire might we create, and Candia, held by Venice, would become the centre of a new Christian empire in the east, rising where the ancient one falls. Let us conquer by yielding—exchange Venice for Candia—and strengthen our sons to avenge the defeat which we avoid."

The senators looked at each other in amaze, but not altogether in displeasure ; they talked in knots. Contarini sat silent, as though watching how the project worked. In the general move, Lionardo Morosini might be seen to approach his cousin and speak to him earnestly ; while Marco turned angrily from him.

" I do but say what Messer Alessandro would have counselled," whispered Lionardo, " had he encountered you on your landing."

" Alessandro ever counsels what is most for the honor of Venice ; and he never, Messer Lionardo, fails to be convinced when I have shown him such reasons as now I tell you." He rose hastily, and moving a step or two from his cousin, he spoke aloud. " Let us not be cast down, most excellent prince, because our perils are great ; for many of you, most excellent fathers, who have been as I have in our camp, know full well that our citizens have lost no jot of their prowess or their fidelity. No, the fortune of war is uncertain, most noble senators ; but our strength is as great as ever to seize the next turn in our favour. Nor is our wisdom so exhausted that we must say we have neither counsel nor strength left us to stand before our enemy, but must fly for safety like cranes before the hunter. Have we lost our reason in the tumult of arms ! Believe it not. I can say, that even the fatigues of the combat have not been able to make me sleep so hard at nights, but what I could devise plans for Venice and her succor. And this is my plan ; sharing in the impatience and devotion of the most illustrious and most noble Messer Jacopo Malipiero, but less in the fiery courage which makes that puissant cavalier so invincible in fight. Let us call upon the Venetians

for aid ; not by decree and the force of law, but by the force of honor and of conscience. Trust me, excellent fathers, this will bring far greater succors than would a forced subsidy. We will not tax them at all, we will not seize upon a single rower ; but we will ask them to give, for the love of St. Mark, of Venice, of their wives and children. We will promise them renown—renown for all ; profit for those that give freely ; and let us, to save our noble power, dispense some of its honors to those who most do devote their substance to our cause. To save the roll of our nobility, by a trifle extend it. High and wealthy merchants are there in this city, scarcely less noble than ourselves, yet by fortune, not so soon reaching this place as we did through our ancestors, are they shut out. If they do give what we do to preserve Venice, they are not less noble ; and let us call them noble. One word more ; if the senate in its wisdom do judge to accept the counsel of Messer Marin Barbarigo, one at least will never leave these his native islands ; but at the foot of the altar of Santo Stefano shall be found the mangled body of him whose forefathers have worshipped there ever since the church was built—whose name is as old as Venice, and fixed to the rocks on which our mansions stand."

Loud was the applause ; and senator after senator rose to say that the Morosini's plan was the wisest. Malipiero rushed across the hall, and grasping Morosini's hand, declared that he had saved the city. Yet did not Barbarigo's party, though few in number, so readily give up their counsel ; and the debate was kept up to a late hour of the day. At length, when Andrea Contarini was asked for his judgment, he spoke, and said that as each had by turns told his seeming, he thought each good and worthy to be done ; but that Morosini's was the one to do first, and Barbarigo's last of all ; therefore, at that present council, the doge would make choice of Morosini's device. And so it was decreed.

CHAPTER XXXVI.

THE patriotic Morosini had not misreckoned the effect of his project. Such speed was made, that before night it was proclaimed in the great square, that Venice, in the extremity of her peril, needed the aid of all true citizens to serve her by their persons or substance ; and that among those who gave most, either of money or men, or who best served the state by their acts, thirty men of the people should be made nobles of the grand council, they and their children for ever ; that each year for ever more fifty thousand golden ducats should be dispensed among others ; and that foreigners should have a farther guerdon, in being admitted as citizens of Venice with all privileges thereunto pertaining. No rest was there in the city that night. While some kept guard, others met in their houses, calculating what they might give ; some using their best wits to discover how little they could keep for themselves ; others to learn what their neighbors would give, and how therefore they themselves might buy the prizes with least cost. Betimes on the morrow, Andrea Contarini took his station in the hall of the grand council, which was thrown open to all who chose to enter with an offering. A multitude assembled at the entrance and in the great square; and as they came and went the bearers of aid were loudly greeted. The first to appear before the doge were two tall and stalwart youths, whose mail and browned faces showed that they had already been in the fight—Donato Bartolomeo and Giovannino, the sons of Guido Everardo; they came hand in hand; and Donato, with a modest mien, declared that he and his brother would give their persons to be disposed of at the pleasure of the senate, with their servant, at their own cost. Next came two other brothers—Marco and Aluise Boni, who promised in like manner to serve themselves, and to provide four bowmen, for two months. Others followed; one offering himself, another his men, others the usual pay of bowmen and rowers, eight ducats and four ducats a month, for different numbers, and different periods. At length came the venerable Bernardino de' Garzoni: after making his obeisance, he said: "Old age, and the near approach of death, most illustrious prince, make me think of others that die and of those they leave behind them; and, therefore, first will I offer to the state two hundred ducats of gold to give to the widows and children of the poor soldiers who are slain. That said, I will ask you to take part of what I possess through the strength and protection of this city—suffer me to pay for one month all the bowmen in your own galley, and all the bowmen of twenty-five galleys for half that time." The doge smiled, and bowed his head, thinking that the aged citizen had done; but he continued—"Farther, I would offer all the profits that come to me for moneys that I have lent. There are not a few small boats that I have, which are not worth mention, but that they may serve some use. Lastly—would I were richer—I do yield up to the state the two sons already at Lido, and the third, my young Giovannino, who will soon arrive from Bologna."

"I begin, Messer Bernardino," said the doge, with a pleasant smile, "to make sure of victory, and to think that both of us may yet live to hear the sounds of triumph once more resounding in Venice."

More followed, until Donado da Cà, supported by a youth, his servant, painfully approached the steps before the throne, and in a feeble voice declared that he would provide ten bowmen for two months; saying, "Moro would I give, and these poor arms should still combat for Venice; but all that my poor means could furnish was spent for my ransom when I was taken prisoner in the last war with the Lord of Padua; and for myself, the worst was done when these limbs were for ever made unfit to serve my country, for they put me to the torture."

"I came," said Marco Storlado, "to offer my son and twenty bowmen; but, in place of this my good friend Donado, I also will go with twenty other bowmen; so that Messer Francesco shall gain little by spoiling one Venetian."

"Well said, good Storlado," cried Raffain Caresini, the grand chancellor, rising from his seat; "and besides that my brother is going

with our bowmen, I will give five hundred, and he shall give three hundred ducats of gold, for the sake of Messer Donado."

"Good sirs," said Donado, "I did never think to find my maiming a source of riches, as now it is; and I would be tortured often and again, could my agony always bear such sweet fruits."

"Then," said Matteo Fasuolo, advancing, "do I hope that my poverty may yet serve the state: in ransom and in ventures seized at sea, the Genoese have taken all that I had, so that the very house I lived in I sold to pay my poor mariners. Some kind friends have fed me of their good bounty; I am so very poor that nought have I but this body, not yet quite past service; and I do hope, most illustrious prince, that Venice will vouchsafe to take it, for it is all I have to give."

"You have given more than any yet," said Contarini; "and you shall tell me your name; for we will set it down as that of the first that gave his all."

Marco Morosini rose from his seat, and said aloud: "I take shame to myself, Messer lo Doge, for that I, who did recommend that we should give to Venice all we could, have given less than the most generous of us all—this worthy citizen, whose name I know not."

"It is Matteo Fasuolo," shouted many voices; while Morosini approached and took his hand. "I cannot," said the senator, "offer so much as Messer Matteo Fasuolo; for my palace, my wealth, my kindred—they are not mine, but belong to my house. But in shame at his noble offering will I give all that is mine—all my moneys and wealth shall be at the use and service of the state while the war lasts."

"Viva Marco Morosini!" shouted those who filled the hall, patrician and plebian.

Morosini still stood beside Fasuolo, when a woman, closely veiled, drew near the throne steps. She was tall, and her walk was dignified; yet a certain timid doubt seemed to arrest her footsteps. Bowing to the doge, she held forth a small bag which seemed to be of some weight. The doge motioned for an attendant to take it, and the woman was about to retire, when the voice of the prince made her stop. "Is this a gift to the state, lady, or is it by some mistake that you bring it here?"

"It is gold, my lord, I think," said the man who had taken it.

"But is it your wish that it should be a gift?" said the doge, still speaking to the woman.

"It is for the state," she answered.

That voice! it thrilled through Morosini with a strange feeling of anger and re-awakened desire; for, though low and faltering, he knew it to be Teresa's.

"But as a gift or a loan?" asked the doge.

"Neither. It is the state's already; and yet it was hardly and nobly earned. My lord, I would say no more, but that it is the state's. Some day you shall be asked to remember that eighty-eight pieces of gold were this day given to the state."

She was retiring; when Morosini, with a half-formed impulse to make her disclose herself, partly through revenge, partly to bring her again into his power, cried—"Stay, my lord; perchance this fair lady offers to the state what is not her's to give. It may be that I could tell her history."

Teresa turned round, and shrunk as she recognized him.

"How is this!" asked Contarini.

"Spare me, my lord," she cried : "I came, trusting to the sacred purpose of this day for protection. What I have done has been for the justification of the injured and the dead ; but do not because I am defenceless make me expose myself to what would now be shame, though it shall one day be honor."

"You speak fair, lady ; and yet your right to give this offering is challenged ; and by one of such high regard, that it needs some stretch of faith to accept."

"Alas! my right to give it is but too simple ; there is none else to claim that miserable gold. Let your faith go so far, noble prince. Your hair has grown white, and yet in your countenance I see the kindness of young faith and the unfaded light of hope ; therefore you should have lived long enough to know how truth will abide and grow even where there is suspicion, or even vileness most foul ; as in rude nature, the flower is hidden among weeds. And if Messer Morosini," she added, drawing herself up, and speaking to him with a firmer voice, "who has guessed my humble self, must needs make me known, and all my misfortunes, let him not think that I will tremble in telling to Venice, before its doge, my poor history. Suffer me to depart."

"You shall receive no hurt, young maid," said the doge, "and shall depart at once, taking with you your gold."

"Nay, keep that ; I disclaim it. It is not mine."

"Why now you puzzle us ; for if it is not yours, you may not give it, and we may not take it. See you none here that would be sponsor for you."

"Alas! no."

"That will I be," said a man who stepped between Teresa and Morosini. At the sound of his voice, both started as though it had been some unearthly sound : it was Sebastian ! Morosini's pale face grew paler ; he clenched his hands and teeth, and stepping forward again was about to speak ; but his son's stern regard arrested him. He folded his arms, in silence, tightly embracing himself to master his panting rage. Teresa clasped her hands, and cried to Sebastian, in a hurried whisper, "Not now— not here ! Sebastian, meddle not with this."

"The riddle grows more difficult," said the doge. "What has brought Messer Sebastian to play so strange a part in it ?"

"My lord, I am from Pelestrina, with a message for your private ear. This is no time for disputes amongst ourselves. We should forget them. Enough that I will answer for this lady with my life."

"But know you on what quarrel ? I cannot suspect ill of one that hath so sweet a voice and speaks so well ; and were I here but as Andrea Contarini, I would take this offering which she has made for the state as most virtuously given : but it is your father that accuses her, and says that it is none of hers."

"Doth the lady say that the gold is hers ?"

"She does, and she does not."

"Then my lord, believe that it is hers to give, but not to keep."

"But your father !"

"He says nothing, my lord. He spoke knowing less than I do."

"How say you, Messer Morosini !"

"That if a son knows not when it is unseemly to gainsay his parent, the parent should stay that ugly sight by leaving the quarrel. I say no more; my lord." Morosini spoke in a low and muffled voice ; and turning round he left the hall.

The man that held the bag looked towards the doge, as if for his order ; and the prince, addressing Teresa, said—"And now, fair damsel, do you still will that we should keep this gold !

Her voice told that she was in tears. "It has been accursed, even to this last moment that I have had ought to do with it ; but it is shameless, and will be blessed for Venice's sake. Keep it, my lord : and say of it, not thanks, but that it is welcome."

"It is welcome. May you be happy, my daughter."

"My lord," said Sebastian, "I divine, though I know not why the offering is made ; and Venice shall one day know why, and for whom I have thus strangely been sponsor. Meanwhile, that which I have to tell you, brooks no delay : suffer me to see this lady properly guarded to her home, and then to attend on you."

"Do so ; you shall find me anon in my private room."

Sebastian took Teresa, still veiled, by the hand, and led her from the hall.

CHAPTER XXXVII.

TURNING to the right as they left the palace, Sebastian directed his way with Teresa to one of the smaller canals, hoping to find a boat to carry her homeward without being too much noted. They did not altogether escape unseen. A man, loitering among the idle crowd, started angrily as they passed him, and pressed forward to stop their way, but he could not make a path through the press until they had got beyond. When he was free, the man looked after them, and seemed to change his mind ; for instead of hastening to address them, he slowly followed, stealthily dogging their steps. At the water's edge Sebastian stood, and looked up and down the canal ; on which their pursuer came up, asked if it was a boat they sought, and he ran off to seek one. Running towards the canal of St. Mark, the man hurriedly looked around. He was choice in his mood, for instead of hailing the nearest boat, he passed on to one a little farther on.

"Tonio !" he cried, breathless with running and his eagerness, "wouldst earn a ducat or two ! Give me your place then, and let me go with your good fellow. Dost not know me— dost not remember Nadale, honest Nadale ! Be assured of your money—I will pay you in gentleman fashion."

"And who will be your surety, Master Nadale ?"

"My surety ! I myself will be it, for I will go with you or your fellow. But despatch, good Tonio."

"Why then Pietro here shall give you his place, and I will go myself," answered Tonio.

Pietro obeyed ; Nadale jumped in, and in a minute the boat stood ready to receive the pair that awaited it. Having taken his seat, and turned his regard for a moment from his companion, Sebastian glanced at the boatman that had been so ready in his service. The face was not unknown to him, and though he could not tell where he had seen it, it occasioned some disquiet to him. The insolent bully, whom he had surprised in Bianca's room, whom he had struck down in the place of St. Mark, was, indeed, little to be known in the new boatman ; that terrible blow of the outraged lover's fist had so battered the ruffian's jaw, that it had been ill to mend, and stood all askew ; the rugged beard swerved aside as though it were for ever blown by a strong wind ; the brutal features were sharpened, but not softened by sickness ; an ashy paleness lent a more deadly expression to the natural villainy of the face ; the sunken eyes, the lids dragged somewhat to one side with the hoisting of the jaw, glared under the contracted brow with a more settled malignity ; and the once sturdy bravo would have been ashamed to own this goal hospital creature for his counterpart. Sebastian had doubted his own faint memory, and imputed his dislike to nought but the man's sinister looks. He distrusted him enough, however, to prevent going nearer to Teresa's house than midway up the Cannreggio ; where he gave their conductor a ducat, and they landed. Nadale watched them as they walked away ; then looking for an instant at the coin, he threw it to Tonio, jumped ashore and followed. He saw them enter the house.

Once more alone with Sebastian, Teresa took his hand, and smiling sadly, she kissed it. "You will think, my Sebastian, it is so dear to me to be saved by you, that I wantonly make the need for it. But chide me not. That miserable gold weighed upon my heart ; and there seemed no way but one to repair my poor father's most cruel, but most generous fault."

"Chide you, my sweet life ! when I chide the sun for shining, or you for loving. But these dangers ever remind me that while I am away, you are defenceless — and how defenceless ! Be it so no more. Taking counsel with myself, I have devised a way to place you in safety. Of all my friends, none is so noble and so powerful as Messer Carlo Zeno, and none of such perfect generosity. Know, too, that he has a wife worthy of himself—a Justiniani ; as indeed, the first was too ; for how could he join himself to what were unworthy ? And so the great lady of Greece, who wooed his early love in honor of his young deeds, and the noble Venetian lady, whom afterwards he chose to be the solace of his riper years,—both were such as befits Zeno. Madonna Caterina, whom I know well, is a most discreet and noble lady. Let me take you to her, and for the sake of the true love and service that I render to her consort, she will afford you safety and protection. Say that it shall be so, and we will again depart at once."

Teresa did not answer for a little while, but looked down, musing ; and then raising her eyes, she said—"It must not be so, Sebastian.

It may be that a time shall come when you may own me, though still unfortunate and disgraced before the world ; but let that not happen without need. Perchance, when Venice has recovered from these perils, the voice of justice and of the humble may be heard, and my father may disprove his false accusers : but not till then—or at least, not while you have trouble enough of arms and dangers—not while Venice needs you with all your high renown, unsullied by taint of suspicion, shall you lead forth the traitor's daughter. Meanwhile, here I am safe unknown ; and with Rosa's watchful care—so faithful, so bold, so gentle, I am safe from harm. Believe me, I will not tempt danger again ; so chide me not in the guise of offering safety to be bought with harm to you."

Nor could all Sebastian's tender urgency drive her from her resolve ; which she justified as he departed, with new protestations that she would thenceforth keep close in her asylum until he should return again.

When he went forth, was it the same evil-eyed boatman that he saw skulking away at a distance !

CHAPTER XXXVIII.

THE year 1380 opened upon the Venetians with the most adverse prospects. In the long and tedious war, although their resistance had been brave and powerful, the Genoese had upon the whole, gained ground, inch by inch ; Chiozza they had so long held that it might almost be considered a Genoese town ; and the whole of Brondolo was theirs. Thus, supported as they were, by Carrara on the main land, they had become something like a strong and conterminous power, such as had never before menaced the Venetians ; whose only powerful neighbors hitherto had been landsmen, and utterly incapable of coping with them on the sea. Within the lagoon, and behind Brondolo the intruding enemy had also a marine force supported by that which it retained within the port of Chiozza ; some time since, a landing had been effected on the island of Malamocco ; and the extent of ground within the power of the Genoese had gradually extended itself ; we have already seen how by the treachery which sapped the strength of the Venetians, a part of the marine force of their foe had penetrated through the barriers into the port of Venice. The long line of islands which separated its peaceful waters from the Adriatic, and really constituted the wall of the city, had been overpassed and nothing now remained between its palaces and the enemy ; its treasury was empty until recruited by the bold measure which the senate had adopted. Its means of defence were still numerous ; no power could easily have seized the city itself, peopled as it was by a race which considered itself at least equal to any in the world, and whose pride and daring were strengthened as the danger increased ; the nobles alone would have formed a band of Immortals sufficient to defend the canals against any invaders for many a day ; to say nothing of the forces scattered over the island   the east of the lagoon ; the greater part of   zlamocco was covered by the fortifications, partly of stone, but more of wood, which had been hastily extended to shut out the invaders, and every point was in possession of a numerous force, chiefly supplied by the Venetians themselves, with whom the small town of the island was filled. We have seen how by that successful treachery which vitiated their councils an important post had been entrusted to the Condottiere Roberto da Recanati, though the jealous policy of the Venetians had stationed a band, whose red sleeves and fresh color showed them to belong to the little army headed by the Englishman, William Cooke, as a guard over the more wily mercenary. Great part of the republic's army, however, was posted on the long littorale of Pelestrina, which stretched from Malamocco to the port of Chiozza; the intervals between the fort at the northern end of the island, and the fortified camp which lay about midway, and thence onward to the south was filled up with hastily constructed towers of wood or stone, connected by palisadoes and trenches which received constant additions, not interrupted by those petty skirmishes between straggling bands, and crossing galleys, to which the war had now dwindled; the Genoese thinking to wear out the besieged.

On this island lay the worst danger of the Venetians. Their treasury was low, and the mercenary troops that now thronged it began already to clamor, and to say, that if Venice could not pay for its salvation, Genoa would buy the city. The troops had been as much as possible disposed in separate bands, with small bodies of Venetian soldiers, picked for their courage and constancy, placed between them; while the high repute of da Recanati had also induced the senate to impose a share of that duty on him. The more discontented of the soldiery were posted about the chief camp in the centre of the rest, cut off from communication with the Genoese. To the south of the camp had been collected a strong force, where was stationed Marco Morosini, and with him was a small guard of native soldiers; to the right were seen, ever alert, the ruddy warriors whom William Cooke commanded, with red vests, well burnished arms, and the long bows of their country; to the left was the flower of Recanati's band, gathered from every part of the Italian Peninsula—the Neapolitan might be known by his big stature and indolent bearing; the Florentine by his compact and active figure; the Piedmontese by his height and presence.

Instead of occupying, as many of the leaders did, one of the houses scattered about the island, and assumed for the occasion by the senate as the property of the state, Marco Morosini chose the more soldierly plan of pitching his tent at the post of duty. A large pavilion—capacious, that his military state might be amply furnished, but bare of all that savored of ornament, had become his dwelling. Here, on the last night of the year, was the senator-warrior seated at a small table, illumined amid the darkness around by a single lamp. He had been telling his project for recruiting the treasury of the city. Near the same table sat Sebastian, whom Pisani had made his father's lieutenant, little knowing, as perchance he would little have heeded, the feud between

father and son; on the opposite side were two men who seemed drawn together by the force of contrast. One, who sat upright in his chair, with one hand firmly clenched on his sword-hilt, where it had lain motionless throughout Morosini's story, was not much above the middle height, but compact and neatly, if not elegantly made; the mail which clothed his broad shoulders, left bare a throat whiter than many a Venetian maid's, and the closely cropped hair was of a sandy yellow, approaching to red as it ran into his whiskers and beard; his round features and laughing blue eyes, gave a good natured expression to his face, which was subdued, but not disguised, by the grave bearing of a military commander; and the frank countenance at once bespoke that generous faith which made William Cooke as well trusted by the Venetians as any of their own race. Next to him was the no less famous Captain Roberto da Recanati, whose tall frame resting partly against the table and partly against the back of his chair, seemed rather that of a lady's gallant than of the hardiest soldier of the time; not indeed but what strength was manifest in his mail-clad chest, and daring, or even audacity in his countenance; but the short black curls that shaded his brow, the well trimmed silken beard and penciled eyebrows, and the soft voice seemed formed rather to impress and to persuade than to command; his long limbs were elegant and slender, even to an appearance of weakness and effeminacy, and his narrow hand and tapering fingers seemed better suited to the jeweled rings they wore than to the hilt of the long sword by his side; his features were small and delicate, but a long and slightly aquiline nose and compressed lips, gave the character of a manly firmness to his face; his large black eyes were somewhat shut, and being set close under the brow, with a sharp and watchful aspect, they imparted to the sleek form of his outline the expression of a serpent; and so he was esteemed; daring above all in fight, Roberto da Recanati was a serpent in council; but accounted unbroken in faith to those who bought the services of his band, none possessed higher fame for the honor of a condottiere. He too had listened to Morosini with motionless attention.

"And thus," said the senator, as he finished, "thus, Messer da Recanati, will we Venetians satisfy the clamors of those soldiers who serve Venice for money, and not for love."

"Say it, Messer Morosini," replied the condottiere, with a smile, "not of those before you. Our men heed little of the cares of state; and those who command, you know, must also serve their followers."

"I know it, I know it well," answered Morosini. "I know, Messer da Recanati, that in you and in our English friend, the state has faithful servants, and that money little sways you. It speaks, indeed, your power over your men, that you have so long kept them silent, while the state, which once paid so freely, has withheld from them their due. It tells us how the fortunes of Venice have fallen, when Roberto da Recanati's men begin to reproach her with her poverty; and I do wonder that these sturdy Englishmen have not done the like."

"You have paid us, Messer Morosini," said

Cooke, "in advance ; so generous has the senate been to us, who have so often served you, that we may yet go on for some time more before we begin to give you credit in our trade. Therefore, pray you, tell the senate, that in striving for money in these hard times, it may leave out the men of William Cooke. And rather will I myself give some little treasure that is mine, than take from Venice what it can so ill give."

"Nay, nay," said Recanati, "you may say as much for me ; though my servants do not follow me quite so blindly as Messer Guglielmo's. But, Messer Morosini, have you told this device of yours to your friend Alessandro ?"

"No ; why ask you ?"

"For many reasons. And first, to know whether he would think it wise that you should surrender so much, unless some good were to be bought by it. And next, to know how soon you can make your citizens give all you ask. I doubt it—I doubt whether their generosity will equal yours ; and whether, even were they so generous, they could find their gold so fast as your friends here in Pelestrina will ask it. Remember, Messer Morosini, it was not my men that asked at first—it is not my men that call out most greedily ; but that here, in Pelestrina, have you some thousands, whom you have hemmed in like prisoners, lest they themselves should take boat, and seize the senate house in pledge for repayment. Remember that this night has been fixed by many of the captains as the last day to which they will wait. And here, while we sit, before the sun begins to sink, may we expect to hear the shouts of some new multitude, demanding that Venice should yield in this hopeless war. It is a hopeless war. I still say that I will serve you ; but I serve against hope. But if I dared to say it, all the danger that Venice has braved might be stopped at once, were some better and discreeter man to lead her councils."

Sebastian started to his feet. "What words are these, Messer da Recanati !—and who has taught them to you ? Treason is indeed ripe among us, when it begins to speak in the mouths of our soldiers and captains. Who has been teaching you, Messer Condottiere ?"

Slightly turning his head, but keeping the quiet softness of his voice, da Recanati replied, "Be less impatient, Messer Sebastiano. We often say things little discreet ; but I believe none have taught me any more than yourself. We all have a choice, and I have taken mine, which is to serve Venice."

"True, true," cried Morosini, "and faithfully. There have been many who do say that Andrea Contarini served Venice better when he was younger. But we listen not to these things, Messer da Recanati ; and if you hear this said, count it only said by the foolish. Here in Venice, I doubt much whether any Venetian could so far forget his birth. And our soldiers are not traitors. We have hired them, and it is the naturalest thing in the world, that if they do not receive their hire, they should forget their duty. But give me your aid, Messer da Recanati—and you, Messer Guglielmo, to pacify these men for two more days ; and if, in that time, I do not bring you some gold, and more promises, take me to pledge, and tear me to pieces among you. To you, Messer Sebastiano, I have permission

to leave this post ; and certain do I feel, that with a son of our house it must be safely entrusted." So saying, he arose ; and in a few minutes he was speeding his way towards the meeting of the senate, for which he had been summoned.

The day was black, and there was little stir among the Genoese. They seemed disposed to leave their work to be performed by the trouble and treachery working among the Venetians ; and they did not altogether count wrongly. The murmurs which had been heard on every side in Pelestrina increased as night advanced ; as Sebastian kept watch with Cooke, the loud sounds that arose behind them in the distance, denoted that some tumult had arisen ; and in making their rounds, they found knots of men talking among themselves. But though rumours had reached even to that distance from the camp, they could learn nothing distinct. At length, so uneasy did Sebastian become, fearing lest the whole fortune of the city should be destroyed by the want of strength to keep in order its own forces, that, leaving his post to the charge of Cooke he set out with a small guard for the camp. As he approached it, bodies of men, hurrying hither and thither, showed that his fears were not altogether unfounded, and that some strange disorder had broken up all regularity. He stopped the passengers occasionally, but could gather nothing more than the old complaint—the soldiers wanted to be paid. The camp presented an appearance of one recently seized by the enemy ; for large bands of soldiers were traversing the ground, singing and brawling. In an open place at the centre, near a house occupied by the Proveditore Vendramini, he found a knot of nobles, who were earnestly discoursing with the men, and among them. To his surprise, he saw that Roberto da Recanati had come before him. The proveditore was urging, with little effect, the old lesson of patience, while Gianni da Pioveri, one of the honestest of the mercenary leaders, was scornfully rejecting that scanty comfort. Vendramini himself seemed as if he doubted his own words ; but at length he pointed to the silence of Recanati, and rebuked the other captains for their lesser patience.

"Aye," replied Gianni, "Messer Recanati is a wiser man than we are ; and doubtless he has his reasons. Perhaps it may be that he is wealthier, and can himself pay his men ; or, it may be, that being more powerful, the senate has given to him the treasure which we poorer soldiers cannot have."

At this Recanati stepped forward, and pressing his hand upon his breast, assured the brawlers that he was no more favored than themselves ; and he appealed to Sebastian to say whether even he had not difficulty in silencing his men. "I do believe," he cried, "and that is the reason that I tell my men, that the senate will pay us our due ; nay, I do believe that long ere this we should have had all that we have earned ; and that it is not that the senate look coldly on us, but that they are poor—that they have not the money—that Venice is quite bare."

"Why, then, if so," cried da Pioveri, "it were better to end the war at once. We are not Venetians ; and if Venice cannot be saved, it were better to hand her over at once, than to risk our lives in a losing war. What is it that we fight for? Does Venice so freely bestow its honors and its privileges on all that serve it? Will it count us her citizens? Will it——"

"I do beseech you," said da Recanati, "to be silent. Messer Vendramini has asked us to delay eight days longer; and though it be eight days, or twice eight days, or any time, I would be content to wait. Indeed, I believe it will be longer. I know not where Venice is to seek her wealth, hemmed in within these lagoon—without merchandize, almost without food; for even the path to Treviso cannot long remain open. And where Venice can find the means to pay us I know not. Still let us serve for our good fame; and if Venice be destroyed, let us fall fighting in her defence, that our name may live in history."

"Why, Messer da Recanati," said Vendramini, "you encourage the men in such fashion, that they are like to die of fear if you talk much longer. I tell you that the senate has new projects; that it is taking fresh counsel; and that before many days have passed, we shall find some plan to satisfy you all. We will sell our houses before we leave our friends unrequited."

"So," cried da Piovere, "you have told us any time these last six months; but I do not hear that any houses have been sold yet. No, we are now resolved: and this night, as many of us as can find boast, will pass straight to Venice, where we will tell the doge, that if we are paid we stay, and that if we are not paid, we shall hold Pelestrina for the Genoese. Therefore, Messer Vendramini, stay me no longer; for our time is past already."

"If it be so," said Vendramini, looking about him as if in doubt, "we must stop this traitor project; and here, Messer Gianni da Piovere, I seize you as a traitor to the state."

"Those seize who have the power; those are seized, Messer Vendramini, who are weak. I will not tell my men to seize you, because I know you mean no harm. But if I do not, count it rather my courtesy than any need I have."

Vendramini's face flushed; and looking to those behind him, he cried again, "Let him be seized!"

Sebastian alone advanced, seeing that none dared to touch the audacious condottiere. But da Piovere, taking him by the wrist, said, "Messer Sebastiano Morosini, look around and see which of us is like to seize the other." Then raising his hand, he called out, "Which are my men? who are with me?" And at the instant a loud shout arose from the entire crowd that surrounded the small knot of Venetian nobles and the grumbling leaders. "You, most noble sirs," said da Piovere, "are our prisoners; as indeed, you have been the whole time that want of pay has made our soldiers your enemies. Therefore fear not; for your danger is no greater now than then."

"And you, Messer da Recanati," said Sebastian, "do you take part with these? Are you one of the enemies of Venice, because you are not paid?"

"My men are so, if you will. But I, like yourselves, am here a prisoner. Think you that I could force my way, or bend to my will this turbulent crowd? Is it so, Messer da Piovere?"

"No, surely not; we have but two parties here—those who join us, and those who oppose us, and any may take which side they will. But I doubt those who oppose us, have small chance of victory. And if you will not be convinced, Messer Sebastiano, we will try it again. Shout once more, my men! Who are for the new bargain with Venice!"

Again was there another shout, loud, prompt, and simultaneous as the former. As it died away, there was a faint echo in the distance.

"Aye, listen," cried da Piovere; "they answer us afar. It is the same all over the island."

"I fear me," cried Vendramini, "that there is no hope for us, Messer Sebastiano, except in letting these cavaliers go on their errand to Venice; and perhaps there the senate may teach them a higher duty."

"Why perhaps it may, if it have money enough," said da Piovere. "Hark again, Messer Sebastiano—they are answering us like two cocks at a distance. Do you think that if we were not of one mind, we could shout so well together? Crow again, companions—let them hear us once more." Those around him obeyed, and once more the shout rang through the market place.

Vendramini drew Sebastian aside. "This," he said, "is fearful. I know not what to do; I command here no longer; and Messer Pisani is overtasked in defending the very canals of Venice. Messer Barbarigo, who is proveditore with me, says nought, and I do suspect that he would yield, and let these fellows pass to Venice. But if once they were there, we must surrender the city to them, or drive them out as enemies; and in either way we are lost."

"Let me," cried Sebastian, "fetch hither our own men, and Messer Guglielmo Cooke; and we will finish the quarrel here in Pelestrina."

"Nay, not so; I have thought of that. But Messer Barbarigo knows that we are too few for the traitors. Alas! alas! that men should thus break their faith. I can devise nothing better than to send to the doge and the senate, to tell them what straits we are in, and to prepare them to receive these their visiters; and I can think of no better messenger and discreeter than yourself. Haste, then, to the city; and while you are gone, we will do our best to stay these impatient men."

"I will go at once, so that none see me. But I would rather that you should take the sword out of these traitors' hands, and scourge them with it."

"Why so I would; but I dare not make the venture alone; and Messer Barbarigo——"

"I will depart. But lead them into your house—the leaders, I mean—that they may not see me go. Farewell; I will bring, either word to deal roughly with these bargainers, or the doge himself."

———◆———

CHAPTER XXXIX.

Vendramini so far obeyed his young friend's counsel, that he prayed da Piovere to confer

L

with him in his own lodging. At first the sturdy condottiere refused, saying that they could as well confer in the open place ; but da Recanati assented ; and in brief time they entered the hall of the house that served the proveditore for council chamber ; Recanati took care to leave some few of his own men near the door. Exhausted with anxiety, the proveditore threw himself into a chair. His colleague sat close to him ; and others entered, taking their seats or standing as they listed. But the heated Gianni da Piovere would not sit.

"And now that we have entered," he cried, what more have we to say ? Think you that I can linger here, while those shouts keep calling me to take boat for Venice ?"

"I would convince you," replied Vendramini, "that the senate must soon have wherewithal to satisfy you. And Messer Barbarigo will say as much."

Barbarigo answered not.

"Messer Barbarigo," cried da Piovere, "is tired of promises—he has grown bare of them, as bare as Venice of treasure. There is nothing left for us but Venice itself ; and that will we go fetch, with your leave, and that of Messer Sebastiano—why he is here no more ! Have we frightened the young man, that he has fled ?"

"Messer Sebastiano," said da Recanati, "is not one to be frightened. Perhaps the proveditore can tell us why he has gone ?"

"Nay, I know nothing," answered Barbarigo, breaking silence for the first time.

"Then shall Messer Vendramini tell us. He says nothing. There is treachery here, sirs. I have not liked this enterprise of Messer da Piovere ; but if he is to be betrayed, then will my honor force me to side with him rather than his betrayers."

"And do you too abandon us ?" exclaimed Vendramini.

"I abandon none. It is we who are abandoned. I see it all—our blood has been spent in vain—the promised treasure comes not, and now spies are sent to spread rumors against us, and to betray us. Da Piovere, I go with you to Venice."

"Be welcome—of all men in the army most welcome," said his brother condottiere. "Let us then dally no longer."

Vendramini looked aghast. He turned a bewildered despairing look to the other nobles ; but little comfort saw he in their faces. Barbarigo sat still and expressionless as marble. Lionardo Morosini looked undaunted ; nay, he almost sneered ; but he spoke no word of counsel. The rest were as dismayed and bewildered as Vendramini himself.

"Stay," he cried, "one short delay. Messer da Piovere, never yet did I ask boon of man ; but now will I entreat of you to grant me this —one other day. Bethink you, that it may to yourself be the saving of honor, with no loss of profit. I beseech you grant me this. Think how great a city totters to its fall, and spare us."

Da Piovere laughed. "Let those shouts answer you, Messer Vendramini ; for I am loth to speak out a refusal to so courteous a gentleman."

The shouting truly was loud and long ; it sounded like a body of men approaching to the rest, and swelling the noise with fresh voices. It was like some mad feast, so shrill and lusty was the cry.

"This," cried Vendramini, "is no echo of yours. There is something new astir."

"Aye, aye, more of them."

"Hark, again !"

All listened. Vendramini started, and flung his arms aloft, wild with joy.

"They shout 'Carlo Zeno !' He is come !"

Barbarigo, too, started and turned pale, like da Recanati, who bent a fierce look on Vendramini, as though he would have smote him. Da Piovere laughed again, crying, "Farewell, Messer Proveditore ; more such pleasant dreams to you." And he moved towards the door of the hall.

It was opened by Edward, who, entering the hall, made room for Carlo Zeno, and his companion Luigi Morosini. Looking around him with a pleasant smile, Zeno said, "I have come in happy time, for my path I found full of lusty soldiers, and their leaders I find in council."

"Alas ! Messer Zeno," answered Vendramini, approaching to take his hand, "you find us in most unhappy time ; for the soldiers that seemed to you so ready, are ready to attack, not to defend Venice ; and we in council here are defeated by the traitors that would lead them."

Zeno halted in his advance. "You speak riddles," he answered ; "I have heard, indeed, through these my friends that came to fetch me, how Venice had been beleaguered by the Genoese ; and I have heard too of treasons in the city ; but surely I see around me none that I know for other than honest men ?" As his eye passed from one to another, it rested on Recanati, and he started, adding, "At least none that I know to be other than honest. Which is the traitor ?"

"Say traitors," replied Vendramini, "for there are more than one. And ask da Piovere ; let him tell the tale."

"How is this, my friend da Piovere ?" asked Zeno, "surely you have not turned traitor ? You were wont to have more skill in the field than in council ; and I fear if you have turned senator, you may have made mistakes. What is it that you want ?"

"Nay ;" answered the condottiere, laughing, as if for shame, "let us talk no more of that : we have wanted, as soldiers do want, either victory or pay ; and now that you are come, we are secure of both. But, in sooth, for a long time past neither have we had to cheer us."

"You shall have both if I can bring them to you ; and pay at least you shall have, for my own means are not exhausted, as they shall be presently if Venice need them all. But you spoke, Messer Vendramini, of more than one traitor. Messer da Piovere is none—where are they then ?"

Vendramini pointed to Recanati.

To Zeno's inquiring glance, the condottiere returned a steady regard. Drawing himself up to his full height, he stood for a moment as if uncertain how to act. His eye turned hastily to the table where sat Barbarigo, and then to Lionardo Morosini and then again he looked at Zeno.

"You are silent, Recanati," said Carlo.

"I was silent, Messer Zeno, because the proveditore spoke of traitors, not of me; but I see that an enemy has come among us, and I am not so easy as da Piovere to think that one man can bring back the fortune and the treasure which the whole senate and people of Venice have lost; we have fought for Venice for many a weary month, and when we ask our guerdon we are paid by being called traitors, and then by some fancy of what one great general is to do for us—I am not safe here, let me pass to my men," and he moved towards the door.

"Not so, Messer Recanati," answered Zeno, stopping his passage; "you shall not leave us in this mood. I would satisfy you as I have satisfied da Piovere before you depart.

"Why then, Messer Zeno," answered Recanati, "count me not one to be satisfied like da Piovere. If my suspicions were slower than his, as Messer Vendramini will tell you they were, once aroused they are more fixed; and I say to you, that a few fair words or a few frowns shall not bow me down; let me pass, Messer Zeno." His eyes grew darker, and again he moved forward; Zeno laid his hand upon him to stay him, but Recanati rudely pushing him back cried, "Violence is then to be used;" and rushing hastily to the door he threw it open, calling out as loudly as he could, "Where are the friends of Recanati! save me, save me!"

"What folly is this!" cried Zeno, "there is none threatens you here, Messer Recanati. Bring back the brawling fellow, Edward, and close the door."

The Englishman essayed to obey, and while he and Luigi seized Recanati by the arm to draw him back, he tried to push the doors close with his foot, but Recanati's men, now pressed into the hall, and the door could not be closed.

Barbarigo had risen from his seat, and with Lionardo and the other nobles had approached the entrance of the hall, but all stood as if bewildered.

"See you not," cried Recanati to his men, "that I am a prisoner—they have called me traitor, and when I would have fled to my people, they have held me fast, I know not for what violence."

Vendramini endeavored to make him listen to the assurances that no harm was intended to him, but he would not be pacified: and while he continued to call out like a man in fear, his people pressed into the doorway and kept others back.

"What folly is this," again said Zeno, "be still, Messer Recanati; listen, sir, to me." As he spake, he again seized Recanati by the arm to force his attention; but breaking from those that held him, the condottiere cried with increasing rage—

"I see, I see, Messer Vendramini, it is my life you seek, but think not you shall buy it so cheap."

And before any one was aware, he drew from his belt a short dagger, with which he suddenly and fiercely struck Carlo Zeno full in the middle of his chest: the blade broke short off, so that the hilt remained in his hand. Like lightning the swords of Edward and Luigi were out of their scabbards, but as he struck the blow, Recanati had hastily drawn back among his men, and the blood which followed the stroke of Edward's sword was not that of their leader. Uttering a loud cry, Vendramini threw himself unarmed between the combatants, exclaiming,

"Back sirs, back; let us not set the whole town in arms!"

Others of the nobles pressed around Carlo Zeno, and seized him to prevent his falling; but still upright as ever, he gently put them aside, and plucking forth from his clothes the blade of Recanati's dagger, he held it up crying.

"The traitor's weapon was traitor to himself, it is but a scratch, signori miei; for Zeno is too old a soldier to travel in war time unarmed;" and he knocked his hand against his breast, showing them by the jangle which they heard that he had a stout shirt of mail under his vest, in which the violence of Recanati's blow had bedded the point of his weapon, though it scarcely touched the flesh beneath. "But sirs," he continued, "are we to be beard-ed thus by a traitor and his band? are we so few or so scantily armed, that this dozen of men can scare us? once more then, seize the traitor."

Himself setting the example he rushed among the condottiere's men; surprised by the suddenness of the attack, and hesitating perhaps to wage open war with so many of the nobles of Venice, the traitorous crew feebly resisted, and in a few seconds Recanati was held firmly by four or five of the nobles, who had now gained courage and energy from the example of their trusted leader. In the mean time, too, others of the soldiery had entered the hall, and when Recanati surveyed their numbers, he resigned himself in sullen daring to the fate that might await him.

"We must," said Zeno, "crush this conspiracy at its root. Let him be guarded; and to-morrow he shall be sent to Venice for judgment of the Ten."

But Vendramini seized the arm of Zeno, and speaking low and earnestly, pleaded for the baffled traitor.

"Bethink you, Messer Zeno," he said, "that this conspiracy began not with Recanati. As he was the boldest to carry it out, so he was the very last to join it. Bethink you that your coming should be graced rather by fresh harmony, than by blood and death: and much I fear me, that if this captain were slain, so enraged would the others be, that our whole army would be turned to foes. His mistake is not greater than da Piovere's whom you so easily forgave; but that he has been more audacious, which also you should forgive, for it is a soldier's vice."

"It is not for me," answered Zeno, "to judge, but for the Ten."

"Nay, it is for us here to judge in times like these. If we send this man to Venice, he must perforce be adjudged to death, but here in this chamber we can forget what has happened."

Calling to him Barbarigo, Vendramini made him join in his entreaties, and seeing that his prayers were of no avail, he would have knelt, but Zeno prevented him.

"Well, noble sirs," cried he, "I have ever found it best to meet and crush danger when first it shows its head, but truly the senate has yet given me no office : it is mine to obey, not to command, and you shall do with Messer Recanati as you will. I have no farther will in this business."

"Then," said Vendramini aloud, "all shall be forgotten. You have found us, Messer Zeno, in most miserable estate, with doubts and treasons amongst us, and discord among ourselves; your arrival shall begin a new history; from this moment we shall have hopes in place of fears ; trust and good faith instead of suspicion and treachery. Messer da Recanati, you are released. Let your men withdraw ; let all withdraw. And while we retire, Messer Zeno, to give you that rest and ease which your voyage must need, one of your friends shall hasten to bear to Venice the glad tidings of your arrival."

"Be it so," answered Zeno ; "and let the messenger be Messer Odoardo, who has so well performed the service for which he was chosen."

CHAPTER XL.

Sebastian returned to Pelestrina before it was light, and learning the joyful tidings that the long-wished man had arrived, he went at once to the lodging which Zeno had chosen in Vendramini's house. Zeno slept. He had sought repose, he said, that he might work the earlier ; and Sebastian sat by his bedside.

Not long after, Zeno awoke, sat up in his bed, and knowing his friend, he said without greeting—

"Sebastian, find me some trustworthy man with whom Recanati has been talking."

"Myself."

"Does he disclose his secrets to you ?"

"No ; perhaps he would think it dangerous."

"Some other then."

"My father is another, and Guglielmo Cooke."

"Neither ; they would not see, the one for his simple mind, the other—know you of none besides ?"

"Of none except a boy, Ranieri Arduino."

"Arduino ! the son of Jacopo !"

"The same."

"And what then is this boy ?"

Sebastian hastily told Ranieri's history, not concealing from his friend even the part that Teresa had in it, and then telling how Recanati had of late seemed to court the friendship of the youth.

"And when was that ?" asked Zeno, who had listened in silence.

"But two days since."

"Bring the boy to me."

Sebastian took his leave and hastened to his tent to fetch Ranieri : with whom, not long after, he returned to Zeno's presence.

"Here," he said, "is the young friend of whom I spoke, Ranieri Arduino."

"Why," said Zeno, "you told me of a boy, but here I see a man."

"Truly," answered Sebastian, "Ranieri grows fast, and if his friends are absent for a short space, they may well mistake how to call him ; and you see his beard now begins to bud, so that he will not much longer be offended with the name of boy."

"In sooth," said Zeno, "he is a tall fellow —you have a sister, Messer Ranieri ; is she tall too ?"

"I think," replied the youth, "that she is nearly of my own height."

"Aye, and but a little while ago you would have been proud to say that you were nearly of her height. Now tell us—Roberto da Recanati has been speaking with you ; what has passed between you ?"

Without pausing for excuses, or lack of thought, the youth told the two nobles, how, early one morning, while he had been loitering about Sebastian's tent, he had been accosted in a soft and courteous manner by Roberto da Recanati. "He spoke to me for some time," said Ranieri, "as if he knew not who I was, and only discovered it from something that I had said ; and then suddenly he cried, ' What, then, are you the youth that gave up his father to the Ten ?' "

"And what answered you to that !" said Zeno.

"I answered nothing, for I felt angry; and yet was he so courteous in his manner, that I scarcely knew why I should be so. I suppose he saw my anger, for he said, ' Nay, be not offended, for I asked only to be sure to whom I spoke to.' And then he said, ' Messer Ranieri, you are discreet beyond your years, and, if I mistake not, you have the full trust of your friend, Messer Sebastiano Morosini.' I told him that I believed so ; and he said, ' Does Messer Sebastiano know the tale that is told of you in Venice !' Then I felt angry again, and I said, Why do you ask ! on which he smiled, and said that he would not ask farther if it displeased me. But so he went on, sometimes asking questions, and sometimes telling me, in dark and doubtful words, that if I chose, I might reach to great distinction ; that I could have high rewards ; and that Messer Sebastiano might grow powerful ; and he thought, from what he knew of me, that I could contrive these things ; and also, as Messer Sebastiano had so far trusted me, that he would not be displeased."

"And what answered you !" said Zeno.

"Indeed I answered very little. At first I felt disposed to tell him roughly, that I would listen to no traitor. But I bethought me that I had better take sager council than my own ; so that I told him I could say nothing, but that I would speak to him again. And thus he left me."

"You should have spoken out," said Sebastian ; "it is not safe to speak with traitors in secret, for always the man that is seen listening to a traitor is thought to be so himself."

"You have told me, Sebastian," interrupted Zeno, "that Ranieri was discreet, and truly I find him more so than you ; for he has found just what I needed. Think you, Ranieri, that this Recanati believes Sebastian to be leagued with you in some bad device, that he spoke of your yielding your father as if it were a crime which you concealed, and Sebastian allowed !"

"So it seemed."

"Boy, have you courage and firmness enough to play with this traitor at his own weapons? Will you, for all the rewards which he would give you, but obtained honestly. help me to circumvent him? For," continued Zeno, turning to Sebastian, "none that has led, either in council or in camp, can push to his end without deceit. It is one of the things that we have to fight, and therefore must we learn how to fight with it, since you never can conquer any combatant if you do not understand his art. The difference between an honest man and a traitor, both using stratagem, is this—that the traitor uses it against all, and for his own bad ends; but the honest man uses it only against traitors, and never for his own ends. You will make a bad general, Sebastian, if you are too proud to use a little of this vile art. That man's honesty is but weak who cannot a little dally and play with it, fearing that it should break down if once he trust it out of rigid keeping. I can see by your friend Ranieri's honest face that he can use some of this cunning, and yet not be the worse; is it not so, Ranieri?"

"I think, Messer Zeno," answered the youth, "that I may well shape myself by your wisdom and conscience, without fearing either disgrace or ill."

"Then," answered Zeno, "we must play a little with our friend's character. You shall make this Recanati think that the most proud and pure Sebastian doth a little relent to his treachery, and that he is willing to join him in the conspiracy, so that it be safe, and, therefore, that he acts rather through you than of himself. Shall it be so, Sebastian."

"I have learnt of Ranieri how to answer, and I will say that I am yours to use as you will."

"Know then, Ranieri, that I suspect this Recanati to hold some secret converse with the traitors here, or in Venice, if not with Carrara. Refuse him then nothing; do all that he wishes; plot, contrive, and compass the destruction of us all; but do it on this sole condition—that you, on behalf of Sebastian, take part in all his councils, and hear all that is done. There may be danger in this, my young friend; but never can man reach greatness except by passing through danger at every step. And as for your good fame, fear it not; for in whatever part you may fall, I will be sponsor for you to the world. Do this, and you will have done me such service, that when I hold victory in my hand, I shall account you to have given it to me."

Flushing full up to the eyes, which sparkled with animation and hope, Ranieri promised that he would do what was needed of him. And taking his leave, he hastened away to regain Sebastian's tent ere his absence could be noted.

"And now," said Zeno, "tell me—the Genoese have gained a footing in Pelestrina here behind us, to the north, and on Malamocco."

"Also to the north of Malamocco," said Sebastian; "for they hold the port of Lido, and the canal within."

'Holy Mary preserve the city! We must drive them from it—at once. To-morrow I will look to our means—to-morrow night Mal-

amocco shall be regained, and Pisani shall sweep clean the canal of the blessed saint of Venice. Set him his task, and none can perform it so well as Pisani. After that—but let us think now of the beginning—by the blessing of Heaven, I will drive before me both traitors and Genoese."

CHAPTER XLI.

CONTARINI had arrived at Malamocco. The whole place to the south-west of where the Genoese had entrenched themselves was in a stir. Recanati's men had been drawn off from the face of the enemy to the farther end of the island, nearer to Pelestrina, and a new force took up the position in front of the Genoese. Among them might be seen a strong body of Uscocchi, and many of Cooke's men. More towards the centre of the island, the soldiers were engaged in striking and pitching tents; those who had already been there moving off towards remoter posts, and drawing their tents closer together, to make room for the reinforcements which Contarini had brought. Every face was changed; doubt and treason were forgotten. More men had come—the prince himself was there, he had brought gold—and Zeno had arrived. While the men were thus working like ants, they were stopped in their labors by the shrill clangor of a trumpet; and those who could be spared were led to the front of the large tent in which the doge had taken up his lodging for the nonce. The day was fair, and the sun shone brightly on the white tents; some of the canvass, indeed, had forgotten its first color, and had assumed many fantastic hues—the sun, too, gleamed brightly on the waters of the lagoon, which was covered with galleys, and burchi, and other large boats which had gathered to the spot. The soldiers stood for a short time in order, awaiting what should happen, when another trumpet called their attention, and a large party of nobles, mostly in arms, but some few in robes, issued from the doge's tent. After them came the prince, and on either side of him were two forms well known to the armies of Venice. On his left, and walking a little behind him, was the square and athletic Vittor Pisani, in arms; but he had hastily donned for the occasion his robe of office—the long red sleeveless robe, buttoned over either shoulder, and the round red cap in which Venice clothed her generals. In his right hand the prince led Carlo Zeno, and at the sight of him and of the robe he wore, the men set up a loud shout; so loud and long, that Contarini did not even essay to make his voice heard, but advancing to the square space between the men, he waved his hand in token that he gave a new general to the army. All the while that the chief stood there, the men continued shouting; so that after saying a few words, that none could hear, the doge retired again with the generals.

The men did not relinquish their busy labors. The day was well nigh spent when the whole of the tents were removed and repitched; and then were arms taken out and scanned to see that they were fit for service. That done, the men gathered into knots and rested in pleasant talk; questioning what might next be done, and disputing whether Zeno meant to strike at once, or to gather new strength before his first blow. Night arrived, and all went to repose.

But the night had not passed, ere the whole were in movement again. With as much silence as they might, great part of the soldiers put on their arms and took their posts, each under his own leader; each uncertain how many like himself might be stirring in the dark, but gathering, occasionally, from the distant tread of men or the clank of arms, that others also were abroad. It was bruited among them that Pisani had left Malamocco before even they had roused them; but each leader, as he passed away from the camp with his men, was silent, and gave no hint of the work before them. Many moved up towards Lido, slowly and cautiously, and often as they went, came messengers, who, speaking to the leaders, passed on and were lost in the darkness.

Within a tent at the edge of the ground still Venetian, were assembled a party of cavaliers, all armed. The troops there stationed, were silent as death: they had been roused from slumber, but they stirred not; and those who watched upon the low wall which the Genoese had built around their camp, or looked out from two taller towers that stood near, could not have guessed that a large force was there lying in readiness for action. Even the Venetians themselves were unaware of the numbers gathering in their rear; and the cavaliers who looked out from their tent, which was open so that they could see at once the line of the Genoese wall, and the tents of their own men, watched also in stillness, talking among themselves almost in whispers. Galluzzi was there, Boemondo Tiepolo, Orso Mocenigo, Alberto Alberti, the senator's son, and Rinaldo Caresini. As they watched, a tall form appeared in the dim light at the opening of the tent, and Sebastian entered. Knowing his errand, all started to their feet, and before he had said the word that all was ready, they had moved to follow him. As they issued forth, they found ranged among the tents their own men; who had taken their posts with such silence that they could scarcely be distinguished from the moveless ground. Zeno's orders had pervaded every part, and had been carried on without haste, but with eager zeal. Sebastian pointed to the wall, above which, against that pale light that showed where the dawn would rise, was moving a solitary watcher. His slow and easy pace showed that he knew not of the movement so near him. "Let us be unseen as long as we may," said Sebastian; "till then, silence is our first duty. But when we once are seen, speed will be our safety. We are to wait here until we know that Messer Navagero has made his attack. He lies in the centre, nearer to the lagoon; and beyond is Malipiero, who also waits for the same signal."

"I doubt," said Galluzzi, "if Malipiero will wait for the graver Navagero."

"He has Soranzo with him, who will keep him in until it is time. Besides, for all he has fought in this war more fiercely than ever he did when his blood was young, he has grown more silent and discreet; and they say that he has waxed marvellously pious, having sworn an oath that he will faithfully serve St. Mark."

"Why then he will keep it," said young Alberti; "for Malipiero has so much of the priest in him, that he would have been in the church, but for his fiery passions."

"Are we not late?" asked Tiepolo; "for it seems to me that the dawn will overtake us before we have crossed the wall."

"It is scarcely the hour named," answered Sebastian; "and it was Zeno's thought, that if the darkness would be the best for the attack, some little light would serve us after we have entered; therefore is it that we await till now. But Navagero must be ready, and we shall soon know when he moves forward. Let us be silent that we may hear and watch the better." So saying he held his peace; as did his companions.

They did not wait long, before the man on the wall, whose motions were a sign to them of the peace still reigning on the other side, stood still. Presently another form appeared near him, and then more; and they moved away towards the left.

"Methinks they have seen something," said Sebastian. "Let our men stand ready to move forward the stage."

"They are at their posts," said the voice of Boemondo; "I have just been with them."

The forms of the men upon the wall now moved more quickly, and while some again had jumped down, the others might be seen running hastily. A moment's silence, and then the shrill blast of a trumpet startled the night: there was a confused hubbub, and then a crash, and then arose up the sound of voices—a tramping,—and the clash of arms.—

"They are at it," cried Sebastian. "Forward! we will give them work here too."

He had no sooner spoken, than a large wooden machine on wheels—a heavy frame supporting a platform at the top, with a drawbridge to let fall upon the walls, and steps behind by which the besiegers might climb it—was dragged hastily forward by a hundred hands. The trench which the Genoese had begun, had made little way in the hard ground, and was easily filled with wood that the Venetians had brought for the purpose. But their noise had drawn others to the wall, and presently showers of arrows began to fall among them. Little heeding that hard rain, they pressed forward to their task. Planks were laid—the stage was driven to the wall—the bridge was lowered, crushing the hand of one man that would have forced it back before it was fixed—many feet trampled upon it—there was a sudden sound of thunder, a glare of light, and the heavy discharge of a manganel swept the floor of the stage. It cast a blasting light full in the faces of the Venetians; and struck by that terrible force, more than one was hurled down to the ground. But Sebastian had pressed on so swiftly, that he had already passed beyond it. He jumped down, and threw himself among the Genoese; and alighting he knew not how upon his feet, dashed his sword into the living mass of men before him. Striking with might and main he pressed forward so lustily that none could withstand his blows; and as he pushed on he heard the constant sound of others jumping from the wall behind him, so that the mere press of numbers began to drive back the Genoese. The tumult had now swelled to an uproar; the sound of arms and of voices might be heard along the whole line of the wall. At first was heard at intervals the thunder of manganels and bombards; but presently they were silent, showing that the surprised enemy had been driven back from the guns.

Meanwhile, a galley had silently been making its way along the seaward shore of Malamocco. It was the same that had brought Zeno from Tenedos. It had nearly the same freight, save that its deck was now more crowded with armed men, whose tall forms and gallant bearing, shewed that they had been picked from among a number. As soon as it had arrived near the Port of Lido, it turned back, and moved along the shore very slowly, as if those on board were seeking for a landing place. It was so; the darkness of the night, and the change which the foe had made upon the island had so altered its aspect, that those on board could not know it again. Near the mouth of the port, the shore jutted out somewhat under the water, but at a little distance from it they knew that there was a better landing, and there, too, they had learnt that the Genoese, little fearing attack from the seaward, had but a weak palisade in place of the stronger wall that faced the land, and turned the corners at the edge of the water. This palisade it was their object to make; but the darkness, and the altered buildings, confused their senses; and while Edward insisted that they had already gained the place of which they were in search, Luigi Morosini was strong in the belief that he recognized a tower which they had passed, like another, he said, which also lay nearer the port than the spot they sought. Zeno left it to them; for the change had been even greater since he departed from Venice, than it was since they had issued from the port that night when they went to bring him back to the city. Edward too, perforce, yielded to the better knowledge to which il Grasso pretended. Already they heard the tumult which arose when Navagero made his attack; then it swelled; the manganels ceased too soon for the trusty leaders of the Venetians to have been repulsed, and they guessed that the wall was passed. Still the tumult ashore went on, and still the galley made its silent way. Edward turned anxiously towards the fresh east wind, which bore them rapidly past the landing place. In the dim light they could barely discern a tower, as it seemed to glide past them; and now Morosini turned the head of the galley to the land. Edward went forward, and, leaning over the bow, tried to pierce the gloom towards the shore; but the beating of the waves told him nothing. He had scarcely regained the stern, before a sudden crash, and some confusion below, told him that the oars on the right side of the vessel had many of them broken, and presently the bottom of the ship itself grated heavily and harshly upon the mingled sand and mud that stretched out in patches from the shore. The cry which arose among the rowers, who had been thrown down, and among the bowmen, was answered by one long, loud shout on the shore; and a

man's figure was seen to arise against the dim light of the sky at the top of the tower.

"Silence!" cried Edward, as he hastened to the stern. "Zanni, run forward and silence those men. Luigi mio, we must get her off as fast as we may, and the darkness which betrayed us, will help us to avoid the Genoese before they know the prize that has fallen to them."

Under the hasty directions of Edward and Morosini, every pole that the vessel afforded, and many of their oars, were now thrust out on the right bow, and the vigorous strain of a hundred arms urged it slowly and steadily back from the place where it had settled. But the wind, which had been shifting as the darkness diminished, now sent them, as in very spite, forward again, and the stem again ground hard upon the sand, though a little farther from the tower. From the noise on shore, and what they could see of the moving figures on the tower, they were aware that the guard had been roused. Without long delay, a few arrows fell amongst them, and some stuck quivering in the deck. Edward could only in part silence the shout of defiance among his own men, which now marked to the Genoese where the stranded vessel lay, and a thicker flight of arrows followed. Some stifled cries, and another shout, though not so loud as before, showed that many of the weapons fell upon something different from wood. Another attempt was made to drive the galley from the shore, but with no better success. And now the arrows of the Genoese fell like rain. Cooped up at the mercy of the enemy, and unable even to struggle against the dangers that assailed them, the Venetians were struck with terror, and ran hither and thither in their confusion. Many of them, leaving their oars, gathered together in the bow, and took counsel among themselves. Some sought under the deck a shelter from the iron storm which raged above; and the boldest among them stood with their arms folded in sullen indifference. A bright flash of light above the tower, and a noise like thunder, was followed presently by a heavy splash at the side of the ship.

"The rogues!" cried Luigi; "that is one of our cannon. They have not yet made them to throw so far, nor such heavy stones."

As he spoke, the murmur among the crew grew louder, and presently a few among them drew nigh, while those behind raised cries to surrender.

"Now, Zanni," said Luigi, "what is it! Have your friends again sent you on some traitorous errand!"

"They say," answered the man, "that it is useless to fight thus, when we have nothing but the dark to meet and the wind: while these good Genoese can skewer us all at leisure, like larks brought to market; and we may be drowned here on this muddy shoal, if we wait till the galley breaks up with the beating of the waves. They say, Messer Luigi, that if we do surrender, and declare that we have Messer Zeno on board; that Doria will be so pleased at that prize, that we shall be saved, and welcomed on shore with lights and feasting."

"Is that what you would have, Zanni! Who gave this counsel—it was not you! Show me the man—show me the Genoese that said this. Bring him here, and fetch me a light, that we may look at him. Is this the price you put upon Zeno, that you think him worth no more than this galley, and all who are in it? or, rather, would it be cheap if all were lost, so that we kept him safely for Venice, who sent us to fetch him? Bring me the man here."

The mariners seemed somewhat abashed, and stood in silence; but the shots behind them did not cease, when the voice of Carlo Zeno was heard loud above the tumult—"Who talks of surrendering!" he cried, "the Genoese? Hark! hear you those shouts—the shout of victory of your fellow Venetians, as they seize the stronghold of our enemies? Hark again: the Venetians have gained the fort. Let us be with them. Olá," he cried, "is there one among you that can swim? Give me a man that will face the waters, ay, and death for me, if you have such."

The sound of his voice was like a spell upon the men—the old familiar shout that they had so often before heard, in tempest and in danger, and had so often conquered by, drove away their fears, while it surprised them into the habit of obedience. Many of them rushed to the stern; where stood Zeno and Edward, who had persuaded him to take the command which Luigi had lost.

"Now," cried Zeno, as the men ran up to him, "which of you can swim best?"

"I," and "I," and "I," cried many voices.

"Nay, I want not more than one, and let me not have any but the best. Tell me, all of you, which is it that is strongest in the water?"

"I am," said Zanni; "they will all tell you so."

"Strip, then, and let me see your limbs, if the darkness will let me. And now, my friend, can you brave a little salt water? Listen then —get ashore, with a rope in your hand, and make us a path to the land; if we cannot get our galley off, we will land where we needs must."

Zanni made no answer, but knitting his limbs, walked slowly to the side, and threw his legs, one after another, over the bulwark. He still hung with one arm firmly over the side of the vessel, until, in its rolling, it came nearer to the water, then, dropping straight down, he cleared a high wave without a splash. Many eyes strained after him, until he reappeared some ten or twenty cubits from the ship.

"It will do!" cried Zeno; "If we could have made a fish do our office, we should not have done better. And now, boys, let us also bestir ourselves. An arrow will find us as readily when we are still, as when we are at work."

Animated by his words, the rowers again strained every nerve, but now to thrust the galley farther towards the shore. The wind favored their efforts, and slowly, and with many a hinderance the heavy ship glided forward. Realizing so soon the success that Zeno seemed always to command, the discipline of the men improved, and they silently drifted in. Another burst of light, however, though it sent the mass of stone far away from the galley, in its course, again disclosed the Venetians to their foe, and the next flight of arrows spent its full force upon them.

"Now boys," cried Zeno, "to your oars; the water is deep here." As he spoke, seizing the rope, of which Zanni on the land held the other, he jumped from the ship, and partly swimming, and partly wading, he dragged himself swiftly to the shore. By the same rude bridge followed others, and more, until the whole were on shore; Edward closing the rear. Still the manganels kept up a fire at intervals, and the better light enabled those on the tower to see them. "This is no palisade," cried Zeno; "but a sound wall;" and he moved towards it to try its height. The ground beneath it was rough, rising in a low broken bank. He began to climb it—he staggered—he fell. At first they thought that he had only stumbled. But as he endeavored to rise, they saw him stagger and fall backwards: he lay quite still. In an instant Edward and Luigi were at his side; knowing that he must be wounded. With his hand he pointed to his throat, and in the imperfect light, they saw that there was an arrow sticking there; but he was silent.

"He does not faint," said Edward, "for I can feel his hand grasp mine. I fear me that he cannot speak." Zeno grasped the shaft of the arrow, which was short and thick, and strove to draw it from his throat; but the pain had weakened him, and he signed to Edward to draw it out. Edward looked close to the wound, and seeing as well as he could for the darkness, he found that the iron still remained in great part outside, and therefore not fearing to tear the flesh, he pressed with his fingers gently on the sides of the wound, and drew the weapon forth.

"Does it bleed much?" said Luigi.

"I can feel the blood on my fingers," answered Edward, "but there does not seem much."

"And yet," said Luigi, "I can feel him clutch my hand, as though the pain were worse. He is choking, and we have no surgeon here."

They watched him as he lay, his limbs quivering slightly, and his strength seeming to grow less; and already they feared that they had brought him to Venice merely to be carried to the tomb.

"He would have us to do something," said Luigi. "What is it, sir?"

Zeno was making signs with his hands.

"I think," said Edward, "that he would have us turn him round." They laid him on his face, and the blood which had flowed into his throat and choked him, now ran freely from the wound. They could feel from the stillness of his hands that he was easier. But how to remove him! Edward looked up once more towards the tower and the wall, and thought, almost with despair, how the wounded man lay, in that narrow strip of ground between the sea and the enemy. He began to deem it the safest to force their way through the enemy, and scarcely had the thought crossed his mind, ere Zeno himself reviving, made a sign that they should lift him over the wall. His wound had now ceased to bleed so violently as it did before, and Edward prepared to obey. His first task was to take the wall; on which he could dimly descry the moving forms of those who manned it. He stood not upon stratagem; but making his men bring their ladders, they were laid against the wall; and while some held them tightly to it, others scrambled up, Edward at their head. He was seized at the top by many hands that strove to throw him back; and sharp was the struggle; but Edward fought for more than life, and after one fierce embrace on that perilous stone couch, both besiegers and besieged toppled in together. By great good fortune, as Zeno had reckoned, only a small force remained to guard that seabound post; and the Venetians had no hard labor to force them back. Without waiting to assail the tower, Edward helped those below to raise the wounded general to the wall; and once within it, they hurried forward, carrying him in their arms, and shouting, "Viva San Marco! Carlo Zeno! Carlo Zeno!" The few whom they encountered fled before them, or throwing down their arms, craved protection; and still as they hurried on, a new standard was unfurled upon the farthest wall by the Port of Lido—it bore the winged lion of Saint Mark. They had come just in time to share the victory, and in the name of Zeno and of Venice to grant mercy to the prisoned Genoese.

Presently there was a new shouting towards the port, and where the wall was lowest they might see above it the mast of a galley pass hastily along; while the Venetians who had already manned that battlement, were shouting as if in triumph, and discharging arrows at the passing vessel. "Pisani," exclaimed Edward, "has done his duty; the Genoese are flying." Another galley was now seen to pass as hastily as the first. They would have carried Zeno within that he might be tended; but he made signs that they should bear him to the port, and there reclining upon the wall, a leech was brought to him, while he looked out upon the lagoon. He watched for Vittor Pisani, whom he had sent to drive the Genoese from the waters of Saint Mark. Already they could see a fleet of galleys hastening towards the port—first there were some two or three fugitive Genoese, straining every nerve to escape the pursuers behind, and to dash through the port now guarded by their enemy. They went on their way, but as they passed, some few drops of blood marked the skill of the bowmen in the fort that made sport of their flight. Then came the body of the fleet, dashing and crowding into the port. There was a space behind them, and two galleys might be seen running a race for the outlet. The one to the right of those who viewed it from the fort, bore the standard of Saint Mark. A cavalier was standing at its prow, sword in hand; by the golden fess upon the blue ground, blazoned on his jupon, it was Taddeo Justiniani. The object of the Venetian was to cut off the path of the Genoese galley, which came more to the left, and which in turn was striving to make the outlet before the Venetian. The race was nearly even; but the Genoese was too much on one side of the channel, and thus its path was a trifle longer. All its men stood moveless on the side next the foe. Every eye was strained as

the two paths drew to a point. They neared the oars of the Venetians ceased for an instant that they might take the galley in its flank; then they beat the water again, and dashed furiously against the other galley; Justiniani standing ready to leap on board at the instant that they touched. The whole of the men in the Genoese galley rushed to its right side, their weight and that of all the things that that they had already passed to that side, bringing it down close to the water, throwing the opposite bulwark high into the air, and hiding the two parties from each other. As they leaped, the Venetians fell against the wet and slippery sides of the galley; many toppling into the water, where they sank from the weight of their arms. The Genoese shouted in derision, as they heard the splash and tumult. One Venetian alone retained his hold: it was Taddeo Justiniani, who had leaped the first, and who was now thrown by the force of his leap right into the Genoese galley, and went running and stumbling alone among the enemy; but no fear mastered his heart. Hastily scrambling to the nearest mast, he passed his left arm round it, while with his right he struck fierce and fast on those who assailed him; the slanting deck gave them a bad footing, and many a man fell under the blows which he dealt from his vantage-ground. Seeing how he withstood so many, the captain of the galley made his men go back to the other side, so that the galley righted, and now from the shore they saw that Taddeo stood with his back to the mast, defending himself against death from the swords that must slay him by their numbers. The Genoese called out to him to yield, while some few went forward to attack him from behind; turning to this new enemy he left the others, and striking the first he met he rushed to the bow of the vessel—he leaped on to the beak—dropped into the lagoon, and strove to swim for the shore, liking rather to yield to the waters of his native country than to the cruel mercy of the Genoese; but his arms were heavy, his strength was spent, he could not even answer the shouts of the friends whose hands were stretched out to him in vain, and before his own galley could reach him, he had sunk to rise no more.

No hostile eyes witnessed his last struggle, for when they would have pursued him as he rushed to the bow of the galley, a fresh assault made the Genoese think only of their own safety; their galley staggered under a violent shock, and before they were aware of it, Vittor Pisani, who had remained to sweep the last of their vessels from the canal, marking the danger of his friend, had come to his help—too late to save him, but not to revenge. Seeing that all hope was gone, the Genoese drew themselves together, determined to sell their lives as dearly as possible; they would not ask for mercy, they would not give it, but hewed down by Pisani on one side, and by the men of Justiniani, who now came on board with little resistance on the other side, they stood to be reaped down in a bloody harvest. Say, when Vittor Pisani stood master of the galley, how many Venetians, after that dance of battle, shared with the Genoese the bloody bed of death!

M

CHAPTER XLII.

After leaving Zeno, it was Ranieri's care to keep himself as much as possible alone in Sebastian's tent, so that no interruption might be offered to his next conversation with Roberto da Recanati, and he instinctively provided for his contest with the crafty man, by keeping ready to his hand a book which he read from time to time, though his thoughts ever wandered to more stirring matters. The day was well nigh spent before the conduttiere came. While he seemed to note him not, Ranieri caught at once the sound of his stealthy footstep; he drew near to the stool on which the youth sat and laid his hand upon his shoulder. Ranieri started round, as if taken by surprise, and looked in Recanati's face like one who would know what he wanted.

"You have not forgotten," began the Florentine, "of what we talked the other day?"

"Truly no," answered Ranieri, "and I have not misused my time."

"Tell me then how you have speeded."

Ranieri paused, and smiling, he replied, "I think that it is not for me to begin to tell anything yet, rather should you tell and I hear more."

"How so;" asked the conduttiere, "what said Messer Sebastiano?"

"I have nothing to tell you of what Messer Sebastian has said, nor shall I. Think of me as Sebastian himself: speak to me as Sebastian, and I will tell you what I say."

"Why this," replied the soldier, "is making compacts with one who keeps in the dark. How can I treat with Messer Sebastiano, if all the talk is on my side? Is it nothing that we offer him such power and such possessions as, though he were to live to be the oldest man in Venice, he never could attain? and we offer it for him or his father at once; it is for him to choose his prize."

"Ay; you offer to give him some small part of what you are losing in despair, in order to keep the rest; and he would lose in your defeat the whole of what he has. You know, Messer Roberto, to what Sebastian may look one day. You know that there is no station in Venice which he cannot enter, having, so young, achieved such high fame. You know that the ducal robe itself has been worn by others of his family; and that it may be so again, even without the aid of Messer Roberto da Recanati. For him the only gain in your success would be one of time—the risk and the danger, I say, are all on his side; and if you would have his aid, you must have it on his own terms. I tell you that I am Sebastian; and that if you are defeated, I alone will take the risk. If you win, more powerful hands than mine shall crown your triumph. Have it so, or not at all."

The conduttiere looked hard and thoughtfully at Ranieri; who leaned his arm upon the table, with his head resting upon his hand, as though he would give the other all his own time for reflection—"You speak in riddles," said Recanati, "and if you fear to speak more plainly, truly we can go no farther in this matter."

"I tell you that the risk is all ours; the gain will be all yours; for you are now losing, and therefore must you have it so, or not at all."

Recanati pressed his lips together, and his black eyebrows met in a fierce frown, as, looking at Ranieri with a new expression, he cried, "How shall I know, young man, but that you are playing with me? How shall I know that I may speak to you as to Messer Sebastiano, with his leave?"

"Why," answered the youth, carelessly, "that is one of your chances: Messer Sebastiano will not appear to you, nor speak to you, while you are losing all, and he can gain nothing but disgrace. If you need proof that he has given me his power, which is no small one, take it in the command I hold here. Think you, that if I were not as Sebastian himself, that I, young as I am, should have the obedience of his men?"

Stepping to the door of the tent, he called out, "Olà, Ordelaffo!" and then walked back to the table. A soldier appeared, and respectfully waited the youth's command.

"Have your men," said Ranieri, "retired to rest?"

"But now, my lord," answered the man.

"Rouse them instantly, for I may need them; and bring them here into the open ground before my tent."

The man bowed and retired.

"It is long," said the youth, as he resumed his seat, "since you were at Florence, Messer Roberto. You must weary of this camp life after the amusements of your own city."

The conduttiere did not answer, but looked at his companion as if half amused and half perplexed. They remained silent for some minutes, during which Ranieri had taken up his book. Presently there was a sound of many feet outside, and Ordelaffo re-entered the tent.

"We await your commands, Messer Ranieri," he said.

"Stay awhile without, sir," replied the youth: "Messer Recanati and I will be with you anon, and may need you or release you to your beds, as we shall determine."

Ordelaffo again retired, with an obeisance.

"You see," cried Ranieri, turning to Recanati, "that I am Sebastian here; and truly I think you will be in danger of little mistake, if I am Sebastian also to you. You will have none other as yet; therefore must you be content with this poor shape of that nobler gentleman, my friend, or you must leave your enterprise. So now, Messer da Recanati, take your free choice."

The conduttiere hesitated; then suddenly putting on a frank manner, he cried, "Be it so, Messer Sebastiano Morosini; I shall doubt no longer. So what say you of your own proper mouth?"

"Nay, nay," cried Ranieri, smiling, "I have still the same answer for you. It is you that are to speak, not I. What say you, Messer da Recanati? How am I, Sebastian Morosini, to know that you have the power you boast? You see me here in Sebastian's tent, leading Sebastian's men, who attend my bidding without, holding Sebastian's powers; but how know I that you have entry into Chiozza; that you have the ear of Carrara, and power to speak for him? I have shown you all that I possess before we began our compact. You have let me see nothing; thinking, perhaps, that so young as I am, I may be ready of faith. But remember, that if I have Sebastian's powers, also I have Sebastian's years, and Sebastian's counsel."

"What would you! You know as much as I can show you—Messer Sebastiano knows how Alessandro da Padova—"

"I know all that Sebastian knows; but Sebastian himself knows not how things have altered since the fortunes of war have altered—how you, (I say it not to offend you, Messer Recanati) being trapped into a difficulty by the cunning Carrara, may be using me to escape from your trouble, secretly, and without the privity of Carrara. Look you, I have shown you all my power; before we go farther, you shall show me yours, if you would have us be allies."

"What is it you ask!"

"Proof that you have the ear of Carrara."

"Why, do you not see the command I have here! Do you not see the secret powers that I have held, and which well-nigh cost me my life last night!"

"I know you, Messer Recanati, for one of the discreetest and astutest of condottieri; and I see, that great part of the hired troops here assembled look up to you for counsel."

"Have you not noted the power I hold over these soldiers; and do you believe that I could hold it, but that I have held the purse—that I have had money!"

"I know that you are the most sought after of all your craft, and that you have been well paid, Messer da Recanati; you have treasure, I doubt not, stored up in Florence."

"Little of that, indeed, as you will learn, if ever you carry on the trade of a condottiere. But how can I give you proof of what you ask, here in Pelestrina! There is no such proof, unless you were to be in Chiozza itself, and see the conference I hold with Carrara."

"Be it so."

"Be it so! but how can it be so! how can any stranger enter that fortress, or how would you venture thither by your own will!"

"As to the venturing, Messer da Recanati, do not believe that any danger will stop me—or if Sebastian thought that it would, I should not now hold the powers I do, or speak to you as from himself. For the rest, take your choice. I will have the proof you named, or you shall not have my alliance."

"In sooth, Giovinetto, you are as difficult to deal withal as a woman; you are so proud and wilful, you ask what is impossible."

"I am not yet so old as you, Messer Roberto, and have not learnt to use that word impossible. When I have been with you to Chiozza we will talk farther."

Ranieri rose from his chair and took off his cloak, as if to prepare for rest; to hint that his visiter might retire. After a short silence, Recanati said, "I leave you then, Messer Ranieri : a rivederci." Recanati stepped towards the entrance of the tent; but then returning, he said, "Have you bethought you, young man, that there is danger in playing too far with men intent upon a desperate game!"

"I have thought of all, and am as you see, unarmed. I am ready to go with you, also un armed, wherever you like. There are some things that we will not trust to any man, and there are other things which we will trust to any. I will not trust Sebastian's fame and fortune in your hands; but this body, comely as it is, and of price to its owner and divers young damsels, you shall have in pawn when you list." He continued slowly unbuttoning his vest.

"You are the boldest spoken lad that ever I encountered. Undress no farther, my friend, for I will humor you sooner than you might think. What if I were to take you now !"

"Why then, as the night is cold, I shall put on my cloak again."

"I will not, however, disturb you so unawares."

"At your own time. But having on my cloak, I will go forth to dismiss the men."

"You are a strange youth, Messer Ranieri. You shall hear from me again , but now I take my leave." And he departed.

CHAPTER XLIII.

THE blow on the Genoese at Malamocco was followed up with such resistless might, that the whole fortune of the war was changed ; and the change might be noted in the altered bearing of the soldiers ranged under the standard of St. Mark. A cheerful confidence was seen in every face, activity and prompt obedience reigned throughout, and the murmurs of treachery were hushed. It were needless to recount how the post of the Genoese in Pelestrina had been assailed like that at Malamocco, and how they craved leave to retreat to Chiozza ; which Zeno allowed, to the surprise of some among his colleagues. "Every mouth in Chiozza," he answered, "does battle on our side." And soon stories were told, how in the night, large bands of prisoners, the people of the town, were carried away from Chiozza to the main land , where they might more readily be fed. But soon the traffic with the main land was rendered difficult ; for Pisani pressed so with his galleys and smaller boats upon every part that the enemy were now driven in upon Chiozza and the neighboring island Brondolo. To do all this Zeno did not wait for the healing of his wound, though that went on apace; but seated in his lodging at Pelestrina, he ordered anew the fortunes of Venice. He sent back the venerable doge to the city, bidding him restore hope and good rule to its troubled people. He watched the bearing of the Genoese, as the toils were narrowed around them ; and while he evoked the whole strength and wealth of his country in one last struggle for death or destruction, he inspired his countrymen with his own resolve, that the Genoese should be driven from the lagoons, or that Venice should there close her history and drown her existence in the reddened waters. Still, too, he watched when the treachery that he knew to lurk among them should show its ugly face or wicked hand ; but it seemed to shrink as the Genoese shrunk within themselves : none was more active than the unconscious traitor Morosini –than the conscious but faithful Malipiero, rejoicing to wield the sword in expiation for his oath-chained tongue—than the vigilant Alessandro, whose dark eye no man could read. Surrounded by uncorrupted bands, Re-canati remained in idleness on Pelestrina. All seemed to go well.

"At length Zeno was whole again, and could bear arms. Pisani was summoned to Pelestrina, and close was the council. Some hours after-wards—the night was moonless, but calm and tranquil—a great fleet of galleys, and of all the smaller vessels that could be commanded, was gradually stealing along the shore towards Chi-ozza, so silently that those in each vessel might have supposed that it was alone, or that only the one or two nearest to it were moving like itself. The whole fleet moved slowly, as if the purpose were not to let a needless sound es-cape, and to keep even the rowers unfatigued. Thus they passed along the low, flat shore of Pelestrina. Its outline showed against the gray side of night, where the dawn was to appear; and how changed from its wonted aspect! No small fisher's house loomed against the sky, no vine leaves danced in the air; but all along were the straight and cornered lines of palisades and bastions, or the sharper angles of tents crowd-ed into that narrow space. On their right, lost in the darkness, lay the safe and quiet waters of the lagoon. It was already morning when they arrived at the port of Brondolo, and those which were foremost, taking a course to the left, made for the shore of the island in the strait. After the galleys had for some time turned in that path, one of them, followed as silently still by those behind, pursued the shore towards Chiozza. The deck of that galley was crowded with a band whose death-like silence denoted the command that swayed them. Near its poop was gathered a knot of cavaliers; some sitting on the boards taking a hasty repose; others watching as well as they might in the dark, the path of the galley through the waters. Carlo Zeno stood by the right side of the ship, and near him were the two friends.

"So far," he said, "our path is smooth and quiet; the spell that we have cast upon the lagoon has lulled the Genoese into the belief that we have grown idle; and perchance to de-spise us. Hear you any sound!"

"Nothing," said Edward, "save the steady splash and rumbling of the oars. But we have yet a good piece to go."

"Ay; our friends in little Venice have their choice of three ways to meet us. They may force us to a battle on the shore; or they may meet us with courtesy, and give us all we ask; or they may think (and it is more likely) to trap us by suffering us to land. Every stroke now gives us a better chance; and unless they have a stronger force on this side of the canal than we have learnt, we could even now land faster than they could issue out upon us. For Pisani, who has gone before, will keep them busy at Brondolo; and I know that we could now jump ashore faster than they can pass the bridge. I have been fearing day after day to hear that they had crowded this place before us to stay our landing; but if this scanty light deceive me not, there lies, as yet, been none on shore. Have you seen any, Odoardo? for my eyes have been more turned to the right here, watch-ing for any lights in Chiozza."

"None; if we knew not otherwise we might suppose all the town deserted."

The course of the galley now became slower for some minutes it glided so gently that might almost seem still; presently it stopped, and a mariner coming towards them asked if it was the general's pleasure to land, for that was the place.

"Be it so," cried Zeno, "go among the men, Sebastian, and let there be no hurry, for we have less need of time than of silence; before we are seen, I would have all on shore, less that I fear to make good our landing, than that I wish to hide our strength. Is it you, my friend, who will lead us to the hollow that I spoke of?"

The man bowed in token of assent. Gradu-ally the galley parted with its living freight, and the sound of footsteps was heard treading carefully and steadily on the shore. The drowsy cavaliers had now shaken off their slumbers, the repose of the short voyage was exchanged for a more active eagerness, and Zeno passed on shore amid a troop whose measured but elastic steps showed the hopes and courage that animated each among them. All was quiet on shore. The troops moved for-ward after their guide, and were lost in the silent darkness. Zeno and his friends remained by the water-side, watching the bands that nim-bly alighted from the galleys, and followed in the same path.

"I am amazed," he said, "at the stillness of the Genoese, and do suspect rather some trea-chery than mere neglect; go, Messer Andrea Donato, take with you whom you will outside these hillocks, and learn if all be clear."

There was no sign or sound of life, except the now steady tramp of the Venetians inland; and the whole of the galleys, and the smaller boats which followed them, had landed their men, before the light could betray them to those within the neighboring city. Following in the rear of the party, Carlo Zeno, who need-ed no guide in treading that ground, led his friends almost on the ridge of the slight rising that separated the little marshy hollows from the part towards Chiozza, until they came nearly opposite to the great bridge, where he placed himself behind a little chapel, so that they might be concealed while they could yet watch. As the dawn began to break, they could see more clearly the Venetian forces; and it was a mar-vel how so strong a band could have found its way to that solitary place, with so little noise or confusion. As the light increased, what had seemed mere shadows of the uneven ground, grew into men; so that a goodly force might be seen, of some two thousand bowmen; but in front, and nearest to the bridge, was a small troop of William Cooke's sturdy Englishmen, dismounted men-at-arms. The morning was chill, but clear and pleasant; and the light clouds that broke away in the west served rather to show the brightness of the sun than to conceal it, as the English band, and a few of the bowmen advanced up the hillock to show themselves to the enemy.

"The sluggards will wait till we go to knock at their gates," said Zeno; "and in sooth I would rather fight them here than there. Stay, what is this?"

As he spoke, a column of smoke, so black and thick that it seemed a solid pillar, rose from the city near the end of the bridge, and fresh masses of it danced quickly above the wall, rising high up in the air, and sailing slowly away with the wind.

"That," cried Zeno, "is no sudden chance, and I marvel, since they must have known we are here, that they have not troubled us before."

"They will be with us anon," answered Sebastian, "for see, here is one running to tell us that they come." He pointed inland, where a man might be seen coming as fast as he could run, and making no stay to answer those who questioned him as he passed each separate band at its post. He made straight for the party behind the little chapel, and came with such haste, that when he made his obeisance he could scarcely speak.

"How now," said Zeno; "have you Doria and all his men behind you, that you come so fast?"

"Messer Gradenigo has sent me," answered the man, "to tell you that we on the other side can see, in Brondolo, a large pillar of smoke rising in the air."

"Ha," exclaimed the general, "is it anything like that?" and he pointed to the smoke near the bridge of Chiozza.

"Why, it is its very counterfeit," answered the man, "and Messer Gradenigo thought it might be some signal."

"They think," said Zeno to his friends, "to enclose us, but I fear them not in Brondolo; for they must eat Pisani before they can feast on us. We may care little for the smoke behind us, so that we watch what this shall bring forth. And it is not long first you see." He pointed to the bridge, on which might now be seen a body of men steadily marching along it. They seemed to become aware of the English and Venetians who showed themselves in front, for suddenly they stopped; but presently they moved forward again, and the whole outline of the bridge showed a moving row of figures.

"Tell Messer Gradenigo," said Zeno to the messenger, "to watch well what he may see towards Brondolo; and let it be his care that none come at our backs, for we shall have work before us in plenty."

The man moved to obey him; but scarcely had he gone ten paces from the chapel, ere a little hissing was heard in the air, and some three or four arrows fell near him, one striking him on the neck, so that he fell badly wounded.

"Why, what is this?" cried Zeno; "have the Genoese some friends in heaven that fight for them?"

"It is likely enough," answered Edward, "for I think the mischief comes from this holy place."

He held out his hand towards a little bell-tower which stood some distance from the chapel. And the general now noticed that what seemed but an appendage to the holy building had been walled about with a strong palisade of wood, as if to block their entrance. All looked quiet, however, and there was no sign that it held any people.

"How like a holy hypocrite this chapel is," said Zeno. "How tranquil—and see that sign of peace and forgiveness," pointing to the cross which surmounted the other end, where

the entrance lay. "And yet from out this belfry have we these treacherous shafts. So often do some holy folks stir up war! As these busy priests will not let us rest, let us even begin our work."

The line of warriors crossing the bridge had now drawn its hindmost end on to the land: there were no more to come. Those who had reached the shore had hastily formed themselves, first into one band, which stood rather to the right of the bridge, and now into another on the left; and both slowly came forward. Zeno stepped as he spoke towards the troop of English soldiers that stood in the van. Another little flight of arrows whistled along as he passed beyond the shelter of the chapel; but they all fell wide, and Edward, who followed him with Sebastian, pointed to the fortune which seemed to bear the Zeno harmless.

Raising his loud voice, that had so often made itself heard against the wind, Zeno spake so that it might reach beyond the English to his own countrymen, and hastily addressed them in one of those short and animated speeches with which he was wont to begin the combat.

"We have buckled on our armor this day, my soldiers," he cried, "with good omens. The sun that shines upon us will dazzle the eyes of those we fight; and you see how God is leading them, little by little, across that bridge, that it may be easier for us to find them than if they were on the farther shore. Truly God stands against wicked and unjust enterprizes, and blinds the eyes of those who pursue them. See how they come on, judging our prudence with a corrupt judgment, taking it for very fear: through their error and your wisdom shall our glory be begotten. Stand quiet yet a little, and silent—But when the time shall come, and I give you the accustomed sign, then crying out, and with a good will, we will run upon them and drive them back, broken and disordered, against the walls which they cannot re-enter. This day shall bring destruction to the daring of our foes, and this miserable war shall have a happy end. For all human things have the same course; nor was there ever so troubled and perilous a tempest that had not behind it a serene calm."

He ceased, and turning towards the foe, he watched the distance as it diminished between them.

"They have one advantage over us," he said, speaking low to his companions—"for if they have few horses, we have none. And yet methinks they seem to gain but little confidence from that; for as they come near, and see our numbers greater than they showed at first, note how they seem to stop and doubt. Gerardo de Mantelaro—that is he on the black horse—is not often so slow in coming to battle; for never was there a braver man, as there is not a discreeter. These holy bowmen at our right will not let us forget them. I must not have them left here to make a panic behind us. Be it your task, Sebastian, to drive them out as soon as we move forward."

After a short pause of silence, Zeno suddenly turned to the men behind him, and crying "Evviva San Marco," was answered by a loud and deafening shout: as the Englishmen rushed forward at his back, a roaring flight of arrows flew from the bows of the Venetians behind them.

The Genoese did not wait the shock in silence, but answering to the shout, rushed forward to encounter it. More than half way did the invaders meet them, and with such force did they rush together, that many in front could not use their arms, but were driven body to body, or were hemmed in among their enemies. Followed close by Edward, Carlo Zeno might be known by his red cap, piercing far and deep among the Genoese; and in a few moments, around him was the thickest of the fight.

Gerardo da Manteloro, pointing to Zeno with his sword, called out to him by name, and cried to his men to seize and bind him. But even his own horse could not bring him near to the coveted prisoner; for so fast did Zeno push forward, and so close was the press of men, that Gerardo's sword could not make way.

The shout of defiance had died away, and in its place was heard the jangling of the mail, as those who wore it struggled in a close embrace; the hacking of swords upon the steel; the deeper shouts of execration or of agony; and for a short space the combat seemed to waver in one fierce convulsive struggle on the spot where they first met.

But the Genoese had been deceived: the number of the Venetians was greater than they had counted from the bridge; and the fierce onset of the Englishmen, headed by Zeno, which seemed to drive the small band through rank after rank, as if each were no stronger than water, made the Genoese behind believe their strength still greater than it was. The soldiers remaining on the bridge had stopped—those who had put their foot on the land began to think it safer to return, and in pursuing Zeno in his fierce career towards the bridge, Gerardo himself had hurried his men backward in what many took for a flight. Turning his horse a little from without the press, he galloped back to the bridge, and strove to stay those who fled, now with entreaties, now with reproaches, and, at times, even with his sword. But the madness of fear was on his men, and rather than face the danger that might be quelled, they thought of nothing more than to reach the bridge alive.

Terrible was the slaughter made by the Englishmen, who backed the fugitives as they ran, carving them behind, and strewing the whole path to the bridge with bodies. As they regained it, the very crowding and crush made them stand. And those on the wall, seeing the danger, helped their friends as they might; turning upon the Venetians the thunder of mangonels and bombards, from which great round stones were hurled with such force that armor even could not resist; and many went then to their last account. Some of the heavy missiles, falling short, fell among the Genoese themselves, and helped the sword of Venice.

Seeing that strange aid, the Venetians gained new strength, and still pushed on for the bridge.

Now was the day of vengeance for that time when the Genoese fought their way into Chiozza by the same road; now the Genoese, as the Venetians did then, fled before greater numbers; but they turned more in coward fear, and abandoned themselves more to agony and distraction. When Zeno reached the bridge, the press upon it was so close that scarce his sword could pierce its way; and still there were Genoese behind him too bewildered to strike, and striving for nought but to scramble past, in the vain hope of reaching the city.

"Push forward, push forward," cried Zeno to Edward; "let us enter with them."

Seizing the advantage of the press, Gerardo now endeavored to make some stand against those who had so surprised him. His horse had fallen over the entangled bodies, and he was on foot. His courage and his sword would have forced a path forward, but that his own men drove him back; nay, sometimes almost lifted him off his feet. Near him was a young cavalier, who now aided him with his sword, and at times upheld him when he would have fallen. Seeing that this man a little stopped the forward course of his countrymen, Edward made towards him, and calling out, that he might not take him unawares, struck him with all his force upon the head. The blow made the knight reel and stagger, but, turning round, he repaid it with profit to him that dealt it. As he struck, Edward knew his face—it was young Francesco Carrara; and though his sword was raised again to strike, the Englishman, remembering where he last had seen him, lost heart to do so. Not so Turnbull, whose weighty form had borne him among the foremost. His sword had broken short off on the back of some flying Genoese, but rushing to the cavalier, who had so rudely assaulted his slighter friend, he struck him with a blow that might have opened a city gate, full upon the chest.

The youth's mail seemed to shrink and crumple under the blow like silk, and in his face which was red with heat and the violence of his toil, turned ashy pale. He did not fall, for the press around him was so close; but he seemed about to sink on his trembling knees, when Edward, seizing him by the arm, raised him up, and cried,

"Push forward, sir, to the city while you may; for there is no victory to be gained here, and you have done more than your due already."

Turning to look where his general was, young Carrara saw that Gerardo had now given up the contest, and was yielding, though slowly, to the backward pressure. Both sides had nearly ceased to fight, and the striving to rush forward had become more like the struggle to enter a church on some festival than the storm of a city.

The wooden bridge creaked and shook under the moving weight. The Venetians halted; some sudden thought checking their footsteps —the bridge groaned and labored like the mast of a ship in a storm, but a hundred fold louder —suddenly there was a sharp crack—then a shrieking tear—and Zeno and Edward stood pressing backwards with their feet at the edge of a precipice, while the broken drawbridge fell suddenly down, and poured forth the living mass upon it into the canal below. For an instant Gerardo, who had almost passed the weaker part of the bridge before it broke, might be seen to cling to the splintered end of a beam partly it gave way in his grasp—partly his hasty hold yielded to the weight of his falling body; and he too was seen struggling beneath. But the fight for life now became how to resist the pressure of the mingled fugitives and pursuers behind, who knew not what had happened. Those in front turned round and cried out to all behind them, friend or foe, to keep back; but they understood not, and already many Venetians and Genoese had been thrust forward into the splash and scramble below.

With a sudden thought Edward seized in his arms the man on whom the hopes of Venice rested; motioning to Turnbull, he made the ponderous Englishman also clasp him; and thrusting their feet firmly forward, the two threw themselves back against the living stream that rushed to the brink of the broken bridge. Never had Edward endured so fierce a struggle. The group swayed from side to side, like the bow of a ship that meets a beating sea. Little by little he could feel his feet move forward, where but a few inches of ground remained before them.

But gradually the pressure lessened; the flying Genoese and the pursuing Venetians began to know the doom that had cut off the path to Chiozza, shutting these out from victory, the others from safety.

Forgetting their strife, the late foes might be seen leaning together over the rail, and watching with fearful earnestness the struggle of the armed men in the water. With most it was short, for the weight of their arms soon dragged them under the surface. Some few, however, had fallen with the broken fragments of the bridge, or had seized them in the water. Among these was the unfortunate general of the fugitives; and when the struggle for his own life had subsided, Zeno called to his followers that they should save the illustrious Genoese, offering them large rewards. Some few hastily joined their sword-belts, and threw one end towards the general; but another seized it, and he himself was dizzy and faint with his fall. The beam that lay beneath his arm rolled over with the struggles of those near him, his head went backwards, and presently nothing was seen but the splash of the water where the cavalier had sunk.

Scared by that misadventure, the fugitives and the pursuers watched each other in listless curiosity. Even the Genoese who remained behind, and who now made their best speed towards Brondolo, were but little molested by those who had so hated them. For the dreadful doom which had struck so many seemed like the hand of heaven: pity and awe withheld the hand of mortal. Recalling his men, Zeno withdrew towards the chapel, pointing as he passed to the heaps of slain, whose mangled features showed how bloody had been the victory of the Venetians. No arrows assailed them from the little belfry, but near it stood Sebastian, with a small band of four Genoese prisoners, bound. Pointing to them, he said—

"There are our captives; there are fourteen dead bodies within the belfry, and twice as many more Venetians lie around it."

"Your triumph," said Zeno, as he laid his hand on Sebastian's shoulder, "has been dearer bought than ours; but it is more soldierly—for chance and some few rotten timbers have marred the work we could not complete. If Pisani has done as well at Brondolo as we have here, Venice has now regained the shores of the Adriatic; and the Genoese hold Chiozza not as a fortress, but as a cage. Still must I leave you here, Sebastian, with enough force to guard the ground we have gained, while I hasten on to Brondolo, to speed Pisani's certain victory; for never has he truly belied his name of Victor."

And so, without resting, Zeno, taking with him Edward, and such of his troops as he judged to be most fresh, moved southwards for the town. He had not seen it since he left Venice, and now he mournfully thought that he was in some strange place, so altered was every part. They came to where once stood the monastery of Cistercian nuns, and there stood a ruin, deserted even by the rude soldiery that had converted it into a dwelling and fort. Still going on, they came to where the town should have begun; but low walls, some of the earliest raised to close in the camp of the Genoese, replaced the houses of the ancient town—more ancient than Venice itself. Here saw they a tumult in front, but it was no battle. The fight was over; the town was retaken, and a host of prisoners remained, while another host had fled as they might to the main land.

As they drew nigh, something seemed to fix the random movements of the Venetian stragglers who had staid outside the streets; and then a little band, slowly moving marched from among them, bearing what looked like a litter. Zeno's party still went forward, and presently they knew that the soldiers had hastily made a litter of their spears, covered with cloaks and such softer things as they could find: on it lay a wounded man; his robe like Zeno's was red; it was Pisani!

"How is this, my friend and brother!" cried Zeno, as he took his hand; "are you hurt!"

"To the death, Zeno; but I have gained one more victory before I die, to show that I was worth letting out of prison. Set me down, my children. I see that you have conquered, for you are here. Is Chiozza taken!"

"It is not; for the way to it is cut off by the breaking of the bridge, of which many died; and the Genoese are locked up in the trap they have made for themselves. But your color goes! Where is your surgeon!"

"There is none here; nor does it need: it is too late. I did but long to see you, and to let you see me under the sun of victory, that hereafter you might remember me as one who did well for Venice. We have caged the foe, and you will drive him out without me. Embrace me, Zeno."

Zeno took his friend in his arms, and stooped over him. So lay the wounded man for a while, locked in that embrace. When Zeno rose, his face was wet with tears; and then the sad soldiers who stood around, saw that Victor Pisani was dead.

CHAPTER XLIV.

The shouts of the victory had died away in Pelestrina, and the day was drawing to a close, when Recanati, so long absent, entered Sebastian's tent. His pale cheek was flushed with a red spot, his silken eyebrows were drawn into a frown, and his delicate features were pinched together with the resolve of a man who is spited by fortune, and has made up his mind to some last resort.

"You know for what I am come," he said.

"I do forget," answered Ranieri; "you must tell me anew."

"Have you repented of your promise—of your wish to go with me to Chiozza; for time presses more than we thought? Or will you give us Sebastian without that idle ceremony."

"I have never yet repented of anything. It will be time to repent, when one can learn to undo what is done. I am ready."

Recanati turned and left the the tent, followed by the youth who would not arm; well aware that arms would in no way lessen his risk, though their absence, by seeming to show greater daring, did lessen it. When they had reached the condottiere's tent, Recanati entered it alone. Presently he returned, and beckoning to the other they again took their way, joined by two more cavaliers, who followed them in silence.

"Who are these?" asked Ranieri.

"They are men who bear us company on an errand like our own, and," he added in a severe tone, "they know you, Messer Ranieri, and will know you hereafter."

"Be it so."

Proceeding to the water's edge, they entered a small boat, in which they were rowed silently, but steadily and swiftly towards the Genoese. When they had come under the town they turned to the right, and went slowly along until they arrived at the mouth of the canal that divides the island. Whispered challenges were given and answered as they passed between the galleys stationed there, and floated within the barrier at the entrance. They landed and as they proceeded through the dark streets Ranieri was aware that scanty troops of soldiers loitered about rather with the air of men in idleness, than of those kept to guard a town invested by the enemy. Occasionally a torch borne by one or other of them showed him gaunt forms, and the vacant sulky languor of men whose spirits had been wearied out.

They entered the same house, and the same hall in which we saw Pietro Emo the night before Carrara had galloped into the place.

Where Emo had stood consulting how to repulse the Genoese, there stood Carrara taking counsel how to to repulse the Venetians.

In his condition he had much altered since he sat with Alessandro listening to the conversation of Marco Morosini with the monk. His frame had grown more meagre and the watchful look of his face, its hardened lines, and more angry eye, explained the wasting of his frame, which still was square and muscular. The color of his cheek seemed more settled on the surface and his hair, grown grayer, no

longer set off his face to so much advantage. Yet was there the same bold and dauntless expression, and the same ready smile, though a trifle bitterer, as he listened to the companion beside him.

This was Doria, whose grave and dignified face had grown more solemn; and he, unlike Carrara, seemed to bear rather than to brave the difficulties that overwhelmed them. And in truth he had more at stake. The Genoese cooped up in Chiozza could barely hope to escape even with life and limb, while the Paduan had gradually managed to withdraw the greater number of his forces; and he himself, cunning, active and fertile in resources, had no fear of escaping from the trap into which he had ventured. The worst to him was that his game went against him. Doria was anxious for his life—his fame, and the existence of the thousands that depended upon him. There was in the grave anxiety of his look a rebuke to the more careless manner of the unscrupulous Carrara.

As an attendant ushered in the small party that interrupted them, Carrara rose and came towards the strangers as though he expected them; but looking beyond the condottiere, his manner showed that he was surprised at seeing him accompanied by others of his own condition, whom at first he had taken for servants. Recanati took him familiarly by the arm, and leading him apart from his companions, spoke to him for a few minutes with earnestness and rapidity.

Ranieri watched them for a little time; but it was not at all his purpose in venturing so far to suffer the soldier to conceal his projects. Once or twice he moved with the intention of stepping forward and interrupting their conversation, but he chose a discreeter course. Turning to one of those who had come with him, whom he had not yet adressed, he said with a sneer,

"It seems that Messer da Recanati has not quite admitted us to his counsels. It may be dangerous to us to buy what we do but half see. The sack may contain a serpent to bite us if we see not to the bottom."

"True," answered the other, "I was just going to think as much," and he stepped towards Carrara and the condottiere, crying, "Pardon me, Messer da Recanati, but those who share the risk must share the council."

"True, true," said Recanati, "I had thought that you would follow me, but—" He stopped on seeing that Ranieri had not remained behind, and that the third of his companions had also pressed close upon him. "These, then, my lord," he said to Carrara, "are the gentlemen of whom I spoke; Messer da Piovere you already know; and this time I hope he will be more discreet. This is Messer Buzzacherino."

"And who," asked Carrara, "is this young gentleman? This is not Messer Sebastiano Morosini."

"It is, and it is not: it is a hostage for Messer Sebastiano; one who has all his power, and will convey to us even to help our success. But Messer Sebastiano will not trust himself with us until he sees better into our chance."

"Why this," cried Carrara, drawing angrily back, "is not the way, Recanati, in which you were wont to make your compacts. It is the compact which the old thief made with the young one; to share the booty if the boy got away with it, but to inform against him if he were caught."

"Those are strict in their compacts, my lord, who have the power to be so. We must take what we can get, and we have too Messer Sebastiano's hostage."

"Aye, a hostage; but say that Messer Sebastiano forfeits it, what were his loss?"

"This young gentleman has a life as sweet to him as his master's, and I think that he will not risk it; therefore it is for him to see that Messer Sebastiano fulfil his part. The young man knows that he lives only while he is true to us."

"Aye, and as for that," said Ranieri, putting on a little more audacity than he felt, "you, too, have kept in the dark as well as Sebastiano. I have only half yet made our bargain, Messer Condottiere, nor shall I close it till I know better what it is you mean to do. You tell me that you have Messer Carrara's word; but I have not yet heard it from him. You tell me that you have projects; but I know them not; and truly shall you not have Sebastiano's men or Sebastian's aid, until I can say for what purpose it shall be given, and what is the gain. You have me here, Messer Condottiere; and this powerful gentleman, whom I take to be the Lord of Padua, can dispose of me as he pleases. Let me never return to Pelestrina, if you will—you, who have gone so far in the contract, stop it if you list. I shall not be missed; or, if I am, no one will lay my life at your account. But if it be that you desire to have me help you, I say I must know in what I give it, and what I give it for."

"A bold youngster," cried Carrara, with a smile; "and Carrara tells you, boy, that no triumph in this world was ever gained but that which may be won by daring and by cunning. Each apart may make a man a ready tool for others' uses; but to make him a master, both must be joined. Now I will tell you what it is we need, and therein lies my boldness; cunning I have no need for. There is but one risk, but one discovery to be made, and all rests upon our boldness. We do desire, having lost great part of our force, to buy over to our own use what we can of the Venetian forces. We have already the company of Messer Recanati; Messer da Piovere has come to give us his, and there are more that may be purchased. We have already in Venice those who, if we approach it in power, will yield to us the rule of the city; but truly should we be well pleased to have more of those whom the people themselves would favor—those who are loved in the streets and in the lagoon, as well as those who are cunning in council. Therefore is it, Messer Giovane, that we would buy the good will of your friend; for as I hear there is none other so young that is so well beloved in Venice. That is what we want. And now for the price. It is Venice. Those who join in this our great enterprise shall share Venice among them—its wealth amongst us all, leaders and men; its rule to those who bring us power, whereof Messer Sebastiano shall have large part. To make this compact, Messer Roberto da Recanati has full power. He is the leader of that Venetian army which will pass over to me so soon as we know all whom we can gain. In him may you trust as to myself. And now, sir, I have told you all; what gage have we that you are faithful?"

"None but that which Messer da Recanati told you of just now, my life. I think, as I have told him before, that the risk is all with us; for you, it seems, have lost everything already; whereas with us our losses are to begin."

"Be it so."

Recanati once more attempted to draw Carrara aside; but Ranieri laying his hand upon his arm, said—

"If we are to be true to each other, there must be open councils for all."

"Nay, nay," replied the condottiere, "I do but wish to ask Messer Carrara's pleasure, and anon you shall hear it. You are a young councillor, Messer Ranieri, and too sharp."

When the two had conversed for a few minutes, the Lord of Padua beckoned to Ranieri, and said to him—

"Now, this shall be your first task: it is necessary to our enterprise that on some pretence the whole of our friends should be called out before the rest of the army in Brondolo, if it may be. Think you that you could so contrive, when the time comes, that some one who has the power should give such order that it might be done without any show of activity amongst yourselves?"

Ranieri thought for a moment. How to do it he did not attempt to consider. The use that it might be put to, was scarcely more distinct to him. Chiefly he thought what would be the best answer for him to make before those with whom he spoke, and in a firm and confident but quiet voice he answered—

"It shall be done."

"Enough," answered Carrara. "You have gained that for which you have visited us in our poor lodging, Messer Giovane. We have learnt that which Messer da Recanati came to tell us, and we need keep you no longer. But," said Carrara with a smile, "a gentleman of your condition must needs lack service, and for your sake I have asked Messer da Recanati to spare two of his most comely, discreet, and bold men to be your attendants. They will help you in keeping true to you trust, Messer Giovane; so you may thank me for this generous act of Messer da Recanati's."

"I will thank you, my lord, some few days hence when you shall ask Messer Sebastiano to confer upon me that office in Venice which I shall then have earned."

"In three days, or never."

Leaving the presence of Carrara, da Recanati and his companions took their leave; and having re-entered their boat, regained Pelestrina in early morn, without observation.

CHAPTER XLV.

RANIERI had not long returned to Sebastian's tent, when two men entered to him; and one of them, a sleek and decent serving man, not much older than himself, taking off his cap, approached with a low obeisance.

The man's manner was humble and respectful, and yet there lurked in his cunning eye and slightly compressed lips a smile of insolent daring.

"We have been told, my lord," he said, "that you need more servants, and that you will take us for your attendants."

"Who sent you!" asked Ranieri.

"Messer Roberto da Recanati."

"I am obliged to him for the courtesy, and what wages am I to give you?"

"Messer Roberto, my lord, is too desirous for you to be served well, to trouble you to pay us; but we are to have, elsewhere, double the wages that you may choose to name."

"Why, then, I can give you generous pay, and yet be none the poorer. Who is your friend here; will he take equal wages with yourself?"

"Battista is an honest man, my lord; but will scarcely ask so much, my lord, as I always have."

"Why then, sir, say that my wages to you shall be a bowman's pay, eight ducats a month; and your friend's, a rower's, the half of that. And you say that you will have double; will that satisfy you?"

"We shall be satisfied, my lord, with whatever you choose to vouchsafe; and I will say to you that never will you have closer attendants than we shall prove."

"I think that I shall never have been so well attended, for look—you see how I have thrown my clothes here all in confusion: you shall enter upon your duties at once, and set them all in order for me."

The man bowed obsequiously, and entered upon his new task as if he had already for years been the young gentleman's servant.

Ranieri was puzzled how to deal with his new attendants. He felt no great fear, though he saw by the man's manner and the blunt daring that appeared in the deportment of the other, that there were set upon him spies who would stop at no extremity; yet embarked as he was in an enterprise that promised more honor even than danger, he was prepared to run the risk with the same temper that men brave the rocks and storms of the Adriatic, and busied himself rather to think how he might out-manœuvre even the great Carrara, and his tool Recanati, than how he might avoid the peril to his own person. It seemed to him that he could even turn this watch set upon him to advantage, and that if he could deceive these spies, who were naturally less cunning than their masters, he might through them more readily deceive the masters themselves. Carrara should have had only Carraras for his spies, and then he might have trapped Venice at his will.

His first task was to confer with Sebastian, both that he might seem to be carrying on the plot into which he had entered with Recanati, and that he might possess his friend of the actual state of matters. He made no attempt to evade his attendant spies, but now he turned to account the art which his sister had taught him, of writing. While the men were busied about the tent, he wrote a short story of what he would tell to his friend, and seeming to put it away, he hid it in his sleeve; the soldiers little heeding that clerkly employ.

He set forth in early day-light to seek Sebastian in Pelestrina. Before entering Sebastian's room, he beckoned to him the younger serving man, and asked his name.

"Giovanni," replied the man.

"Then, Giovanni," said Ranieri, "I would have both of you attend me where I am going, but keep you closer to me than your friend Battista; for however useful a sturdy arm may be, I deem you to be the discreeter man; therefore you keep closer to me, but yet not so close as to offend the noble with whom I am going to confer; for Messer da Recanati may have told you that he is ready to take offence—and yet he is a gentleman, whose favor your master most needs."

Ranieri's familiar manner had already in part disarmed the cunning spy, and he bowed with more respect than he had yet shown for his master-charge. They entered the room. Sebastian was right glad to see his young companion return in safety; but observing strangers with him, he somewhat smothered the expression of his pleasure. Nevertheless Ranieri embraced his friend with more than wonted fervor, and while he did so, thrust the paper he had written into his clothes at the back of his neck, saying in a quick low tone,

"Read this and say nothing."

"Dear Sebastian," he continued aloud, "I have, you see, returned, and better attended than I went, for my friend Recanati has lent these excellent servants for my use."

Sebastian was silent, not knowing how to answer, and Ranieri continued; he told Sebastian that he had been whither he knew he was to have gone; and that the friends whom he had seen, wished him to cause an order to be issued for the whole of the troops to be drawn out on a day to be fixed, as if to see their strength; and," added Ranieri, "let it be done; for then shall we see our strength."

And presently he took his leave.

No sooner was he gone, than Sebastian feeling like one in a dream, hastened to pluck out the paper that Ranieri had thrust under his clothes, and read it. It ran thus :—

"I have seen Carrara in Chiozza. He has gained, through Recanati, the troops of Piovere, Buzzacherino, and some more whose names I know not. If the troops be all drawn out, they will show their strength, and entice others, and declare for Carrara. He offers you a large share in the government of Venice, having many friends therein. I have promised that the troops shall be drawn out. The men who are with me are spies, to kill me if I betrayed Carrara, therefore remember that in thinking of what I say to you aloud. Tell Messer Zeno of these things, and let him do as may please him."

Sebastian was struck with amaze at the youth's daring and his danger; and he instantly went to Zeno, with what he had heard and the paper.

"Ah! the traitor," cried Carlo, "I did suspect as much; but scarcely could I have thought such daring and such discretion in so young a man as your friend. His promise shall be ful

filled I see it all. And you say he was dogged by two of Recanati's men. Aye, Roberto
has the sting as well as the cunning of the
serpent ; but we will foil him by his own scheme.
Can you count, Sebastian, upon your men, or
has this traitor been poisoning their ears ?"

"No, my lord ; they are faithful ; and so I
think are all. Since Ranieri did not tell of any
more, I should suspect that there are no new
traitors ; but it is likely that those whom we
have already marked, have returned to their
falsehood. These I can name to you, and
these must be watched."

"They shall be so. Give you order that
Recanati's troops be brought here on the morrow, and stationed with da Piovere's behind
us here, towards Brondolo. Now forsooth do
I feel that I am driving these traitors before
me, while they think they are running their
own course. On the day after it will be the
Lord's day, and we will rest ; but for the next
day we will contrive a plan to defeat and use
these knaves."

<hr>

CHAPTER XLVI.

THE morning was bright and sharp ; and as
the men moved hither and thither to take their
alloted station, every one looked alert and ready
for action. All had been disposed as Zeno desired. Recanati and his own force had been spe-
cially summoned from Pelestrina, and so had
the remainder of Sebastian's men, who had been
left there under the command of Ranieri.

In the open ground between the town of
Brondolo and Chiozza, were arrayed the whole
force that Zeno had gathered to the spot ; the
severals bands standing in compact bodies, at
intervals ; the view of the whole broken by the
tents that had been raised. Far in the rear,
Recanati was at the head of his men, anxious
care gradually giving place to a daring hope, as
with the advance of day the whole of his project
seemed to go forward to his wish. Near him
stood da Piovere ; the burly soldier dissipating
in a restless activity the mixed anxiety and
shame which moved him as he thought that the
day had come when he was to betray the patron
who had so often shared his dangers, improved
his fortunes, and had even so lately forgiven his
treachery. Near him also stood Ranieri, in
whom the suspicious Recanati believed that he
had an instrument as willing and as cunning as
himself, embarked with a good faith in his
treacherous enterprise. Ranieri's bearing was
such as to strengthen his confidence. The youth
was clothed in gay and well made arms, given
to him by Sebastian. He felt no alarm at the
approaching crisis of his fate. The danger was
as far too great for his own control, as for him
to oppose. And he placed his trust in God, and
in the fortune of the day, throwing in his safety
as a stake in the game where the prize was to
be an honor so much above his years. Thus,
while he still was with Recanati, he had nothing
to distract his mind from the immediate task
before it, and he set himself to advise the condottiere in the disposal of his men, and in his
own demeanor towards Zeno, as though he
were heart and soul in the successful issue of
the scheme

"Now, Messer Ranieri, that we have gone so
far," said the mercenary, " it were well to tell
you the immediate purpose that we have. See
you here," he continued, as he stepped apart
from his band to command a better view of
their array, " these men are mine ; those beyond
belong to Messer da Piovere ; and those again
on this side to Buzzacherino ; and on this, and
on this," pointing as he spoke, " we also count ;
the whole of this body, strong as it is, belongs
to us and to our scheme. Then there are your
own men or Messer Sebastiano's whom also we
may count with us. Is it not a good show ! We
are ill placed here, and must find some way
presently to move more to the front ; but there
is time enough ; for it is yet full early ; though I
have told those who are to receive us, never to
think it too soon, but to watch for us even from
midnight. I do believe that when we declare
ourselves, more will join us than Messer Sebastiano ; for already have friends of mine
spoken to Messer Vendramini, who has been
very hopeless ever since he found the troops so
discontented at Pelestrina, and truly we can
offer much to those who seek our favor. This
then our plan : being all here assembled in our
strength, we shall first strive to know how we
may increase it, and having gathered all we can,
look you, we march to Chiozza, which opens its
gates, and straightway we are joined by all the
force it can bring to the field we already possess.
Carlo Zeno may have heart for the fight, but the
sword will break in his hand. There are dangers
which even a secret shirt of mail cannot turn
aside."

"The scheme promises well, so that nothing
occur to interrupt our path."

"To interrupt us ! what can occur ! We have
the path in our own power : it is straight before
us. See you here ; there is nothing that lies
between us and Chiozza, but that palisade, the
gates of which we hold as soon as we will.
What can occur ?"

As he spoke, a gentleman came to them and
said, that the generalissimo desired their presence at a council, wishing to learn the condition
of all the men and their stores. Recanati looked
at Ranieri, as much as to ask if he had heard of
this council !

"Perhaps," said Ranieri to him, in a low
voice but smiling, " this may be one of the ac-
cidents of which I spoke ; for it is more than
either you or I meant."

"It is no matter," answered the condottiere.
"Accident or design, it yet may serve our purpose. Let us go. I will but return to tell da
Piovere that he may keep my command until I
come back, and that we will go together.

Whether some suspicion crossed Recanati's
mind that made him more anxious to keep the
youth by his side, or whether it was that he always worked in doubt and distrust, certain it is
that he seemed more anxious than ever not to
miss Ranieri. The young man obeyed his wish ;
and showing no distrust, accompanied him to his
post at the head of his men, but when they arrived there, they found that da Piovere had already repaired to the council to which he had
been summoned, and one of Recanati's officers
told him that he had seen many other leaders of
the different bands on the ground repairing to
Carlo Zeno's tent.

"Why then," said Recanati to his companion, "we must go perforce; for it would be amiss to remain outside, unknowing of what passes."

The distance was not so great but a man might walk it in less than a quarter of an hour. They entered the tent, and the condottiere cast around a hasty glance. He suppressed the surprise he felt when he saw Zeno accoutred in full armor, as if ready for action, the white and azure bars, of eight pieces, blazoned on his surcoat; all the nobles by whom he was surrounded were also in arms: near him stood the provveditore, Vendramini, Marco Morosini and his son, Pietro Emo, Edward, William Cooke, and many trusty leaders of the Venetian armies, even some whose men were not upon the ground. The condottiere had not expected to find so full a council. Not far within the entrance of the tent stood da Piovere, and the companions of Recanati's conspiracy; and he was somewhat reassured, when among the group near Zeno, he saw Alessandro da Padova, Lionardo Morosini, Marian Barbarigo, and Pietro di Bernardo.

There was a general silence. Even the few whispers that passed between those who stood near to each other might almost be distinguished in the general stillness. The principal group stood perfectly mute—Zeno seeming to await some farther event. As they went in, Ranieri would have stepped over to Sebastian, but Recanati suddenly grasped his wrist, and drew him close to his side, pressing to take up their station in the midst of the small knot of leagued captains.

"I did but desire to ask," said Ranieri in a whisper, "the meaning of this council."

"It is well," answered the other, "but we can wait."

Though he studiously forbore to meet the eye of Recanati, Carlo Zeno had noted his entrance; and soon afterwards stepping a little forward he said aloud,—

"I have summoned you all, gentlemen, my very good companions, to learn from you the state in which our forces now are. The power of the Genoese has sunk so low, that but a little more struggle will throw them entirely within our reach. To make the blow the quicker, to make it the more merciful to ourselves, it needs that we should have our utmost strength for a last attack. Therefore would I know in what condition are our men, and in what mood; for if they are not with us in their hearts, their arms can little avail us; and I would take Chiozza only by the help of those who desired to seize it with me. We have had amongst us, as it has been said aloud in Venice, foul treachery. It has even shown its face before our sight; but that was when the fortunes of Venice seemed at their lowest. The favor of heaven always maketh men kind, and I am fain to believe that now we are in our strength, there are none that seek to abandon us. Therefore have I almost forgotten the treachery that showed itself amongst us—of that, no more; but I would learn from you, who so well can tell me, how are your men furnished with arms, whether they are well contented with the provision that they have had, and in what state is their discipline. Are they prompt to obey? ready to advance at a word? ready to fall back at a sign? and especially those who are most strange to us, and owe less love and allegiance to Venice. Messer Guglielmo Coco shall first tell me whether his men are faithful as ever. Stand forth, excellent sir, that we all may hear your answer."

"My lord," replied Cooke, answering in English, "I think that when you command you will know no difference in the bearing of my men from what you have found before."

"I need scarcely translate our friend's answer," said Zeno, "for it is what we all expect. And you, Messer da Piovere, are your men as sturdy as ever, as bold, as generous, and as faithful as their leader? Stand forth, sir, that all may understand what noble soldiers are your men, and how much they deserve their excellent leader."

The old soldier's color went and came. He turned pale at first, and then flushed to a purple red; and as he swayed from side to side, hesitating whether to step forward, or not, whether to speak or remain silent, he muttered some scarcely intelligible sounds.

"How is this, Messer da Piovere," cried Zeno. "Nothing has happened amiss! Indeed I saw your men as I entered, and truly I thought that never saw I a finer band. Come hither to me, my good friend, and if some doubt has assailed you, tell it softly to me here, and we will find a remedy."

As he spoke, Recanati's face had grown gradually dark and angry—his cutting glance had passed from the old condottiere to Sebastian and Ranieri, and to the high conspirators whom he saw engaged among the Venetian nobles. Placing his hand stealthily towards his fellow soldier, he struck him in the side to recal him to himself, and said, in a low voice,

"Answer, answer; let your answer be what it will, speak at once."

Mechanically obeying both commands, da Piovere stepped forward towards the general, stammering as he said,

"My lord, I trust you suspect no ill!"

Recanati saw da Piovere leave his side with impatient anger, and turning to his companions, he said, in an under tone,

"Look after our young friend here. You shall account to me for this, sir."

"Be discreet," answered Ranieri, "there is nothing yet wrong if you can but silence that old babbler, who has no more rein upon his tongue than a child; therefore speak you as soon as you can to stop him."

Recanati bent another hasty regard on Ranieri, doubtful whether to trust him the more, or to suspect him the more for the calmness of his reply.

"What means this?" cried Zeno, "has something befallen our friend da Piovere? It may be that his companions can tell us; and you, Messer da Recanati, may perchance explain how comes it that this excellent old man is so strongly moved?"

Recanati at once suppressed all outward sign of the rage and doubt that now consumed him, and he answered with a smile, "Our grayheaded warrior is as shame-faced as a girl; and therefore is it, that in the presence of so many your words have moved him."

Motionless for an instant, Recanati looked from Zeno to Ranieri; and then he said to the general, in a stern voice that rang in the silence of the place.

"I see that Messer Zeno still ungenerously suspects me; that I have been betrayed by spies set over me, and that I can no longer seek honor in the service of Venice."

Suddenly the fire of his eye grew fiercer, and moving with a rapidity that the eye could not follow, he snatched forth a short dagger from his side and plunged it into Ranieri—not waiting to pluck it back, but rushing towards the entrance.

"Seize him," cried Zeno.

He was gone. The men who had stolen behind the group of conspirators to seize them at a given signal, rushed forward and captured Ranieri and those near him. But the chief had darted through their confused rank, like a swallow between the branches of a tree.

"Pursue him," again cried Zeno.

The men darted from the tent in pursuit; the whole place was in confusion; swords had been drawn at the first act of violence, and there was a general move to follow the fugitive.

"Stop, sirs, stop," cried Zeno, holding up his hand; "let us not check each other's way. He has already escaped, or we shall find him in bonds. Follow me who lists, but let us go orderly."

The agile Recanati would far have distanced his pursuers, but for the most untoward accident. As he rushed headlong from the tent, a soldier of the guard without crossed the path, and the flying cavalier dashed against him. The soldier was struck down on the spot, and Recanati, stumbling over the falling man fell at full length upon the ground. The soldier, bewildered and angered by the sudden assault, grappled with his assailant and called loudly for help.

"Release me—release me!" cried Recanati, "I have a message from the general."

The angry man heard him not; and some short time had passed before he could tear himself free from the grasp that held him. As he rose he saw that he was surrounded by the band from which he had fled. Nothing daunted, he drew his sword and again dashed forward, pushing desperately for his onward path, and striking those who opposed him with such impetuosity that even the increasing numbers that now assailed him from every side could not altogether resist his progress. In the skirmish, some received the blows from their fellows that were meant for him; many a hand grasped his clothes, felt them torn apart with fingers chafed by the rapidity of his motion; and more than one hand thus thrust forward was hastily snatched back in bleeding agony. Still he made way, when Zeno issued from the tent, and seeing how matters stood, hastily sent round some few who yet were fresh, to place themselves full and close together in the condottiere's path; while, with Morosini, Edward, and others of his friends, he stepped towards the desperate traitor.

"Yield yourself, Messer da Recanati," he cried, "there is no longer hope for your flight. Yield yourself, if you would have mercy. He heeds me not; the blundering fools hinder each other and fight on his side. Who will stop him for me! for if he escape, Venice may be lost."

At the word Edward sprang forward, and calling out to the soldiers to leave his prey, he rushed upon the traitor himself. Recanati turned to his new foe. Despite his exertion, his face was pale with rage and settled purpose, and losing no time in words or attempts at flight, he threw into one fierce blow at the neck of Edward, whose head was unarmed, his whole intent to destroy at one sweep that hindrance to his flight. Edward but half avoided the stroke, which alighted partly on his neck and partly on the edge of his mail, writing in a deep red line of jagged flesh and iron the strength and fierceness of the Florentine. The other too strove to make the first blow do the whole of his will, and he aimed his thrust full in the face of Recanati. It struck him on the chin and glancing down between the bone and the edge of the mail wounded him deeply in the throat. He staggered.

"One more blow for Venice," cried Zeno.

Edward's arm obeyed the will of its leader; and his second stroke cleft the falling traitor across the eyes, and he fell a dead man.

By this time the open space outside the tent was in the utmost confusion—men running hither and thither, shouts echoing in every part, and a large moving crowd keeping up a continual scramble to see what was passing in the circle around the combatants.

"We must silence this," said Zeno, "or we shall have the traitor's men upon us. Bear in the body. And let us at once dispose of these infected hands. Where is Sebastian?"

"I am here," answered the man himself.

"I had thought that you were with your wounded friend: how fares he?"

"I am here too, my lord," answered Ranieri, "with nothing worse than a bruised cut upon my shoulders." Stepping close to the general the youth said to him in a low and earnest voice, "Did you, my lord, understand my message? there is a path open for us into Chiozza, if we use it betimes."

Zeno smiled; he was pleased with the boldness and spirit of the youth, and more so with his discreet cunning.

"It is all planned, Ranieri mio; and you, if you are not much hurt, shall take your share in it; for none of us can so fitly be the guide, since you know what is passing on both sides, and you are known to both. It is all done. Sebastian, hasten to your own men, and let Messer Guglielmo and the other troops whom you have in readiness quickly move around those of this traitor here. And now let me have some sharp fellow among your men."

Sebastian beckoned to a soldier, who approached them.

"Can you look frightened, my brave fellow?" said Zeno.

"I will try, my lord."

"Why then run to Messer Recanati's men. You know where they are stationed; run and shout as if for your life, *that Messer Recanati is betrayed,* and that they must hasten to his rescue. Now, stand no longer, but run and let us see how fast your legs can go." The man scampered off as if he ran for a footrace; and presently he had passed the tents that hid him from their sight. "They will already have heard the tumult; let me have another such fellow, Sebastian."

Sebastian again summoned one of those that stood around.

"Now, my man," said Zeno, "see if you can run as fast as our friend: follow him and say that *Recanati is dead*. Shout it aloud, and let them hear it well—*dead, dead*;—mind that they hear that."

That man too ran off, and presently was out of sight. Sebastian and Cooke, with other officers, had already left Zeno's side to take the head of their men; and the general himself with Vendramini, Morosini, and the guard following them close, now took the path that had been taken by the two soldiers. In a little time they came in sight of Recanati's men, and there, as they expected, they saw all confusion; a large number already hastening with fire and anger in their looks, towards the part where the nobles had come. Leaving his friends Zeno stepped briskly forward alone, and standing erect he held his hand on high. The mutinous soldiers stopped, as if uncertain of their purpose.

"What is it you want, my friends!" he said in a loud and pleasant voice; "what is it you seek!"

"Da Recanati, our captain; our Recanati," shouted the men; some few again moving forward.

Again Zeno raised his hand.

"Your Recanati," he cried, "is dead; he would have betrayed you, as he would have betrayed us; and for his own gain he would have led you to death. He had deceived you, for he told you that he was strong while he still was weak. He told you—answer me, did he not?—that Messer Morosini's men were your friends who would be on your side. Now look you here." He waved his hand around. "These are Messer Morosini's men who surround you. Look behind you—they are the men of Messer Coco. You are surrounded and divided in every part, and the prize that da Recanati had promised you was hopeless. Tell me your wishes. They shall not be denied."

As he spoke in a pleasant manner, the men looked round, and seeing that truly they were encompassed on every side by close bands that kept marching slowly round and separated the disordered mutineers in more and more places, they were daunted, and standing sullenly still, they yielded to the command of Zeno.

Had it been any other they might longer have resisted; but Zeno's fortune was accounted too irresistible not to overbear the courage of men who had lost their leader, who knew not the path to pursue the enterprise to which he would have led them, and who lacked confidence in each other.

Zeno again spoke—

"Fear not for yourselves; it is your captain that was the traitor. You were betrayed, and yet again in the triumph of Venice you shall reap that guerdon, you shall have that spoil which he would have denied to you. Go back to your tents and rest you; more at leisure I will confer with those among you in whom you trust, and we will contrive how you shall be provided with leaders, and how you shall be paid. Does that please you! Some of ye answer me."

"Aye, my lord," cried one near to him, "we

must be content perforce, since it seems we are prisoners, and truly you speak us fair."

"I speak no fairer than I will do. Back to your tents, and on the morrow, if need be, you shall again be led forth in the battle of Venice. Messer Vendramini the proveditore will lead you to your tents. You know him for a friend of old, and you know how highly he is esteemed in Venice."

As he had said, Vendramini and other of the nobles approached Recanati's men, who went the way they came slowly, and perchance somewhat sullenly; casting on either side no pleased glances at the close ranks that formed a barrier to their path and opened as they advanced to let them pass with their Venetian leaders.

Seeing that his purpose was thus done, Zeno turned round, saying—

"Now your second task begins, Ranieri. Come hither."

He laid his hand on the youth's shoulder, and seeing him wince, he said—

"I had forgot your wound, and it is often that the love of friends will thus hurt us in pleasing itself. But your cut has not taken the color from your cheek. It was well for you that Recanati was in such haste, for he did not often aim so ill. Have you still strength to do our bidding?"

"I believe, my lord, that all who serve you will go on as long as you please to command, for I do not see that any draw back when you bid them go forward; nor will I be the first to do so. I am only too fortunate in being chosen while so young and helpless—"

"Young truly," cried Zeno, "but there are many older who have given me less help, with all their years, than you have in these few days. We shall yet task your strength and courage still farther, and you may remember that if we now push you within the very reach of death, you are making your good fame faster than any of us have made it."

"I think, my lord, that one reason why you are so well served is that you over-pay your servants with too much praise."

"Why, then," answered the general, "consider that I have paid you in advance, and if I have put too much in your treasury, you shall still earn it. And now for the first time, Giovinetto mio, you shall enter into most grave and solemn council. Come with me to my tent where you shall be taught your task. But this I will tell you before we enter, that old man da Piovere has wits so feeble that he cannot keep his own honesty, but must even let his will lie abroad to be handled by every knave that will steal it. Thus I account it not his knavery that he is a traitor, but rather that in his person da Recanati himself was two knaves. Now this old man is very free of heart, so that you may easily turn him to your purpose, good or bad; therefore will we, shaming him sorely, make him very penitent, and you will see that he will do our bidding as easily as he would da Recanati's. He went with you, did he not, when da Recanati took you to Chiozza?"

"He did."

"Why then he shall go with you now, for then seeing him as well as you, the Genoese will put more trust in you. But this is what I would tell you, lest we should be mistaken in da

Piovere's good intent, or lest he should be even yet more feeble than we account him, and should fall from his word—we must be shielded from the dangers of his weakness ; therefore he will go with you as a companion ; but with him shall be, to keep close by his side, even as you were watched, some three or four stout fellows, who, at the pointing of your finger, shall despatch him at your feet. And now tell me, Ranieri mio, if you can steel your heart like a man to do Venice this duty ?"

" My lord, I have given myself up to you to be fashioned as you list, knowing that you are the wisest workman in Venice, whose order we have only to make good. Therefore whatever you think fit to command, I think, because it is so commanded, the properest to do."

CHAPTER XLVII.

Soon after they had entered the tent, a general movement might be observed among the soldiers, who were marched in close bands from the rear towards the edge of the encampment fronting Chiozza ; and on all faces might be seen that anxious and unsettled, though pleased look, that men exhibit who are bent on some unknown enterprise, which they believe to be important. This movement was yet unfinished, fresh hands were still quietly taking up their station, when Ranieri and da Piovere, attended by some few of the soldiers attached to Zeno's person, issued from the pavilion.

Ranieri walked with a quick and confident step. His eye glowed, but his compressed lip marked the effort of his young mind to put restraint upon his bearing worthy of the enterprize.

The old soldier looked dejected and shamefaced ; but still was there an effort to be bold and cheerful ; while in the alacrity of his step and the closeness of his attendance upon his young companion, he seemed to show that there was no need for the guard that had been placed about him to secure his new fidelity. The stepped to the band, picked from among Sebastiano's men, stationed nearest to the palisade, and with a brief delay issued at once towards the town. As they came in sight their movements grew quicker, and their march turned to a run in a feigned flight.

To give color to the trick, another band headed by Cooke, pursued them for some short distance in counterfeit hostility, but quickly drew back as if engaged with fresh combatants in the rear. Ranieri slackened his pace, and forming his men into better order, they still kept on a hasty march towards the bridge. The draw-bridge was raised ; behind it stood a thick crowd of the besieged troops ; and in the midst of them was the veteran Doria, watching the issue of the movements on the opposite side. Long had he stood at his post expecting the signal for his army to issue from the town ; and now, when he saw Ranieri flying before his pursuers, the delay seemed in part accounted for—Recanati's enterprise must have failed. The fugitives had come far upon the bridge, and still no sign was made that the upraised draw-bridge would be lowered.

The youth cried out as he still pushed on, " Lower the bridge, sirs, if you would not have us slain."

" How is this, Giovinetto ?" cried the Genoese commander. " We have not seen the signal ; and our compact was, that we should issue to you, not that we should admit a strange band into the town."

" Aye," answered Ranieri, "so would it have been if we could have promised success ; nor yet are we defeated ; but traitors have been amongst us, and Messer Roberto has been obliged to forget the signal, while we fought for our lives."

" Where is the captain ? And is this the whole strength that he was to bring us ?"

" Not so, he is still behind, and will be here anon, but he remains to guard the rear, while we bring off as many as we may ; for a large part of the army has joined with us. Still Zeno will not let us off so easily, but that we have had to fight our way, and you must find room for us in the town if you would keep us for your own service. Lower the bridge, sir, that a path may be made for us."

" I cannot lower the bridge until I see the signal, or until Messer Recanati himself shall come to make a new compact."

" What ! a compact with Carlo Zeno and an armed host at our heels ! Lower the bridge, sir ; or if you will not lower it, in sooth we will go back to Zeno, for he will treat us with less cruelty than those for whom we have deserted him. Rather would I have the mercy that Zeno will show to traitors, as he may truly call us, than stand here parleying with one for whom we have shed our blood, yet who refuses us shelter. See you not Messer da Piovere, who has been separated from his own band ; and look you here, how I have been wounded in the shoulder. Truly will God bring destruction on those who thus forsake their friends. Lower the bridge, sir, or we will go back—will we not, men !" cried the youth, in a loud voice, as he turned to his followers.

" Aye," shouted a hundred voices.

" How know we that your tale is true, that we should open a way into our town," said Doria.

" True ! do you ask for the truth of our story ! —why, will not our danger—will not this very blood tell you that we have no time to contrive falsehoods ! And see, here come more of us. If you do not lower the bridge I will go back, and say that you cast us off, and that we had better make peace with Zeno, while yet we have arms in our hands ; for we are so strong, sir, that we yet may make terms for ourselves with Zeno before he has quite conquered us. Only that we thought to join our friends and to increase our strength, Messer Recanati would sooner have sent me to open a path for him into the town. Let down the bridge at once, or we return."

Doria still hesitated ; but after remaining for some moments silent, he suddenly started like a man who has cast aside some dreaming doubts ; and with a wave of his hand he signed for the bridge to be lowered. Its creaking joints had scarcely ceased their sound, ere its shaken timbers, late so hastily repaired, were pressed with the tread of Venetian soldiers : in a few minutes. Ranieri and da Piovere stood among their men before Doria at the open gate of the town; which was crowded on the top and on every side by anxious spectators; while the space within was peopled by the bands that stood ready to issue forth.

"Where is Messer Carrara, my lord," asked Ranieri of the Genoese, "that he is not here to confer with us at such a moment !"

Carrara has been watching here since sunrise, and he left us but just before you came, for I sent him in to rest while I should watch."

"He had better be sent for," said the youth, "since you say that some new compact must be made; for while our companions are marching to the town with an angry foe behind them, it little behoves to have in front that which will stop our way. If the old compact is not enough, my lord, let us have a new one at once; for I do believe that Messer Recanati will not arrive so long as he can keep back the Venetians; and when he does there will be little time for us to stand here at the town gate making terms to enter it or not—send for him at once, sir, that Messer da Piovere and I may make the compact with him now."

"You speak boldly, youth," said the venerable commander. "I did but talk of compacts while I doubted. It is too late to doubt now. But keep your men together, and we will make compacts after you are in town. March your men, and we shall see them safely disposed of in the piazza."

"Nay, my good lord," answered Ranieri with a sneer, "those who doubt, wake others' doubts, and I will not leave this gate while I see the path for my hard pressed companions uncertain. Let your men stand back, for there will not be room for us; and truly when Messer Recanati comes, we shall be in haste to shut the gate behind his back."

While this converse had proceeded, another band, and yet another had come, flying from the encampment; hasty steps already resounded on the bridge. Ranieri's companions began to press hard upon the soldiery stationed under the gate; and turning with an angry glance to the old condottiere, the youth said,

"You are silent, Messer da Piovere; we want your tongue here as well as your hand; why do you not help me to make a path for our men !"

The old man flushed like one rebuked, and then called out in a loud voice, asking Doria to order back his own soldiers. The Genoese commander complied; he motioned them back, and a few steps more placed the front of Ranieri's troop within the gates. Still more of the Venetian soldiers now crowded behind them. More and more came on, still keeping up a semblance of flight. More and more again, till it seemed that the living stream would never cease to pour over the edge of the hill.

Doria's frowning brow grew thoughtful and gloomy, as he saw so large a force now hold the bridge and the gate, and pressing in towards the town. Privately he sent one to summon Carrara, while others went among his own men and bade them stand firmly to their posts, making a narrow path for the Venetian fugitives.

"I do not see," he said, with a look of grow-

ing suspicion, to Ranieri, "that much fighting passes yonder. Let your men march in, sir, for we ourselves must keep the gate, and the bridge is overcrowded. March in, sir."

"Anon, anon," answered Ranieri, scarcely heeding him; for not far off he saw Willian. Cooke, and but a little behind him Sebastian and Carlo Zeno with a whole troop of Venetian leaders following close upon their general: "I have told you, sir," he said, turning to Doria, "that I will not leave the gate until my friends have entered it; and I shall stand to my word."

"Nay, youngster, it is I who command in Chiozza as yet; therefore, I say, move on, if you would not be roughly handled. We will close the gates upon you and keep you out, if joining us you obey not our command."

"Zeno was pressing forward through his men, whose passage was now blocked, and already he was upon the drawbridge, when Ranieri, seeing that the time had come to relieve the bridge of its choking load, turned to Doria, and said,

"Now, sir, we will go forward."

There was something in his look that alarmed the Genoese with a suspicion of the truth. Glancing his eye hastily towards the bridge, he saw, threading their way through the dense mass of soldiers, a long line of cavaliers, too many and too august in their bearing to be the condottieri with whom the compact had been made; while Recanati himself was still absent. Suddenly drawing his sword with violence, Doria said,

"None shall enter the town, young sir, until Messer Recanati comes before me;" and raising his weapon he signalled for his men to advance. They were not slow to obey. The path into the town was walled across by the crowded soldiery of the Genoese, who began in their turn to press upon the intruders; while Doria cried out to Ranieri,

"Stand back, sir, or I shall strike you down."

His arm was raised. Ranieri heeded it not, so intent was he in watching Zeno's advance—there was something in the gallant bearing of the lad, and even in the manly beauty of his form, that made the stern old warrior spare the blow while yet he might, and dropping his weapon he pushed the youth with the other hand towards the bridge.

Ranieri turned, and starting swiftly from the stalwart veteran, he shouted, loud and clear,

"On, men, on; now for Chiozza. Viva San Marco !"

"Viva San Marco !" shouted the men; and in an instant the place where Ranieri had stood chaffering with the ancient noble, was filled with the din of arms. The sudden rush of the Venetians headed by Ranieri and da Piovere, who took vengeance on the surprised Genoese for the shame of his own wrong and treachery, had carried them far into the town—a town now crumbling to pieces in that long, wasteful war. Pressed behind by their friends, they drove back Doria and his men a great distance before they came to a stand. Bewildered by the suddenness with which their new allies had turned to invaders, the Genoese soldiers struck at random and stood to their ground less obstinately than was their wont. Ranieri resting his fortune upon the deeds of that day, dashed madly forward, and a few far on in the town were engaged in the unexpected fight before their distant general could give them order to resist.

So it went on. It was more a scuffle than a combat. Those who newly issued from the houses into the streets were forced back by the strangers, who had now little to do but to drive the herd before them; so panic-stricken and bewildered had the once bold possessors of Chiozza become. Their limbs were weakened by bad food, and still more by fear; and when the cry of "Viva San Marco!" rang in the open place before the podestà's palace, many who heard it before and knew that the town was taken, believed that some visitation from heaven had destroyed the power of the Genoese. Overpowered by numbers,—so pressed in the crowd that he could not wield his sword, Doria yielded himself a prisoner; and as Carlo Zeno came before the palace, the place seemed suddenly re-peopled by its old race—so utterly had the baffled Genoese been routed—so joyous and so multitudinous was the throng that shouted the national cry of triumph.

"Well done, Ranieri!" said the general, as he struck the youth on the shoulder; "let us hasten in to the palace; perchance the arch traitor may still be there, and our victory may be crowned by the capture of Carrara."

At the word the whole band of nobles around him again pressed forward and entered the palace.

CHAPTER XLVIII.

As the Venetians entered the palace, Alessandro da Padova, who had kept close to Zeno with Marco Morosini, took the lead, and running before them as though he would show his zeal, and almost take the palace by himself, guided them to the principal hall. It was deserted. On a chair near a table lay Carrara's cloak, and near it the cloth that he wore upon his head in exchange for his helmet, after the fashion of his family.

"Seek him through the house," cried Zeno, speaking aloud, above the din that broke the silence of the mansion.

Many hastily left the room at every door. Zeno with his friends and Morosini followed the way that Alessandro went; and after running up a small staircase, they found themselves in a room less than the one below. Here also some clothes of Carrara's were left in haste. A little bed in the corner was still smooth, for he had not slept that night; and on the table lay a few papers, that in the haste of the flight, he had forgotten. They were the spoil of the conquerors. Beneath the bed was a small box, which Sebastian hastily dragged forth. It was fastened—some twenty hands presently wrenched the lid from its hinges. The box contained nought but papers like those upon the table. They were poured out hastily, and hastily glanced at.

Suddenly every eye was turned at a loud cry from Alessandro; his look was fixed intently upon one of the papers that had been snatched from the box. His eye glared as if he had seen

an apparition; and yet there was in it the fierceness of a bitter triumph, which showed that it was not fear that had possessed him. He stood transfixed; his outstretched hands, both grasping the paper, shook with eagerness as he read it.

"What is it, Messer Alessandro!" cried many voices.

"It is the compact between Doria and Carrara," said one.

"It is a bill of exchange," said another with a laugh, "which Messer Alessandro fears that he must share with us."

"I think," cries another, "that it is a letter from Messer Alessandro's mistress to the Lord of Padua."

"What is it, man?"

"Would that I had not found it," he said solemnly. "This indeed might make Venice rue her victory: read it, Messer Vendramini. The proveditore alone should read it; and read it aloud, sir, that none may doubt hereafter what it is which we have found in this accursed box."

Vendramini took the paper, and at the first word a frown of dismay contracted upon his brow. He looked around him uneasily, like a man who almost fears what he has to say; and then taking breath that his voice might be heard, he read aloud :—

"*To the Most Noble Lord, Messer Francesco da Carrara, Lord of Padua.*

"Excellent Sir and most dear Friend—

"I have received from your secret and trusty messenger, Messer Jacopo Arduino, the sum of gold which you entrusted to him and of which he has given me the full weight; for he is an honest and zealous, though a very poor man. But he told me that you had well paid him for the service. And, indeed, I know that you are ever generous, not less to those who are poor and little worth your consideration, than to those of high station and esteem. I am happy that I could serve you in the matter wherein you have paid me by this gold; and I should have been pleased still to serve you, though you had not been so free to pay me my due. Ever you may count upon me; and while I may seem most your foe, and most eager against you in my place among the Venetians, my countrymen, still believe that you have no servant so willing to your command, as

"Your most humble and loving Friend,
"CARLO ZENO."

All around devoured the words as they were read by the proveditore; every eye glancing in dismay at Zeno, who stood unmoved.

When Vendramini had finished, Alessandro said, in a loud voice,

"This then is the plot that has been amongst us — this the hidden treachery of which so many have spoken. We have the other traitor in our power, that trusty messenger that took to Messer Zeno the gold sent by the enemy of Venice. It was Jacopo Arduino; it was the father of that youth that is now before us—the servant of Messer Carlo Zeno. We are too late to catch the chief traitor, and we know (for Messer Carlo Zeno has told us) that Ranieri Arduino was in Chiozza but two nights since. It was an easy way for Carrara to fly

O

from his compact with the Genoese, now that the power of Venice was rising to crush him. Oh! we see it all, Messer Zeno; for no traitor ever yet threatened Venice, but his treachery was exposed, and brought him to his own ruin. I accuse him before you my lords—before Messer Vendramini—you, Messer Marco Morisini —and you, Messer Leonardo, and all of you—I accuse Carlo Zeno of treacherous conference with Messer Francesco da Carrara, long time ago, when this gold was sent, and also now, but two nights ago, when the son of that same messenger came to Chiozza; and my evidence is that paper in the proveditore's hands. I accuse him before the state; and now if he escape, be not mine the fault."

"Traitor in your teeth, Alessandro da Padova!" cried Sebastian fiercely. "Look me in the face, man, while I tell to these nobles that I know you of old for an unblushing traitor, that has sought to compass the ruin of Venice. This is some juggle. Alessandro had brought here the paper which now he would foist upon us."

"Aye," cried Alessandro with a loud laugh, "traitors are ever readiest to talk of treason. See how true a servant Messer Sebastiano has been to the general that would have betrayed Venice. Ask his father, the noble Marco Morosini, that faithful senator, how he has done his duty as a son! All can be witness that I took the paper from the box which we found here. I ask you Messer Vendramini if you saw me not?"

The proveditore nodded.

"Why, Messer Zeno does not deny—he has not said that he did not write the paper; ask him."

All turned to the general.

"It is my writing," he said, "and at the proper time I will say wherefore I wrote it. But now, since this gentleman has accused me, let the matter come before the senate and the Ten. It has ever thus been my fortune, that when most I have triumphed, then some sudden blow has struck me. And it may be that Heaven never gives us such high fortunes (for to conquer in the name of Venice is the highest fortune that can befal man) without some great affliction, lest we should grow too proud and think that it is we who have done it, and not our blessed Lord, who to the prayers of San Marco vouchsafes glory and safety to our city. I shall not escape; but let me be guarded. Be you who have shared with me my victory, my guards; for this shall be the favor that I will ask of you, that I shall have no baser guards than those whom I have led to our triumph."

"Let others then be guarded too," said Alessandro—"I accuse him, that boy Ranieri Arduino, whose traitor father is already in our prisons. And you," continued he to Edward— "but no; I know nothing that touches you. You have been the close companion of Messer Carlo Zeno; but you may be innocent, and never will I accuse upon mere suspicion, or stretch accusal to make it fit my fancy rather than plain knowledge."

He glanced at Sebastian for an instant: but his eyes quailed at the steadfast regard that met them. Alessandro looked at his foster brother; and Marco Morosini started forward. Wearied with seeing the lead taken by others, he had worn a dull and listless look, which even the heat of battle had not quite cleared away. But as Alessandro's accusation went on, the senator awakened: his eyes flashed a sterner fire, and a gleam of fiercer pleasure dawned upon his face—

"Say on, Alessandro," he said. "Spare not me. If Venice demands it, forget our friendship; for I see that you have more to tell."

"I obey; though fain would I spare the son for the father's sake. I know your unparalleled audacity, Sebastiano. We have been alone, and I well know that, if you had your will, he who refused to serve your treachery would be the victim. I know you; but bold as you are, I will match your boldness. Not a father's just anger, not love for your country, nor shame before him you would have tempted, can blanch your matchless insolence. You then, also, I accuse. And know, my lords, that in secret converse, under cover of the night, this bad, bold young man, swearing me to secrecy before I guessed at crime so horrible in one so young tempted me with promises of power, if I would join a dark conspiracy to force his honored father on our ducal chair; saying forsooth that Contarini was old and helpless; and—but I will say more before the judges. Let them not escape. They would have destroyed us; but we will bring them to justice, and God defend the right."

"Silence, vile blasphemer," cried Sebastian. "Will none seize the traitor! Is it not enough that here in the moment of victory he thus foully accuses a name, the very sound of which revived the fortunes of Venice! Will not one of you, lords, seize the wretched traitor that seeks escape in a tale so extravagant that even by crossing the threshold the dream that transfixes you with wonder shall be dispelled."

Alessandro pointed, with a smile, to the paper in Vendramini's hand.

"I told you," said Zeno in a quiet voice, as he laid his hand upon Ranieri's shoulder, "that there was peril and risk to be braved; but I did not think, my son, that we should share so high a triumph, and then presently be partners in such deep distress. But I fear not; as you can face danger, so I see by your steadfast eye that you dread not accusal; I fear not that we shall both regain our honor."

The youth could not answer, but taking his fellow prisoner's hand, he pressed it fervently to his lips.

Surrounding the accused victors, some out of respect, some with eager suspicion, the whole company moved to leave the house; and in a short time all stood upon the deck of a galley, as they bore the conqueror to re-land in his native city, a prisoner awaiting judgment.

CHAPTER XLIX.

THE place of St. Mark was thronged, the crowd thickening towards the water's edge in the piazzetta. Often in the course of this war have we thus seen the heart of Venice filled with her people, but how were they altered since they were summoned by the knell that sounded the captivity of Chiozza! then they were stout of limb, ruddy with health, but full of anger and fear; now faces were pale and sharp with fasting, and many a stalwart limb had shrunk to a sinewy leanness, that betokened yet feebler estate; but hope was in every eye, and lank cheeks began to round their outline with the smile of gladness. Each day had brought tidings across the lagoon of losing fortunes for the Genoese. Zeno's attack on Chiozza had already got wind; and now all eyes were strained to catch the first sight of the boat bringing news of triumph, as it should enter the canal between the island of St. George, and the Giudecca. A shout! some few saw a boat between the buildings: it passed them—it crossed into the grand canal, the crew waving their hands, their caps, a sword, or a bow; —they cried out incessantly; and at last their words grew into shape—"Zeno has conquered! Chiozza is taken!" In the piazzetta they echoed, "Zeno has conquered! Chiozza is taken!" —they echoed it in the great square—and apace the roar of triumph spread abroad into the city. The boat's crew landed, and anon every man of them was seized and passed from hand to hand to recount the battle and the victory. Presently came another boat—afterwards another; and soon many that flocked from Chiozza, in the race to bear the tidings, announced the approach of Zeno's galley. Again the joyful tumult subsided in the fixed attitude of expectation: a galley is seen in the canal beyond—it passes between the buildings —it comes across the grand canal: 'tis he!— Zeno stands on the deck, a well-known circle round him: he lands; and shouts, which make the arches of the ducal palace ring again like bells, welcome the hero that brings back to Venice the gifts of his prowess. Tenedos and her own Chiozza,—tokens of the march of her power in the east, of Genoa's repulse on the Italian waters. Amid shouting of voices, Zeno stood and looked around. He spoke not—he might as well have whispered in the storm; but he laughed pleasantly, and then, at the sight of that familiar and ever-trusted face, thus in its loving joy a mirror of the bright fortune which it had brought to Venice, up rose a louder swell of exulting welcome. Zeno turned his eyes on his companions. A circle close around him answered his look in beaming eyes, that joyed in his triumph less because they shared it than because it was his. Beyond them were some few that looked askance, distrustful how he might act— obey his doom, and submit to their vengeance; or turn against them the ready tumult of the Venetian populace. He whispered a few words to Sebastian. Thus, amid the storm of greeting, he landed, and, still guarded by his friends and foes, entered the ducal palace.

It was like passing from the tempest of the open sea, into the safe, silent waters of the harbor, to enter the tranquil hall where sat the senate, awaiting in solemn repose the arrival of the conqueror. Carlo Zeno took his station before the doge, and baring his head, he said in a clear and loud voice,—" Most illustrious prince and most excellent fathers, it has been vouchsafed to me, by the mercy of heaven, to declare to you, that Chiozza again belongs to Venice, and that there are in the waters of our lagoon, no strangers except our good allies and our prisoners. For the unhappy Genoese, who have been more audacious, but not more criminal than those who have attained safety in a hardy and difficult flight, I have been bold enough to promise the clemency of the republic; and the only guerdon that I venture to ask for myself, is, that the last pang of this most signal war may have been struck by that rush of triumph that bore the standard of St. Mark into Chiozza. Of others whose great daring and cunning wisdom helped me to that victory, I will speak when the senate shall give me leave to recount the story of this long battle." The doge was about to rise, but Zeno interrupted him, " Pardon, most excellent lord,—but before you make that answer to my tidings which your generous motions would dictate, you have yet more to hear, for this tale has a most strange sequel, as others will unfold. I pray you hear the rest."

There was a pause. The doge looked from one to the other, expecting that the next to speak should show himself. Zeno's friends turned to Alessandro da Padova, but he stirred not; and at length Contarini asked, " Who is it that would address the senate?"

" Marco Morosini," said the senator himself, stepping forward from the group behind Zeno. " The task is mine, since none other will undertake it." He spoke firmly and cheerfully; his face was less pale than usual, and less stern; and his words flowed from his lips with a freer confidence. " I accuse Carlo Zeno of treachery."

Had the earth gaped beneath their feet, the senators could not have started more. A sharp buzz ran through the hall, but it was stilled at once, in the self-stifled eagernesss to hear. Zeno and his friends alone were unmoved in aspect.

Contarini's venerable face flushed so red that his beard and hair showed a more snowy white, and he started eagerly from his seat; but, suddenly recollecting himself, he said in a calm voice,—" This is a most strange charge indeed, Messer Morosini. Say on; for till we hear more we are lost in wonder. Say on."

" Truly, most excellent prince, it is most strange; but, alas! most true. I accuse Carlo Zeno of treachery. I accuse him of a secret alliance with Messer Francesco da Carrara, the Lord of Padova; of having been paid in gold by the said Messer Francesco, for secret services rendered against the safety of Venice. I can lay before the senate the receipt of the said Carlo Zeno for the gold thus traitorously paid; I will produce from the prisons of the republic the messenger that carried that gold— a wretch already known in Venice for the crimes that taint him and his blood; with other proofs that may make us marvel, but not doubt the deviltry that has turned our puissant soldier into the most dangerous of the traitors with which Venice is accursed. That is my charge; and with all speed I will submit ample proof thereof before the senate, or before the signory, or the Ten, as may seem most meet."

There was a dead silence, none knowing what to say or think at so monstrous an event in the hour of triumph.

" What say you, Messer Zeno?" asked Contarini, in a cheerful and confident voice; "is this accusation true or false?"

"It is, my lord, most false. Messer Morosini has been cozened; for no noble of Venice could be the deviser of this villany, except he were bewitched. Let me know this charge, let me have time, and I also will have proofs and witnesses; for I do partly know or guess the authors of this stratagem to destroy me, for that I am the faithful servant of Venice."

"Be it so: both sides shall bring their proofs; or until we have proofs, the charge is merely incredible. We will not stay you, Messer Zeno, from the embraces of your family; but when this matter is done with, Venice will know how to acknowledge the services which she can record, but cannot repay."

Alessandro whispered to his foster brother, and Morosini again spoke. "Messer Zeno will pardon me, but it is not safe for the republic that those so gravely charged should walk free and unrestrained in our streets."

Contarini threw himself back in his seat, bewildered and disgusted at the odious office to be thrust upon him; and he traversed the assembly with his eyes in search of counsel; but none offered. All were dismayed, and sat as if in a dream.

"Why this," cried Zeno, "is more paltry than the rest; but if the laws cannot be satisfied without the custody of this poor person, it is theirs."

"Take heed, most noble fathers," cried Alberti, suddenly rising; "lest we bring a new danger upon us by our own folly and crime. Who amongst us, not spell-stricken by envy, believes this charge against our deliverer? What if there be proofs, as we are vainly promised? Can one man collect such proof as would gainsay that evidence which we already possess?—there it stands—Carlo Zeno himself, and his whole life. If my very eyes saw him, here sword in hand, striking down our venerable doge, should I not believe rather that my eyes were sick and my brain mad, than that so monstrous a sight were true? To believe these hideous fables, because men can muster what they call proofs—proofs well enough, perchance, to prove common things—is to overturn all belief: we can have strong faith in nothing, if the first aspect of some riddle is to take our faith captive to follow it from the straight path. But, I say, it is not safe to mistrust our own better faith: the people do not follow these nice and fantastic sophistries; they take the common wisdom, the broad faith, the belief that masters the heart and instincts and love of men; they look to the life of Zeno —they will believe in that until you bring them equal proof—another life—until Zeno shall have lived a second bad life to disprove the first. I say it is not safe to disappoint their faith. Already—for they have heard already that now we sit in judgment on our deliverer, —already they murmur. The people ask, where is his triumph and his guerdon—they ask, is it true that he, the conqueror, is a prisoner accused? They call for him, that they may see him free. Am I disbelieved? let any of you go forth, and see if it be safe to carry the reconqueror of Chiozza this day to prison. There is treachery in Venice, and truly the self-same treachery that has planned this accu-

sation—aye, treachery—I read it in the very act of accusing with ready faith so good and great a man—that self-same treachery, if you do gratify it, will find such opportunity in the storm you rouse, that some other hideous crime will spring up and flourish. Go forth, and see if the joy of the people be not changing to a fierce and anxious cry for Zeno. It is not safe, I say to imprison him—it is not wise, it is not virtuous. Let us not do it. If there be charges to be brought let those that choose— that dare — bring those charges, with their proofs; and when we see those proofs, if they be strong, let us then begin to believe; but until that be done, let us not turn aside from our great content this day to sit and ponder idle calumnies; as if the bad dreams of the guilty, were of equal account with the great deeds of the good and mighty, that we should put them in the scale and solemnly watch for the turning of the balance! Let us not finish off this great triumph with a foolish and bitter jest."

There was a swelling murmur of approval, and many essayed to speak, and then each gave way to the rest. As they gradually sat down, one remained standing; it was Vendramini, who had moved from among the officers of the army, and had taken his place.

"Not one of you, most excellent fathers," said the proveditore, "is more disposed to befriend Messer Carlo Zeno than I am; and yet I do in some sort hold myself answerable for the safe keeping of him as an accused prisoner; since with my own eyes I have seen that which could not have been devised beforehand, giving in some sort proof to this charge; he was accused before me; to me was he given as prisoner: and I claim at least the declared license of the senate to be released from my office before he is allowed to go."

There was again a rising murmur, when Barbarigo stood up, saying—"Messer Vendramini says truly: this is not a matter to be dismissed thus hurriedly; and it were better for the honor and dignity of Messer Zeno himself that we should proceed carefully and regularly on without these hasty frolics, as though we took example by the mad populace."

The discretion of the respectable Vendramini had cast a chill upon the assembly. Lionardo Morosini was moving to speak, when Alberti started to his feet before him.

"Say that, profiting by our trust, being really guilty, but set free, Messer Zeno were to fly— what would that be but exile for evermore? and what punishment so great as degradation or exile could strike so great a criminal? Is it death? If you think so, bare that majestic form, and ask of the scars that fret the walls around Carlo Zeno's heart, what dread of death lurks within. Let him be free; and if he is guilty, let the trust of Venice be the monument of her generosity and the reward of those great services which, done before the world, cannot be doubted. That is what I say; and if you, illustrious senators, think with me, be not silent at this moment when our honor stands at stake; make my poor voice strong with your loud assent."

Uprose at that appeal many a senator, then more, and more, and more again, with loud mingling of voices.

Contarini also arose, and, lifting up both his hands, he looked around: all was silence, as he said, "I learn from your gestures, and the tone of your voices, most noble sirs, that Messer Alberti has spoken your will."

"Aye, aye."

"A will worthy of this assembly! I do then speak your pleasure—Messer Zeno, you are free. Venice receives with gratitude the great gifts you bring to her; but the first of all rewards for the victor awaits you, the needful repose in the arms of your family. More at leisure, we will accept the account of your services and your victories, and rest assured that your just pledges shall be fulfilled."

Carlo Zeno bowed, and was about to retire, when Marco Morosini, listener to frequent angry whispers from his foster brother, again stepped forward:—"If it be the pleasure of the senate that, on the faith of those brave deeds which are strangely mingled in man's life with the wickedness permitted by the Heavenly will, there are others not less criminal who have not such claim for dangerous indulgence.—I accuse that youth who stands by Messer Zeno—his name is Ranieri Arduino—him I accuse of holding secret and treasonable conference with the Lord of Padua, in Chiozza, but two days since, if I mistake not: know that he is the son of that man who bore from Francesco da Carrara the gold which was paid to Carlo Zeno—gold which Carlo Zeno acknowledges to have been paid in this letter which I here hold—one of the proofs that do so pleasantly amuse Messer Alberti."

Here was a loud shout; but Morosini angrily continued: "Nay, I gainsay not the pleasure of the senate, that Messer Zeno should go home to bestow that gold in safety"—another shout—"but let not all our criminals think to escape: let not the spy and servant of da Carrara, Ranieri Arduino, go loose about our streets. Another whom I accuse stands next to him—Sebastiano Morosini."

There was a sudden move, and a short hasty murmur ran throughout the assembled senate. The doge cried,—"Your son!"

"My son, unhappily my son! but thanks be to our Lord and to St. Mark, Marco Morosini, not a harsh or unloving father, is more Venetian than father; and alas! that unhappy youth is little of a son, less of a Venetian. He is leagued with that boy, younger in years, but older in vice, to betray the republic. I have done my duty—let them be secured."

"Since I am free," cried Carlo Zeno, speaking before the doge could answer, "let me once more be heard in this senate, from which I have been so long absent. Know, then, most excellent fathers, that of all the servants Venice has, none is more faithful than these two, with myself accused before you. Of Messer Sebastiano Morosini, whom in some strange madness his father hates, and accuses to destroy, I cannot, without long delays, recount all the high services; for to his discretion, to his zeal, and to his skill and courage do we in great part owe it that our troops were able to preserve their faith, that the conspiracy of Roberto da Recanati was defeated, and that we could turn that perilous conspiracy to our use in making a path into Chiozza. But to this youth," cried Zeno,

laying his hand on Ranieri's shoulder,—"young as he looks—he is yet younger than his tall limbs and steadfast countenance would let you think—to this boy do we owe that we have entered Chiozza, and that this day it is ours. With a ready cunning that outstripped the lessons I taught, with secrecy equal to any here in the dread Council of Ten—be it said without offence—and braving death, be it was that shaped and opened our way into the town; and the way being open, this young form was the first that pushed in among the Genoese, piercing the wall of their closed ranks with the swiftness of his rush, and finding safety in the very daring and desperation of his courage that made him meet the danger faster than it would come, so that the blow ever fell behind his onward course. To put these two in your prisons and leave me free, were to send my body abroad, and imprison my honor and victory. If it so please you that these must be prisoners out of this triumph, let me also keep my rank and be the chief; for to be the chief of such as these, wheresoever they are, is the highest honor for me. I cannot go free without them; and if these mad charges can outlive the fancy of the moment, think not that we shall fly them. I will be surety for these two my friends; and if you doubt my word,—who here will be surety for me?"

Alberti rose, but scarcely before many others; ere they were well standing, more followed their example; and but few, save Lionardo Morosini, Barbarigo, and the secret friends of Alessandro, remained sitting.

"I see," said Zeno, "monsignore, the senate will be surety for us."

"Be it so," replied Contarini; "this charge against your officers is the same as that against yourself. Messer Zeno, happiness attend your welcome home!"

Zeno bowed, and, still keeping his hand on Ranieri's shoulder, he walked forth from the hall, attended by Sebastiano, Cooke, Edward, and others of his friends; while many of the senators, leaving their places, followed to do him honor by bearing him company to this house. As he appeared in the place of St. Mark, the people raised a great shout to see him free; and they too followed as he went, so that to do them pleasure, as it was his wont not to thwart the harmless humor of the moment, he went all the way on foot; the crowd forming a rude procession, which lined the sides of the canals, and filled a fleet of boats on the water, often separating and rejoining again in making turns down divers streets. At length they came to Zeno's palace, and his followers took their leave, that he might not be incommoded on first returning to his home. Only his nearest friends and companions entered with him. In the hall stood a noble dame, dressed all in black velvet, which well became her full and matronly form. Her face denoted a ripe age, yet was it round and fresh and comely. Her eyes were grave, and on her cheeks was a deep flush, which turned to pale as her noble lord entered. Zeno took her in his arms and kissed her fondly, and when she hid her face far in his neck, and her brave body shook with sobs, he went on kissing her shoulder as though forgetting the eyes that watched them. None turned away at the sacred sight, yet the

look of none could offend. At length, lifting her gently away to look in her face, Zeno cried,—
"The sight of thee, Caterina, makes me young again; and truly am I deceived; for years have gone on, and ever when I come back I find thee as fair, as tender, as blushing as the dear girl I wedded."

"And you have returned, Carlo, and in health and victory—and yet accused!"

"What! you have heard! Know you not, that to be successful is ever to be envied, and to be envied accused! It is one of our honors, and is well shared. But we are weak, my life, with our voyage and with talking against our foes; and these my good friends, companions in battle, in victory, and in calumny, must be companions too in this our home and in our hospitality. Show you the way, for I have forgotten my own house."

CHAPTER L.

Not long after they had entered, Ranieri drew Sebastian aside. "Is it not true," he said, "that Zeno is the kindest as well as greatest of men; for certes while busy in affairs of state he thinks of the affairs of each one amongst us, as if they alone filled all his thoughts. But now he called me apart and said, 'I can see, my boy, that you do not eat because your will is elsewhere. Go: bring your sister here, for nowhere will she be so safe as with Madonna Caterina; and as soon as Venice has settled herself after this turmoil, we will have your father out of prison where he has put himself. I was wrong,' Zeno said, 'to leave him so long to run after his bad fortunes. But bring your sister straightway to this her home and yours.' Truly has the ill fortunes of our house begun to turn. But I scarce can tell where you, Sebastian, have bestowed my sister, and you must be my guide."

"How willingly! I did already pray her to let me lead her to this house, knowing the noble generosity of those that own it; but now that Zeno's self sends you to fetch her, she will not refuse."

In a few moments, the two youths were in a boat darting towards Canareggio, along the canals now growing dark with night; and but few more saw them at the door of Pierotto the fisherman's house. They knocked, but no one answered. Gently pushing the door, Sebastian found that it was already open. The room in which they were was almost dark, so that they could ill see the scanty furniture in it.

Not far from the door lay something long and moveless. Tightly grasping Ranieri's arm, Sebastian pointed to it in silence. They stooped over it; it was a man—the aged fisherman, cold and stiff in death. On his head might dimly be seen in the fading light two fearful gashes; one that severed his skull almost to the eyes, and dabbled his silver locks in gore, now hardened in a dark crust. Leaving the body, Sebastian led the way to an inner room; it was silent and deserted. They went up a flight of stairs; but nothing was heard save the echo of their steps. Still without speaking, for he knew that one only thought

filled both their minds, Sebastian again more closely looked through the whole house, within the bed once warmed by the dear form they sought, but now cold that dreary night—under the table, behind every door. All was still. Hastily repassing the dead body, Sebastian, followed by Ranieri, left the house, and entered Rosa's, hard by.

Hearing them as they opened the door, she came forth from an inner room, with a lamp in her hand.

"Rosa," cried Sebastian, "where is Teresa?"

"At her home. Know you not the way? I will show it you, for I was going but now."

"Nay, we came from it, but she is not there. The danger has sought her, Rosa; there has been mischief in Pierotto's house; for Teresa has gone, and the poor old man lies dead and murdered."

Rosa sent that sharp searching look into Sebastian's face which they do who hear news that they dare not believe; and then, without stopping, she rushed forth. The light she bore was blown out at the first breath of wind; but not staying for another, she threw the lamp back into her house, and ran to her dead neighbor's, followed by the two youths.

Again they searched the house through, its blank silence striking more drear from the waxing darkness of the night. Again they stood by the dead body.

"See," whispered Sebastian, "the head is towards the door: his slayers struck him down while he barred their issue. The Ten should know of this."

"Not through us," exclaimed the girl; "they will know of its perforce, but let us not help them."

"Know you then," asked Sebastian sternly, "who hath done this crime?"

"Alas! no; but I can guess not far off Teresa had, as I think, but one enemy, and that for your sake, Sebastian. The Ten may find that a man has been killed, and may discover the real murderer; but that one enemy that paid the murderer, and possesses the secret, has defied the Ten, and can ever do so. Him I can reach; and I here promise you that I will answer and restore the dear lady, or I will die. Alas! Sebastian, see how faithful old Pierotto has thrown down the sweet remainder of his harmless life to stay the path of her ravishers—not to conquer them, poor weak old man! but to be in his willing death a witness, and a gage of love and faith to solace her misery: and if he so loved that gentle lady, how must we to whom she was the life and the hope!" Kneeling down, Rosa bent over the body, and hiding her face in both her hands, she wept.

If for a moment he had doubted, less Rosa's faith than her ill companionhood, Sebastian doubted no longer. He stooped to raise her from the ground; but still kneeling, she clasped his hand, and, with bitter sobs, asked him to forgive her.

"For, what, Rosa!"

"For that I, marked out for misery by my sins, dare to think that I could serve one so excellent, and have dragged upon her dear head the ruin that I alone deserved. Dear lady! she held out to me a hand from heaven, and I have seized it to drag her down among these infernal devilries."

" Speak not so, Rosa, but still hold fast by the love and hope she brought us ; and rather think that now in you alone is the hope of me and of this her brother. I believe you, and that you alone can reach that enemy—the enemy of all that is good in Venice. Let us but know where she is, and presently no power in the city shall hold her back from our grasp."

" I promise you," she said, in a firmer voice, rising : " the night will not last long, and betimes I will seek him. Leave we this door open, that the early passengers may see the the body, and take order for paying its just honors. Hasten away, that none may see you. Farewell." She parted from them as they went forth into the open air ; and the two friends left the place on foot, that none might so readily mark their presence near the house of the murdered man.

CHAPTER LI.

FROM the moment of the return to Zeno's house, Edward had cast about in his own mind to devise the means of once more speaking with his mistress, who had remained unseen since the conference before his departure for Tenedos. Ever since he had come back from that enterprise, his patience had been tried to forbear a new attempt to gain audience of the lady ; but from day to day Venice had been fighting for life or victory, and his conscience would not let him be spared from ever hasty service. Now, there was a lull after that long storm ; and the loud voice of his impatience, better heard, quite mastered him ; so that, thinking of no other way, he resolved to make known his bold and little hopeful love to Sebastian ; which hitherto he had not done, because he feared to bring some new trouble on his friend. Now, even that thought gave way before his eagerness. But when he had come to that resolve, in vain he sought him whom he wanted ; for Sebastian had already been carried away by Ranieri. After traversing every part where he thought his search might be gratified, and being at last assured that, through some anxiety for Teresa, the two had gone, Edward wandered out of doors and towards the Morosini palace, uncertain what to do ; but hoping that chance might favor his intent. The day was already darkening, when he passed the church of St. Stephen ; but he came even to the door (which was closed, for the night was chill and gusty) without descrying any hope of making his way, except by entering in at once ; and that he feared to do, knowing that his enemies had returned to the house and were astir. He trod back upon his steps, and then again approached the door many times ; and still it showed the same unmoved and sullen front, as if mocking his mingled will and fear to attempt an entrance. After some time, as he loitered about, he was aware that a man who stood near to the house was watching him. He was somewhat angered at being thus spied upon, but he stifled his displeasure, and bethought

him that he would go farther and wait longer before returning the same way , hoping that the man would then be gone. But the other, as if guessing his purpose, now sauntered across his path. As well as he could see by the dim lights in that narrow street beside the piazetta of St. Stephen, the fellow was meanly, or rather beggarly dressed ; the careless moving of his lank limbs, for he had never a cloak to cover his short doublet, denoted extreme feebleness or indolence, or both, and no less reckless insolence. With a coarse, harsh voice, made husky and thin, as if by the starvation that had scourged the poor in that time of trouble and dearth, the man bade him good even.

" A happy night, good man," answered Edward. " Do you want aught of me, that thus you watch and follow me ?"

" I am no beggar, my worthy sir ; but rather it seemed to me that it is you who want something, and perchance I might not dislike to serve, nor to be paid for it in coin, honestly earned."

" But who is it that would serve me ?"

The man hesitated ; and his voice sounded as if he grinned, when he replied—" Say that I belong to the household of yonder palace."

" Is it so !" asked Edward ; the man's manner making him doubt. " Do you know Messer Morisini ?"

" Messer Marco ? aye ; a most noble gentleman, my master ; though I am too humble to have his regard. Shall I bear a message to him for my lord ?"

" Know you Messer Sebastiano ?"

" Do I not know him ! Truly I am not likely to forget him, for the gifts that he hath bestowed on me ; though in the freeness and bounty of his heart he forgets them himself, excellent gentleman ! Shall your most generous gift be for speaking with that comely youth ? But I fear he hath not returned ; for I have known the return of each, and him I have not noted."

" It is not with him I would speak," said Edward, now believing that the man did belong to the house. " Know you the Lady Angiolina ?"

" That most sweet and lovely young mistress ! Do we not all love her as if she were our mother ! Sir, the Lady Angiolina is a saint. Is it some letter that I must bear to her ? for she can read, as I am witness. I do think that for the carrying of letters our gallants used to give gold ; and I am assured that I do not now speak except to one who is generous in good gifts, as my most beloved young master, good Messer Sebastian."

" You shall have gold. I would speak with the lady—I have a message from her brother. Can you compass that ?"

" You are answered in your own promise : what could not be done for gold ! Even for silver one can do much ; but, then, no gallant gives silver, lest a baser coin should shame the lady."

" Why, then, take this—it is gold."

" I know it by the feel : it is heavier than silver, my lord, and softer, and richer, and warmer to the touch. I have learned to know the difference ; for I have often taken the two pleasant metals in the dark."

" Often ! Why, then, what is your service !"

"I am so humble in the house, that I am nobody's servant, and therefore am everybody's; so that what I lack in salary I ofttimes get in these gifts."

"Well, let me see the lady where she is, and as I enter, you shall have the fellow to that; and again as I come out you shall have a third, if I reach this place without let."

"Follow me, then." And he led the way to a door more at the side of the house. They had scarcely reached it when he stopped and whispered—"Stand by; here goes one that has more eyes than all the rest in the palace."

Edward drew up close against the wall, like his companion; and then he heard the step of a man at some distance behind them. He came on apace, walking straight towards the little door, and entered. By his stature and heavy stride, it was Alessandro Padovano. Edward remained unmoved till his guide stepped forward; but the man again whispered to him to wait till he saw that the path was clear; and he followed Alessandro. In a minute he returned, and beckoning Edward, led him into the hall, where he placed him in a dark corner, and again disappeared. After a longer delay, the man came back, and cautiously leading his follower up the stairs and through some antechambers, he brought him to one smaller than the rest, dimly lighted; and then, still whispering, he said—"The lady is in there, through that door. It is your business to announce yourself, and say why you have come. You will know your way out again?"

"I think so."

"I will wait for you to guide you; but be not too quick, for I have other work to do. I suppose there is no fear of that." And with that Edward was alone.

With a beating heart, he approached the door that had been pointed out, and knocked upon it. "Enter," cried a soft voice within. He entered, and saw that he was in a saloon, of small size, but sumptuously furnished. On a couch was seated Angiolina; on a table near, but too far off for reading, lay an open book, with a lamp; on the ground, leaning against the couch, stood a lute; and thrown over the other end of the couch was part of a mantle of red velvet, half way over which marched a stately stream of embroidered gold, that stopping in the midst, showed where the worker's needle had stayed. The lady, however, seemed to have been engaged in none of those her recent tasks; but as if, after having left one for the other, she had sunk to sleep; for when he entered she moved her feet off the couch, to sit upright. Shielding her eyes from the light, she looked across the room; seeing an unwonted form enter there, she rose in wonder; and then, knowing who it was, she clasped her hands, and cried—"Ah me! Messer Odoardo! why come you here?"

"Dearest lady, need you ask!" cried he, hastening towards her, and kissing her hand, like one whom lack of time emboldened. "Does it anger you that I should come again, after the words you vouchsafed to hear, and the sweet assent you gave them; or is it that the long delay to return has made you think me recreant, and I have lost the blessing, scarcely won?"

"Neither, indeed it is neither. But to see you here fills me with fear for your danger; I scarcely know why—indeed, I know nothing, but that Venice has been in danger, and is now happily restored to safety; wherein I know of my own heart that you have helped. But still I mark that this good fortune has not made my father kinder to his child, after so long an absence; why I know not. Nor has Sebastian returned to the home he left. I know nothing but that I have been along so long, fearing all, and having no word of comfort."

"Recreant indeed that I was, not to care for that!" cried Edward, tenderly folding his arm round her, and sitting by her side. Her face sunk on his shoulder. "Alas! alas! grieve not so, sweetest lady; but all good hope comfort you. Our Sebastian is safe."

Angiolina wept for a space without stirring; her tears falling fast and gently, like a steady, silent summer-rain, that darkens, but restores the face of earth. Raising herself again, she said, "Forgive me, Odoardo, for meeting you with this humor; but the dreary months have passed all in thought of those dear and absent, with not a word of tidings save what has passed through the mouths of all Venice; and I, who had almost learned to forget everything except the weariness of that lonesome stillness, now melt again into hope with this sad way."

Edward again kissed her hand, and strove to reassure her with many words of solace—stories of Sebastian's deeds, of Zeno, of Ranieri, of Teresa; for Angiolina, in her simple desire to learn all that concerned her brother, suspected no secret towards Edward, and asked freely. And thus, by being to her the sole one in all that house that satisfied her heart with those needful explanations which should have been furnished her by one of her own kin, he reached a place of greater confidence in her affection; so that all at once he seemed to stand to her in place of all family-love—the only one in that time who knew her heart, and was within its reach. Again she suffered him to draw her towards him, and she leaned her head on his shoulder; while she listened, he told her of Sebastian's dangers and honors, fears and hopes; tears bedewed her eyes, and he stole them with kisses ere they fell to waste; she asked him of his own deeds, and when he told, instead, his love, and crowned his words with a kiss on her warm, swelling lips, she only sighed. They looked into each other's eyes, and saw there, under trembling lids, the light clouded over like the mist that dims the surface of sparkling waters under the trees of a summer even—the sweet mastery of passion unresisted by the will. None had taught the young girl to suspect; she suspected no wrong, and there was none to suspect in Edward's loyal heart; but in that converse was all else for the time forgotten—the hour, the place, their enemies—all.

Abruptly and violently clanked the door as it was suddenly opened, and a man strode into the room. It was the foster brother!

———

CHAPTER LII.

When Edward was left alone in the little antechamber, his guide hastened back upon his steps, and passing down stairs, he crossed the hall and entered another apartment, as one familiar with the house. He staid not in the first room, but went straight to an inner one, in which stood Alessandro da Padova, without his cloak ; making some change in his attire, like him who had come from a long journey."

"How now ! who is this !" cried the foster brother, angrily ; "what now, Nadale ! Do you fly from death, that you enter thus unmannerly !"

" I fly to keep up with time that runs apace," answered the fellow, roughly ; "and they are wont to take free license, and to be freely forgiven, that bring welcome news."

"Jest not. Go into the next chamber, and await me there."

"Nay, my time will not await the picking of chambers. I have some wares for you, Messer Alessandro ; a venture which I have made for your market."

"I have given thee no task."

"Truly no : I say it is a venture, what think you of a lady ?"

"No jests, I say. You have been drinking, ribald. Await me without !"

"Nor drink neither. I have a lady that you would have taken had you dared ; that you would buy to sell again, and here she is for you ; as good as new, and yet cheap. What will you give for the Lady Teresa Arduino—taken without your privity—all safe and secret !"

Alessandro listened, chiding no more.

"I have her. Messer Sebastiano hid her away among the poor folks at Canareggio ; but the Ten do not look so close after the poor, especially in these times, when a few women the less makes a few less to feed. I saw him when he led her from the grand council. I knew him and his fist by the aching of my jaw ; I played boatman to him, for the love I ever bear him,—and he paid me for it, sweet gentleman !—I stole upon her just when the victory made everybody mad,—with none but an old fisherman to help her ; I brought her away. Now say—she is yours—cheap—I have a fancy for selling her cheap ; or, if you will not buy, I will keep her, a nightingale in a cage, to amuse o' nights, in token of memory for dear Messer Sebastiano, my most excellent friend."

"Is this true !"

"True as Messer Sebastiano's love. Say the word, and the goods shall be landed here in half an hour."

"What is your price !"

"Ten ducats—golden. It is not too much for the wares."

"I will buy her. Keep her till I demand her here. Now go."

"But that is not all. Messer Sebastiano hath a friend,—a most brave young gentleman."

"Ranieri, Teresa's brother !"

"No : the Englishman—Odoardo we call him ; a most brave young gentleman, best known in Venice as the gallant that did such deeds for the love of la Gobba."

"The Englishman ! I know him. Have you him too for sale !"

"Not quite. Now bear me without loss, and

P

you shall have him at no greater cost. One ducat, one golden ducat—cash—on the nail—only you paying it me instead of him, as he has promised."

Alessandro threw one on the ground, saying,—"You make money fast, Nadale."

"Aye ; trade varies. Now it is all dull, now brisk. But we are poor. Messer Odoardo gives his gold into your hand ; you make us pick it off the ground ; still I love your pride, Messer Alessandro ; and for the gallant, he is here."

"Here !"

"In this house. He has given la Gobba a rival,—none other but our good lord's daughter, Madonna Angiolina ; and now he is with her, losing no time, you may be sure."

"Are you mad !"

"Nay, go to her lodging, and see."

"But how got he entrance !"

"I brought him."

"You ! how then, ruffian, dared you !—Do you desire to be scourged or hanged, that thus you serve me !"

"Nay, good Messer Alessandro, I am no servant of yours, except in courtesy. You pay no salary, but only by the job ; and I am too poor to refuse jobs that fall into one's way. Besides, it was better to let the fish enter the net, than to frighten him away by disturbing the waters. He has not yet had time to steal the bait. Haste to them, and you shall have him at will ; and as for the Lady Teresa, she shall be kept at your bidding."

Alessandro left the room with hasty strides ; an instant brought him to Angiolina's favorite chamber ; and there his malignant eyes were gladdened with the sight of the Englishman, Angiolina folded in his arms. For an instant he gazed on their astounded faces ; and what a tumultuous rush of thought swept across his brain in that second of time ! Teresa in his power—Edward—Angiolina—Zeno ; the need to increase his own might, to crush his toes and save himself from crushing, in few brief days : Rosa, her troublesome pride, ruin tottering in the balance, to fall on him or to be hurled by him : the sight of the young girl, whose growth to womanhood he had scarcely noted, now clasped in the arms of love, suggested to the schemer a new stroke—she should be his—he would buy her of her father with Teresa ; and thus should he strike to the heart of those who had braved him till he had madly chafed—Edward, Sebastian, Rosa ; thus too advancing his iron power and estate to be more mighty in Venice. Raising his arm, he exclaimed in a hollow and stern voice,—"What audacious caitiff has thus betrayed the honor of this most noble house ! Alas ! Messer Odoardo, even I deplore this shame and peril for mine enemy. And you, most miserable lady !—But it is not for one so humble as me to act here. Leave that shameful posture, lest the sight should strike blind him whose honor is above all in Venice."

Angiolina started from her seat, shrinking in fear from Edward.

Rising, too, the Englishman fronted the foster brother, and cried,—"You have surprised me, Messer Alessandro, in the house of one who is my enemy, though I am not his ; but dishonor there is none, save in base suspicions."

"Be it so, be it so ; but this, I say, is above my office." He looked round the room as if considering ; then returning to the door by which he had entered, he took a key from it, and going out, he locked the door ; leaving the lovers alone.

All pale and trembling, Angiolina put her hand to her head, as if to collect her thoughts. Edward drew near, and again passing his arm round her, he begged her to have no fear. At the sound of his voice she started, and turning to him, she cried,—" Oh, dearest Edward, fly ; let them not find you when he returns.—But alas ! alas ! there is no way out of these rooms but this, and Alessandro has barred that way. Oh ! do not resist,—yield—and they will let you depart."

"Speak not of flight, sweetest,—it is for the guilty to fly : nor of yielding, where nought has been taken to yield except that which cannot be given up—the faith and truth of love."

" Hush, hush ! they come," cried she.

There was the sound of distant voice in the ante-rooms, but they passed, and no one came. Long time thus the lovers waited in doubt, still imprisoned, but still alone. Voices passed again ; and still no one broke upon their strange solitude ; which more terrified Angiolina with the delay, while doubt and waiting wearied even Edward's words of comfort. Thus crept on the night in silent fear.

CHAPTER LIII.

ALESSANDRO crossed the great ante-rooms to Morosini's own apartment ; and in a private cabinet he found the senator himself. Morosini paced the floor : the great and doubtful struggle in which he was engaged kept him restless. Alessandro entered without haste, and walking to the window, looked out in silence, waiting till the other should address him ; for ever it was his aim to make all things seem to begin with his patron. Nor could Morosini long withstand the wonted attraction ; for stopping in his course he asked, as if the foster brother knew his thought,—" But, Alessandro, are we all prepared ?"

" Most amply ; and right soon will those be here who will give us their aid and counsel. Before they come, there are other matters whereof I would speak with you, strangely involved. There was, if you forget her not, one Teresa Arduino."

Morosini suddenly drew nearer, intently listening ; but just at that moment a serving man entered to them, and told Alessandro that certain gentlemen desired to speak with him. " Is it Messer Barbarigo ?" asked the Paduan. The man bowed. " Bring them in here. They have come too soon, by some minutes ; but they must first be served."

Not long time passed before Barbarigo entered the room ; and in the greetings might be known Luigi da Molino by his heavy voice, Pietro di Bernardo by his gay manners, and Lionardo Morosini by his bold and careless bearing. The courtesies over, Barbarigo unfolded

the business of the night, " We have come, Messer Morosini," he said, " seeing the danger in which Venice is placed by the treachery that menaces her existence, seeing the trouble that you had even to make heard your just accusal, to take counsel with you as to the means of providing for this peril, and bringing your charge to full proof." The plan was, to collect evidence of Zeno's intelligence with Carrara, from divers quarters known to Messer Alessandro da Padova, and thus to bring shame and defeat, not only on Zeno, but on Contarini and his supporters ; greatly advancing Morosini's power in the senate. And Carrara himself was to be made a witness. " Start not at that name, Messer Morosini," said Barbarigo : " Messer Francesco is a defeated man ; in defeat, he has learned with his happy discretion and right noble heart, wisdom and virtue ; and he generously deplores the ill that he hath worked on Venice, desiring rather to repair it than to continue it, and so to disarm some part of her rightful vengeance." Morosini had indeed started. He would have disclosed his interview with the monk in Carrara's castle on the coast, but Alessandro hindered him. And it was not very difficult to persuade him that this plan, beginning among grave and faithful senators, his chief supporters, was not only safe, but the surest means to overwhelm his enemies ; Carrara being really an altered man and a penitent.

" And I," said Lionardo Morosini, " would summon yet another witness. Carlo Zeno is threatened with prison, and we all know to what prison leads, especially after serving Venice : let us promise him pardon, safety, and new power hereafter, and he will yield to our assault —forego his resistance to our proofs, and accept as our bounty what we shall give." Small favor found his proposal with the rest, and being alone he was soon silenced ; though still muttering that it were a wise scheme. For Lionardo was one who trusted much to force, boldness, and extravagant projects ; which often brought him through dangers that he sought and others foresaw.

It was agreed, for greater secrecy and the better conduct of the matter, that the Paduan should go to seek the evidence of Carrara, and to learn his mind on the matter. And, having other affairs that awaited their absence, Alessandro so managed, that the visiters wasted little time in the conference, but agreed quickly, and then departed.

When they were gone, while Morosini was lost in the strange projects which had been so rapidly unfolded, the foster brother somewhat suddenly accosted him, saying,—" You will bear me witness, Marco, that never in your life (signal as have been your endless bounties to me, and however deep my gratitude) have I flattered that weakness and vice which most holds you in bondage. And yet hath something occurred which makes it now seem that I must do so. Teresa Arduino——"

Marco again listened.

" You remember her ! she has fallen into my power, and I cannot find it in my heart, if I would not help you in these light matters, to be a secret hindrance to you. She is in my power and, being so, in yours. But it is not that of which I would speak," added the foster brother seeing that he had fixed the idea in Morosini's mind to such purpose that it was sure to arise again spontaneously,—" it was of a far other matter. In all these services of yours to Venice to I ever feel that more could I aid you if I were not so weak and of so little account." And on that head Alessandro talked long; until, having brought his brother to be in such mood that it seemed most to advance the power of both to devise some way of enhancing the foster brother's power, he continued,— " Now, therefore, be not displeased at my boldness, if I presume too much on your noble generosity and your patience. If you desired to give me greater esteem in Venice, there is one means—to let me be your son—your son by marriage. That the fair Angiolina would find a nobler spouse is most true ; but what alliance of that kind is needed by your house ! Nor let it disturb you that I am accounted your brother in milk ; for, be it known to you, really it was not so ; but my father was a nobleman of Florence, secretly married to my mother, also a Florentine lady, who was poisoned, as some suspected, by reason of that marriage. I was nurtured in Sienna, and only sent to Padua, for safety, after the age of such nurture as a woman gives. Let not this amaze you, for I can bring proofs such as will satisfy you and all that may need, though I have heretofore forborne, because to have disclosed the truth would have brought me no fortune ; my father's substance being all wasted, or passed to others ; and it might have parted me from you, in whom all my love and duty abided. I can, I say, bring proof." Now herein Alessandro had no intent to deceive Morosini, but merely to save him, by telling him the tale thus privily, from the seeming to join in a fraud ; but he spoke so firmly and confidently, that verily the senator was deceived. He answered not—the foster brother neither desired nor expected him to answer ; his mind was too fully occupied ; the prospect was too new and too sudden for him to conceive it ; and Alessandro left the seed to take root, and grow into a project of the patrician's own thought. " Think not of it now," said the Paduan ; " if you approve not, pass it by as an idle jest ; but it might help me in your service. Yet while I talk, even now, your dear daughter may be seized from us."

" Seized ! Angiol na ! St. Mark forbid ! what —can Sebastian——-"

" Be not impatient. Not Sebastian—though indeed your quick suspicion outruns my slower wit, for Sebastian's friend it is that has invaded your house."

" My house !"

" Aye, your house. He is here, even now ; and, but that I discovered the thief in time, in the Lady Angiolina's chamber, even now the house might have been bereft."

Morosini laid his hand upon his sword, and would have rushed from the room, but the foster brother staid him.

" Bethink you," he cried, " that I have made all safe ; the thief is a prisoner ; and by a noble forbearance you must will abash and humble your enemies, and most exalt your own dignity. The lady is of a tender and dutiful heart, as I have full well noted ; and let that be your trust. Bid her, and she will drive away the miserable man who is lured by her beauty. Thus may you set the duty of the one child against the crimes of the other."

" Alessandro," said the noble, " ever are you my best friend—watching and guarding all—even over myself ; and now to your generous pleading does Angiolina owe the forbearance of an offended father. Lead me to her "

CHAPTER LIV.

SILENTLY sat the lovers, still awaiting Alessandro's return, when footsteps hastily and directly nearing the door startled their sense. Angiolina fled from her seat upon the couch, and stood, turned from Edward and from the opening door, leaning her hand upon the table for support, her head bent down.

The key turned in the lock, and Alessandro, throwing the door open, made way for Marco Morosini. Angiolina gave no sign that she noted her father's presence, except that the arm on which she leaned trembled more. Edward folded his arms, and awaited the senator's approach. Morosini slowly crossed the room, surveying the lovers alternately, with no rage in his glassy eye, with no surprise, but with a composed displeasure, that set forth the dignity of his tall form, drawn up to his full height. First he fixed his eyes on his daughter ; and when his footsteps ceased, as if she knew that cold and cruel gaze was upon her, she trembled yet more. In a low and subdued voice he said—" Angiolina !" and the girl still keeping her head bent down, and her back turned to him, raised one hand to hide her face, hidden though it was already by her averted posture and her drooping hair. Having thus felt his untarnished power, Morosini turned towards the Englishman, saying—" And you, Messer Inglese, what reason can you give why you have thus untimely entered the house of a stranger ! Tell me why you have stolen into the most sacred part of this my house—you who are leagued with the boldest traitors to Venice ; tell me why this treachery to me who have never injured you !"

" Messer Morosini," replied Edward, " there is no treachery. Treachery and guile were useless here. You have me doubly in your power, in that I am here alone among all your household, and in that you are the father of those whom I love, and especially of this most excellent lady. Though you summon all your people, the sword which, as you have seen, did me good service in rougher fields, must not be drawn in this presence. Therefore I am as one without hope from treachery or force, if indeed from anything."

" Fear not, sir, no force is meant to you. Morosini is not wont to need force to maintain his just power. You count on a show of bravery to advance your arts ; but none is needed."

" There is no art—there is no guile, nor aught but two things so little uncommon that they should cause small marvel—love and misfortune. My blood, most noble sir, might well match even with the oldest in Venice ; nay, I can claim conflicting honors, for both Saxon and Danish kings are among my forefathers ;

but the ruin of my race has fallen upon the fortunes of my kin: those whom the Normans least could conquer, most did they hate; and, like my father, have I sought better fortune and freer life in foreign lands. I have served Venice too much as you yourself would serve her, for love, to make profit by the service. I have no fortune that could make me bold to claim your daughter; yet perforce I could not refrain from love—why should I feign to deny it?"

"And so are here to steal what you dared not beg?"

"I ask what alone I can give—truth. Better fortunes may some day shine upon a not luckless sword."

"Knew you not, Messer Inglese, for you have dwelt long with us, that the noble women of Venice are not to be won by swords, nor to be given against the will and order of the state? This is childish idling. You are young, and I will not sternly punish your fault as I might. But the Lady Angiolina is younger, sir, and must learn that the daughter of this house is not to be given away for trifling words or the sport of youth. She knows the duty she has forgotten—she at least among my children knows to obey a father's voice, and she will tell you, even more fitly than I, that you must come no more."

Morosini paused, and there was a dead silence.

He resumed—"You hear what I said. Depart."

"I have heard no word from the Lady Angiolina."

"You shall not wait long, then. Angiolina, say to Messer Odoardo as I have said."

Angiolina turned. Her face was pale, and bathed in tears. She cast down her eyes, not daring to raise them; but the unbroken silence urged her to speak, and she lifted her eyes imploringly to her father, as praying him to spare her. With outstretched arm and cold constancy he pointed to Edward. She trembled, her lips parted, the breath seemed scarce to stir them—but the words fell chill on Edward's ear—"It is as my father has said."

Morosini turned to the youth, something like a proud, disdainful smile shadowed his face. "Thus do the daughters of Venice speak. You are satisfied?"

"Not so, Messer Morosini. You speak in your daughter, and she echoes your words in fear. I have said, use your power against me, and I resist not; but never will I render up my plighted troth to the Lady Angiolina, except at her command, freely given."

"You speak like a boy. Begone, sir."

"Never, except as I have said."

Morosini hesitated; and Alessandro, here first interposing, said—"If Messer Odoardo is so dainty in refusals that he must have this one repeated, let him, Messer Marco, have his wish: your excellent daughter does not so ill know your honor and her duty, but what she can say her lesson by herself."

Angiolina, too, turned once more to her parent. She struggled to speak, forcing out her words as if they would have stifled her. "Father mine," she said, "I have obeyed you. Of your bounty grant me this—all I ask: to

let Messer Odoardo have his will in this little wish." The words were simple, but Angiolina was ever simple and harmless, and had seldom, even of the stern Morosini, asked in vain.

The senator again paused, as weighing Alessandro's counsel, and then he said to Edward, "Be it so: we will indulge you even thus fantastically, in hopes quite to smother and extinguish your vain and injurious hope, young man, out of mercy to yourself; but think not that you can safely forget your own discretion, for there is no escape from this chamber except with my will."

The noble and his foster brother left the room, and the lovers were once more alone. Edward drew near, and again passed his arm round Angiolina's almost lifeless form. She resisted not; but no scarce perceptible bend to meet his encircling arm now acknowledged his embrace. Her face was not averted, neither was it turned towards him. He took her hand: it trembled with fear, not tenderness. He stooped to see the better into her face, and there he saw seated but one overmastering passion—submissive despair. That aspect, so wan and strange, struck an icy chill upon his heart, and its despair seized upon him. Uttering a little stifled cry, he suddenly left his hold, and turning away, he covered his face with his hands and wept.

His passion somewhat roused the girl, and laying her hand on his shoulder, she said, "Odoardo—Odoardo mio, do not kill me outright with grief. We have been wrong—or, rather, I; for I ought to have known, and saved you this. Be patient, you who can seek elsewhere for comfort."

Edward caught her in his arms, and cried—"Tell me now, Angiolina, what is your own free choice and will. Say that it is to abide by truth, and by my deep, lasting love, and I will leave you in pain—but leave you still to hope one day to win you perforce;—say that you take back your favor—that it is your own choice—and I obey."

"Alas! I have no choice—or, rather, my choice is shaped for me. I cannot will other than I have said."

"And is that your choice, without fear or force?"

"I have no cause to fear, except for you. That is my wretched choice."

Edward gazed on her face. It had changed not from its pale devotion to obedience. One farewell he asked, and he kissed her on the mouth. Her lips were cold and still as the dead. It seemed as if some hideous dreary spell had changed his companion, and that the living lover which late he held, had turned to some strange being with heart and sense closed against him. Gently he unclasped his arms, and taking one last look at that moveless countenance, he left the room.

Morosini and Alessandro stood in the antechamber, and the senator started forward as the youth issued forth; but seeing him alone, they only looked, and staid him not. He bore his despair in his front, but with calm firmness; which answered unabashed the challenge of insolent exultation lurking under the cool pride of the two as they suffered him to pass on

He descended the stairs, not forgetting his path ; but before he reached the hall, his guide started from a dark corner, as if he had been waiting for him.

"You have been long," said the man, in a low voice. "I feared to miss you ; for I dared not venture above, hearing Messer Morosini's step. But I shall put you safely without."

Edward made no answer, following in silence. They issued into the deeper darkness and chiller air of the night.

"Do not, in your happy dreams," said the man, the ready grin sounding in his voice, "forget your servant."

"You have earned your fee," said Edward ; and he put the third golden ducat into the fellow's hand.

"Ah! signore mio, I have earned well tonight ;" chuckling and chinking his gold, that Edward might hear it as they parted.

When Edward had left them, Marco Morosini went to the door of his daughter's chamber, and would have entered ; but having looked in, he stopped. She lay supine along the floor. Alessandro looked over his shoulder ; but neither moved towards the stricken girl ; with such fear and shame will the aspect of despair palsy the boldest hearts. "It were well," said Alessandro, "to send her maids hither ; for they understand these passing maladies."

On that license, Morosini walked away ; leaving others to succor his child in her misery.

<hr>

CHAPTER LV.

AFTER taking a few hours' repose, Ranieri was roused by a summons from Carlo Zeno ; who had left his bed betimes, and was found by the youth in a closet, seated at a table covered with papers. Zeno had laid aside his general's robes, and was dressed in the loose gown worn by the nobles of Venice in their homes, with a small round flat-crowned cap upon his head ; a garb which well set off the majesty of his form, and the simple, almost homely, bold blandness of his face.

"I have sent for you, Ranieri mine, after my wont, because I want a service done." His companion smiled : Zeno's service was his best honor. "I want a messenger," continued the noble, "who is quick, fearless, and discreet ; trusty, yet little likely to be missed ; and one already joined with us in this trouble, and therefore not to be harmed or marked out for a new conspirator. I could choose either you or Sebastiano ; and it likes me not to take either of you away till your sister be found ; but while you have the best right to seek her, I do think that Sebastian hath not his heart the less bound in the matter, and may prove the keenest in the search. Therefore do I ask you. You will take this letter to Messer Francesco da Carrara, whom, most likely, you will find in Padua ; or, if not, go to him wherever he may be. Having given it to him, he will listen while you tell him how this accusation has been brought against me, and you, and all of us ; and you will say that I want his testimony to absolve me,—either his license to declare wherefore this gold has passed between us, or whatsoever

may seem fit to him. When can you do part?"

"This instant."

"Go then. But take with you some two or three of my most comely and best furnished servants, for your better show ; and this bag of gold, to spend as beseems you. For your own dress, you need care little, since nature has dressed you out so well, and given you so comely a mien, that you need no clothes to mark you noble. Farewell. Return with all your best speed."

Ranieri kissed his master's hand, and left the room. Zeno betook to the table, and busied himself in reading the papers piled around him, the close record of his acts since he left Venice, to be submitted to the senate ; and now to be set in their last order, after the unceasing activity of his latest achievements. Still he read, when the door was opened, and a servant entered ; saying that a gentleman would speak with him.

"His name?" asked Zeno.

"He will not say, my lord," answered the man, "but by his voice and manner, I guess him to be Messer Morosini."

"What, Messer Marco?"

"No, my lord ; his cousin, Messer Lionardo Morosini."

Zeno was silent for a moment ; and then he said, "bring him hither." He pushed away his papers beyond the reach of his visiter's sharp eye to read them ; and, leaning back in his chair, marked the entrance of this, the most audacious of his foes save Alessandro da Padova.

Lionardo was wrapped in a cloak too plain for the splendor of slashing and embroidery affected by the nobles, and on his head he wore a cap to suit his humble covering ; like one who sought to avoid notice without. Entering in, he doffed his cap and threw open his cloak, as seeking no disguise where he was. Zeno rose, and slightly bending, with a pleasant smile he pointed to a seat near and over against his own ; and both being seated, he awaited what his visiter should say.

"I have come to you, Messer Zeno," Lionardo began, "on a strange enterprise, with little regard of danger to myself—less from you than from others ; and, to be frank with you, I must crave your generous forbearance and secrecy."

"My forbearance you surely shall have Messer Lionardo Morosini ; but, until I hear more, I know not whether I may be secret."

"Why then I must be silent. And yet you can lose nothing in the promise ; for it only binds you not to tell that which, not knowing now, you cannot tell ; and mostly concerns your own safety."

"Messer Lionardo, if I did think that I should gain my own safety by keeping secret that which ought to be known, I would rather not know that safety than pay for it with unlawful concealment. But I like not that others should run into vain dangers on my behalf ; and so I will even keep your secret. Do you meanwhile forbear, and tell me not what I ought not to know."

"I shall tell you little but what you must know already." And Lionardo went on in discourse, now bold and heedless, now cautious and reserved, to declare to Zeno how certain great people were leagued to recover Venice from the dangers into which she had been brought by the misgovernment of Contarini and his friends; how those ill-judged rulers had made an enemy of Carrara, when he desired to be a friend, and were thus the real provokers of the war of Chiozza; how Zeno himself, as one of Contarini's friends, was devoted to destruction; and how he might not only be safe, but share triumphs before unknown, if he would help the rescuers of Venice in their great work—men with whom he would hold it no shame to consort, did he but know their names. While he spoke, Lionardo often fixed a searching regard upon the other's face, watching what his words might do, to make Zeno befriend him or turn a bitterer enemy. Zeno the while kept a steadfast countenance, with no poring looks; but rather a scarcely shown smile, as though he were somewhat amused. Yet was not the intriguer the less watched. "And now," he said, "I am in your power, Messer Zeno; and therefore you may choose whether you will destroy me or make yourself one of our greatest leaders; for in sooth there are amongst us those who, in such case, would be leaders no longer, and others who would grieve little at the change."

"You need fear nought from me, Messer Morosini; but rather shall you ever command my good services. Not that I would stay, for you among the rest, that torrent of danger which you are letting loose upon yourselves; for it is no justice to pick out favorites among culprits, and to reserve a pardon for those who seek to secure both sides, gambling for the chance of conspiracy while they would forefend the dangers by making friends with those who must discover it. Be not angered because my speech is frank: I am not the worse enemy for that; and I am so much bounden to you for this good-will to me, that my sword shall never strike you, should we meet. But I will think no more of this. I will not win either safety or profit in secret and crooked paths; I will rather fight and defend myself in broad day. I scruple not, on needful occasion, to use craft, yet only in rough war, or with those that use nought else; but those that meet me openly, and in good faith, shall never be deceived by undermining deceit from me."

"Then I have failed in my enterprise, and let all that has passed here be forgotten."

"Be it so: but why should not some good come of our friendly encounter? These schemes, Messer Lionardo, are not suited to your free, bold nature; you are skilful, I dare to say it, in contrivings; you are bold to execute; but you cannot keep a coward secrecy, nor brook the slow reckoning of conspiracy—as your coming here is proof. Leave it, Messer Lionardo—choose the bolder and the nobler side, and that which best befits you."

Lionardo listened gravely; but when Zeno held his peace, he laughed, and answered, — "Your counsel is excellent, but I have sought it too late."

"Nevertheless think upon it."

"In any case I count on your discretion. Farewell!" And he left Zeno to his papers.

CHAPTER LVI.

RANIERI used such good discretion and speed that he travelled without let of any kind until he arrived in the presence of Carrara. The Lord of Padua was seen in a different guise from that he wore when Ranieri met him in Chiozza. His anxious look had passed away; and if he had not the aspect of bold cunning with which he listened to Marco Morosini and the counterfeit monk, he seemed contentedly grave, like one who takes fortune as she comes, with equal mind. He wore a loose dark colored silken vest, without confinement or belt at the waist, reaching down to the knees, showing the hose on the leg; and on his head a cloth folded not unlike an eastern turban, only scantier, after the manner of his house. He sat without rising as his visiter entered, and started somewhat when he saw the youth; but he bowed courteously. Ranieri delayed not with his message, but in the briefest and plainest word told his story, and claimed Carrara's testimony for his master. Carrara heard him out; and then putting on rather a stern countenance, he said "Messer Giovinotto, we have met before. What is your name?"

"Ranieri Arduino."

"The Arduino are a strange and varying race! Where have I seen you?"

"In Chiozza."

"In Chiozza! Aye—a spy."

"The servant then of Messer Carlo Zeno, the general of the Venetian forces; and now the servant of Carlo Zeno, your friend."

"You are a bold youth! Did you not tremble to venture hither?"

"I thought not of it, but only of serving the kindest and best of my friends; and if I had, no messenger from Carlo Zeno's bidding need tremble to enter Francesco da Carrara's palace."

"Good," said Carrara, smiling; "bolder still! ever if you are bold, be so to the full. You count rightly on your protection, and we must not question your allegiance. But enough of that. Tell Messer Carlo Zeno that his bidding shall be obeyed, and he shall hear from me in Venice. Trust me, I will not be too late; so that you have sped as well now, sir youth, as you did in Chiozza; and if all my friends had been as faithful and as bold as you are, you might then have missed your aim."

Ranieri reverently took leave.

Scarcely had he departed, when another was ushered into Carrara's presence — the tall square form of Alessandro da Padova, dauntless and unabashed; not bolder than the messenger who had, unknown to him, gone before, but with a fierce instead of gentle bearing. Carrara rose from his seat with the air of him who desires to be on equal terms with a dangerous guest. Not that he could overtop the towering form of the adventurer; but standing, he could more freely speak, turn, and even think.

"Be welcome, Messer Alessandro. What news from that Venice whose victory is your defeat?"

"News, my lord, of reviving hopes, if you will lend your power in aid. Not to stay you long—nor myself, for I must return betimes—I am messenger to you from Messers Barbarigo and your friends in the republic, who have already half won the field. Messer Marco Morosini has joined us even more usefully than ever; and now he knows how we are to invite your alliance. He at last is one of your friends."

"Why that is most excellent—if it were a year or two sooner."

"You may jest, Messer da Carrara; but the thing is good, happen when it may; and you shall yet retake, not only Chiozza, but Venice itself after your own best fashion—that is, by cunning instead of force. We have, too, so assailed Contarini through one of his best props, that he cannot but fall: we have, and partly by your help, already brought Carlo Zeno to be a prisoner before Venice: and now you may smile again, for we made bold to accuse him of a secret conspiracy with you."

"With me! Carlo Zeno!" cried Carrara, angrily. "How is this!"

"Be not surprised, nor take it amiss, for we will make it all turn to your profit." And he recounted how, when Chiozza was captured, the paper was found proving that Zeno had received gold from the Lord of Padua; how he had been publicly accused on that proof; how many more senators had been gained over; and how, in brief time, there was good hope of making Marco Morosini doge of Venice. He told how he himself was to be the son-in-law of the future doge; wherein, by the bye, he claimed Carrara's help. "Thus, my lord, you see how Contarini's power decays before us. At present our only demand from you is that you should aid us in bringing home this crime to Carlo Zeno. Give us proof—whatever the gold passed between you for, give us proof of his treason. This service shall hereafter help to reconcile you to Venice—no difficult task for your so many and so powerful friends, when once they have their own doge. For we are now so many—though all do not know all their own allies—that even the twisted and manifold elections of electors can scarcely prevent the last vote from turning up our own man for doge."

"Good! That is all!"

"All as yet."

Carrara pondered, and took a step or two away. Then turning to Alessandro, and raising his face, he said, "Say to Messer Barbarigo, that they shall hear from me in Venice."

"I counted on your aid," exclaimed Alessandro, with an exulting smile. "The manner of your proof may best be left to you. My lord, I crave license to depart; for my presence must not be missed in Venice."

"You do well to return right speedily; and I will make no delay. But first make this house your own for some hasty refreshing of yourself, and then you shall have leave."

"Not a moment, my lord; for every minute that I lose is dangerous."

"Farewell, then You shall scarcely outstrip me."

CHAPTER LVII.

The day was rapidly closing when Alessandro regained his noble foster brother's palace;

but so intent was he upon his plans, that he scarcely noted the change from light to dark, or the familiar path he followed. Little thought the brawny boatmen, as they made their barque fly across the waters, that Venice would have shuddered and shrieked aloud at their approach, had it known the danger that lurked in that noveless and silent form; little feared the citizens that now strolled at ease across the piazza of St. Stephen, the evil genius of the city, as he stalked by with hasty strides. He saw the dangers before him, but felt his strength wax with the need. Carrara crushed and baffled in the field, yet still powerful, seemed more than ever ductile to his will; his foster brother grew stronger to use, and more willing to be used; his most powerful, most contemptuous, because least mindful enemy, his chief hate, the virtuous Carlo Zeno, appealed for mercy against his accusal, to tribunals filled with those whose honor or whose wisdom he had corrupted; his own advancement by marriage, too long delayed, only awaited his matured contrivance; and as he neared the fair city rising from the waters, he sneered at the thought that the great republic itself was but a tool to further the designs of a bastard adventurer. He landed and trod its paved way as if the place were already his own. None crossed his path as he entered the palace and went straight across the hall to his own apartment. Within the house it now seemed almost dark to him who came from without; but every corner was too familiar for him to need a light; and occupied with his own thoughts he moved rapidly on, careless of looking around him. He had already made some steps into his saloon, when from a seat that he had not noticed rose up into the dim light of the window, the form of a tall and stately woman. He knew that it was Rosa Bardossi; and he started as he saw her, with a sting of fear and anger; for in all the triumphant career of his thoughts he had met with no let or hindrance, till now arose before him his only obstacle—arose before him where least of all he could have looked for it. Stopping, he stamped with sudden anger, and cried,—" But how is this! is it you, Rosa, and here! how have you dared to come hither!"

"It is I, Alessandro," replied the woman, calmly; "would that I were not here."

"And know you not that I have said that I will have no woman with me in this palace; that none should follow me, none in the world!"

"I know that you have said so, and while you held that law I never came."

Alessandro was silent: it puzzled him to understand her words; but not caring to trouble himself with searching deep into her feelings, for now they little imported him, he at once assumed that she was jealous. He felt half glad of the pretext for anger, and already saw in the quarrel the means of removing her. His growing disinclination, too, gained strength at finding so weak a passion in her who had heretofore ruled even him more than he liked; and it was with a heartfelt sneer that he said,—" I did not think, Rosa, that you were so far like other women as to be a spy upon me for jealousy! I have no woman here, and I will have none; last of all such a one. Go at once, before we grow more angry."

"I am not jealous, Alessandro; and I do not suspect you of so much love that you have enough even for me, much less for more. It is not in love that you have brought others here, and yet perforce must I follow."

"What is it you mean!"

"Give me back Teresa."

"Teresa! What is this! Am I Teresa's keeper, that you should ask me for her! What idle folly is this! Go!"

"You are not Teresa's keeper; but I was. I am accountable for her, and I will have her. Think not to put me off with idle pretences. If you thought me not one to be jealous, so I think you not one to make silly pretences, that are seen through even before they are finished. Teresa is here—she has gone from my keeping, and none other would have dared to take her."

"Why, then, I say I took her not."

"Prevaricate no more, Alessandro. She has been brought to you. If your own hands had done all your evil deeds, you would have less to answer. Give her back to me, or I must do what truly I should grieve to do, even more than it we had not quarreled ; for I would not have my truth and service to that good lady take the shape of revenge. Give her back to me, Alessandro, before farther harm is done."

"I will pretend with you no more, Rosa. The woman I have not taken, and I have her not here ; but she has been taken, and she is kept for my use, being not the first prisoner that I have kept in store to serve my purpose at need. Know that she is necessary to my plans, and threaten no more ; for that is the idlest of all. You have no power save through me. Be content to know that you cannot have her. Go home and think no more of this thing."

"Not so, Alessandro ; you know not the strength of my will, for hitherto it has jumped with yours ; but now that you will not have it with you, you must feel it against you ; and in truth I will have the lady back in safety, or, as I said, it shall be worse for one of us two."

"I have said it ; you shall not have her. Go home, Rosa ; go home."

Rosa was silent—not that she felt quite baffled, for she had not thought that the Paduan would give up his prize so easily ; but her heart trembled at the contest which still she had resolution to begin. Alessandro moved away from her, as if to leave the room ; not desiring to force her away, and yet determined to end the conference.

"Stay," she cried. "Alessandro, I must have this lady at all price : there is nothing that I will not yield to have her by gentle means or by force ; you have refused her at my asking, and I must seek other aid. Hitherto I have not troubled you. All that you have done, wrong as right, have I seen in silence, and suffered to pass by. But this I will not suffer—this I will not allow : I shall call the aid of Sebastian. Aye, you listen to me now. I will have the aid of Carlo Zeno——"

"Silence, Rosa ; there is danger in what you say ; be silent."

"I care not for danger, for in this I will have my will. I say that I will have the help of Carlo Zeno : and you must needs know that if once Zeno help me to hunt throughout your secret places, and follow you in all your tools, I can no more stop him than you can stop the sea after the dyke is once broken. Now give me this lady, and think no more of me. Give her to me, and I trouble you no more."

It was Alessandro's turn to be silent. In the bold career of his thought as he entered the palace, he had stumbled upon an obstruction in his path. It had too often crossed him before ; but now as he strove to overpass it, it seemed to rise before his feet, and he felt like one in a dream, to whom some little thing that hinders his way grows up to be a monster threatening him with destruction. His was not a heart to quail or to turn tender where danger threatened himself. Before Rosa had ceased speaking, he had resolved to rid himself of this trouble. Rosa was with him alone ; it was dark ; he had but to move his finger to fasten the door ; there were weapons, many of them, within his reach ; his sword was by his side, and his dagger too. As to blood, if it had to be spilt, he could have cleared away that sign. Whatsoever his hold, bad mind should wish to do within that room, he could do, and could so contrive that none should ever call him to account ; and yet perhaps the thought of raising his hand against the girl who so audaciously braved him, scarcely entered his mind. His left hand grasped the scabbard of his sword, as the familiar habit of an angry man, but he had no thought of using it ; and yet the thought that was in him, more than rage, made his firmly-knit limbs tremble. It was with a hoarser voice that he said,—"Rosa, you have spoken too far. You threaten me with Sebastian and with Zeno ; let them come : I shall be too strong for them. But, Rosa mia, I would not part with you thus ; I could, you know, stop you in your way to Sebastian ; I could do so that you would never reach him ; but heretofore have I trusted you, and I have said that rather will I brave the danger that lies in your knowledge than close my mouth to the one in the world whom I have loved best. Go : fetch whom you will to destroy me ; I will not yield, but I will run this risk ; and for the love that was once between us I will suffer the peril."

After a little pause, Rosa replied,—"You now try my constancy with a new wile, but it will not serve you, Alessandro. It is right and good that I should have back this lady, and have her back I will. You are in no danger from me ; your secrets are safe as ever, so far as I know them ; for not even torture shall force them from my lips. But I will have back the lady, even though I call all Venice to fetch her ; and I know not—you may know, but I know not, whether, if I bring your enemies into this room, they may not learn more than I mean. So give her to me without more words, and, for the love that was between us, let your schemes be marred so far."

"Rosa, you have conquered more than any yet conquered me. You shall have her. You shall have her safe as when last you saw her ; only this I must crave, that some few days you wait, that I may yield her up without quite spoiling my fortunes. Trust me, you shall have her."

"And how soon!"

"You are impatient. Say that you wait three days ; two days, if you will. You shall have her in two days, and as safe as when she left you :—will that content you? Leave me two days in peace—two whole days,—and on the third day, even at sunrise, or before that, the lady shall be brought back to you safe and well. Will that content you?"

"Your voice sounds strange while you say this, Alessandro; I never heard it sound so before. Do you speak in good faith?"

"I have told you, Rosa, that while in all the world I have used guile and force and cruelty to meet the evils thrust upon me by my base birth, to you alone I have been frank and kind. Even as men whom they fain to have been enchanted, and who have had some fatal place left where you might strike them to their death, so am I invulnerable to all the world, yet doomed myself to make this one place where I can be stricken. Leave me now. The lady shall be with you on the morning of the third day."

"I will take that promise, Alessandro. Two days you shall not see me, and on the third day the lady shall return, or I will again come to know why it is you keep her: farewell."

She turned from him and went from the room. Alessandro could not say farewell, for the word stuck in his throat. He listened to her footsteps soon lost in the distance of the wide hall. He waited still longer, and at last, knowing that she must be quite gone, he went out again into the air, and had already walked a few steps, like one bent upon a journey, when a man stopped him.

"A most happy evening to you, Messer Alessandro," said the coarse but feeble voice of Nadale. "I had well nigh missed you; for I came to ask when I should bring home that piece of goods that I have in keeping for you?"

"I, too, was seeking you: follow me, and we will talk within." Alessandro turned back; and presently they were in his own room.

"I was saying to you, Messer Alessandro," said the fellow, with his brutal ease, that I want to know when I shall bring home that piece of goods; for it keeps ill, I say. For all her fairness and her pretty voice, the lady is stiff-necked, and as fierce as a she-bear. I had three good strong ones with me when I took her that night, for I would not trust myself, seeing that I have been a poor, weak wretch ever since her friend so favored me in the piazza. How can a man be strong whose jaw is so twisted that he cannot chew his victuals? and I tell you that it takes me some hour to get through a loaf, though it be no bigger than that fist. I thought the old fisherman was enough for me; and truly I should have found him too much, but that after the lady had fainted, one of the others got him down cleverly with a knife. Well, and now I have her at home, she will not eat, she looks as if she could eat well enough, for she never weeps or moans, or such things; and though I try to move her spirit by sneering at her young gentleman who put my beard in such disorder, and any other fancies that I can think of, still she eats not; and in sooth she has not eaten nor drunk any thing since I carried her away. I dare say she thinks it is poisoned; and I cannot convince her how silly it would be to buy wine to poison her withal, when I could finish her at the cost of wiping my knife."

Q

While the man was talking, Alessandro paced the room in thought, but half hearing what he said.

"Tell me when I may bring her home, Messer Alessandro?"

The Paduan stood still. "You may bring her here at once, into this palace; but not into my lodging here. I will provide a room for her before you bring her. You will be the freer to do some other duty for me. Do you know Rosa Bardossi?"

"Rosa Bardossi? No; I know no other Rosa but one whom you know of too."

"It is the same—she I mean who lived near the old fisherman."

"Aye, I know her."

"She is to come to me in three days; but I wish not to see her—she troubles me." Alessandro drew from his breast a purse, and opening it, he slowly took out some money which he placed in Nadale's hand.

"One—two. They are ducats, I think, Messer Alessandro?"

"The same; if they are not so, give them back to me, and we will fetch a light, that you may have your price."

"No, no—they are ducats; I know them by the feel. But they are only two."

"They are only two. Here are two more, which I will give you for this—that you shall let me know when you have finished."

"Why, you give me but two to bring you the news, and two to—you know what: there is no sense in that sort of bargaining, Messer Alessandro."

"You never have more than two?"

"No, I know; but this is not a common sort of business. Besides, you give me only two to do it, and yet you give me as much as two to bring you the news. Your own price is against you."

"Talk no more, ribald. So away, or give me back the money."

"Nay, nay, I meant no offence, signor mio. Truly, I may have to walk as far to earn these two ducats in my left hand here as these two in my right. Where may I find the lady?"

"You know where she lives."

"Aye; but I did not know whether you would like it done at home or abroad."

"I care not which, so that it be done as secretly as you can do, and have done before. Let us have no more words about it; be gone."

Nadale started, and shambling out of the room, he cried, gayly jingling his ducats—"A most happy evening to you, Messer Alessandro."

CHAPTER LVIII.

Sound was the sleep of Alessandro that night; for strong in body and mind, few things ever disturbed the few hours that he alotted to his bed. He was aroused betimes by a servant, who told him that one desired to speak with him. Hastily donning his clothes, he repaired to his saloon. When he entered, a young man, who was lounging carelessly in a chair, rose briskly to greet him.

It was young Francesco da Carrara, who saluted him gayly, but not too familiarly. "Be well, Messer Alessandro, I come a messenger to you."

"Your father is quick, Messer Francesco, as is his wont. What says he?"

"This.—But first tell me, is Messer Marco Morosini of the signory now."

"He is so."

"That is well. Let there be a meeting of the signory, to hear what the Lord of Padua shall disclose touching the thing you wot of, and there shall be one there to declare it. Can that be done?"

"Doubt it not."

"And forthwith?"

"This day, if you will. But what message has your father bethought him to send?"

"Why, that must not be known till it be delivered; for with all his craft, as Messer Alessandro knows full well, he ever uses to mix something that is true to give it the better show. And this matter, he says, will have more force on men's minds if it come suddenly. It were better that you should be astonished than be forced merely to seem so."

"Most true. Will your father's message be ready for the signory this day?"

"At what hour you please."

"Why then you have brought it? Say at once; for the signory will sit anon, in expectation of your father's visit."

"Be it so. But first for another matter. Before I leave this house, I would see the lady Angiolina." In spite of his habitual self-command, Alessandro started. "Fear not," continued Francesco; "I am no importunate suitor; but it concerns me nearly to see the lady."

"I had thought, Messer Francesco, that your suit prospered not well, since you came no more after that night."

"Talk not of it, Messer Alessandro. If I knew that I had a rival, perchance I might let him know how far I prospered, and how pleased I was."

Alessandro hesitated. "I would not do aught that might displease the lady Angiolina."

"What is it you fear, Messer Alessandro? I too will do nought that can offend her; still less be so humble as to—but enough: I seek but a solace of my mind."

"Have you conversed with your father?—for I would not that he were wronged."

"What is it your fear? We do not use to tell our fathers of all our loves; least of all where we fail; or they must be men of bolder face than I am that would do so. Shall I see her?"

"You shall."

"And alone?"

"Alone; and at once if you wish; for she rises betimes. Wait a while, and I will see if you can be admitted."

"You will not say that I am come."

"I will say nothing." The foster brother left the saloon; but presently returning, he beckoned, and Francesco followed him.

"You know whither I lead you?" said Alessandro.

"No."

"To the terrace; whence you came that night that you visited it in secret, and then met me

so maladroitly in this hall, and were somewhat roughly rebuked."

"Now I remember well; but I remember not the rebuke. I met no one."

"Your memory is gay, Messer Francesco, and dwells not upon what is displeasing."

Francesco answered not; for he knew not Alessandro's purpose in speaking thus; as indeed he could not remember the rebuke which was not made to him, but Edward. Alessandro gently opened the door of the terrace, and letting his companion in, closed it again. Angiolina walked on the other side of the orange trees; but at the sound of the closing door, she turned. How changed! The full round face and form had fallen to slenderer proportions; the rich blood that mantled in her cheek had flowed back to the heart, and the darkness of her skin did not conceal the paleness; the eyes once so gay and sparkling, were now softer, sad, and steadfast, as fixed on mournful thoughts; and her bearing was slower—a little gain of dignity at a dismal cost. Yet looked she so gentle, so graceful, and so tender, that love itself burrowed her mood, and worshipped her less in the rapturous adoration that her growing beauties once awakened, than in a tender submission that bowed itself yet lower before her fallen spirit. She started not when she saw Francesco, but moving a step or two to meet him, she held out her hand. He kissed it right humbly.

"Is it yet safe for you to venture so far within a Venetian house, Messer Francesco?" she asked.

"None is more welcome in this house this day than I am, lady mine; and it is for you to say whether I have ventured too far."

"I spake not with that meaning, but only thought of your safety."

"Why, then, Angiolina it is of your safety we must talk; for, my life, though it makes me a happier and a better man to see you, yet I came, believe it, not for that, but solely to see if I might serve you."

"Serve me, Francesco! In what?"

Francesco looked round, to see if he was watched. But the door was firmly closed, and Alessandro had really left him alone; for the Paduan had no pettiness in his guile, and he little feared or cared for a rival. Francesco again took his companion's hand, and kissing it respectfully, he said,—"Do you remember, Angiolina, that night when we conversed together here?" Angiolina turned away her head: she did remember, not only what passed between them, but the sweeter things that had passed afterwards; and still she felt a kindness towards the young lord of Padua, for that he seemed to belong to that dear night. He continued :—"Angiolina, you then, my sweet, in your kindness, told me that I asked for your heart too late. Dearest lady, when I heard that—I do not know why, but I believe that the love of one so good as you makes the lover good in all that concerns his love; but when I heard that, my own love became less in my esteem than yours, and I wished you happier than I could be." Angiolina pressed his hand. Moving from him, she took a seat; but then, while she covered her eyes, she held out her hand to him again. He learned from its trembling why she had sat down. "Angiolina, dearest, I fear, from what I see in your aspect, that you are not happy,"—again she pressed his hand in answer—"but know not if you yourself are aware of all that threatens you. Tell me this, Angiolina, and pardon me if I offend you; for I ask it only with most humble interest in your service,—tell me, was Alessandro da Padova he of whom you spake that night!"

"Francesco!" cried Angiolina, turning to him; her astonishment overmastering her grief.

"Angiolina! you do not mean that it was! Tell me, sweet; for the doubt troubles me."

"How could you think it! But much more it troubles me to hear your question."

"Then, Angiolina, still more I fear to tell you all; but it must be done. Do not say any name out loud, for I cannot tell who may listen. Know you that Alessandro dares to seek your love!" The girl listened in terrified amaze. "Aye, I have so learned it, that there can be no mistake; but thus it is." Angiolina grasped his hand with both hers; she glanced around, as if she sought some flight; she would have spoken, but speech failed; and looking with helpless terror in his face, her head sunk on his shoulder. He passed his arm round her waist, and went on. "Dearest Angiolina, be not thus in fear; it cannot and shall not be, if you will trust me, and use but your own courage. Did you not know of this before!" Without rising, she shook her head. "But I do suspect your father does." A little shudder passed over her. "Now tell me, Angiolina mine, who it was that you thought of when you spoke that night—tell me, and shame not to speak freely to your old playmate." Angiolina rose from his shoulder, and again turned away. "Tell me—you will not fear to tell Francesco—who was in your thought!"

In a voice that he could scarcely hear, she said,—"I thought then of one you know not."

"His name!"

"It was Odoardo, l'Inglese."

"The Englishman! I know him well, and so did all in Chiozza. Why then, Angiolina, I owe him a life; and I shall pay him more richly, if I give him love. Does your father know of this gentleman!" She nodded. "And hence your unhappiness. You need say no more, but this—Do you consent to remain in love to be given to Messer Alessandro da Padova!"

"Forgive me, Francesco," she said, turning to him, "if I do not thank you as I ought; but I am so wretched and so scared! Oh, my dear friend, save me from that, and I care not what happens."

"Why then, sweetest life, be of good courage; be discreet, let me bestow you where you ought to be bestowed, and thus I will rescue you. This have I had at heart in coming to Venice. And now that I may do it, I must bid you farewell."

"How faithful and generous have you ever been to me, Francesco; and how ill have I repaid you! Why do these things happen—why am I so unhappy as to be too well loved by you who should love one as good as yourself."

"Sweetest, I told you, on that night, that if you would love me and have me, I should be the better and the happier man. That was too high a fortune for me. But yet am I better and happier for that I love you; for that I may serve you; and for that you speak to me thus.

I have warred for Venice, but now much more bravely for one kind word, or to conquer from grief and give to tenderness one tear of those dearest eyes. Farewell, my sweet friend: think of me ever, if not as one who loves." He kissed her hand; but putting the other on his head as he stooped down, Angiolina kissed him, first on the forehead and then on the eyes. "Be silent, and be of good heart," he said, as he left the terrace.

CHAPTER LIX.

So long had young Francesco remained with Angiolina, that when he reached the ducal palace he found without the door of the hall in which the signory were sitting, a messenger who had been sent to seek him, and to usher him into their presence. The dignity and power which he was to encounter could not repress his feeling of amusement, almost of sport, at the confusion into which he was sent to throw the republic. It was some revenge to him for the humiliation which he had endured as his father's proxy when he last stood before its high officers; but he repressed any show of this careless feeling, and entered the council chamber with the courteous yet dignified manner that set forth so well his slender but manly form. Meeting first the eye of Contarini, seated in the chair of state at the head of the table, he bowed courteously, and then to the nobles round the board. There he saw Morosini; and among others whom he knew less well, he was glad also to notice Vendramini and Alberti. The presence of Lionardo Morosini was less welcome; but it struck no fear into young Carrara's heart; and on second thoughts almost seemed to favor the progress of his designs. All were silent, as if awaiting his admission; and the first words that greeted him were from the doge, who said, with his pleasant manner,—"Welcome to Venice, Messer Francesco; I hope your noble father is in health!"

"I am glad to see, noble prince, that your own health is the same that has ever attended you through life, and so will my father be pleased to hear. He is well, and none the worse in the hope that now these luckless wars are over, he will live in the friendship and favor of the republic."

"You have your father's looks so strongly, Messer Francesco, that when you entered here I could think the years had rolled back again; and now I see that you do not lack his cunning speech, for all you look so free and gay. We await to hear your bidding; for we have been told that you have a message for us from the Lord of Padua."

"I have, my lord; and would it were all as pleasant as I could wish; but be it what it may, it will stand as a gage of my father's desire to serve your city, and to wipe away for ever that enmity which has come between you. Before I begin, let me crave that protection which, ere I have done, I may well need; since angry and fierce will be the rage of some."

"Follow on, sir, with your message; you shall be protected."

"There is among your prisoners one Messer Jacopo Arduino!"

" There is."

" He was imprisoned on a charge of treason, for that he had been practising with the Lord of Padua ?"

" He was "

" My lord, I will declare all which that unfortunate gentleman has done for the Lord of Padua. My father had need to send to Messer Carlo Zeno a certain sum of gold—why and to what end I will explain hereafter, since for that among other things am I come—but needing to send this gold, and privately, he lacked a messenger who would do that service, and yet whom he could trust to do it faithfully even though he should know that Messer Jacopo Arduino, being in trouble for want of means, was in Padua striving to borrow money of a lender who had often given it him before, on the security of the house which he still possessed in Venice. But the man, fearing wars, would not lend him the money, nor even buy the house; as Arduino wished him to do. My father hearing of this, sent for Messer Jacopo, whom he had known in better time, and asking him what money he needed, partly to advantage that unhappy gentleman, and partly in payment for his own service did give him what he needed, upon condition that he should with all speed convey the gold I spake of to Messer Zeno. So faithfully did Messer Arduino do that service, that, as I have learned, he spent all his own money in voyaging to find Messer Zeno, which he did at Tenedos, on his return from Constantinople. And for that good faith, and nothing more, hath Messer Jacopo been imprisoned · and, as I hear, he was given up by his own son ; so great wickedness is there in this world ! My lord, that wretched gentleman's imprisonment disgraces justice : let him be released ; and I myself will be hostage that I will make good what I have said of him. But, if it so please you, when he is released, let him be desired to attend here at such time as you shall appoint, as a witness to what I have farther to disclose."

" You ask boldly, Messer Francesco," said the doge ; " but we are in great part aware of what you have now disclosed touching Messer Jacopo Arduino ; and on your assurance, I see no difficulty here. That is not all you have for us to hear ?"

" My lord, Messer Francesco da Carrara, as you well know, has waged war with Venice on certain quarrels that he had, and as he thought justly. Others too that had quarrelled with the republic made common cause with him, and as they thought justly ; and, being thus opposed to your high city, they, as I need not tell you, joined together for the furtherance of their separate quarrels, though each might enter little into the several purposes of the other ; therefore, my lord, though Francesco da Carrara fought by the side of Genoa, and Genoa by his, yet had he little concern in what Genoa had claimed of you ; but rather used the republic as an engine in the quarrel which you had forced upon him ; for as is his wont, he sought to use against your most strong power every engine that he could find ready to his hand. And yet, as we know, alas ! full well, so strong has your power been, that, with all his art, and all his resources he was vanquished. Still, I say, he used all the engines

that he could handle ; and I do believe that none among you who is skilled in the arts of war will think that in doing so he abandoned either his honour or his duty to the most holy God. My lord, in your own city he found other engines which also he thought it no wrong to use—many of your nobles, powerful and right willing to his service. And yet among them, my lord, he found men of so little faith, that even in that treachery, as you would hold it, they kept not to their bond, but rather strove to use him for their own ends ; and in doing so, lacking his more noble heart, they did not fail to bring his name into most hateful report ; so that whereas he wished Venice to fear him as a foe skilled in force and in cunning of state, these base men had made him seem as bad as one of their own crew, and ready for the vilest means. I know full well, my lord, that Francesco da Carrara has been suspected in this your city of crimes, that would drive him from the earth and bring upon him that perdition in the life to come which not even the intercession that all require could wipe away. Therefore, my lord, and also wishing to show to you, now that these wars have gone, how thoroughly he desires your friendship, he has sent me to make plain those his secret stratagems, which have been thus perverted. And now, my lord, I shall need that protection which I have claimed, and some trust from you before I go farther. Before I say more, I must crave that you cause to be seized and kept safe, one Alessandro da Padova, who has long been the servant of my father, Messer Francesco da Carrara—but a most treacherous servant."

At the sound of that name one seated at the table started so violently that every eye was turned upon him. It was Marco Morosini, who jumped back in his chair, but then mastering himself, struck his fist hard upon the table, and there kept it, as though he was prepared to hear and witness all without betraying fear or farther surprise. The others too started, and looked from Morosini to young Carrara in amazement ; save Contarini, in whose face there was no change. He looked round the table, and then at the young Paduan, saying, " These are dangerous words, Messer Francesco, and rather fitted to be heard by the Ten than by us—these are matters that we carry before our council of the Ten ; but since your father is a foreign prince, and we have admitted you here, we will listen to the rest of your message : speak on."

" Most noble prince, I may not say more until that man be arrested." He drew a paper from his breast. " I have here a list of names which it may be I must farther touch upon. It may be so ; but were I to say more before that one bad man is arrested, all that I might have to advise the government of this republic might be rendered in vain. I will, if you bid me, say on ; but better would it be that we had that man safely here, that you might learn from his own lips great part of what I would say to you, and that he might not spread abroad untimely what must follow."

There was a pause ; and Contarini spoke in a low tone to Vendramini, who sat next him. The converse extended from those to others, Marco Morosini alone remaining silent, and unmoved in the fixed posture that he had taken.

" I will retire if it so please you," said Francesco; "that you may consult in freedom; but that I do not speak vainly I will call a witness if you doubt—and I do think that the doge does not doubt—but I say if you doubt whether this man ought to be here in safety before I open farther what I have to say, ask Messer Marco Morosini."

Morosini sprang from his chair, his face deadly pale, then red; while his flashing eyes filled with tears of passion, and the hand he rested upon the table trembled with an unknown dread and rage. "It well suits," he cried, "the great but base enemy of Venice to scatter these charges among her faithful nobles. Like all true men, ever have I hated Francesco da Carrara; and for that hate—for that contempt and scorn—which now before my very eyes——" He sunk down on his chair, suffocated by the passion that could not find its way, while the rest of the signory regarded him with astonishment.

Lionardo, who had begun to glance uneasily at each face—at the bold messenger from his doubtful ally—at the dangerous paper which the young man held carelessly in his hand, now began—"Messer la Doge,"—but then repenting as soon as Contarini turned to him, he said that he would not interrupt the council. The doge continued his converse with Vendramini; who closed it in a somewhat louder tone of voice, denoting his belief that he had said enough. Contarini rose from his seat, and said—"Messer Francesco, it seems to us that this gentleman of whom you speak should be seized; and at your peril be it to make good the reasons for his seizure. He shall be seized; and now say on."

"Not so, my lord; I may say little more until I know that this man is not running loose to warn his brother traitors of what they have to fear, before you yourself know it. Nor am I sure but what, even now, ears listen to us that might do the same."

Again Morosini started from his seat, but Alberti dragged him down, and in a quick and angry manner Contarini asked—"What mean you, sir! speak out, or leave your words unsaid."

"My lord, I shall speak out; and I have to crave that what else I say may be said before the senate; for to you, and to the senate, and to all Venice my message is directed. But this I will tell you now in answer to those fierce glances the which Messer Marco Morosini gives me, that his were not the ears I spoke of. Messer Marco Morosini, noble prince, is an honorable man; still I will say that it behoves him, in virtue of his honor and of his faith to Venice, to let no word that I have spoken go forth from this hall until I have spoken before the senate; and now, my lord, I await to know that Alessandro da Padova is in custody, and that the senate is willing to hear me farther."

Again Contarini spoke with those nearest to him; and then, raising his voice somewhat loudly, he said—"This young man has brought among us more trouble than I foresaw. Whether he will be able to make good the words he has spoken so boldly, it is for time to show. With all that audacity which has made Venice suffer so much in his father, we know not whether he has that father's wisdom and discretion. It looks little like it, and truly it seems to me that he has ventured into this hall, sacred to your councils, to make sport of Venice and its highest

names. Still we have him here to answer for his words; and being challenged thus boldly, it behoves us also to answer for ourselves; and I trust, noble sirs, that you will think it good that this Alessandro da Padova shall be seized forthwith, and brought with this young Francesco da Carrara before our senate; and also that none of us who are here, and who are it seems in part accused, shall leave this palace or stray away from this council, until we have heard the rest of Messer Francesco da Carrara's speech. My lords, it touches us nearly; it must not be otherwise. Never did I feel, since this bonnet was forced upon my head by the will of Venice, that I stood in a post of so much danger as now I do. But truly he little merits to have so honorable a force put upon him who would scruple to meet any danger, having at stake the welfare of the republic; and I say to you, that if any man of you, and even myself should leave this building between what this youth has said, and what he shall say, he may be accused of treachery, at least to the high fame of his race. I do believe that Messer Marco Morosini will repulse all accusal."

"Messer Marco Morosini," interrupted Francesco, "is not accused. He knows, but he is not accused."

"Be it so," continued the doge; "I hope young man, that your audacious accusations will be disproved; but having gone so far, they must be disproved. Meantime excuse the freedom of my speech; and if it please you, you shall be made a prisoner too, if you will vouchsafe the hospitality with which I would detain you."

"My lord, it was my intent to crave your bounty, both that I might still be protected until my task is finished, and also that you might not doubt my honest purpose. For when my task is done," he added gayly, with a fierce little smile that became him well, "if any noble would desire to make me answer for my words, it will not be difficult for him to find me."

"Messer Francesco, I will lead you to my apartment; but you shall excuse me if for a time I return to this council, to give order for what you have desired. Let me attend you." So saying, he led his visiter from the hall.

In a few minutes Contarini returned, and again took his seat and began to advise with the others about the arrest of Alessandro Marco Morosini sat like one listening not, but half dreaming, until suddenly starting, he exclaimed, "It must rest upon this; let Alessandro be seized, Andrea Contarini, and let the senate decide. I say no more, except before the senate; let Alessandro be seized," he added fiercely.

"We are agreed, then," said Contarini, look in around him. He started. "But we are not all here—one is gone." Every eye hastily ran round the circle. Lionardo Morosini had left it.

CHAPTER LX.

Not long after Contarini had given the order for Jacopo's release, the prisoner issued from the gates of the palace, a free man. His hair was whiter, and straggled down his shoulders in scantier locks; his face was more haggard and anxious; his limbs covered with those same decayed clothes that he had worn for years, were shrunken; and he tottered like a very aged man. Yet his countenance was cheerful and almost gay as he looked around him—but then starting he covered his eyes with his hands, for they could not endure the unaccustomed glare of the sun, nor even the light from the tiles under his feet. With impatient but faltering steps, he turned into the piazza; hastening with what speed he might to the stone bench that ran along the front of Saint Mark's cathedral; and there he sat down to rest, wearied with the stone-throw's journey that he had come. For though like a caged animal, he had daily paced his cell, the short space gave little exercise to his limbs; and he who had travelled Italy and the east with firm and elastic steps, could now scarcely totter across the square of St. Mark. He sat not long; for he was impatient to reach his home; and presently rising, he went forward with better strength. He came to the door of his house. It looked not different from what it had; not more—not so dreary as when he left it; for now the sun was renewing his strength, and cast some glow upon the dingy walls. The door was shut; but on pushing it he found it was unfastened. He entered and heard the sound of voices. Crossing the hall, he went up stairs, and turned into the rooms where he had last left the beloved inmates. No one was there. He went on into Bianca's bed-chamber; the bed was there, and the bed-clothes; but all was in disorder, and dust lay upon the very sheets—the dust of months. His brain, dizzy with long confinement, became more bewildered at this strange desertion. He scarcely comprehended what to fear, or what to hope; for vague surmises chased each other away without staying long enough to be understood. He went back into the sitting room; and there he found the same scanty furniture that had served his daughter, all as dirty as the bed. He felt that they had gone long ago;—whither? The sound of distant voices again struck upon his ear. With feebler steps, for he had not found what he sought to cheer him, he again went down the stairs; and standing in the hall, he listened to hear whence the voices might come. They seemed to be those of women in brisk and careless conversation. He followed the sound, which led him into what was once the busy kitchen of his mansion; and there were three or four strange women, who started and looked afraid, as he entered. One was washing some clothes at a sort of sink, while the others stood leaning against the wall or sitting on tubs and such things as they might, chattering with the woman at work. When they saw that sudden and strange appearance of Jacopo Arduino, the master of the house, their faces reflected the whiteness of his own; some taking it for a ghost; others fearing rebuke for being detected in their intrusion. Though they knew him, to him they were unknown; for he was not used much to mark the faces of strangers. For a while he stared at them in amaze; then seeing that they were afraid, he said, "Fear nothing, my good women, for I could do you no ill if I would. I am Jacopo Arduino, to

whom this house once belonged, and does now; but it seems no longer to be mine, since I find it deserted by all that marked it for my own. Tell me, where are they all gone? where is my wife, Madonna Bianca Arduino?"

"It is Messer Jacopo," cried one of the rest, "the Signora Bianca's husband;" and again the women stared at each other and at him.

After waiting awhile, expecting their answer, he asked once more, "Where is she now—Madonna Bianca?"

At that question, the women put on a very doleful look; and several speaking at once, they cried,—"Ah, Messer Jacopo, do you not know what has happened? Do you not know where your wife is?"

"Why, that is the very thing I ask you. Tell me you," he said, speaking to the woman who was washing; and from her he learnt, in a broken and unconnected way, how his wife had died; how his daughter had gone no one knew whither; and how his house so long remained deserted, until these poor women had ventured within, that it might, they said, sometimes be cheered by the sound of Christian voices.

Jacopo turned away, and went out of the house. His poor wife, Bianca, was at rest, he thought, and he should never see her again; and the thought made him sad; but still with his restless mind he less dwelt upon the past than now most eagerly desired to find his daughter. He issued from the door, and stood a little, questioning which way he should go; and then, without having determined, he walked the way his feet happened to lead, and wandered on, through the lanes and by the canal sides, and over the bridges, to San Fantino, to San Stefano, to Canaraggio; scarcely knowing why he went, but fancying he was doing what he could to find his child. So he would have wandered on till night, but that he chanced to see his own lengthening shadow; which reminded him of the order that he should return to the palace; and to that he now bent his way; still he strayed a little here and there from his path, and thus it happened that he came down to the water-side near San Giovanni Bragorà.

Ill fortune was it that led Alessandro da Padova to that same spot that day! He came on with his strong and proud strides, but his face was darker than ever; for he had found from Lionardo Morosini, who had sought him out, enough to show that he had been betrayed, not only by name, but in all his plans. He had been to Barbarigo to warn him of their danger, though still keeping back a part. To see if he had learnt more, he had been back to the wayward Lionardo Morosini, who laughed and told him not to fear, and so angered him that he would have struck the scoffer dead, but for the trouble it would have brought. Already in his heart he had devoted two ducats to Nadale for Lionardo's service. He had been to Nicolò di Bernardo, to Luigi da Molino, and to others of the conspirators, telling them to watch and be together; and now he was on his way to the palace, that he might be near and ready to direct any resistance to the fate that threatened him. Yesterday—that very morning—the fate of Venice, and his own triumph, seemed within his grasp; now all was gone; destruction hung over him; and he only debated within himself whether he should fly, or whether he should stay to turn to his purpose the little chance that remained. With angry defiance he determined that he would brave it out; and if he fell, at least that numbers should be destroyed with him. And now he revolved in his mind how many he could drag down in his own ruin; counting up as he walked, and lashing his anger in the thought of the names of all whom he had summoned to aid him, as victims to celebrate his fall. He walked on with his face held up, but his eyes upon the ground, reckoning these fierce and deadly purposes, when Jacopo Arduino, who knew him well, laid his hand gently upon his breast, to stop him, and said in a kindly voice,—" Tell me, Messer Alessandro, if you know where I may find my daughter Teresa?"

The sudden hand laid upon his breast, the pleasant voice, and the simple question startled him more than the swords and voices of a legion could have done. He drew back. He saw before him, released from prison, one of the men whom he hated merely because their purposes were opposite. The weak and despised Jacopo Arduino, too foolish even to hate well, stood released from his troubles. In his weakness he had controlled them; and the fetters fell from his limbs as if of their own accord, for he had not vigor to have snapped a silken thread; while Alessandro himself, who could have taken the strongest man of Venice in his grasp and wrenched him to his will, whose massive head had planned such schemes that the policy of kingdoms was turned to his purpose, and who had helped to draw upon Venice foes from the farthest Mediterranean, from Hungary, from France,—whose power but now seemed the strongest in the senate, and the stronger for being secret,—this powerful man now trembled at the destruction which threatened him in the very vastness of his own projects. In the midst of his malignant tribulation came this voice, this question searching into his unknown crimes, as though simplicity itself could reach farther and know more than guile. A passion of envy raised a tumult in his soul, and fiercely pushing Jacopo aside, he cried, "Stand aside, fool! what care I for your daughter that I should know, or answer you if I did!"

Jacopo staggered back, and nearly fell; but the spirit that was in him was roused by Alessandro's unmannerly attack, and, hastily stretching forth his arm, he seized the Paduan's cloak as he passed by, and said,—"These angry passions, Messer Alessandro, belong to guilty minds; and for your rude denial of my daughter, I think you know more than you will say."

"Let me go, ribald!" cried Alessandro, growing more angry; "or I will throw your worthless body into the water."

But Jacopo still held his cloak.

Alessandro grew more angry. He seized the other's wrist, and tore his hand away. But now the light and fragile man felt the use of the good food which it had been Contarini's care to let him have, and his pale face blushed with anger and exertion the rosy red of a young girl. As Alessandro tore his hand away, the other seized the strong man's cloak, and hindered his progress. The Paduan spoke no more. He did not try to snatch away the grasp of that other hand; but with teeth clenched, breathing short and quick, he placed both his hands under his antagonist's arms, and, half lifting him from the ground, raised him to the water's edge. Jacopo saw the fate that was meant for him; and now he struggled for life. He threw himself on the ground; he twined round Alessandro's legs, and with desperate activity strove to entangle himself in the murderer's limbs, crying out ever and anon with sharp shrieks for help. His cries were heard, and people who had seen the struggle came running from a distance. Alessandro now strove to shake off the living net into which he was entrapped, anxious merely to get away; but Jacopo, who understood him not, still kept his hold; despair made Alessandro's anger fiercer. Again he seized the fallen man; and still in their struggles, they drew nearer to the water. A rough hand seized the Paduan from behind. He turned his face;—it was Turnbull, who putting his knee in the tall man's back, drew him with force to throw him down. Rising with a sudden effort, Alessandro threw off the big soldier; and at the same time Jacopo, who saw relief at hand, was less desperate in his grasp, and fell back exhausted. Alessandro hastily stepped forward. The crowd around him were now eager to see some disaster, and when he moved, they too stepped forward to chase the flying man. Turnbull knew him: he was abashed at the ease with which his potent hold had been shaken off; and, angry at being baffled, he turned to the eager crowd, and pointing to the Paduan, he said in English, "Aye, my masters, there runs a spy of Messer Francesco da Carrara's." The people understood nothing but that dreaded name: but Alessandro was not unknown; his proud and fierce manner to those who thought his station even lower than their own, while they saw him using the luxury and power of a noble, made him envied; and now that he was pointed at in his flight, suddenly he became a criminal in their eyes. They pursued him, and seized him; while Turnbull, half afraid to meddle with a man so powerful in the state, stood by shouting to see the Venetians thus handle their countryman. For a little while, with blows and rapid strides, Alessandro made his way along the bank of the canal: but presently he stopped; he struggled; the crowd swung backwards and forwards with his violent exertions; he fell; and, held by a score of hands, he was lifted flouncing and kicking to the edge of that water into which he would have thrown another. "Throw him in " was the cry; but amidst the storm of voices those who held him spoke and moved with a purpose of their own. They stopped; and instead of throwing him in, they walked some few steps farther, and carried him into a many-oared boat, which in a few minutes was thronged. It moved; the ropes were cast off, and then a knot of men who had been busy towards the stern, were seen to hold their still struggling victim aloft. They threw him overboard, and with a new impulse, a sheet of oars on either side dipping like wings into the water, the boat shot a head. As he fell backwards into the waves, Alessandro was lost in the splash; but presently he might be seen dashing his hands about, and writhing hither and thither. They had fastened a rope to his feet, which dragged him along in the water. An instant he lay still upon his back in the roaring wake of the boat; then suddenly bending forward, he snatched with his right hand at the rope which dragged him. One moment he held it; but exhausted, blinded, choked with water, fainting and weak, his fingers relaxed; his bent up form once more stretched out in the stream; his arms floated over his head; and, as the boat went on, it now dragged, with clenched hands and glaring eyes, a dead man.

While Jacopo still sat upon the ground, a little way up the calle leading to San Giovanni, a woman stooped over him, and, resting her hand upon his shoulder, asked him if he was ill. "Not so," he answered, rising and looking at her cheerfully. She was a tall and dignified woman, and he could scarcely tell whether to account her a lady or one of the common sort. Seeing her still look inquiring, he continued, "I am not hurt, though I have been roughly handled."

"What has been amiss with you?"

"Excellent lady, I scarcely can say what has been amiss. I was walking here but now, and I met a gentleman—I do not know him well, yet he scarce could have been offended by my freedom—I met him here, close by, and did but ask if he could tell me where I should find my daughter Teresa; whereupon he seized me, and would have thrown me into the water, but that I was rescued."

The woman looked at him more closely; then she said, "You are Messer Jacopo Arduino?"

"The same; but since you know me, perchance you can tell what I wish to know. I have not long been free, and going home, I found my house deserted. Can you say where is my daughter Teresa?"

"Would that I could, for I seek her too; but I hope in a little while that she will be restored to us."

"How, then; is she lost?"

"Messer Arduino, I can say no more now; but I will lead you to one who will tell you better, Messer Sebastiano Morosini." As they moved to go, Rosa said, "What has been this tumult which I see?"

"It is the same tumult of which my little question was the beginning. When that gentleman I spoke of tried to drown me, these compassionate people prevented him; and then falling into anger because of his struggles, they have seized him and drowned him; and I fear some mischief will come, for the Ten cannot but hear of it; so that I am scarcely out of prison before I fall into new troubles, and I know not where to go for peace."

"And who is it then that you asked this question of?" inquired Rosa, looking more startled at Jacopo's fatal news than he himself seemed in telling it.

"It is one Messer Alessandro da Padova."

With a sharp stifled sound, like a shriek drawn inwards, Rosa let fall Jacopo's hand; and dashing through the crowd rushed to the water's edge. There in the distance she saw the boat still moving forward; but now more slowly. She looked around her. All the faces were strange, save one; for as she looked, a man newly joined the crowd outside, and peered over to see what was the matter. She did not know him by name, but remembered somewhere to have seen that dead and distorted face. It was her follower Nardo. Others had now grown cooler, and were watching the boat; at times talking to each other, and laughing as they recalled the struggles of the drowning man; so that a constant buzz was kept up. Rosa stood quite silent. She made no appeal for help, for she had no hope either from their will or from their power of rescuing the miserable man; but she strained her eyes to see whither the boat would go. Not long after, it turned round, and came back again towards the shore; but more slowly than before, for the rowers were tired. A hand took hold of her arm, and she saw Jacopo, who would have led her away; but in a low voice she desired him to leave her. Puzzled what to do, for her passion and peremptory manner were beyond his contrivance to overcome, and yet not wishing to leave her, he stood silent by her side.

Presently there was a regular tramp of feet, and a loud voice spoke some words, as if by one in authority, to make way through the crowd. Nothing drew Rosa's gaze from that distant object upon which it was fixed; but all other eyes were turned upon the spot, and there was seen an officer with some few soldiers, and by the side of the officer came Ranieri and William Cooke. Jacopo stared upon them, for even since he had been in prison the youth had grown so tall and so broad, was so bronzed with braving the weather, and had so much fuller a fringe upon his lip, that the father scarcely ventured to claim his child aloud; and so he stood waiting to see what would happen. The officer spoke to some of the people nearest to him, and then to Ranieri; who pointed to the boat, which had now come nearer, and spoke in his turn. They waited until the boat had drawn still closer, and then four of the soldiers, getting into another small boat, rowed towards it. The larger boat stopped, as if those within were in doubt. The soldiers held up a flag to show what they were, and then the others, not daring to move, either to come nearer or to fly, remained quite quiet, but some unloosed the rope by which the dead body was towed at the stern, and it sank. When the small boat came up, the soldiers did not go on board; but, rowing past, they stopped near to the place where they had last seen the body. There was scarcely a sound or a motion either on shore or on the water. Every look was turned upon the little boat, and the soldiers in it kept their eyes fixed upon the water's face. So they stood for many minutes; and then, not far off, they descried a little darkness on the water; for the body had risen again to the surface. They made towards it, and seizing it, they took the rope that was still fastened to its feet, and slowly dragged it to the shore. As it was lifted out on to the land, the body, with the eyes still open, was so rigid with the dying struggles, that the arms could scarce be forced down to its sides.

No sooner was it laid upon the ground, than Rosa, pushing her way to it, knelt down beside it. The soldiers would have moved her away, but Ranieri prevented them, and they waited to see what she would do. She did not kiss the lips, nor embrace it, nor weep; Alessandro's cruelty and base intents had expunged her love, and now that end so fitting to his crimes had made the hideousness of his nature revolting even to the sight; but laying her hand upon the breast, she clutched the wet clothes, and turning to the soldiers, asked,—"Where do you carry this?"

"To the doge," replied one.

Ranieri stooped over the kneeling woman and putting his arm round her waist, he said in her ear,—"This is no sight for you, Rosa mia, nor does any real duty keep you here. Let me take you home; or rather, for I may not leave the service I am on, let me send you home by this my friend, a most excellent English gentleman."

Rosa looked at him, and following the motion of his hand, looked also at Cooke, who stood lost in admiration at her strange bearing and her majestic aspect. "No, Ranieri," she replied; "I will follow this,—I will follow this, for none other will—until I see where they bury it."

Ranieri stood irresolute for a moment, and then speaking to the officer, he said, "It were as well to let her have her will; for perchance it will not grieve her more. Those who have sent us may find a use in her presence. Let her come; but let us treat her gently; for well I know that this man's death, for which none in Venice should grieve, will be a bitter stroke to her." They raised the body from the ground, and were about to bear it away, when their passage was barred by the people that stood around them. The officers of the doge stopped in surprise, and they were now aware of a different manner in the people, as though bent on farther mischief.

"What is this?" cried the officer. "Stand out of the way, men."

"There is another spy with you," cried a man with a hot and angry face. "Another spy besides the drowned one, and one more besides that other!"

"Which are they?" said the officer; "we know of none but this dead man."

Nadale, whose crooked face Rosa had seen among the people, whispered to the spokesman; who said,—"There he stands by your side; that tall lad, I do not know his name." He pointed to Ranieri.

"Know you what he means?" said the officer to the youth.

"I know nothing," answered Ranieri, "save that where there are traitors, there are likely to be more such; and by his words I should suspect that flustered fellow to be one."

The officer asked the man, if he knew not Ranieri's name, how he knew him to be a traitor?

"Why, they say so," answered the man.

"Who says so? Show me who has spoken to you of him."

The man glanced around to find his teacher, and then he pointed to Nadale, who had moved a little farther off; but before he spoke, Ranieri's eye, too, had found out the ruffian's face, easily known among thousands; and with impatient tones, he cried,—"Sieze that man; we may want him more than any in Venice." Nadale cast at him a look of hate and fear; and then twisting quickly round, he made a plunge to force his way through the crowd. It was wedged too closely together, and even the struggle to yield way to him only entangled it still more. There was a hot and tearing scramble

—he was siezed by many strong hands, and he stood a sullen captive in the grasp of the soldiers. "You need not hold me so tight!" he cried. They unloosed their hold as they closed around him, and brought him forward. He drew nigh, his eye fixed intently on Ranieri; to whom he muttered,—"You think, boy, to have your revenge; but—" One more desperate rush he made, this time at the youth; and a knife flashed in his hand as he flung it back for a blow—his wrist was seized—he turned, and met his new foe face to face;—it was Jacopo, who had followed the ruffian's murderous eye: they closed—the weakened ruffian, strong with the madness of rage,—the feeble prisoner with the parent instinct: now they bent this way, now that, too fast for those who hovered round to seize and part them: once Jacopo wrenched his man with elbow down nearly to the ground —then the father's spine nearly broke as he was strained back:—they hugged—they parted —the knife clanked upon the tiles and dabbled them with Jacopo's smoking blood—he fell back, wildly catching Ranieri in his arms, to shield with his body him whom he could not any longer defend; his arms relaxed—and the doubting son knew his father as he slid senseless to the ground. Nadale stood still, watching the ruin he had made—he stared—he staggered dizzily —his eyes closed, and a choking sound rose in his throat;—bending forward, he spat upon the ground: it was blood! Of old, Sebastian's arm had smitten him with a mortal sickness. He sat down upon the ground beside the wounded father, and sought no farther escape. His captors stood by without word or motion, stricken with awe at the sight of the death written in his face; awaiting to see whether he would live or die before them. Stricken were they with awe, but scarce with pity, save to think how unpitied was the wretch in his agony. The struggle passed; he laughed, a sneering chuckle, and cried sharply,—"Aye, take me where you will; and if you take me to Monsignor lo Doge, I will tell him such fine things as will make your hair stand on end, and flutter stout hearts in many a palace. Many a good story has passed between me and this drowned gentleman here."

"How is it with this wounded man?" asked Cooke.

"He lives," said Ranieri. "It is my father, Guglielmo; how strangely met! You shall bear him to the palace of good Messer Zeno, and I will make account of him where he should have been anon, with Messer Francesco before the senate. Raise up that dying caitiff; for he must go where he cannot walk."

And the strange party moved away, the crowd in bewildered amaze, offering no farther hindrance.

◆

CHAPTER LXI.

In the ante-room to the senate hall the party to whom Ranieri had served as guide, and almost as leader, were stopped by the attendants; and while the rest were detained until orders should be received for their admittance, he was allowed to pass at once. A single

R

voice : ck on the youth's ear as he entered and drew his eyes to the erect and comely figure of young Francesco da Carrara, who addressed the assembled senate with the easy rapidity of one far on in his speech. His voice it was alone that rang in the vaulted hall, although there was that indescribable whispered sound which is felt rather than heard where great numbers are collected in silence; so that Ranieri knew before he turned his eyes around, that the place was crowded. The whole senate of Venice seemed to be there; for not a seat was empty; and rapidly glancing at the amphitheatre of faces, in the midst of which sat the venerable Contarini, he saw the endless variety of passions depicted in each countenance. Near to Contarini sat Rafaino de' Caresini, the grand chancellor; as composed but as intent as the prince himself. Not far off, among the members of the signory, was Marco Morosini, erect and pale, his red eyes winking rapidly, as though they smarted under the light; but his limbs firmly fixed, prepared to brave whatever might ensue. Beyond him was Barbarigo, pale and anxious, and many a year older in his aspect. On the other side of Contarini was Leonardo, contented, almost gay. Among the senators was Malipiero, who watched the orator like a wolf with a growing fire in his eye. At the farthest end of the benches which extended to the left of the door round the three sides of the eastern end of the chamber, sat Carlo Zeno in his place, but not in the midst of his fellow senators; and nigh to him stood Sebastian, Edward the Englishman, and Luigi. As noiselessly as he could, Ranieri moved slowly round by the western side of the chamber, passing from group to group of the attendants, to avoid any interruption of what was going forward; and he learnt from the first words that struck his ear, that Francesco da Carrara had already delivered good part of his message.

"That," said the speaker, "was after the lord, my father, had left Chiozza; and he did not learn it until he had returned to Padua, on which he sent me here. Such, my lords, was so much of my message as I was free to tell the signory before craving audience of yourselves."

"Your pardon, Messer Francesco," said the doge; "you told the signory the name of the person who had thus betrayed both Venice and your father; faithless even in his treachery."

"I did; and I shall tell it to the senate; for, most excellent prince, I have much farther to tell yet. My lords, I have already told how that unfortunate gentleman, Messer Jacopo Arduino, as a kind friend, (for such, though unhappy and poor, he is,) had carried from my father this gold to Messer Carlo Zeno. In all that my father has done, that gentleman (I mean Messer Jacopo) took no farther part: he was only used as a trustworthy person to carry the gold secretly and safely. And now, my lords, I will tell you why that so much suspected gold was sent. While Messer Francesco da Carrara was yet young, he was, as you know, discarded by his family, for I know not what differences that are apt to arise between the young and the old —I see Messer Pietro di Bernardo smiles; but I can tell him that between the young and the old Carrara there have been none of those differences; for Mes-

ser Francesco is too wise to forget what he himself was.—I say that when Francesco was young, he was discarded by his family for a time, and therefore was in some trouble and difficulty; for if he had ready hospitality throughout Italy, since his presence and his prowess bestowed honor on every court, yet were there times when alone the help of a father could have availed him. Now, being in that trouble, he found himself at Asti; where for some occasion of private need,—(I know not what, and it does not matter;) he wanted the sum of 2,000 ducats. Of all his friends whom he could think of as likely to pleasure him freely, without asking reasons or justifications, Messer Carlo Zeno seemed to him the best; and to Messer Carlo Zeno he sent, saying only that he was in trouble for want of 2,000 ducats of gold. Before he thought he could have an answer there came to him two gentlemen, who had travelled all the way from Turin on horseback, almost without drawing bridle, (Messer Zeno was then staying at Turin,) to bring him this gold. In after time, when both had grown older, Messer Francesco da Carrara would have paid back this money; but while Messer Zeno ever told him that he needed it not, so Messer da Carrara, for all he was so powerful, as Venice can tell, never had such abundance of gold that he could easily repay it; since one part of his power has grown out of that generosity which makes him think too lightly of these matters. But now, when this great quarrel between Venice and Carrara had come to such pass, that truly it seemed one must destroy the other, it weighed upon my father's mind that he should hold money belonging to Messer Zeno. And he was eager to pay it, for two reasons; first, because he would not have one of so high station in Venice be a creditor of his while he was working the overthrow of the republic; secondly,—and this was the strongest reason,—because he knew that Messer Zeno, with so great love for his country, would not stop in spending his whole substance for his benefit; and therefore to keep back the money was not only to take an advantage of Venice in her need, such only as might beseem some base usurer, and not a high and mighty prince, but also it was to do great harm in his private welfare to Messer Zeno; and therefore, I say, Messer Francesco da Carrara cast about to find one by whom he could send this gold to Messer Zeno; and I have told you how he sent it. That, my lords, is the great issue of all this conspiracy between Messer Carrara and Messer Zeno, of which you have heard so much. And now that you may believe what I say is true, I will appeal not only to Messer Carlo Zeno, but to Messer Alberti his friend, who well knew this story before, though also he knew that Zeno's generous mind would take offence if it were first told abroad by any but Francesco da Carrara himself. And farther I might bring to you from afar the evidence of Messer Girolamo Fazio, who was then staying at Turin, and who I know, for all the war that there has been between Venice and Genoa, would now come from his own country to be a witness in the cause of Messer Zeno. Also Messer Alberti can tell you that I could bring this witness from Genoa."

When young Carrara paused, Alberti rose up in his place, and said that it was true, and that also the reason was truly said why he had not before disclosed the case.

"I, also," said Andrea Contarini, "can in some sort say that I know this to be true : for I do remember hearing it told as a reproach against Messer da Carrara, when he was a youth (though I was then in nature years), by Messer Fazio, whom I met at Florence; and he told me that he knew it partly by accident and partly because Messer Zeno, not having so much money with him, had in turn borrowed it of that most noble Genoese. But when I heard of this passing of gold between Messer Zeno and the Lord of Padua, truly I had forgotten that early date, and thought that it was merely a fiction."

"Most noble prince," continued Francesco, "I think that I have satisfied the senate of that now so simple a matter; and here, most illustrious fathers, I have to claim what already I have claimed of the doge, and what now again I ask of him with you—protection ; for here begins the dangerous part of my embassy. My lords, so eager is the Lord of Padua to show that all enmity to your republic has past from his mind, that verily he is disposed to make known to you even the schemes with which he thought to work your overthrow ; so that truly you may see that hereafter he means to hold no reserve by which again he could compass aught against you. My lords, if there has been treachery among you, also that treachery has turned against himself; and the shameless traitors have striven not only to work for him against Venice, but to make a tool of him ; as though great princes could be the playthings of base and obscure men; and men, too, of the basest. Monsignore, I ask you to place before the senate that man of whom I spoke, and whom I now name, called Alessandro da Padova."

"I have given order for his arrest," said the doge. "Let him be brought in. You, I think it was, to whom I gave the order," said Contarini to one of the attendants.

"No, my lord, it was Pietro Vantini."

"Is the man taken ?"

"He is taken, and yet he cannot come ; for strange events have not yet ceased in this our city : they have brought, not the man but his dead body."

"His dead body! How is this ? I told them to be careful that he was not hurt."

"They found him not alive but dead ; and dead they have brought him higher."

"Send Vantini before us; and let him bring the body, that we may know the truth."

The attendant disappeared. A low murmur, like a rising wind, ran through the assembly ; the senators conversing with each other in whispers while they waited ; when a man's voice told them that the servant had returned.

"Messer to Doge," said the man, "there is the body here ; but we cannot bring it in for a woman who is with it, and will not let it leave her ; and we know not whether to part her by force, or to bring her in too."

"Who is she ! These strange disorders must be abated, for there is no longer a fell and dangerous war to be their excuse. Who is she !"

"My lord, we know not."

"With your pardon." said Ranieri aloud, stepping forward, "this woman was one well known, too well known for her, to Alessandro da Padova; and he lying in the muteness of death, she, perchance, may in some part suffice to speak for him."

The words were scarcely out of his mouth, ere Marco Morosini started up as if stung with sudden passion, and cried aloud, "What strange and horrible times are these, that even before our faces the senate is thus braved ! What strange and horrible times, that in our own city, by traitors, is the man we seek basely murdered almost in our presence—that men, and women, and boys, come with brazen fronts before us, treading our sacred hall as though they trod the tiles of the streets, and chattering thus ! Who is this boy that boldly braves the majesty of the senate ! Who is this boy, I say !" The doge was about to answer ; but without heeding him, Morosini continued—" I know him—I know the boy; he is the son of that traitor Jacopo Arduino, a miserable man who wasted his substance, and then fell to treachery. He is the son of that traitor whom you, most excellent fathers, have thought it wise, and fit, and decent for yourselves to pardon, without a judgment, upon the word of that young viper that has come to us from the main land, the son of Venice's arch enemy. I know the boy—himself double traitor ; a traitor with his father, and a traitor to his father, whom he basely sold to the servants of the Ten for the gold which was paid to seize Carrara's messenger—Carrara's base accomplice in poisoning the waters of our wells." A growing sound of voices now outchid this burst; and Morosini, remembering himself, said, "Forgive me, most excellent fathers, that I speak thus passionately ; but there are among us men, as I believe, faithful men, charged with heinous crimes ; and I see, on the word of the fiendish serpent that has come among us, and on the babbling credulity of easy and presumptuous age, the worst of criminals set at large to begin their practices anew. You are rewarding the traitors, and destroying the watchmen of our city : beware —beware what you do."

"This, my lord," said Francesco, "is something which I do not understand. I know not what it means ; though I know and will tell you how Messer Morosini himself may be concerned in these dangerous treacheries."

"Infamous ribald !" shrieked Morosini ; but those near him rose too, and forced him to sit down ; while with loud commands the doge restored order.

"Noble senators," said Contarini, "before we speak farther of the matter in hand, I will in brief tell you the story of this youth who has spoken so boldly, and whom you see stand here unmoved at this storm which he has raised. Look at his face, and tell me if I am wrong in believing that a countenance so frank and steadfast, cannot be the face of any such double traitor as we have heard him called ! I will not keep you long, scarcely an instant. This Messer Jacopo, as you have heard, was a most poor gentleman, and his wife was dying, even in great part with the pressure of poverty and sorrow ; the which seeing, Jacopo, being somewhat a desperate man, and hearing how we had offered reward for his seizure, resolved to get this same reward for the help of his family; and thus it was that with all the strength of a father's power, he made this youth to go before the governor of your city and claim the reward for seeming to sell his parent. That is the tale I have heard; and that I believe. Its truth we can prove at a fitting time."

"And from whom comes that little novel?" cried Morosini, without rising.

"It was told me by Messer Carlo Zeno." Morosini laughed.

"We can prove it, I say, at more fitting time; when we will judge farther of this matter. And these truly are matters which rather should be brought before the Council of the Ten than before the senate. But it has been your pleasure to receive this message from the Lord of Padua, through that noble gentleman, his son; and to hear his message, we must hear it as he would deliver it, with all the proofs it is his choice to bring; or we do him wrong, and wrong our dignity, in revoking what we have granted. These things will we farther prove for ourselves in the proper mode and time. It is now our part to help Messer Francesco in giving us his message. Say again, young man, what you would have said of this young woman that clings to the dead body and will not leave it."

In the same voice, as though there had been no interruption and he said it for the first time, Ranieri repeated, "This woman was well known to Alessandro da Padua; and, he lying in the muteness of death, she, perchance, may in some part suffice to speak for him."

"We will admit her?" said the doge, interrogatively; and none dissenting, he motioned to the servant; who left the hall, and returned with others bearing the body of Alessandro. Beside it walked Rosa, whose hand, still firmly clutched the wet cloak of the drowned man. She looked around with an unchanged face on the potent assembly, as seldom faced by women. When they placed the body on the ground, as if knowing that it would not be suddenly removed, she left her hold and stood with it before her at her feet.

Breaking the silence, the doge said, "How was it that this man was slain?"

"My lord," said one of the bearers, "he was drowned by the people after they had rescued from him Messer Jacopo Arduino; whom he would have thrown into the water. They set up a cry that he was a spy of Carrara's, and thus they slew him. He was dead when we came up with them."

"We must look farther into this. Let some of those who slew him be seized, that they may account for it. We must purge the city of these disorders; for its quiet must not thus be broken. Venice is growing as rude and riotous as many another city; even Florence herself might cast back the worst reproaches in our teeth. Look to that, Vantini. Here, Messer Francesco da Carrara, in such state as you see him, is the man whom you have demanded."

"My lord," answered Francesco, "the man can no longer speak: that might matter little, for seldom did his speech go direct to the truth. But I have a worse difficulty here than his dumbness. Who is this woman? That she is

his so faithful companion I might suspect her to be of little worth; but still I would not grieve any woman's ears with the things I have to say."

"You have heard what the youth Ranieri said of her. Would you wish her to be removed?"

"There is no need," said Rosa, who had listened unmoved. "There is no grief remaining for these ears to learn. Be not amazed, Messer Francesco da Carrara, nor think that I cling to these miserable remains solely through love. It is not on earth that any man should be quite abandoned; but if I were to leave them, would this unhappy wretch be utterly left by all. Therefore will I see them to the last, so long as they remain upon earth. Speak on."

"There is a boldness in your words," answered Francesco, "which removes my doubt. My lord doge, you have in your presence another prisoner, whom people used to call la Gobba; let her be brought, and her son; and while they are fetched I will proceed."

"Go fetch her, Vantini," said the doge; "but her son we have not. When the woman was seized, Messer Francesco, the son, who played the spy upon his mother and upon the other traitors, disclosed their practices to us. I believe first to the man that lies dead."

"Aye, my lord," said Francesco; "to no other. But cannot the son be found?"

"We need not seek him far," said Vantini, "for we have him without."

"Bring him in then," continued Francesco, "with his mother; for such is the pleasure of the doge. Most noble senators, you will remember, and you knew it long before the Lord of Padua, that he was most foully accused of sending to Venice, for that deadly purpose of which Messer Morosini spake but now,—to poison the waters of your wells. It was a calumny most foul. Say that Francesco da Carrara were so base as to seek the destruction of the innocent and the helpless, still had he in Venice most true friends; aye, truer friends than those who were ready to aid him in what in them was treachery, for they were Venetians. But he had in Venice at least one friend, or those whom that friend held most dear; and rather than triumph by such means, he would have abandoned the whole war. Think you that he would thus have invaded the palace of Carlo Zeno? Can it be said,—did ever any man say the word—that Francesco da Carrara was faithless to the friends of his person? Never. But I will show you how this calumny began. There it began," pointing to the dead body; "and here comes one who may tell you how it went farther, though I doubt me; for see how bent and palsied she is." he added pointing to la Gobba; who was led in by two men with slow and faltering steps. "Whether that tottering hag will have the memory or the power to tell, in her house was it that this conspiracy was made—a conspiracy, not to poison the wells of Venice, but to make the people of Venice believe that Francesco da Carrara was guilty of that deadly crime. She might tell you from whose lips the words first came."

All were silent; while the old woman, whose decent garb and good condition showed to what obscure abodes Contarini's humanity penetrated, stared around her in amaze; and then dropping her eyes upon the ground, she remained sunk in the passive helplessness of extreme age.

"What is her name?" said the doge.

"We do not remember, my lord," replied Vantini. "She was called la Gobba."

"Speak to her, and see if she will answer."

Vantini spoke: he asked her if she knew him, if she remembered the poisoning of the wells, and other questions; but, at times shaking her head, or groaning with an ostentatious display of her feebleness, or grinning with idle delight, as if a glimmer of sense revived her her faculties, she made no intelligible answer. The doge addressed her from the throne in vain: Francesco was alike unsuccessful. Carlo Zeno pointed to her; and Edward, drawing close, asked her if she remembered him. She grasped his hand, and looked as though she would have spoken, but it died away in a murmured laugh.

"My lord," exclaimed Vantini, "she is a babe again."

"Bring in the son," said Francesco.

Vantini went out, and returned with two more supporting Nadale; and one behind followed with a stool, which he placed for the ruffian to sit upon, for he was too weak to stand. He sat him down between the body, and his mother where she stood. As he sat he folded his arms, and cast his eyes around. For all the frown upon his face, and the haggard paleness, and the twist of his jaw, there was a lurking smile; and he slowly passed his eyes from face to face, as if from the throne of mortal sickness he braved the throned power of Venice, and so took his parting revenge of fortune.

"This, then," said Francesco, "is the woman's son. You are Nadale?" The man turned his eyes to him in answer. "Know you that aged woman?"

"Ay; a son does not forget his mother in a year; though sons may so alter that mothers will forget them. I am not what I was then, even if she had the wits to know me. But others are altered too—and more may change before we have finished, Messer Francesco da Carrara."

"You say true. Can you make her tell us who it was that first spoke of poisoning the wells in Venice, for we cannot?"

"No; no man can make her answer. Her wits have gone. Can you not see it in her eyes? And did you ever see any with her wits left that had so wet a chin? There is no farther good in her but to be buried. But I can tell you, and I will tell you all." And then he called out in a loud and hollow voice, as if he defied the senate itself—"All!"

"Say it, then—who it was; and you will remember, most noble senators," added Francesco, turning to them, "that what words I have said this man cannot know: he speaks alone on the teaching of the deeds that have been done." He waited the answer.

"He that first spoke of poisoning the wells of Venice," said Nadale, "lies there;" pointing to the body. "He made me get some fellows that I knew to confess that they had done it,

and told me to confess; and he promised that he would rescue us, and so it was; save that those others, poor wretches that were of no use but to confess——what became of them I know not: and also that old woman went to prison, and was left there, that the tale might not die away."

"And no wells," asked Francesco, "were poisoned?"

"Ay, were they. They were poisoned by terror and fright; for I tell you, that after that, no water tasted sweet for many a day. But there was no other poison thrown in; it did not need that, for the trick worked well enough without."

"And this was the man," exclaimed Francesco, earnestly, "that was so trusted; who sat even by his proxy in the senate! This was the man whom Marco Morosini—"

Marco Morosini rose up. He tried to speak; but his teeth chattered, and his lips trembled.

"I accuse not Marco Morosini," said Francesco, "as yet. It is enough that he was the servant of this drowned traitor, who held in his single hand the whole mischief of Venice. But we must have you speak farther," he added, to the man. "You must know, most noble senators, that throughout, and especially after, the war of Chiozza, the aim and purpose of this traitor was to drive Andrea Contarini from that seat, and to seat there no other than Marco Morosini. I do not wonder, Messer Morosini, that you are moved; but hear me out. For this purpose was it that Andrea Contarini was to be struck by beating down Carlo Zeno For this purpose was Venice terrified by the crimes of Francesco da Carrara, which he had never devised; because Venice was to be enraged against Carrara, that he himself might hold no power in the republic, save such as this dissembler chose to vouchsafe. And there were those who helped Alessandro Padovano in this double scheme: one is here." He turned and beckoned towards the group of attendants that stood at some distance behind him: a man dressed like a monk came forward. "This man," continued the young Lord of Padua, "Messer Morosini has known — right innocently—as a prisoner with himself; and he can tell you where that was. Throw off your pious gown, Marco." The man obeyed, and uncovered a soldier's mail. "Were Messer Pietro Emo here, he would tell you whither this stout soldier led him one night from Chiozza; but he being away, others can say."

"I do begin to think that I have dreamed all through my life," exclaimed Marco Morosini; or rather that now I wake from life into a dream of death and doubt; so strange a juggle is it that Messer Francesco unfolds, or does himself put upon us."

"I unmake, not make the juggle. This man, craving for him your protection, most noble prince, shall abide your pleasure here in Venice as a witness for the service of the Ten. But there were other aids that the Lord of Padua found—even among yourselves in this your senate: I will not hold your astonished ears in pain. These are their names——"

So many started in their seats at the sound of these words, that it almost seemed as if the whole senate were moved

"They are——"

He was interrupted. "One name," cried Lionardo, "I will give you: it was Lionardo Morosini." Disregarding the start of astonishment in all around, he said with a faint laugh, "You have a witness more than you counted for, Messer Francesco."

"One name has been told to you, most noble senators—the others are these: Ser Luigi da Molino, whom I do not see here; but before you, besides him, there are, Ser Marin Barbarigo; and now I think that pair of pale faces will tell you, before I say the names, that there are also Ser Nicolò di Bernardo, and Ser Pietro di Bernardo."

"And what of my most excellent cousin Marco!" cried Lionardo.

"This: he knew of your treachery, but did not disclose it. He might have joined it; but I will say that the treachery of Messer Marco Morosini lies drowned there." His finger pointed at the body.

"And what," cried the sharp and angry voice of Malipiero, "what of me! for ever and anon I see your eye, Francesco da Carrara, turn with a cunning leer on me." Renewed astonishment seemed to possess the senate, as traitor after traitor had been exposed in its own body; but when the chivalrous Malipiero seemed thus by his passionate defiance to confess a fear of accusation, many a one thought that the doom of all honor had come.

"Hold your peace, Messer Malipiero," answered the young Paduan; "and remember your compact. I will say to the senate, that in the war a violence was put upon Messer Malipiero, whose power and hostile councils Carrara had so often felt; but if Venice had no worse traitors than Malipiero, truly it would be more for the honor of her nobles."

"It is not enough," cried Malipiero.

"Hold your peace, sir; I will give you no farther answer now. Let us go on with what is before us; for that is enough to fill all our thoughts."

"Stand by the doors," said Contarini. "Let them be guarded, and let none pass out."

"I have now fulfilled my duty," said Francesco. "I have told you all; and in doing so I have made known how earnest is the desire of Francesco da Carrara to secure the friendship of the republic. What farther remains for you to inquire, it is for you to judge. The traitors who have betrayed both you and him I have made known to you: deal with them as you will. He has no revenge for them; but their safety must not be bought with your peril in time of peace, or with his dishonor at any time."

"No," exclaimed Morosini, in a firmer voice than he had yet spoken; standing erect, and holding forth his right arm as he turned to the doge—"No; Messer Francesco da Carrara has not told you all. He has not told you of another traitor, another even of the unhappy blood of Morosini, who erred through too much love to Venice; but I, the traitor, will follow—with, I trust, a nobler wish—the example of my cousin Lionardo. You have not been told that I not only knew of this treachery, but that I had consented—yes, start not, monsignor—that I had consented to join with Messer Francesco da Carrara the elder. But if that my crime shocks you, my countrymen, remember that throughout I believed the rule of Messer Andrea Contarini most dangerous to Venice. He provoked the enemies most powerful to destroy us; he did not gain the friendship of citizens most able to defend the republic; and in all his measures, not only did some mischance defeat them, or partly defeat them, but those who were ablest to perform were neglected; and thus it was that I—even so humble a man as I am—at every turn, was thwarted in my efforts to serve our city. Long persuaded of this bad rule, and at last believing that in his sincerity, of which you have token this day, Francesco da Carrara, the father, was a better friend to Venice than Andrea Contarini, I had, and I stand confessed before you, consented to league with him unknown to the senate: that I did so, unknown to the senate, was a fault, a most grievous fault and crime. Now, it is only left for me to crave from the senate that punishment which is my due; or license, at least, to seek that penitence which henceforward must be my chiefest glory. And let me farther say, that never should this have been, had I not too far trusted one whose commanding power is seen even in the number of instruments that we find him to have possessed in this our senate; I mean that terrible traitor whom till now I loved as a brother."

Morosini's form was still erect; the echoes of his loud, clear voice, still rang throughout the hall, when a movement near the dead body, to which he pointed, drew every eye from him. It was Rosa, who, taking a step or two forward, burst forth,—"Let not the mocking penitence of a coward before disgrace deceive you, senators; let not the fallen alone suffer, and all the crime be charged upon him alone who cannot defend himself, though best of all he would have repulsed assault had he been here in life. Think not that Messer Marco Morosini is alone so exalted in his crimes. Truly under that high dignity he conceals such coward baseness, as each man here would scorn to be his fellow. Ask him where is that ill-used lady, Teresa Arduino? Ask him, who, for her sake, followed with false accusal that unhappy gentleman, her father!—who rudely violated the sacred quiet of her dying mother!—who, when she most nobly came before the great council, to render up the gold for which her father had sacrificed himself, rather than eat the bread of his misery,—who it was, that even then would have tortured her with public disgrace, to force her to his vile intent! And let him tell you where she is now. Ask him, there, as he stands!"

The senators looked at Morosini. He stared at Rosa in pale bewilderment.

"He will not answer you," she cried, with increasing energy; "then I will tell you. Seized by that distorted ruffian—seized by the order of that too faithful brother—she is now in Marco Morosini's house."

Again the senators looked at Morosini. He glanced from eye to eye, as if he sought escape—he gasped—he burst into tears. Again drawing himself up erect, and mastering his passion by a violent effort, he said—"I confess it—I do confess this also. It is fit, most excellent fathers, that my disgrace should come all at once; so that my penitence may be quit and clean from the beginning, and that I may at once renounce these hateful sins."

A harsh chuckle answered him; and Nadale exclaimed, "In sooth, there are more cunning ones, Messer Marco Morosini, than we thought for. I know not where this girl has learnt to see through our schemes. And yet," he said, laughing again, "there are things which she sees not. Now, look you, noble sirs; see how she stands by to guard this man's body. After we had got it on shore, you might have seen her walk by its side, holding it every step by the cloak; so faithful was she. Now, you see, she thought that this man had loved her; for how could she tell otherwise? It is not wet or dry clothes that can teach you whether a man loves you or not. So she walked even into this hall; for I saw her brought in, still clutching this man's body. You have been sitting, noble senators, side by side with traitors, and you could not tell that the honest men had turned traitors, like Messer Marco Morosini there; you saw no difference in him before and after——'

"Silence this ribaldry!" exclaimed the doge. "Remove him if he speak."

"Nay, hear me out, and I will tell it you in brief. This damsel, or woman, or lady—for I know not what to call her—as you saw, noble senators, still clutched this man, believing him her lover. I ask you how she could tell what he would have done to her had he been alive? how could she tell that he had paid me these two ducats, good gold," taking them out, and tossing them in his hands, "to make her as dead as he now lies? I took the ducats in pity to the girl, meaning to tell her; and now we are both the safer that he lies thus."

Rosa, who had turned deadly pale, looked hard upon the ruffian, and asked, "When was this?"

"Aye, now she is altered too; but you see we do not know these things till we find them out. It was last night; you had but just left him."

"It is false. You have no proof."

"Nay, I will tell you why he said it. He said that you were in his way, and that you were coming again in two days, but he wished you to come no more; and then he gave me the ducats. We all know what that means. Aye, you look as if you believe now; and I will tell you why you were in his way; for that, too, I can guess, though he did not tell me: he was going, and that noble penitent there can bear me witness, to marry the Lady Angiolina; and I think if he had married her, you would have been troublesome. Look at Messer Morosini, he does not gainsay it; and Nadale finished with another chuckle.

Rosa searched into his eyes to see if there was any show of falsehood lurking there—she looked at the dead body of the overbearing and lawless Alessandro—a shudder passed over her as if she were cold—she folded her arms across her breast, and turning from the two, the living and the dead ruffian, she walked away from them; her steps tottered, and she would have fallen, but running towards her, Sebastian and Ranieri caught her in their arms, and drew her aside under an open window.

"Remove the body," said the doge, in a gentle voice, "that it may not meet her eyes again."

A new voice arrested every ear, as Carlo Zeno, rising in his seat, said, with a grave but not angry face, "I could wish, most excellent fathers, that all here had as much reason to be contented with what has passed as I have; but it may not always be so; and yesterday others' triumph was my peril. Let us not imitate the wrong-doing we have suffered from. Our noble visitor has truly said, that Messer Marco Morosini's fault lies dead and drowned there. You see from the plainest tokens that he is truly penitent. There is no charge against him. Let him go forth, and repair the wrong he did in grievous mistake. For others that have been more strongly accused, they must have justice done to them; and let us hope that the justice may also prove mercy. For that unhappy lady, let her stand excused, since on every side most grievous wrong has been done to her. She shall be cared for; and the lady who is now known to be in Messer Morosini's house, will also be well bestowed; for of that house are her best friends. And I have to crave that, for the present, this sick man, who has scarcely yet been accused before us, may be left to my care; for him I will use to bring farther proof of the dangers which have come to Venice. He shall be safely restored when claimed by the officers of justice."

"Be it so," said the doge; "we owe you some guerdon, Messer Carlo Zeno, for the wrong that we have suffered to be put upon you; and our guerdon shall be, that you shall have the freedom you ask to serve so many unfortunates, and to give one more of the thousand services that you have rendered to Venice."

"Do with me as you will," cried Nadale, "but what will you do with this witless old woman? See how she winks and nods. She is sleepy with the sleep of death, and pines for her bed of stone."

"Great wrong has been done to her," answered the doge;—" in human ignorance, great wrong—and she shall have what amends she may, in reverend care of her foolish age, with nought to do but to breathe the free air of Venice."

"Andrea Contarini," said the ruffian, "if there were more men like you, there would in Venice be fewer men like me."

"One word more," cried Morosini, rising proudly—"If I understand aright, I am free I will ask of you, Messer Zeno, and of all of you whom it may concern, that you will do me this last favor—to come to my house this night, some two hours after sunset; for I have there a duty to perform of which you shall be the witnesses."

"We will attend you," said Zeno.

Morosini walked across the hall to leave it. His path lay near the foster brother's body. He stopped and looked where it lay; once so deftly powerful, now a helpless lump. A shuddering pang passed over the senator's breast as he gazed upon it, and thought how that vigorous life had gone for ever, never again to guide his way, even to crime. "Unhappy that he was, Vantini!" said the noble. "We all do sin, and he was not my foe, save in too great love. Will it please you to speak with me hereafter! for I would do penance for him who served me so indiscreetly ; and gold shall flow for his salvation and favor in the sight of heaven. We must all make our peace, good Vantini ; and this shall remind you of your errand." He drew forth a poniard, curiously wrought with jewels. "I shall need such no more." A loud sigh burst unwilling from his bosom, and he strode from the hall.

CHAPTER LXII.

MAP TO MOROSINI left the palace with impatient steps. His boatmen feared to interrupt his angry taciturnity, and took him homeward at a guess. He entered his palace as if life and death depended on his speed. His first words were, to order a high banquet to be prepared ; his next to summon the holy man who was wont to confess him. With him he spent long time ; and issuing forth from his chamber with a more composed aspect, he passed to that of his daughter.

Angiolina had so far forgotten her hopes, that she had also forgotten much of her griefs ; yet, remembering what Francesco had told her, she started in affright at the solemn aspect of her father, expecting the dreaded demand.

He took her by the hand more kindly than ever he did in his life ; and kissing it with a show of respect that she had never before seen, asked her if she would listen to him, for he had much to disclose ! In amaze at his newly-born humility, she signified assent by her silence ; and he went on ; "Never, daughter mine," he said, "have I had before to make so grievous a disclosure as now behoves me ; seeing that nothing can be more terrible than for a father to humble himself before his child. But first tell me, Angiolina, if ever you have found me other than indulgent to you, other than kind !"

This, she thought, was to lead to the terrible announcement. She drew away from him, looking round her in vain for help ; but no Francesco was there, no Edward, no Sebastian ; and she felt at her father's merey. Clasping her hands, she cried,—"Oh, father mine, kill me if you will, but tell me not what is in your thoughts, for it is too horrible !"

Morosini started with surprise ; for an instant he thought that his paternal penitence had pressed too heavily on his daughter's tenderness; but then, seeing her terrified face, and noting that she seemed to expect him to tell something as if she knew already what it was, he divined that there was more in her fear than he knew of. Others had left him in enmity ; some in treachery ; some in pride ; Alessandro in death ; and now the last of all who had once surrounded him was to be driven away in fear at he knew not what. Doubt and disappointment stung him with anger ; and stamping his foot, he asked Angiolina in a louder voice, what she meant.

Fright made her silent, until a sterner question forced her to speak. "The espousal !" she said,—"that terrible espousal !"

"What game is this that you play upon me ? Am I an idiot, that I wander about the world to be made its fool ! What espousal have I put upon you ; what espousal know you of but the one that I prevented ? Is it that you speak of in such terror !"

"Alas ! no ; the other,—I speak of the other."

"Of what other ? tell me, daughter," cried Morosini, looking at her in still greater doubt. He remembered Alessandro's scheme ; but Angiolina's knowledge of that treachery seemed to rise up in his path with a new shape, like the smoke and flame that rise up before the feet of him who treads the treacherous ground about a volcano.

Angiolina's fear was too great for caution ; she had resigned herself up to her fate ; and expecting death, or worse, she answered,— "You mean me to wed with Messer Alessandro da Padova."

Clenching his teeth and fist, Morosini started away and walked a few paces from her. That last wrong which he had meditated, and which he had thought shut out from all knowledge, was then known, and he stood before her not only a culprit in himself, but cruel towards her. Then he remembered Alessandro's proclaimed treachery, and how he himself had abandoned his foster brother to obloquy ; he remembered too his new penitence, and his more sacred life, now beginning ; and, lifting his eyes up to heaven, he took comfort to himself in the remembrance. He turned to the trembling girl, and speaking yet more solemnly, he said, "My daughter, I pardon you these doubts ; as indeed what should not so great a sinner pardon ! I scarcely know, and not knowing can scarce confess, what mad thoughts may have been chased across my mind. But dread no more ; for he whom you fear can affright you no longer ; Alessandro da Padova is dead."

"Dead !"

"Dead. He is dead : the victim of his own crimes and treachery, too late known to me. He has fallen under the violence of the outraged people of Venice. The dreadful story you will learn too soon ; and my time now is short, for I have other things to prepare. Fear no more, either, from me—I command no longer. I am a sinning and a stricken man ; humbly craving pardon from all," he added, with a bended head, but his form erect and chest expanded, " craving pardon, my daughter, even from my children. Know, my daughter, that beyond the sacred circle of this palace I have been, even as other men are, erring. I have gone astray in my ambitions, in that I have been misled by men of less generous blood ; and I have gone astray in those shapes also which it less behoves a noble lady to hear. For these things I have stood somewhat abashed, even before the senate ; and likewise before him whom now we must account the chief of our family, Sebastiano Morosini. Conscious of these my great wrongs, I have made a resolve to repair them as far as in me lies ; and if I have given Sebastian offence, I shall do so no longer. I will cancel all reproaches. But here I owe a tenderer duty, and am willing to bow to an uncontrolled will. I have grown accustomed, Angiolina, now that I am old, to great crosses. Him whom I thought my faithful friend, Alessandro Padovano, have I found a most heinous traitor. You do not start, but truly it is so; and I fear that he may have betrayed more than I thought for. I have grown used, my child, to think that those who own me for father have right to deal with me as they will, and no longer can I regard Sebastian as other than the chief of my house; but you, my sweet daughter, have ever treated me not as your enemy; and therefore is your will stronger over me. I have caused you sorrow. I did it, little wishing for your grief, but rather thinking of the honor of our house, and of your highest good. And now I have come before you, to humble myself, and to say that it is at your choice to leave your father, to add one more—perhaps the bitterest grief, but still but one more—to the many griefs that cannot be avoided; and you shall say. I do revoke what before I commanded, respecting that young Englishman; and now it shall be at your will to take him if it so please you,"—a sudden flush warmed Angiolina's cheek; the senator continued—" and to leave me to that fate I seek. How do you answer;"

Angiolina laid her head upon her father's shoulder. Like the well scourged dog, that sees the gate thrown open but dares not pass it, she looked at the liberty that was offered to her, and dared not take it. The sight of it only made her thraldom the more bitter. Her father had removed her worst fears—she owed some gratitude to him for that; Edward, Sebastian had left her; Francesco had let Morosini return before him; she had no help in her weakness, and could not but yield. Had she used more courage when Edward was present, at the first contest with her father, perhaps she might now not have seen that liberty in vain. But she had yielded up her spirit. And now, when her father humbled himself, and seemed to place his power in her hands, she could not, for shame, repulse him in his lowly condition. She did not love him more; and she hid her face in his breast, partly that he might not see it, and partly that she might suffer, but not meet his caresses. As she rested against him, she thought that of all others he had been her coldest enemy; yet he alone was left to her. All else she had chosen to forswear; and with a kind of bitter grudging, mixture of aversion and pity, as she thought how the world had been spoiled by him for both of them, she clung the closer to him, and wept much.

Morosini pressed her tightly to his bosom; and raising his eyes he said in a loud, firm voice—" May Holy Mary bless thee, my child! Angiolina, I expected this, and know that Marco Morosini was not to be quite deserted. Joy is not for man on this earth, my child; but we will share our griefs together."

A servant entered and told him that guests were come. " And is the banquet ready!" he asked. " It is, my lord." " Lead them, then, to the saloon. Now, I am ready for them! You, Angiolina, I will bring to the guests when the time comes; meanwhile, I must seek that lady, who, to my shame, has been brought to this house." So saying he left her.

CHAPTER LXIII.

Morosini's guests were true to the appointed time. Sebastian re-entered his father's house with a presentiment of his increasing power, and viewing its lofty walls with new feelings, now that he regarded them as containing Teresa. And Edward came, uncertain what might happen—both hopes and fears too vague to assume a distinct aspect. Luigi Morosini also came, Alberti, and many of the senate who owned an interest in the house. There might be some twenty or thirty guests. Servants with lighted tapers awaited them in the hall, and led them in silence to the saloon. There some time they waited; but Carlo Zeno did not join them; and they marvelled that Morosini did not appear to bid them welcome. At the hour after sunset they came; and the host who was so studious to receive his guests with courtesy did not show himself. The guests talked with each other; first amused with Morosini's altered habit; then they began to wonder, and then the wonder so filled them that they grew silent. Thus passed a full hour; the silence from time to time broken as some new guest came. Still no Morosini; and Sebastian began to feel a darkening doubt that the promise to surrender Teresa was a juggle, even in the midst of the senator's great penitence.

A little noise of approaching steps and voices, with lights, made them think that Morosini was coming: it was Carlo Zeno, with Ranieri. He looked round with a little mistrustful smile, like a man who thought he should be expected to make some strange disclosure, of which his own mind felt the burden. Sebastian hastened towards him, and asked the reason of his long stay.

" Do you not know that I have been before the Ten !"

" The Ten ! No. On what behalf?"

" As accused. I had scarcely left the senate, ere the officers of the council sought me; and I found my judges all prepared."

" But who had accused you !"

" Luigi da Molino, the Avogadore."

" Da Molino !—himself a prisoner !"

" Himself a prisoner; but his charge against me had been received and must be gone through. He afterwards took the place of accused; for all the proofs were so close and well prepared, with the help of what I had learned through these my friends, of the witnesses sent by the Lord of Padua, and of Lionardo Morosini, who sought atonement for his crimes in full disclosure, that their misdeeds were all brought home to them right speedily. Strange tales has Venice to learn, of stratagems to let the Genoese into our lagoon; of those who contrived their entrance into Chiozza, which cost us so much to regain; and of the accomplices of Roberto da Recanati. Aye, Messer Luigi, you are amazed; but if men were as innocent as you, more of them would thrive as lustily."

" But you have not said—what crime remained for them to charge against you !"

" That I had conspired with Francesco da Carrara, and taken a bribe from him to prevent the reconquest of Chiozza."

" And how long did they hold you with such fooleries !"

"Until," said Ranieri, whose strange and unwonted countenance, angry and sneering, now drew attention—"until they had punished him "

"Punished him!" cried many voices.

"Aye, punished."

"Be still, Ranieri," said Zeno, smiling; "or the Ten will claim another prisoner."

"Tell it us, Ranieri," cried Sebastian, little heeding Zeno's interruption.

"I was not there, and learned it only from Messer Zeno himself. But it was so—they punished him."

"For what—for what! Was he not acquitted then, as by the senate?"

"Acquitted and punished too. They acquitted him of treachery, but punished him for lending aid to a foreigner who has since become an enemy of the republic, and for receiving money under any pretext, even his own due, from one at war with Venice."

"And the punishment?"

"A fine of two thousand ducats. They would have imprisoned him; but—"

"Hush, hush! Ranieri," said Zeno, gravely. "Remember the Ten. But where is our noble host! Are we too late to have his welcome!"

"No," answered Sebastian;—"we still attend him, and marvel at his long delay. Your strange tidings have made us forget that in a greater wonder; and both again in marvel at the calm and contented air you wear with this reward for all you have done and given to Venice."

"It was done and given to Venice, Sebastian: if wrong has now been done me, it is not by Venice, but by some few men who have mistaken, not abandoned, their duty. There is no harm done; for, blessed be our Holy Mother, our fortune can spare the fine."

"You should grow fat, Carlo Zeno," exclaimed il Grasso, "if content make men so. But what was done with the traitors?"

"Their guerdon is harder: Marin Barbarigo and Luigi da Molino will come no more forth from prison, but waste their days in close penance; Pietro di Bernardo—I think some of the council could not forget his pleasant ways—will spend one year in prison, and then will seek his happiness abroad, never to return; and Lionardo Morosini's penitence has obtained him the like favor. Da Carrara's man, Marco, bore hard upon Lionardo, remembering that all but fatal thrust of the sword at the bridge of Chiozza."

"And was not my cousin, Marco Morosini, spoken of with his friends?" asked Luigi.

"By none. He was not accused. I think men believe that he was more tricked than tricking; and they leave him to his own punishment—the cloister—for that is on his mind. It had nearly been mine for life."

"For life!" cried Ranieri. "How so, master mine?"

"Know you not, Ranieri, that I was destined to the church, and might by now have been pope; but when I had charge of Patras, while yet a boy, I defended it from attack; and ever since that I could not let the sword out of my hands?"

"Nor the book neither," said Luigi, "since you read enough for a clerk."

"Aye, that habit stuck to me too."

"But," said Alberti, "touching the Ten, and Marco Morosini——"

"Nay, your pardon! let us talk no more of that, lest he surprise us, and feel offence. His is too hard a trouble of shame and peril to be added to; and if I mistake not, here he comes, by the sound of footsteps."

It was not Morosini; but more servants appeared, to light the guests to the banquet-hall. As they passed from the saloon through the hall, another guest joined them, and mixed with the group, so as to draw little notice. More than one marked that it was Francesco da Carrara; but, grown used to strange events, they watched him without challenge. They entered the banquet-hall.

Morosini was there, alone. Many years seemed to have gathered upon his head in that single day. Save that the fiery red of his eyes reminded them of his weeping in the senate-hall, and that there was a trembling about his mouth and nose that told of the working passions which had agitated him, there was a greater dignity in his manner, and he looked prouder than ever, if more serene. With a pleasanter courtesy than usual, he bade them welcome. He took Sebastian by the hand, and grasping it firmly, bent to him in silence, and sat him to the right of the chair at the head of the table, with Carlo Zeno on the left, and the others in posts suitable to their rank; then taking the head, the banquet proceeded. Little was eaten; and although he pledged all round, little was drunk, except by himself. "You do not," he cried, "Messer Alberti, answer me freely. You spare the wine as if it were bad, or as if we had many such meetings." But invitation could not make those eat or drink who were lost in expectancy; some merely wondering what he would do, and others waiting to hear from his lips the fate of their life.

"And now," he cried, "since you will not join me in this high revel, most noble guests, I will ask you to do honor to one who must henceforward honor you here. I will not recount what already you have heard recounted to-day—I will not recall those painful deeds which I need not tell you to my shame—how there is one whom I was bound to honor and protect, but to whom I have done some wrong. If in that son, noble Venetians, there was some pride, some warring against fatherly control, do I not confess that that pride has run in the blood; and that even higher control than that of a father has been warred against by a Morosini! You have seen my sins laid bare before you; and it does not befit one of our noble race, when thus convicted, to shrink from the confession of his wrong. Therefore have I thought it not only to confess, but, as you saw to-day, to avow it in full; and if for me all earthly glory is gone, then is it my right and my duty to seek a more sacred glory. And thus, most illustrious nobles, have I resolved, in rendering justice to my noble son, to seek a higher inheritance than any which I hold of the republic. Now, and from henceforward, I yield up to Messer Sebastiano Morosini all that portion which I hold in the wealth, and property, and power, and privileges of our house, even as it has come down to us since this great

republic has existed; and from this day, Messer Sebastiano Morosini shall take the place of Marco. For be it known to you that it is my resolve to seek in holy penance, with admission to one of our sacred orders, that forgiveness which I have not deserved, but which is obtained through the goodness of our Lord, and the intercession of our saint, Messer San Marco. Thus do I retrieve, by a holy sacrifice, the shame that I might have brought upon our house."

The guests were silent. Many had suspected his purpose when he invited them at the senate; many rejoiced more than they cared to tell him; and all looked for what further he had to say.

He went on. "In the next matter I cannot speak with so much boldness. And here I have to crave the trust of Messer Sebastiano Morosini, and of Messer Carlo Zeno, and of all who take concern in it. You were told this day that a lady had been brought to this house—Madonna Teresa Arduino. Most illustrious nobles, she is not here."

The whole company started. Sebastian drew back in his seat, and looked upon his father with surprise and a new suspicion. Ranieri and some others started up; and there was a confused murmur of questioning, which was stopped by the voice of Carlo Zeno. "Let us hear Messer Morosini; we can ask farther when he has done."

"She is not here, I swear by the blessed Virgin and the most holy Saint Mark; and if the sacrifices I have made this day are not pledges that I speak the truth, then may my salvation be for ever destroyed. If uncourteously I have detained you after I bade you to this house, it was, most illustrious nobles, that I felt shame to meet you, and sought in vain for her who is lost. I did believe her to be here; but some strange cheat has been put upon me, and upon you, for I cannot learn that ever she has been brought hither. You doubt me; I see that Messer Sebastiano Morosini doubts me too; but here in this place I give my person in pledge as hostage for the truth of what I say. And after I shall have told you all that is known to me on that head, you shall seek the whole of this palace through, still holding me prisoner until the lady be found. And thus I surrender myself prisoner to the keeping of Messer Sebastiano Morosini." He then told them all that Alessandro had said to him when last they spoke, and how that had made him believe Nadale's accusation to be true: but how, upon searching through the house, he could nowhere find her, nor could any of the servants say that a lady had been brought there.

Without speaking, Sebastian rose from the table; others followed him, and searched the house through. They questioned the servants, but could learn nothing of the lady, and perforce they were constrained to believe that Marco's words were true.

When they had reassembled in the saloon, Morosini again pressed them to receive him as their prisoner, hostage for Teresa; but Sebastian would not have it, nor would Zeno allow it.

"The words of a man at the gate of the cloister," said Zeno, "must not be doubted; or where would our doubts stop! It was not alone the love of the sword that stayed me from the cloister, but that I could not thus answer for my own words, seeing that so sacred places must not be entered by falsehood. We will seek for the lady elsewhere. That ruffian who has beguiled us and Messer Morosini, and he is in safe keeping, shall disclose to us where she is, and wherefore he has put this cheat upon us at the last; and meanwhile better were it that we should be deceived, even in so mortal a matter, than that we should dishonor our nature by mistrusting Messer Morosini."

"You speak," said Morosini, "as behoves your noble nature; and now with your leave I have one more duty to perform, and have to crave your patience for a short time longer." He retired and kept them waiting for a little while; and then he returned with Angiolina, leading her into the midst of the saloon. Sebastian for an instant forgot his own care, and looked to see what courage his friend had for the unknown trial that awaited him. Edward was pale, but motionless. In the cold and steadfast aspect of the girl, the Englishman saw no glimpse of hope for himself; and he half foresaw what was to follow. He would have left the place; but chiding himself for that faint-heartedness, he resolved to stay even for the smallest chance.

"Be it known to you, illustrious nobles," said Morosini, "for, after so much has been laid before you, all may be known, that there is present amongst us an accomplished gentleman, who has sought, and, I will say it, obtained the love of a daughter of the house of Morosini. I did no more than any other in the world might have done, in forbidding that a daughter of our house should be led away by a stranger, of whom we knew little. By and in me, the house of Morosini has fallen; my pride must be humbleness, and no longer do I dare to say that that most excellent English gentleman, who has served the republic so well and so faithfully, even as well and as faithfully as though he had been born of us, is in any way inferior to so great a fortune; therefore have I and do I now revoke and regard as null all that I have said to forbid that gentleman from his pretensions. Messer Odoardo, for all that I have said that may have given you offence, I now most humbly crave your pardon, and shall not go content from the world without I bear it with me. Tell me, sir, that I have it."

Edward's cheek flushed, and he felt a glow of anger pass over him as the man spoke. What had Morosini done that should change his mind! He knew not; but yet there was something in the senator's abject humiliation which forbade him to spurn the beggar, even as he would have forborne to trample on a man grovelling at his feet. He said, "If you seek it so earnestly, Messer Morosini, my pardon you have."

"Sir, I thank you. And now, as I have said, it lies with the lady to make her choice, whether she shall prefer the world, its joys, and all that it and you can offer her, and leave as others have done, her father in his age and shame; or whether she will make choice to share with him his misery and penance, and retire from the world to a sacred quiet. It is for her to say." He drew back a step or two from her, as if to leave her free.

Sebastian started forward. "Do not speak," he said, "Angiolina; do not answer now." And then, turning to his father, he cried. "You carry your tyranny, sir, with you, even into your penance, and the most cruel passions into your sacred life now beginning. You have prepared her for this, and she is too gentle to withstand you. Leave her free—let some days pass over—let her breathe a fresher air ; and then she shall answer, for then she would have a will, which she no longer has now."

"Messer Sebastiano Morosini," answered his father, with a most forced calmness, "you speak somewhat before your time, as though I were already buried in the cloister. But I will not gainsay you, for already you are to me the head of this house. Sir, the lady shall speak when it shall please her; even now, or any day hereafter, she shall say that she shall leave me, or that she will follow me. I put no force upon her. Let her say the word, and I leave this hall and this palace alone, saying nought against her. I put no force upon her. Her will is as free now as the wind itself."

"It is not so ; you have cast a spell upon her. I see it in her bearing ; for who would know in this pale and trembling and silent girl, what my sister Angiolina was ! I ask of you, my lord father, to say what she was, and what she is now ; and who has done it but you, and therefore how is it that you call her free !"

"She is free in my disgrace. Whatever has been, is no longer ; and what she says now is her own will. My penance will not brook to wait for your delays. I go now ; and I go alone, or with a companion. Interrupt me no more."

"Marco, Marco !" cried Luigi il Grasso, stepping between the father and daughter, "this must not be. Your rash and cold austerity will kill our sweet Angiolina. Leave her with us, and we will cherish her as the dearest daughter of our house."

"Be it, I say, as she wills. But stand you aside, Luigi ; you have no office here, for you know not what it is to be a father."

"Edward," said Sebastian, impatiently, speaking to his friend, in English, "will you not say a word to her !"

Edward approached the still silent girl. He took her hand, and looked into her face ; but it did not answer him. Pale and silent, her eyes were fixed upon the ground. Edward would have spoken, but his heart froze within him. He dropped her hand ; and leaving her side, he answered in his own tongue—"She has not strength for it, Sebastian. I cannot put that force upon her."

A brisk step across the floor broke the mournful quiet of the room, and a new voice called aloud upon Angiolina. Her face met the sound with a look of not unwilling surprise ; but then a new fear seemed to possess her face, and it became as pale as before. It was Francesco da Carrara.

A quick murmur of subdued astonishment burst from all around. Both Angiolina's brother and father drew nearer to her ; and resuming his fiercest pride, Morosini asked, "By what right is Messer Francesco da Carrara in this my palace ! Small friendship has there been between our houses, and this day has it been destroyed forever. I would not chase away a guest, Messer Francesco—"

"Cross me not in this, Messer Morosini," answered the young Paduan. "Trust to me, or to your daughter's angel purity, that nothing shall be done to offend you. But I would not see her thus leave the world, nor let her go, without knowing that she departs at her own will and pleasure ; for in this we are all her servants."

"Messer Francesco—"

"Say no more, Messer Morosini ; I will speak with your daughter apart, though still in your presence, or you shall slay me here as I stand."

"There are others here, Messer Francesco," cried Sebastian, "to whom you must answer for this strange interruption : by what right do you enter here, or speak thus !"

"Talk not of rights at times like these, Sebastiano Morosini, when all goodness may be lost for want of boldness. Trust me, I will do you no wrong, nor yet to Messer Odoardo."

Edward remembered that night when he had first seen Francesco. He remembered what the youth then said to Angiolina, and what Angiolina to him. He remembered too how he himself had already served his foe, sparing him at the bridge of Chiozza ; and the same good faith now moved him. "Let him have his way, Sebastian," he cried ; "I will be his hostage."

"Twice my guardian !" exclaimed Francesco ; "and yet I shall strive to do you better service even than you have rendered me."

None hindering, he drew Angiolina to the farthest end of the chamber. She suffered him to lead her ; she leaned upon his arm. There was in the gay audacity with which he braved everything and everybody, something in which her too yielding nature put more trust than in all the rest. Perhaps it was too that his love, less absorbing than Edward's, stood to her as a gage of his good will and fidelity, but yet threatened no evil from its impetuosity.

"How is this, Angiolina mia," he said in an under tone ; "will you make no end to what you will sacrifice ! You are too tender to be most cruel ; for want of some little sterner stuff, you cast away your friends, one by one, until none is left you ; and now you cast away yourself."

"Not so : rather say, Francesco, that I preserve myself. Alas ! what have I seen but danger and misery ; and why should I not seek safety where our Holy Mother vouchsafes it !"

"This is no answer. The blood rises in your cheek to contradict you, Angiolina. It is no cold and aged piety that tears you from the world ; but merely the grasping will of that man who has no scruples in his heart. What end of goodness or piety can you thus gain ! Tell me this, and I will suffer you to go."

"Do you call it no end of goodness or piety, Francesco, that I should serve heaven, and fit myself better for that blessed state !"

"Still you do not answer me. And bethink you, Angiolina, that heaven will gain little even thus. By so much more pious that you become, withdrawing from the world, so much more careless of good shall I become in that world which you have left. For while you are in it, there is to me a sacred presence that keeps hope and goodness in my heart. Let me be left thus quite alone, and you know not how wicked I shall become; so that, take us two together, and the account with heaven will stand where it did. I was content, Angiolina, that you should throw away my fortunes; but this is more than I can bear—to see you throw away your own. Say only the word—the word you wish in your heart—and it shall be stopped. See how many friends you have. Count them there—all but one. Say that word, and all will defend you and keep you safe. Or shall I say it for you! Or let us fly at once, and I will carry you away from the strife, and keep you safely till you choose to return."

"No, Francesco; whatever I wish, there is a duty to be done. You forget, but I cannot, that there is one who has been left by all, save myself; and I dare not brave the mischance that might befall, if despair were driven into that proud soul. No; all that you have said only makes me believe that the danger lies in the world. I am not strong enough for it. I do not know that what I do is wiser or better than what you would have me do; but I know that it is all that I can do; and I fear that were I to study it deeper, I might go astray. You must give me up to my fate, and remember that I was not worth a better one." She pressed his hand, and would have moved back towards her father; but Francesco held her for a moment. "Farewell, then, Angiolina," he cried; "and remember, that if ever you need a servant who will do your will without asking reasons, you have Francesco da Carrara." He kissed her hand. Her own trembled in his; and laying her hands on his shoulders, she said—"Of all that I leave, Francesco, truly I believe that none have ever been so kind to me as you have. Farewell, my dear friend." Whereat she kissed him on the mouth, and moved away. There was silence in the room, all wondering at the strange conference they had seen, and at its stranger end. Her steps trembled, and she faltered as though she scarcely knew where she was going. "Angiolina," cried her father. She moved towards him—her steps quickened —she ran into his arms. Folding them round her, he pressed her to his heart, and said to his son—"There is a love the child may feel for its parent, Messer Sebastiano, which the head of the house of Morosini may not know. This is too sacred for your violence. Let us depart. For some days we will crave an abode in this our ancient palace; when once our home is found, it shall remain yours. Farewell." None hindered him as he led his daughter from the room.

CHAPTER LXIV.

From the Morosini palace Carlo Zeno hastened home with his friends, bound upon extorting from Nadale a better knowledge of Teresa's place of concealment. Edward was pale, and still trembled from the suffering within, and Sebastian would have had him retire to rest; but

he answered, he could not rest in Venice , and he would not leave the quest they were on until Teresa should be rescued. Together they sought her captor.

The ruffian had been thrown into no dungeon. his sickness being a sterner gaoler than any that could have been put over him; and with a humane policy Zeno had had him confined in a pleasant room on the ground floor of his palace, where he lay in bed, with servants to watch over him. Sebastian would have released his master from the trouble of meddling with the man, but Zeno would not let him. His authority, he said, might make the rogue more readily confess. And therefore, taking with him only Sebastian and his two companions, he entered Nadale's chamber.

The sufferer lay in a softer bed with finer sheets than he had ever pressed before. But little will mortal agony feel slight luxuries; and the manner in which his arms were cast about, one here and the other there, as he lay on his back with his face turned to one side, showed how he writhed under the burthen that oppressed him. He was dozing; but the sound of footsteps as they approached his bed awakened him. He started at his four visiters, as though they were spirits that he saw in the room.

Some time all remained silent, staring at the man; and then Carlo Zeno began:—"How is it with you? Has the physician seen you and given you ease?"

Nadale was silent still for a few moments, almost as if he had not heard; and then his cheeks suddenly reddening and his eyes flashing with heightened fever, he cried in a low husky voice,—"Why do you ask! To what use am I to be put, that I am thus cared for? I tell you that I am past using, and that if I were still a good tool, those are gone whom it was my humor to serve. Why do you come to pester a dying man?"

"I would not have you die," answered Zeno; —"your life might be useful to me, and should not be unhappy to yourself. But say that you are dying,—I would have you leave the world as easily as you may, carrying with you what recommendation you may for the Heavenly mercy. And how can that be my friend, if you depart with falsehood on your lips?"

"What is it now! What mean you! Never talk in riddles to a dying man, for none must hurry so much. Talk plain, or my answer may be cut short before you have finished your fine speeches."

"Why then I will learn wisdom from you, and be brief: Teresa Morosini is not in the palace where you said she was."

Nadale laughed.

"Miserable ribald! is it thus you mix the talk of death, and falsehood, and laughter, on your mortal pillow!"

"Go; leave me · I can only sleep. I have no strength for aught else."

"Not so; we must know where this lady is; and until we know that, no force will we leave untried."

Nadale laughed again a low chuckle; and turned round upon his bed as if to compose him to sleep. The secret of Teresa's abode was to die with him !

"Think not you can get off thus, fellow!" cried

Sebastian, " to we have you in our power ; and in truth will we make you declare where you have hid the lady."

The sick man turned his head, and seeing Sebastian, he started up more fiercely than before ; resting on one hand while he shook the other at his questioner ;—" Ha ! is that you ! I expected you here—I looked for you,—misbegotten animal ! You who struck me down, and now come begging to my bed. It is blow for blow ; and now say, wretch, who strikes hardest. This is what I lived for ; and you get nothing more from me. This is why I do not lie down on my back and die at once. Stay there—you may stay ; it gives me content to see you."

Zeno drew his younger friend back, to moderate his rising anger ; and again spoke to the man, in a calm but stern voice :—" My friend, I would have you, for your own sake, go out of the world with ease of body and of mind ; but truly will I not lose even for that what is more precious to us all. We must know where this lady is at any price ; and if you will not say freely, we must make you tell us."

" Make me ! Why look you, do you see this face ! Do you see how it is twisted ! I say to you that every mouthful of food I eat tells me how my beard is tangled with this ruin here. Ask him who made it so ; and now know, that since it was done, my work has been to bring him with the strong arm under my feet to trample on. I have him there. Now say what price you think he is worth. What will you give me for his ransom ?"

" What you ask."

" Why then," said the man, throwing himself back on his pillow, with a little laugh—" you shall not have him." Then rising again at once, he continued, " Would you have tidings of the fair lady, Messer Sebastiano !" Sebastian was silent. He could not crave—he could not refuse the offer. Composing himself on his pillow, the man went on in a slow, steady voice, watching Sebastian's face as he spoke. " I took her away—you know what for—for Messer Alessandro, I guess, to make a bargain of with his foster brother. She is tall—she was strong —and truly it cost us more to master her than it did the miserable old fisher who would have crossed us. One day she would not eat ; but then I told her"—and he laughed—" that Messer Sebastiano would never find her if she left the world in that way ; and then I found that the bread and wine that I put for her used to go. You have been busy with me this day. Yesterday I was watching to meet with our friend Alessandro. It is two days—stop !" he counted on his fingers—" it is three days ; yes, it is thrice clear days—four days ago, I placed food for her ; well, that would have gone, and it is three clear days——"

" Cease this ribaldry," cried Sebastian, moving towards the bed, " or I will squeeze the truth from your throat." Edward and Ranieri held him back.

Nadale answered with another laugh. " I am equal with you, nobles, and can throw away money as well as you. We can bid against each other and I will beat you. Go ; you are foolish. What is the rest of my life worth that I should bargain for anything that you can give ?

All that it is to me now belongs to the past, gone by ; that I have to make up that I have made up, and having done it I am ready. Go to your beds."

" This trick shall not serve you," said Zeno " Ere we go to our beds, if you speak not, I will have you moved from yours to one less easy ; and the question shall be wrung out of your limbs if it flow not from your tongue."

" Do it—do it. You shall wring from me groans and shrieks, and all I suffer shall serve to tell you how I prize what I now hold, and how I know that others suffer more. I am ready for you. Let us come. I can walk yet," and he made a move as if to rise from the bed ; but sunk back with weakness. Zeno turned away the great mind that had faced all dangers, and had feared to brave no artifice of war, was struck with dismay in the encounter of infamous despair and mortal sickness. Death and depravity ruled in that dying bed. Sebastian's blood boiled in his veins, but he kept the end of his tongue between his teeth, lest he should displease his leader ; and thus they looked silently on the sick man, while he closed his eyes as if he were forgetting them.

Ranieri laid his hand on Zeno's arm, and putting a finger upon his lip, to signify that they should suffer the man to sleep, he drew them away from the bed. " We shall not," he said, whispering, " force it out of him thus. He is the master of us on this field, and he knows it. But trust me and I will yet humor him. Leave it to me. Let you and Sebastian here, who keep his flame alive, withdraw. I and Edoardo will stay with him ; and soon shall we learn how we shall compass his defeat."

Zeno looked at Sebastian. " Ranieri is better than us all," he said ; " and in faith, Sebastian, I can tell you that he did more to take Chiozza than all the rest. Let us leave the youth this fortress also to conquer, as he will have it so. Put your trust in San Marco and Messer Ranieri, and your fortune shall be more blessed than if I took the adventure, for all I am so great a man in Venice. Let us take his counsel."

In silence Sebastian obeyed ; and as they withdrew from the chamber, Zeno said, " I will not sleep, Sebastian, to-night ; but I will watch apart, ready if you shall summon me for your peril. The thought of that dear lady whom I have learnt to love on your report will keep me awake, and I may yet help you more humbly than our good master, Messer Ranieri. You may better watch near this door, but meddle not with the youth, for truly I think he is more cunning than any three of us could match."

When their friends had gone, Edward, half divining Ranieri's scheme, sat himself down in the shade, which Ranieri made still darker by putting out two of the lamps that were burning. Then he sent the men who had watched before away ; seating himself near the head of the bed. Long time it seemed to those that watched ; while the sick man often turned sharply round, as though suddenly stung with what he lay upon. He groaned and muttered in his sleep, and then threw his arms apart, and sighed as though he were weary of the night. He raised himself up in the bed, and looked around, fixing his eyes on a jug that stood near him. Ranieri knew his wish, and starting up with noiseless alacrity, brought the water to the bed. Nadale looked into the jug, and then at Ranieri, with a malignant and suspicious glance. "None but a fool," he muttered, "would poison a dead man. It would be wasting the drug." He took a draught, and lying down again closed his eyes. Not long after he rose again; and again Ranieri tended him. "The water has got warm," said Nadale; "maybe, with standing near this fire that is in me."

"You shall have some colder," answered the youth; and leaving the room he brought fresh water. The man drank again. "Aye, that is cold now. When you are hot you learn to think this coldness sweeter than the best wine; and this is no summer heat." He lay down: the draught seemed to have composed him, for he moved about less. Some real sleep seized him. Edward approached the bed to see how matters went on, and to learn Ranieri's intent: but the youth still motioned him to be silent, and to draw back. Resting his elbow upon the bed, Ranieri whispered in a soft voice, just above the man's ear, "Nadale, would you escape?" Nadale opened his eyes, and fixed them on the other. Then, with his little laugh, he whispered and distinct "No," and closed his eyes again. Ranieri held up his hand lest Edward should move, and then he said again, "Nadale, would you escape?" The sick man started up. "No," he cried, angrily; "get you gone. What is it you pester me for? Do you think that I am losing my wits, to be fooled by a boy, when Carlo Zeno, and Sebastiano Morosini, so strong as he is, have been driven with defeat from my bed? Hold your tongue, boy, and give me the water." Ranieri reached him what he wanted, as tenderly as a son serving a father; and the dying man again composed himself to sleep. "Nadale," repeated Ranieri, "would you escape?" He did not move. He lay still as if he chose not to hear. "Nadale, would you escape?" was uttered again, and yet again. The man really slept; he dreamed, and talked in his dream, and counted the ducats that Alessandro had paid him. "Two for killing Rosa, and two for taking the news to Alessandro. No more of that business," cried he, laughing; "Messer Alessandro has gone before me." He rose up in his bed; his face was now redder; his eyes wandered, dancing so fast from side to side, that a fantastic mirth seemed to light up his haggard and distorted features. Ranieri again held up his hand, and Edward drew closer into the shade. With a pleasant face, Ranieri busied himself to collect the man's clothes. He handed him his hose, and then his doublet: the sick man ever and anon talking and chuckling; then throwing the things aside and sitting still; while Ranieri stood by and folded his arms. At length the work of dressing, never so strangely carried on, was fairly finished. Nadale stood upon his legs, and balanced himself. They held him up bravely, and turning to his attendant, he laughed merrily at the jest. Ranieri laughed too, and placed his finger on his lip, to make Nadale understand that he should be quiet, lest they should hear him. "Aye, aye," answered the delirious ruffian; "you can trick me, and I can trick them; so that the trick can go round. Well, every man has his day. Messer Sebastiano Morosini had his; I have had mine; and now your turn is come, as young as you are. Do you remember when we fought for a knife, and how that maiden hugged you? Well, I have her fast. And what if you are tricking me out of her. Messer Giovinotto?" He walked feebly towards the door.

Ranieri's heart beat so that it might be heard in the stillness, as he supported the staggering man.

Nadale stopped: he stood firm and strong upon his legs; he looked his companion full in the face; then, suddenly and spitefully, he bit his thumb at him, and breaking out into a loud laugh, scrambled back to his bed, and threw himself upon it.

Again Ranieri motioned to Edward to keep quiet; and drawing close to him, he sent him from the room to bid Sebastian that he should not hinder them if he came forth; "for," he said, "I have not lost yet."

Alone once more he tended upon Nadale, with such quickness and such silence that the wayward sufferer's wishes seemed to fulfil themselves. Never had his pillow been so smoothed, —never did the burning sheet he so light upon him,—never did his hands dispose themselves so easily; and over and anon Ranieri whispered, as sleep fell upon the crazy brain,—"Would you escape?"

Once more Nadale arose. He was more silent now, and he leaned often on his new friend's shoulder, as he adjusted his clothes. "See you here," said Ranieri with a whisper, drawing forth his purse, well filled by Zeno's generous bounty, "this is what my master has left me; for we will not escape empty handed." Nadale took the purse and weighed it with an absent air in his hand. "Is it gold?" he asked. "Of the best," answered Ranieri. "Two ducats," muttered Nadale, "for killing a woman, and two ducats for telling her lover of it. That is not much. Why you, stripling, make a better trade; and yet you have no more wit truly than to pay a man for escaping?" Starting, he added with a fierce cunning,—"And for what else?" He threw the purse upon the ground. Ranieri picked it up and put it back into his hand. The man took it mechanically; and when Ranieri moved to take it back from him again, he clutched it with a perverse anger. "Put it in your pocket, good man, or you may chance to lose it; for your hands totter. No! I will have half; for it shall not be all yours." "Half!—half!—be it so. We can talk about that outside; for you are master here, you know;" and he moved towards the door again. He walked steadier now, and Ranieri sought to give him no more help than he needed. He laid his hand upon the lock, but could not turn it well. "Hush! hush!" cried the youth; "what a noise you make. Leave it to me, who am at home here." The door stood open, and the fresh air pouring into the room seemed to revive the feeble prisoner. "Aye, that is cooler," he cried; "but I must have another drink of water before we go." It was in his hands almost as soon as asked for. Ranieri set down the jug silently by the door, and they went forth. They crossed the wall. Edward had already set the outer door open, and they issued forth into the cold night. They walked on. Presently Nadale stopped, and said fiercely to his companion,—" Well, now I have escaped; will that suffice you? I am not to be watched home. Do you think, stripling, that I have lost my wits? Stand you back here."

" Farewell then," answered Ranieri ; "but how shall I get half of the gold?"

" Why you shall fetch it to-morrow."

" But how, if I know not where you live?" Nadale laughed, and ringing Ranieri's hand, cried,—" Farewell ;" and he tottered onwards.

Ranieri watched him as he went ; letting him gain as far an advance as he could keep him in sight ; and then he walked forward too. He had not gone a great way before his two friends joined him, creeping close to the houses. But the wandering dreamer cast little regard backwards ; and as he went his pace grew faster ; so they were fain to draw nearer lest they should lose sight of him. And so he staggered on ; now, jostling against the walls of some narrow calle, now balancing upon the edge of a canal. The luck that waits on drunkards and madmen seemed to keep his footing safe, and still he staggered onward.

" His pace holds out well," said Edward.

" To my seeming," answered Ranieri, " it grows fainter. He could scarcely stand when he was dressing, and I fear that with that heated running, he will scarcely last out. Look how he stumbles!" And as he spoke the man did stumble, but recovered himself. He stumbled again and again, and then he vanished, flat upon the ground. With quickened pace the friends drew near him. He was motionless. Ranieri turned him upon his back, and placed his hand upon his heart. One moment he held it there, and there was a faint beat.—" There is some life left," he whispered, " if we could but rouse it. Sebastian, run back, and fetch me some wine."

" Wine!" exclaimed Edward, " it will kill the man."

" Aye, it will kill him, but the fuel will make the flame flare up first ; and we want but a little more of his life to serve our turn."

Without farther question Sebastian flew to do his bidding.

" Kneel you here behind him," said Ranieri, " and let him rest against you, while I stand to speak to him if he rouse." But the wretch's head dropped back as if in death upon Edward's shoulder, and he spoke not a word while he waited. " This is frightful," whispered Ranieri, " for if he die who shall say where this hidden murderer was wont to lurk ; and yet in his den is there all that Venice holds most precious to some of us." Edward did not answer ; he felt the weight heavier, and truly feared that the man was dying.

There was a sound of footsteps in the dark, quick and quicker, and Sebastian came to them.

" Have you brought a cup too?" asked Ranieri.

" It is here," answered Sebastian.

" Well thought of ; fill it full."

He held it to the sick man's lips, and instinct still prevailing, the lips sucked up the draught. So deftly did the youth tilt the cup that not a drop was spilled. The glassy eyes unclosed, the faint gleams of a clouded moon flashing coldly upon them.

" Why how it this?" said Ranieri, presently ; " you need something stronger than water now." Again the full cup was held to the fevered lips.

" That is hot and cold too," said Nadale.

" But it makes you stronger! Can you stand now?" and he helped the man to rise, motioning his two friends to draw back unseen.

" I might have slept there," said Nadale, laughing, " if you had let me be."

" And yet you would not let me follow you? Will you drink some more of this strength, and you shall pay it me back when we get home?"

The man drank again ; and Ranieri could tell, from the fierce tottering of his hands, how the fever had grown upon him. After he had gulped down the draught, he panted and coughed for breath. The flame had indeed begun to flare ; but his legs, if wilder in their movement, were stronger now, and again he staggered onward.

He stopped.—" It was not our bargain, giovinotto mio, that you should go home with me. You know each man has his home, and yours lies behind there."

" And so it does ; but can you stand alone?"

" Aye, bravely."

" Farewell, then ; and if you fall I will be by to help you."

" Why, then you must follow me," said Nadale, with a bewildered laugh.

" Why, then I will follow you if you need it ; but now I shall leave you." And he drew back, suffering his companion to stagger onward alone. And so he went, down this street and that lane, till they found they were reaching a poorer quarter of the city. Once or twice the pursuers feared that footsteps would cross the drunken man's path ; but they turned aside ; and still he went forward, like one that made no doubt of his way. Onward, onward, more and more closely followed, as he grew more regardless and headlong in his course, until his pace abated. He had drawn nigh to his lodging, and now took the more leisurely step of a man who feels he has arrived at home. He stopped, and placing his hand upon a door he looked back, to see whether he was still unwatched, as he hoped. It was too late ; the wretch's game of hiding was up ; and running forward, closely followed by his friends, Ranieri helped the tottering hand of the dying man to open the door. Nadale turned fiercely to them as they pressed upon him,—" Keep back!" he cried, seizing Edward with desperate violence. Short was the struggle. Clutching the miserable wretch by both arms, Edward forced them together, and shaking the spent ruffian, he threw him upon his back into the open house. A short hoarse cry burst from Nadale as he fell,—there was a stifled sound of choking in the dark, and his limbs struggled—it ceased. The silence was as intense as the blackness of the night within the house.

" We have no light," whispered Ranieri, " and how shall we find her in this darkness? The place seems deserted."

" Hush!" cried Edward.

" What is it!"

" I thought I heard a voice."

Sebastian had already moved towards it in the dark ; he stopped and listened.

It cried, " Sebastiano!"

They heard him dash against a door—his

hands wandered madly about it—it opened—it closed—they knew that he had gone.

By the dim light that came from the window Sebastian saw in that other room, in a corner, a bed; and on it, leaning forward on one hand, while the other was raised in the act of listening, reclined a woman. Rushing towards it, Sebastian threw himself upon his knee to be on a level with the bed, and clasped her in his arms.

"I lived for this," cried Teresa, as she sank, fainting, upon his shoulder.

To procure a boat,—to carry her to the palace, where Zeno himself received them in the hall,—to consign her to the care of Madonna Zeno,—all was the work of but little time. Her swoon changed to a deep sleep; from which awaking, she called for Sebastian, and from his hand she took her first food.

That night Edward left Venice.

CONCLUSION.

Some years had passed—Andrea Contarini had sunk to rest, and reposed in the church of San Stefano; and Antonio Venier was doge,—when, on a bright and sunny day, our friend William Cooke entered the palace of the Morosini. His gay attire—the English soldier had chosen scarlet for the loose silken doublet which reached to his hips, and the blue cloak which floated behind him as he pressed forward, was slashed in every part to show its white lining, and crusted with silver; the blue cap on his head setting forth the crisp yellow curls that just showed beneath it—attire so gay denoted that he had been engaged about some holiday work. He hastily passed the hall, and through two or three rooms, until he found two ladies.

Both were tall; but the dark glowing cheeks of the one who was seated, contrasted strongly with the extreme fairness of the lady bending over her, employed in teaching her the art of embroidery. For a rich vest lay in the lap of the seated lady, and busied her fingers. Rosa was the pupil. She was clothed in a dark murrey colored gown, whose loose sleeves, falling back as she moved, displayed the noble outline of her arm. A line of white parted the dark dress from the deep, but more brilliant brown of her neck. Her countenance was grave but contented, and she seemed absorbed in her work, as she followed the guiding fingers of her instructress, Teresa. Madonna Morosini was clad like her companion, only that she had chosen a hue of silver gray. So bright and clear looked one, so dark the other—both so beautiful, that they might have stood for a picture of night and day. Both looked up as the condottiere entered, and received him like one who was not unexpected.

"Whence do you come, Messer Guglielmo?" asked Teresa.

"I come from Saint Mark's, where the new procuratore has been conducted to pay his devotions."

"Is the ceremony over, then?"

"It is all done. It took no great time to do; yet, if I mistake not, never were there greater numbers pouring into the grand council to elect a Procuratore di San Marco than came to the

election of Carlo Zeno; and when he came out all Venice seemed in the piazza."

"Venice was forced by its conscience to pay that long owed debt; and now, though it has done its best, though it has given to Carlo Zeno high honor and rank almost equal to the doge, without the dangers and troubles that beset the prince, how poor is that payment for all the wrongs, the hardships, and the wounds that Zeno has endured in the service of the republic, and even at its hands!"

"I could think, Madonna Teresa," answered Cooke, "that you were out of Venice in speaking thus of it; for tongues, I ween, are beginning to grow less bold. The nobles are so heaping up the power of the state, that they are giving away their own. Zeno is content, for all the bad profit that he has made of the republic."

"Aye, he keeps no count on his own side. How did he look?"

"Pleased, as ever he does when he meets his countrymen in friendship; and in his new robes he looked more dignified than ever; they seemed to suit his grayer hair. Though, methinks, he never showed so gloriously as in the crimson robe and cap of a general, at the head of his troops."

"Was Sebastian there?"

"Aye; and though I say it to you, madonna, I would have chosen him amongst them all for the most splendid."

"Why now you are flattering me, Messer Guglielmo, through my husband; but I notice that in these holiday times all become flatterers. It seems as if pleasure made an over abundance of delight, so that men fall to throwing it away like largess among their fellows."

"No; I say but as it seemed to me. Your father was with us too—that is, among the grand councillors, as befits him since his blood was ennobled for its deeds and sacrifices in the time of the war of Chiozza. You could tell us, lady, they say, of one sacrifice then made, of certain gold."

"Name it not, Guglielmo; the memory sickens me with the taste of the despair that then brought death into our house."

"The despair has past. Messer Jacopo was of the gayest, and younger far than when I knew him in those doubtful days. But there were others whom you would little expect to find. When the procession entered the church, there were in it Messer Francesco da Carrara and his son, who have been guests with Zeno. The Lord of Padua has lost his stoutness of late years. I think he still misdoubts Venice, and that towel-like cap upon his head, with the loose vest and cloak in one, reaching to his knees, make him yet more like an old woman than any even of the senators."

"And was Francesco altered?"

"The son? Why yes, he has gained the portly bearing that his father has left. He bore himself, I thought, less gayly than he used to do, though more audaciously. I do believe none so mourned for the loss of the Lady Angiolina as he did; though Edward seemed to take it more to heart at the time. It might yet have been better for Venice if one of its daughters had used her arts to tame that bold and cunning man. Perchance the Lady Taddea

T

d'Este may tame him, for they say he truly loves her. But another guest was there who concerns you more nearly."

"You do not mean Ranieri?"

"No; we could not see him anywhere, and Sebastian said that he lost sight of him earlier in the day at the palace of Da Riva. Are there girls hidden there? It was not Ranieri. Long time ago Messer Zeno wrote to Edward——"

"He is here!"

"He is. Messer Zeno had asked him to be present at his election; but having no answer, he had thought the letter was lost—as well it might be on so long and doubtful a journey. But Edward has come; he arrived in the midst of the ceremony, and not to interrupt it he hid himself among the crowd in a corner of the church until all was over; and then he found out Sebastian. Never, I think, did men hug so close as they did; and then Sebastian led him to Zeno, who embraced him, and in turn led him to the doge; and Messer lo Doge would have had him for his guest, but he would not be parted from Sebastian; and so he is coming here anon."

Teresa clasped her hands with delight; and Rosa started from her seat. "And how," cried Teresa, "did he look?"

"Not ill—neither well nor ill. You might say that he is not altered in anything—yet when I saw him, then did I know how little time had done against Sebastian. I cannot tell in what Edward is altered, but he looks an older and even a graver man than he was; but the change is not so bad in him as in old Francesco da Carrara. I left them talking with the doge. Sebastian bade me come to tell you, that you might not be startled; and he bade me say that Messer Zeno will come with them; for there is new surprise—Carlo Zeno has been appointed ambassador to England. They say that he was appointed many days ago, yet staid that his election might be passed, so that he might carry his new dignity with him; and now he goes without delay."

"Why then," said Teresa, "we should be ready to receive our guests as is most fitting. Do you go back for them, Messer Guglielmo, or do you stay their coming?"

"I will await them here."

Teresa left the saloon, and Rosa would have followed her; but, seizing her by the wrist, William Cooke detained her. She looked round at him in surprise. He seemed to lose all his boldness; and the hardy soldier, muttering some unintelligible words, drew back. Amazed at his bearing, Rosa still looked at him; and recovering courage, William Cooke again took her hand. "Madonna Rosa," he said, "will you pardon what I say, since I am a rude untaught man, and moreover have but little time to say it in; as indeed I think I never should have said it but for that—but that I must say it in so short a time. I fear from your look, that you do not, as I had hoped, know what it is I have to tell you, so that I must fain say it all for myself."

Rosa still paused; she did now guess his meaning; but yet it was so new to her, and she had guessed so little before, that she remained silent, not knowing how to answer.

William still gazed upon her, as though gathering courage from the last word; and then, speaking with a little start, as if he made a plunge, he said,—"I love you!"

Rosa did not withdraw her hand—she did not start—she looked no sterner, but gently pressing his hand, she said, after a short silence, —"Messer Guglielmo, you know not what you say. I am not to be loved thus. You see me in the palace of Morosini: I live, I breathe, I speak like others; but mine is a life not like others' life. I was spoiled early—poisoned by falsehood and mistake, and would have been utterly destroyed, but that Teresa saved me even from myself. You do not know these things. Learn them of Sebastian. Tell him that I told you to learn them; and you will come back no more."

William still held her hand in silence, gazing in her face as she talked of what they had never spoken upon before. She seemed to him in that new light, still so beautiful and so admirable, that in his admiration he forgot even what he would have said.

"I have offended you," said Rosa, "and I would not do that; but it is my ill fortune which has made me before injure those whom I least would injure."

"Offended! No; but I was thinking how wrong you were in saying that I knew not these things. I have known them before from Sebastian; for he was aware before I dared to tell you, how much it behoved me to hear all that concerns you. Do not say, Rosa mia, that your life was spoiled, but rather that it was bettered by your hard trials, and rather think it presumption that so rough a soldier, without high degree, or wealth, and almost without country, to ask the hand of the dear friend of Sebastian and Teresa."

Rosa now withdrew her hand, and moved a pace or two away. "I know not how to answer you, Messer Guglielmo, since I would do you no hurt; and either way, it seems, I must. It is most true that my life was spoiled when young. It had gone wrong—not for my fault, but for a curse that was put upon me. It had gone wrong even in this, in love; and if Teresa saved it, it was only to be done by snatching it away altogether from the wrong path that it had taken. In that path I left love, and to regain life I have foregone it forever. Such love, I mean, save any but that which I bear to her."

"Rosa, it is not so. If I had Sebastian's tongue or Teresa's, I would soon show you otherwise; but you silence me, because I cannot talk; and never before did I feel how poor is the art of him who can only wield a sword, when now I must yield up all that can make life most precious to me for want of a few words. If you do not find compassion for me in your heart, there is no hope for me, and that now I crave of you most humbly."

"Speak not so, Messer Guglielmo; it suits not any to be humble to me."

William would have retaken her hand; but at that instant Teresa returned. She returned still as gay and joyful with the expected arrival as when she left them; but stopping, she glanced in dismay from one to the other as they walked somewhat apart, and showed in their faces the pain they felt. "Why what has befallen!" she cried. "Rosa!—Guglielmo!—What miserable tidings have you brought, Guglielmo, that has made you both thus!"

"I brought no tidings, Madonna Teresa, that were miserable, until they became so after they were told. Ask Rosa what they were; or,—for I know not why I should conceal it,—I will tell you now that I have offered to her the honest heart of a soldier, and she has thrown it back to me. That is what I grieve for, and she grieves perchance in pity; and so I bear away with me not so gay a face as I brought with me; that is all."

He would have departed; but Teresa stayed him, and making him repeat all that had passed, she said, when he had done, "No, Guglielmo, you are right, it must not be so. We must not lose so true a friend as you have been; and if there is but one way to bind you to us, why truly I think I must use it." Taking his hand she put it in Rosa's.

It was not refused now. Guglielmo kissed the hand he held with a grace more like what Teresa had seen in Sebastian, than in her secret heart she could have expected; but love makes men equal in many things.

"And do you think, Rosa mia," said William, with still doubting delight, "that you can exchange for this the cold rough climate of our distant island!"

"Of England!" cried Rosa in dismay.

"Of my own country."

Snatching away her hand, Rosa cried,—"No, not that; ask me not to leave Venice." And she threw her arms round Teresa, still looking towards her suitor in affright, and clinging to her friend like a shipwrecked mariner who grasps some tree growing at the water's edge, and turns in terror to the still threatening waves.

Bending towards her, Teresa kissed her on the forehead and said,—"No Messer Guglielmo, you must not ask this; for I doubt whether either of us could bear so much. You would but carry away a dead wife, and kill Sebastian's. Rosa and I have suffered together as few women ever suffered. We clung to each other while we were wounded, and our wounded flesh has grown into one, and may not be parted. If you wed Rosa, you must wed also her country and her friends; nor need you suffer wrong in that, for where Rosa is there you can be."

"You put upon me by force," answered William, "what I dared not have thought of. But Messer Zeno has bidden me to his service, and I may not leave it. He needs an Englishman for his guide and interpreter in his embassy, and having chosen me, I must not forswear so honorable a service."

"Nor shall you; Rosa shall be hostage for your return."

"You bind me to a condition which is to me new life and happiness, and I can only answer by giving myself up to you, Madonna Teresa, for a slave."

"You shall be as you are Sebastian's friend."

"Sebastian's friend at your bidding."

Teresa again gave him the hand he sought, and it was not drawn back; but still Rosa's other arm clung round her friend.

They heard the sound of approaching voices, louder and louder still, and Sebastian entered the room with Ranieri and Edward. The Englishman would have kissed Teresa's hand; but embracing him, she kissed him on the mouth, and welcomed him back to Venice; knowing he was Sebastian's dearest friend, and remembering how on that night when his heart was quivering with the grief that killed his joys for ever, he had remained in Venice to aid Sebastian in seeking for her. After their first greeting, many words of old remembrance and inquiry passed between them. Three young children were sent for that he might see them—a boy, already like Sebastian in beauty, height, and noble bearing; a little girl, too round and fair to tell what she was like; and a younger infant lost in its own clothes. These dismissed, still talk went on, until more new comers were heard without. Edward's voice sunk to a whisper—the first question that had entered his mind was the last to be asked—"Angiolina!"

"Angiolina loved," answered Sebastian, "in spite of the cloister, even to *the last*,—two years after you had left us."

Zeno with a troop of companions entered the saloon, which now filled with guests pouring in from the pageant. Awakening from their sad remembrances, Sebastian and Teresa received their friends and the guests with fitting courtesy, holding them in talk, while the banquet was prepared.

Edward drew aside unobserved; and chance leading his steps from the bustle of welcome and congratulation, he walked into a smaller room that opened from the saloon. He gazed out of the window, scarcely conscious that others in idle wandering, had entered the same cabinet, until Ranieri touched his shoulder. He had sunk in a dismal and bitter dream; tears, few and hot, starting from his scorched eyes, at the memory of hope so cruelly gone for ever.

Looking round, he turned pale, and grasping Ranieri's arm he said:—"What strange and blighting sight is this that enters to us! I should know that man, but little thought to see him here."

"The Father Eremitano!" asked Ranieri. "Yes, you know him. It was Marco Morosini. He went into the convent of San Nicolò da Lido. He is often here."

The man was all but unchanged. His head was bald of its hair at the top, and what remained around it was grayer, but he was not more gaunt than he had been. If his neck bent now and then in humility, his head was raised again as proudly as before. His eyes shone with as glassy a stare and his form was as erect. His friar's gown was scarcely more sober than the clothes he used to wear, and he trod the halls that once were his with as much of a master's step. Stricken down where he stood upon earth, he had mounted the floor of heaven to be upon a vantage ground over friend and foe; and thus he had regained the house he yielded to his son, and held that, and all other earthly possessions besides, by a heavenly right to his use. His eye glancing around rested upon Edward. He knew the Englishman at once and marked his sadder mien. One triumph at least he had accomplished on earth; and the sad face of Edward was a pledge of it

Walking across the cabinet, so that all who stood talking in little knots turned to see what led him by so sudden and straight a path, he approached the Englishman and took him by the hand.

Edward snatched back his hand, and recoiling, stood speechless in amaze and anger at being thus hunted out by the dullard's obstinate malice.

Dreading some mischief, Ranieri hastily left them to seek the interposition of Sebastian or Zeno; while those around, knowing the Englishman's story, gathered round to see what would follow in that strange encounter; none more eagerly curious than the still fiery Malipiero,—who hated still Marco Morosini, the senator, but cowered before the monk.

Father Eremitano stood unrebuked. A grave and placid smile quenched the exulting fire that lurked within his eyes; a holy passion seemed to move his voice; and he said aloud, so that all might hear—" It is long since we met, Ser Inglese,—changes have happened by the will and for the glory of the Most Holy; since all who are mortals suffer. But doubt not," he added, raising his voice yet higher——

"Stand back, sir!" cried Edward: his voice was broken and choked; his lips and cheeks, dappled with red and white as the blood-tide dashed in wild anarchy through his veins, quivered with passion; and he tossed his hands before him, as he would thrust back the unwelcome visitation.—" Leave me—let me pass away from you in silence. You cannot by miracle will back the mortal years; or undo the curse you have been. Heaven grows hell in your presence."

"Doubt not," continued Eremitano, his loud voice flowing on again, unchecked; "Doubt not that I forgive you, as I hope we are all forgiven." He looked around to see whether any would gainsay his holy office; and he raised his hand with two fingers stretched forth in the act to bless.

Edward maddened under the hideous spell. "Stand away, infamous being! You come from the tomb, exulting in death; and beware lest I hurl you back."

A loud murmur arose among the guests that crowded round, shocked at the impious bearing of the alien towards the holy man; and in his reckless and irreverent passion they forgot the wrongs shadowed in the distance of the past.

Brought by Ranieri's solicitude and the sound of loud anger, Zeno and Sebastian, with Teresa, Rosa, and many more, came into the crowded room, and slowly forced their anxious way towards the Englishman, bent on recalling him from his delirium.

With uplifted hand, the friar still pressed forward.

Edward leaned back, shrinking from the loathsome spirit that hovered over him.

"Bless thee, my son!"

A blow, loud and heavy, was hurled full on the gowned breast; and the tall friar staggered back.

Swords flashed in the air, and one darted like lightning into the rash man's breast; the point gleaming out between his shoulders for the instant before it drew back.

A loud mingling cry and shriek from behind burst away through the bewildered crowd for the friends that came too late; and Edward was seized as he fell in the cradling arms of Rosa; while Teresa knelt beside him, Sebastian leaned over.

Zeno turned to the friar. "Leave us, Marco Morosini: your holy garb cannot hide you from cruel memories, and its sanctity is endangered here."

Eremitano was once more erect and calm, as he ever studied to be. "Beware, Carlo Zeno, —beware, Sebastiano Morosini! I forgive and bless; but a sacred rigor moves the Holy Office; and those who harbor impious traitors to our church tempt a terrible fate."

"Go, sir. We who are unstained with intent of wrong dread not the Holy Inquisition; but here is agonized grief, and what is greater than us all, death. Let peace be in this place of misery."

Eremitano's face flushed: he moved forward, as if for contest; but stopping, he raised his eyes and hands mechanically to heaven, and in a loud voice cried, "Peace and forgiveness be upon us all, even upon the proud and the humble—upon them that strike and them that are stricken." And so saying, he left the place.

Teresa had pressed a veil which she held to staunch the blood that welled forth in a bubbling stream. Seeing the wounded man turn fainter, she passed her other arm round him, and cried, "Alas! alas! dear friend of my lord and love, what can we do to ease you!"

"Nothing, sweet lady, but what has been done and what you are doing." His voice was weak and broken.

"Go fetch physicians," cried Zeno. William Cook and Ranieri both rushed out. "And leave us, sirs," added Zeno to the guests, "alone with our friend."

"And seek the father Onorio," said Sebastian; "his benign tenderness will sooth where we cannot heal. Whose hand was it, Edward, that struck this fatal blow!"

"What matters! It was Morosini's—or mine own;—and it has done for the best."

"Ah! why is our house doomed to be thus fatal to you, my friend! Can you forgive us!"

"Forgive you! Say, Sebastian, that I am forgiven for this unseemly brawl—but I was mad. Thank you. Who was with your sister, when she lay thus, Sebastian!"

"Teresa and Rosa."

Throwing his eyes upward, Edward glanced in Rosa's downcast face; so moveless had she been, that he forgot his pillow lived; her tearless eyes watched him without a motion, the brow fixed in a regard of steadfast ministering pity. He saw how she had watched the departure of her who had gone before. He looked at Teresa. She bent against him, thus hiding her eyes, drowned with tears. "Your hand, Teresa." She gave it into his, and looked into his face. So had she suffered once before—so had she companioned her sister to the portal of death.

Sebastian stooped over his friend—"Zeno! he is dead."

THE END.

HARPER'S LIBRARY OF
SELECT NOVELS.

Mailing Notice.—HARPER & BROTHERS will send their books by Mail, postage free, to any part of the United States, on receipt of the Price.

BY THE AUTHOR OF "JOHN HALIFAX."

JOHN ESTEN COOKE'S NOVELS.

HENRY ST. JOHN, GENTLEMAN;

Of "Flower of Hundreds," in the County of Prince George, Virginia. A Tale of 1774–75. By JOHN ESTEN COOKE. 12mo, Cloth, $1 50.

This charming story depicts the social life of Virginia in the time of Governor Dunmore, and is full of happy, effective touches. The characters and the scenes of old Virginia are finely sketched.

LEATHER STOCKING AND SILK;

Or, Hunter John Meyers and his Times. A Story of the Valley of Virginia. By JOHN ESTEN COOKE. 12mo, Cloth, $1 50.

Without a trace of the audacity and extravagance which are so much in vogue with many recent American writers of fiction, this unique story of Virginia life quietly winds its way to the heart of the reader by its simple touches of nature, its gentle pathos, and the admirable harmony and fidelity of its coloring. The author has a rare perception of the capacities of character for dramatic effect.—*N. Y. Tribune*.

PUBLISHED BY HARPER & BROTHERS, NEW YORK.

☞ Harper & Brothers *will send either of the above novels by mail, postage prepaid, on receipt of $1 50.*

PARTISAN LIFE WITH MOSBY.

By Major JOHN SCOTT, of Fauquier, Va., late C. S. A. With a Portrait of Colonel Mosby on Steel engraved by Halpin, also one by Jewett, and nearly Fifty Illustrations, embracing Portraits of Field Officers and Captains of the Battalion, a Map of Mosby's Confederacy, and numerous spirited Illustrations of Fights, Raids, and Humorous Incidents. 8vo, Cloth, Beveled Edges, $3 50.

This work is the history of the Battalion which, under the command of Col. John S. Mosby, achieved so great a fame in the Virginia campaigns of 1862, '63, and '64. It has been prepared for publication by the express sanction of Col. Mosby, and has the patronage and co-operation of the partisan chief, his officers, and men.

Partisan warfare, as established and conducted by Col. Mosby under the Partisan Ranger Law, introduced a novel and very effective instrument of defense against the march of invading armies. The explanation of this system afforded by the author was derived from Mosby himself, and exhibits the partisan leader in his true aspect as the co-operator of Lee.

The author served under Mosby during the memorable campaigns, and is a native of that portion of Virginia which was the scene of the principal operations of the Battalion. His material is drawn not only from the actors in the strange history, but many a thrilling and many a humorous incident has been derived from spectators of the fierce drama. The impartiality of history has been preserved, and the generous acts or heroic exploits of Mosby's opponents have been frankly related.

The women of that region were often connected with "Mosby's men," sometimes as actors and sometimes as spectators. They appear in this volume under their own names, and the important part they acted in these strange scenes is fully recorded. "With this feature omitted," remarks the author, "it would be impossible to draw a truthful picture of the stirring and memorable scenes of which I treat. It will impart to much of the narrative the high coloring of romance, for Love, with its enchantments, is ever ready to attend upon War."

The skill and prowess of the officers and men under Mosby is related with every particularity of detail, and the work affords not only a complete and exhaustive record of the achievements of the famous Battalion, but also an inside view of social life among the partisan, showing how they lived by "boarding round" when off duty, how they amused themselves in camp and on the march, and how they loved as well as how they fought. Hundreds of anecdotes and incidents, nearly fifty engravings and portraits, and a map of "Mosby's Confederacy," illustrate and beautify the volume.

PUBLISHED BY HARPER & BROTHERS, NEW YORK.

☞ Harper & Brothers *will send the above work by mail, postage paid, on receipt of $3 50.*

HARPER'S WEEKLY FOR 1864.

WITH the opening of the year was commenced the *Eighth Volume* of HARPER'S WEEK-LY, an Illustrated Family Newspaper, devoted to Art, Literature, Popular Information, and Politics.

The general aim and scope of this paper are too well known to require special explanation. In politics it will continue to advocate the National Cause, wholly irrespective of mere party grounds. Whatever Administration honestly endeavors to put down the present Rebellion and to restore the Union, will so far receive the cordial support of the Weekly. Ample provisions have been made to maintain the Artistic and Literary Departments of the paper.

HARPER'S WEEKLY has regular Artist Correspondents with every great Division of our Army, who will furnish sketches of every incident of importance in the War. The Conductors are, moreover, in daily receipt of valuable sketches from Volunteer Correspondents in the Army and Navy in all parts of the country. The Publishers will gladly welcome such sketches from members of our forces in every section, and will pay liberally for such as they may use. The Weekly has already contained more than *Sixteen Hundred* Illustrations of the War, and the Proprietors are warranted in promising that the successive numbers will embody a thorough and exhaustive ILLUSTRATED HISTORY OF THE WAR, in its current phases.

From THE METHODIST, *a Weekly Religious Newspaper :* Rev. GEO. R. CROOKS, D.D., *Editor ;* Rev. J. M'CLINTOCK, D.D., *Corresponding Editor.*

HARPER'S WEEKLY.—This periodical merits special notice at the present time. There is probably no weekly publication of the country that equals its influence. More than one hundred thousand copies fly over the land weekly; they are read in our cars, steamboats, and families. Our youth especially read them, and as the family newspaper of the nation its power over the forming opinions of the next generation of the American people is an important item.

It is abundant, if not superabundant, in pictorial illustrations—a means of strong impression, especially on the minds of the young. Both by its illustrations and its incessant discussion of the occurrences and questions of the war it is a "current history" and "running commentary" on the great event, and there is probably no literary agency of the day more effective in its influence respecting the war in the families of the common people. Most happy are we then to be able to say that this responsible power is exerted altogether on the side of loyalty. No paper in the land is more outspoken, more uncompromising for the Union, for the war, for even the policy of the President's "great Proclamation." When the rebellion broke out we did the publishers the injustice of some anxious fears about their probable course on the subject.

Steadily have they kept up with the Providential development of its events and questions; not only abreast of them, but, in important respects, ahead of them. No periodical press in the nation deserves better of the country for its faithfulness and "pluck" in all matters relating to the great struggle. And we should do it injustice were we not to add that, with its outright loyalty and bravery, it combines commanding ability. The editorial leaders which is continuously flings out against all political traitors and flunkies strike directly at their mark. They are evidently from pens both strong and polished. On even the astuter subjects of policy, finance, &c., it is eminently able. And it makes no mistake in supposing its readers capable of an interest and of intelligence in these respects. American families look keenly into such questions, and with such a really educational force as this paper wields, it is especially right and commendable that it seeks to elevate the common mind to the higher questions of the times. The American people will not fail to notice and to remember the courageous and patriotic course of *Harper's Weekly* in these dark times of hideous treason, and of more hideous, because more contemptible, semi-treason.

TERMS.

One Copy for One Year	$3 00
Two Copies for One Year	5 00
"Harper's Weekly" and "Harper's Magazine" one year	5 00

An Extra Copy of either the Weekly or Magazine will be supplied gratis for every Club of TEN SUBSCRIBERS, *at $2 50 each ; or, Eleven Copies for $25 00.*

Volumes I., II., III., IV., V., VI., and VII., of HARPER'S WEEKLY, handsomely bound in Cloth extra, Price $5 00 each, are now ready.

Muslin Covers are furnished to those who wish their Numbers bound, at Fifty Cents each.

* To Postmasters and Agents getting up a Club of Ten Subscribers, a Copy will be sent gratis. Subscriptions may commence with any Number. Specimen Numbers gratuitously supplied.

Clergymen and Teachers supplied at $2 50 a year.

As HARPER'S WEEKLY *is electrotyped, Numbers can be supplied from the commencement.*

The Publishers will send *Harper's Weekly* free to any Regiment or Ship of War which may supply them with the name and address of the officer to whom it should be forwarded.

HARPER'S WEEKLY is probably read in more households than any other American weekly publication. It is therefore the best advertising medium in the country. Only a limited space is devoted to advertisements. The price for the insertion of advertisements is *seventy-five* cents per line, except for the last page, for which the rate is One Dollar per line.

Harper's Magazine for February.

IT has from the outset been the aim of the publishers of HARPER'S NEW MONTHLY MAGAZINE to furnish a periodical containing so great an amount of matter in every department of literature, presented in a form so attractive, and at a price so moderate, that it should be indispensable to every cultivated American reader.

The Magazine has contained several of the best Serial Novels of Bulwer, Dickens, Thackeray, Lever, Trollope, Reade, Miss Evans, and Miss Mulock, besides Essays, Tales, and Poems from the foremost American and British writers.

Historical and Biographical Papers, especially those relating to American subjects, have formed a distinctive feature of the Magazine. These papers alone, if published separately, would cost more than the price of the Magazine.

The results of the Explorations and Adventures of the most distinguished travelers have been presented in careful abstracts.

The Editorial Departments comprise a careful summary of the history of the times, comments upon the current topics of thought and remark, and an immense collection of anecdotes and facetiæ, furnished by hundreds of voluntary correspondents.

Wherever Pictorial Illustrations could add to the value or interest of an article they have been freely used. The Magazine has contained nearly nine thousand engravings, executed in the best style of the art.

The result of the enterprise has exceeded the highest anticipations of the Publishers. The Magazine gained at once the foremost place among American periodicals; and its circulation has for years exceeded, as it now exceeds, that of all other periodicals of its class issued in the United States. No effort or cost will be spared by the Publishers to insure that the Magazine shall maintain the position which it has won.

The Postage Law.

HARPER'S MAGAZINE is charged 24 Cents a year, instead of 36 cents, as heretofore: Postage to be paid in advance, yearly, semi-yearly, or quarterly.—(Section 36.)

HARPER'S WEEKLY is charged 20 Cents a year, instead of 26 cents, as heretofore: Postage to be paid in advance, yearly, semi-yearly, or quarterly.—(Section 35.)

HARPER'S PICTORIAL HISTORY OF THE REBELLION is charged 2 Cents a number, instead of 3 cents, as heretofore.—(Section 36.)

NEWS DEALERS may receive their packages at the same rates pro rata as are paid by subscribers: That is, at the rate of 20 Cents for 52 copies of the WEEKLY, and 2 Cents for each copy of the MAGAZINE, and may pay separately for each package when received.—(Section 36.)

MANUSCRIPTS and PROOFS passing between Authors and Publishers are charged as Printed Matter (one half Cent per ounce), instead of as Letters (6 cents an ounce), as heretofore.—(Sections 24 and 34.)

The Twenty-seven Volumes of the Magazine contain matter equivalent to more than two hundred duodecimo volumes. Most of this is of permanent value. A complete set of the Magazine will therefore be a desirable acquisition to any private, public, or school library. The Publishers will furnish these in sets, neatly bound in Cloth, for One Dollar and Eighty-Eight Cents per Volume—$50 76 for the whole, nett Cash, the freight to be paid by the purchaser. The same amount of matter, with an equal number of illustrations, issued in ordinary volumes, would cost more than Three Hundred Dollars. Any single volume will be sent by mail, *post-paid*, to any place in the United States within 1500 miles from New York, for Two Dollars and Fifty Cents; or any single Number for Twenty-five Cents.

TERMS.—One Copy for One Year, $3 00; Two Copies for One Year, $5 00; "HARPER'S MAGAZINE" and "HARPER'S WEEKLY," One Year, $5 00. And an Extra Copy, *gratis*, for every Club of TEN SUBSCRIBERS, at $2 50 each; or, 11 Copies for $25.

Clergymen and Teachers supplied at $2 50 a year. The Semi-Annual Volumes bound in Cloth, $2 50 per volume. Muslin Covers, 35 cents each, *Nett*; when ordered to be sent by Mail, *Eight Cents* additional must be remitted for postage.

www.ingramcontent.com/pod-product-compliance
Lightning Source LLC
Chambersburg PA
CBHW021121020726
47500CB00003B/871